"What are you doing here?" Marisa demanded huskily.

"An odd question, *mia bella,* to put to your husband when he visits your bedroom on your wedding night."

She sat rigidly against the pillows, watching him approach. Lorenzo was wearing a black silk robe, but his bare chest, with its dark shadow of hair, and bare legs suggested that there was nothing beneath it.

"It is quite simple," he continued. "I wish to kiss you good-night. To take from your lovely mouth what you denied me this morning—nothing more."

Renzo took her by the shoulders, pulling her toward him, his purpose evident in his set face.

"Let me go." She began to struggle against the strength of the hands that held her. "I won't do this—I won't." She pushed against his chest, fists clenched, her face averted.

"*Mia cara,* this is silly." He spoke more gently, but there was a note in his voice that was almost amusement. "Such a fuss about so little. One kiss and I'll go. I swear it."

"You'll go to hell." As she tried to wrench herself free, one of the ribbon straps on her nightgown suddenly snapped, and the flimsy bodice slipped down....

SARA CRAVEN was born in South Devon, England, and grew up surrounded by books in a house by the sea. After leaving grammar school she worked as a local journalist, covering everything from flower shows to murders. She started writing for Harlequin in 1975. Sara has appeared as a contestant on the U.K. Channel Four game show *Fifteen to One*, and in 1997 won the title of Television Mastermind of Great Britain.

Sara shares her Somerset home with several thousand books and an amazing video and DVD collection.

When she's not writing, she likes to travel in Europe, particularly Greece and Italy. She loves music, theater, cooking and eating in good restaurants, but reading will always be her greatest passion.

Since the birth of her twin grandchildren in New York City, she has become a regular visitor to the Big Apple.

THE SANTANGELI MARRIAGE

SARA CRAVEN

~ FORCED TO MARRY ~

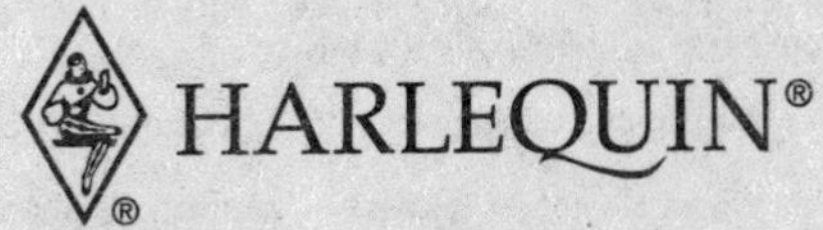

TORONTO • NEW YORK • LONDON
AMSTERDAM • PARIS • SYDNEY • HAMBURG
STOCKHOLM • ATHENS • TOKYO • MILAN • MADRID
PRAGUE • WARSAW • BUDAPEST • AUCKLAND

ISBN-13: 978-0-373-52725-0

THE SANTANGELI MARRIAGE

First North American Publication 2009.

This edition published by arrangement with Harlequin Books S.A.

www.eHarlequin.com

Printed in U.S.A.

THE SANTANGELI MARRIAGE

CHAPTER ONE

THE glass doors of the Clinica San Francesco whispered open, and every head turned to observe the man who came striding out of the darkness into the reception area.

If Lorenzo Santangeli was aware of their scrutiny, or if he sensed that there were far more people hanging around than could be deemed strictly necessary at that time of night, and most of them female, he gave no sign.

His lean, six-foot-tall body was clad in the elegance of evening clothes, and his ruffled shirt was open at the throat, his black tie thrust negligently into the pocket of his dinner jacket.

One of the loitering nurses, staring at his dishevelled dark hair, murmured to her colleague with unknowing accuracy that he looked as if he'd just rolled out of bed, and the other girl sighed wistfully in agreement.

He was not classically handsome, but his thin face, with its high cheekbones, heavy-lidded golden-brown eyes and that mobile, faintly sensual mouth, which looked as if it could curl in a sneer and smile in heart-stopping allure with equal ease, had a dynamism that went beyond mere attractiveness. And every woman looking at him felt it like a tug to the senses.

The fact that he was frowning, and his lips were set in a grim line, did nothing to reduce the force of his blatantly masculine appeal.

He looked, it was felt, just as a loving son should when called unexpectedly to the bedside of a sick father.

Then, as the clinic's director, Signor Martelli, emerged from his office to greet him, the crowd, hurriedly realising it should be elsewhere, began to fade swiftly and unobtrusively away.

Renzo wasted no time on niceties. He said, his voice sharp with anxiety, 'My father—how is he?'

'Resting comfortably,' the older man responded. 'Fortunately an ambulance was summoned immediately when it happened, so there was no delay in providing the appropriate treatment.' He smiled reassuringly. 'It was not a serious attack, and we expect the Marchese to make a complete recovery.'

Renzo expelled a sigh of relief. 'May I see him?'

'Of course. I will take you to him.' Signor Martelli pressed a button to summon a lift to the upper floors. He gave his companion a sidelong glance. 'It is, of course, important that your father avoids stress, and I am told that he has been fretting a little while awaiting your arrival. I am glad that you are here now to set his mind at rest.'

'It is a relief to me also, *signore*.' The tone was courteous, but it had a distancing effect. So far, it seemed to warn, and no further.

The clinic director had heard that Signor Lorenzo could be formidable, and this was all the confirmation he needed, he thought, relapsing into discreet silence.

Renzo had been expecting to find his father's private room peopled by consultants and quietly shod attendants, with Guillermo Santangeli under sedation and hooked up to monitors and drips.

But instead his father was alone, propped up by pillows, wearing his own striking maroon silk pyjamas and placidly turning over the pages of a magazine on international finance. Taking the place of machinery was a large and fragrant floral arrangement on a side table.

As Renzo checked, astonished, in the doorway, Guillermo peered at him over his glasses. 'Ah,' he said. '*Finalmente.*' He paused. 'You were not easy to trace, my son.'

Fretting, Renzo thought, might be an exaggeration, but the slight edge to his words was unmistakable. He came forward slowly, his smile combining ruefulness and charm in equal measure. 'Nevertheless, Papa, I am here now. And so, thankfully, are you. I was told you had collapsed with a heart attack.'

'It was what they call "an incident".' Guillermo shrugged. 'Alarming at the time, but soon dealt with. I am to rest here for a couple of days, and then I will be allowed to return home.' He sighed. 'But I have to take medication, and cigars and brandy have been forbidden—for a while at least.'

'Well, the cigars, at any rate, must be counted as a blessing,' Renzo said teasingly as he took his father's hand and kissed it lightly.

His father pulled a face. 'That is also Ottavia's opinion. She has just left. I have her to thank for the pyjamas and the flowers, also for summoning help so promptly. We had just finished dinner when I became ill.'

Renzo's brows lifted. 'Then I am grateful to her.' He pulled up a chair and paused. 'I hope Signora Alesconi did not go on my account.'

'She is a woman of supreme tact,' said his father. 'And she knew we would wish to talk privately. There is no other reason. I have assured her that you no longer regard our relationship as a betrayal of your mother's memory.'

Renzo's smiled twisted a little. *'Grazie.* You were right to say so.' He hesitated. 'So may I now expect to have a new stepmother? If you wished to—formalise the situation I—I would welcome…'

Guillermo lifted a hand. 'There is no question of that. We have fully discussed the matter, but decided that we both value our independence too highly and remain content as we are.' He removed his glasses and put them carefully on the locker beside his bed. 'And while we are on the subject of marriage, where is your wife?'

Well, I walked headlong into that, thought Renzo, cursing under his breath. Aloud, he said, 'She is in England, Papa—as I think you know.'

'Ah, yes.' His father gave a meditative nod. 'Where she went shortly after your honeymoon, I believe, and has remained ever since.'

Renzo's mouth tightened. 'I felt—a period of adjustment might be helpful.'

'A curious decision, perhaps,' said Guillermo. 'Considering the pressing reasons for your marriage. You are the last of the line, my dear Lorenzo, and as you approached the age of thirty, without the least sign of abandoning your bachelor life and settling down, it became imperative to remind you that you had a duty to produce a legitimate heir to carry on the Santangeli name—both privately and professionally.'

He paused. 'You seemed to accept that. And with no other candidate in mind, you also consented to marry the girl your late mother always intended for you—her beloved goddaughter Marisa

Brendon. I wish to be sure that advancing age has not damaged my remembrance, and that I have the details of this agreement correct, you understand?' he added blandly.

'Yes.' Renzo set his teeth. *Advancing age?* he thought wryly. *How long did crocodiles survive?* 'You are, of course, quite right.'

'Yet eight months have passed, and still you have no good news to tell me. This would have been a disappointment in any circumstances, but in view of the evening's events my need to hear that the next generation is established becomes even more pressing. From now on I must take more care, they tell me. Moderate my lifestyle. In other words, I have been made aware of my own mortality. And I confess that I would dearly like to hold my first grandchild in my arms before I die.'

Renzo moved restively, 'Papa—you will live for many years yet. We both know that.'

'I can hope,' said Guillermo briskly. 'But that is not the point.' He leaned back against his pillows, adding quietly, 'Your bride can hardly give you an heir, *figlio mio*, if you do not share a roof with her, let alone a bed. Or do you visit her in London, perhaps, in order to fulfil your marital obligations?'

Renzo rose from his chair and walked over to the window, lifting the slats of the blind to look out into the darkness. An image of a girl's white face rose in his mind, her eyes blank and tearless, and a feeling that was almost shame twisted like a knife in his guts.

'No,' he said at last. 'I do not.'

'Then why not?' his father demanded. 'What can be the problem? Yes, the marriage was arranged for you, but so was my own, and your mother and I soon came to love each other deeply. And here you have been given a girl, young, charming, and indisputably innocent. Someone, moreover, you have known for much of your life. If she was not to your taste you should have said so.'

Renzo turned and gave him an ironic look. 'It does not occur to you, Papa, that maybe the shoe is on the other foot and Marisa does not want me?'

'Che sciocchezze!' Guillermo said roundly. 'What nonsense. When she stayed with us as a child it was clear to everyone that she adored you.'

'Unfortunately, now she is older, her feelings are very different,' Renzo said dryly. 'Particularly where the realities of marriage are concerned.'

Guillermo pursed his lips in exasperation. 'What can you be saying? That a man of your experience with women cannot seduce his own wife? You should have made duty a pleasure, my son, and used your honeymoon to make her fall in love with you all over again.' He paused. 'After all, she was not forced to marry you.'

Renzo gave his father a level look. 'I think we both know that is not true. Once she'd discovered from that witch of a cousin how deeply she was indebted to our family she had little choice in the matter.'

Guillermo frowned heavily. 'You did not tell her—explain that it was the dying wish of your mother, her *madrina*, that financial provision should continue to be made for her?'

'I tried, but it was useless. She knew that Mama wanted us to marry. For her, it all seemed part of the same ugly transaction.' He paused. 'And the cousin also made her aware that when I proposed to her I had a mistress. After such revelations, the honeymoon was hardly destined to go well.'

'The woman has much to answer for, it seems,' Guillermo said icily. 'But you, my son, were a fool not to have settled matters with the beautiful Lucia long before you approached your marriage.'

'If stupidity were all, I could live with it,' Renzo said with quiet bitterness. 'But I was also unkind. And I cannot forgive myself for that.'

'I see,' his father said slowly. 'Well, that is bad, but it is more important to ask yourself if your wife can be persuaded to forgive you.'

'Who knows?' Renzo's gesture was almost helpless. 'I thought a breathing space—time apart to consider what we had undertaken—would help. And at the beginning I wrote to her regularly—telephoned and left messages. But there was never any reply. And as the weeks passed the hope of any resolution became more distant.' He paused, before adding expressionlessly, 'I told myself, you understand, that I would not beg.'

Guillermo put his fingertips together and studied them intently. 'A divorce, naturally, could not be countenanced,' he said at last.

'But from what you are telling me it seems there might be grounds for annulment?'

'No,' Renzo said harshly, his mouth set. 'Do not be misled. The marriage—exists. And Marisa is my wife. Nothing can change that.'

'So you say,' his father commented grimly. 'But you could be wrong. Your grandmother honoured me with a visit yesterday to inform me that your current liaison with Doria Venucci is now talked of openly.'

'Nonna Teresa.' Renzo bit out the name. 'What a gratifying interest she takes in all the details of my life, especially those she considers less than savoury. And how could a woman with such a mind produce such a gentle, loving daughter as my mother?'

'It has always mystified me too,' Guillermo admitted. 'But for once her gossip-mongering may be justified. Because she believes it can only be a matter of time before someone tells Antonio Venucci exactly how his wife has been amusing herself while he has been in Vienna.'

He saw his son's brows lift, and nodded. 'And that, my dear Lorenzo, could change everything, both for you and for your absent wife. Because the scandal that would follow would ruin any remaining chance of a reconciliation with her—if that is what you want, of course.'

'It is what must happen,' Renzo said quietly. 'I cannot allow the present situation to continue any longer. For one thing, I am running out of excuses to explain her absence. For another, I accept that the purpose of our marriage must be fulfilled without further delay.'

'Dio mio,' Guillermo said faintly. 'I hope your approach to your bride will be made in more alluring terms. Or I warn you, my son, you will surely fail.'

Renzo's smile was hard. 'No,' he said. 'Not this time. And that is a promise.'

However, Renzo was thoughtful as, later, he drove back to his apartment. He owned the top floor of a former *palazzo*, the property of an old and noble family who had never seen the necessity to work for their living until it was too late. But although he enjoyed its grace and elegance, he used it merely as a *pied à terre* in Rome.

Because the home of his heart was the ancient and imposing country house deep in the Tuscan countryside where he had been born, and where he'd expected to begin his married life in the specially converted wing, designed to give them all the space and privacy that newlyweds could ever need.

He remembered showing it to Marisa before the wedding, asking if she had any ideas or requirements of her own that could be incorporated, but she'd said haltingly that it all seemed 'very nice', and refused to be drawn further. And she had certainly not commented on the adjoining bedrooms that they would occupy after their marriage, with the communicating door.

And if she'd had reservations about sharing the house with her future father-in-law she hadn't voiced those either. On the contrary, she'd always seemed very fond of Zio Guillermo, as she'd been encouraged to call him.

But then, Renzo thought, frowning, apart from agreeing to be his wife in a small wooden voice she hadn't said too much to him at all. Something he should, of course, have noticed but for his other preoccupations, he conceded, his mouth tightening.

Besides, he was accustomed to the fact that she did not chatter unnecessarily from the days when she'd been a small, silent child, clearly overwhelmed by her surroundings, and through her years as a skinny, tongue-tied adolescent. A time, he recalled ruefully, when she'd constantly embarrassed him by the hero-worship she'd tried inexpertly to hide.

She hadn't even cried at her own christening in London, which he'd attended as a sullenly reluctant ten-year-old, watching Maria Santangeli looking down, her face transfigured, at the lacy bundle in her arms.

His mother had met Lisa Cornell at the exclusive convent school they had both attended in Rome, and they had formed a bond of friendship that had never wavered across the years and miles that separated them.

But whereas Maria had married as soon as she left school, and become a mother within the year, Lisa had pursued a successful career in magazine journalism before meeting Alec Brendon, a well-known producer of television documentaries.

And when her daughter had been born only Maria would do

as godmother to the baby. A role she had been more than happy to fill. The name chosen was naturally 'Marisa', the shortened form of Maria Lisa.

Renzo knew that, much as he had been loved, it had always been a sadness to his parents that no other children had followed him into the waiting nurseries at the Villa Proserpina. And this godchild had taken the place of the longed-for daughter in his mother's heart.

He wasn't sure on which visit to Italy she and Lisa Brendon had begun planning the match between their children. He knew only that, to his adolescent disgust, it seemed to have become all too quickly absorbed into family folklore as an actual possibility.

He'd even derisively christened Marisa *'la cicogna'*—the stork—a mocking reference to her long legs and the little beak of a nose that dominated her small, thin face, until his mother had called him to order with unwonted sternness.

But the fact that Marisa was being seriously considered as his future bride had been brought home to him six years ago, when her parents had been killed in a motorway pile-up.

Because, in a devastating aftermath of the accident, it had been discovered that the Brendons had always lived up to and exceeded their income, and that through some fairly typical oversight Alec had failed to renew his life insurance, leaving his only daughter penniless.

At first Maria had begged for the fourteen-year-old girl to be brought to Italy and raised as a member of their family, but for once the ever-indulgent Guillermo had vetoed her plan. If her scheme to turn Marisa into the next Santangeli bride was to succeed—and there was, of course, no guarantee that this would happen—it would be far better, he'd said, for the girl to continue her education and upbringing in England, at their expense, than for Renzo to become so accustomed to her presence in the household that he might begin to regard her simply as an irritating younger sister.

It was a proposition to which his wife had reluctantly acquiesced. And while Marisa had remained in England Renzo had been able to put the whole ridiculous idea of her as his future wife out of his mind.

In any case, he'd had to concentrate on his career, completing his business degree with honours before joining the renowned and internationally respected Santangeli Bank, where he would ultimately succeed his father as chairman. By a mixture of flair and hard work he had made sure he deserved the top job, and that no one would mutter sourly 'boss's son' when he took over.

He was aware that the junior ranks of staff referred to him as 'Il Magnifico', after his namesake Lorenzo de Medici, but shrugged it off with amusement.

Life had been good. He'd had a testing job which provided exhilaration and interest, also allowing him to travel widely. And with his dynastic obligations remaining no more than a small cloud on his horizon he had enjoyed women, his physical needs deliciously catered to by a series of thoroughly enjoyable affairs which, the ladies involved knew perfectly well, would never end in marriage.

But while he'd learned early in his sexual career to return with infinite skill and generosity the pleasure he received, he'd never committed the fatal error of telling any of his *innamoratas* that he loved her—not even in the wilder realms of passion.

Then, three years ago, he had been shocked out of his complacency by his mother's sudden illness. She'd been found to be suffering from an aggressive and inoperable cancer and had died only six weeks later.

'Renzo, *carissimo mio*.' Her paper-thin hand had rested on his, light as a leaf. 'Promise me that my little Marisa will be your wife.'

And torn by sorrow and disbelief at the first real blow life had struck him, he had given her his word, thereby sealing his fate.

Now, as he walked into his apartment, he heard the phone ringing. He ignored it, knowing only too well who was calling, because the clinic would have used the private mobile number he'd left with them—which Doria Venucci did not have.

He recognised that, if he was to stand any chance of retrieving his marriage, she was a luxury he could no longer afford. However, courtesy demanded that he tell her in person that their relationship was over.

Not that she would protest too much. A secret *amour* was one thing. A vulgar scandal which jeopardised her own marriage would be something else entirely, he told himself cynically.

As he walked across his vast bedroom to the bathroom beyond, shedding his clothes as he went, he allowed himself a brief moment of regret for the lush, golden, insatiable body he'd left in bed only a few hours before and would never enjoy again.

But everything had changed now. And at the same time he knew how totally wrong he'd been to become involved with her in the first place. Especially when he'd had no real excuse for his behaviour apart from another infuriating encounter with Marisa's damnable answering machine.

So she still didn't want to speak to him, he'd thought furiously, slamming down his receiver as a bland, anonymous voice had informed him yet again that she was 'not available'. She was still refusing to give him even the slightest chance to make amends to her.

Well, so be it, he had told himself. He was sick of the self-imposed celibacy he'd been enduring since she left, and if she didn't want him he'd go out and find a woman who did.

It had not been a difficult task because, at a party that same evening, he'd met Doria and invited her to a very proper and public lunch with him the following day. Which had been followed, without delay, by a series of private and exceedingly improper assignations in a suite at a discreet and accordingly expensive hotel.

And if he'd embarked on the affair in a mood of defiance, he could not pretend that the damage to his male pride had not been soothed by the Contessa Venucci's openly expressed hunger for him, he thought wryly.

He stepped into the shower cubicle, switching the water to its fullest extent, letting it pound down on his weary body, needing it to eradicate the edginess and confusion of emotions that were assailing him.

It could not be denied that latterly, outside working hours, he had not enjoyed the easiest of relationships with his father. He had always attributed this to his disapproval of Guillermo's year-long liaison with Ottavia Alesconi, having made it coldly clear from the beginning that he felt it was too soon after his mother's death for the older man to embark on such a connection.

And yet did he really have any right to object to his father's wish to find new happiness? The *signora* was a charming and cultivated woman, a childless widow, still running the successful PR company she had begun with her late husband. Someone, moreover, who was quite content to share Guillermo's leisure, but had no ambitions to become his Marchesa.

His father had always seemed so alive and full of vigour, with never a hint of ill health, so tonight's attack must have been a particularly unpleasant shock to her, he thought sombrely, resolving to call on her in person to thank her for her prompt and potentially life-saving efforts on Guillermo's behalf. By doing so he might also make it clear that any initial resentment of her role in his father's life had long since dissipated.

Besides, he thought ruefully, his own personal life was hardly such a blazing success that he could afford to be critical of anyone else's. And maybe it was really his bitter sense of grievance over being cornered into marriage that had brought about the coldness that had grown up between his father and himself.

But he could not allow any lingering animosity, he told himself as he stepped out of the shower and began to dry himself. He had to put the past behind him, where it belonged. Tonight had indeed been a warning—in a number of ways. It was indeed more than time he abandoned his bachelor lifestyle and applied himself to becoming a husband and, in due course, a father.

If, of course, he could obtain the co-operation of his bride—something he'd signally failed to do so far, he thought, staring broodingly in the mirror as he raked his damp hair back from his face with his fingers.

If he was honest, he could admit that he was a man who'd never had to try too hard with women. It wasn't something he was proud of, but, nevertheless, it remained an indisputable fact. And it remained a terrible irony that his wife was the only one who'd greeted his attempts to woo her with indifference at best and hostility at worst.

He'd become aware that he might have a fight on his hands when he'd paid his first visit to her cousin's house in London, ostensibly to invite Marisa to Tuscany for a party his father was planning to celebrate her nineteenth birthday.

Julia Gratton had received him alone, her hard eyes travelling over him in an assessment that had managed to be critical and salacious at the same time, he'd thought with distaste.

'So, you've come courting at last, *signore*.' Her laugh was like the yap of a small, unfriendly dog. 'I'd begun to think it would never happen. I sent Marisa up to change,' she added abruptly. 'She'll be down presently. In the meantime, let me offer you some coffee.'

He was glad that she'd told him what was being served in those wide, shallow porcelain cups, because there was no other clue in the thin, tasteless fluid that he forced himself to swallow.

So when the drawing room door opened he was glad to put it aside and get to his feet. Where he paused, motionless, the formal smile freezing on his lips as he saw her.

He could tell by the look of displeasure that flitted across Mrs Gratton's thin face that Marisa had not changed her clothes, as instructed, but he was not, he thought, repining.

She was still shy, looking down at the carpet rather than at him, her long curling lashes brushing her cheeks, but everything else about her was different. Gloriously so. And he allowed the connoisseur in him to enjoy the moment. She was slim now, he realised, instead of gawky, and her face was fuller so that her features no longer seemed too large for its pallor.

Her breasts were not large but, outlined by her thin tee shirt, they were exquisitely shaped. Her waist was a handspan, her hips a gentle curve. And those endless legs—*Santa Madonna*—even encased as they were in tight denim jeans he could imagine how they would feel clasped around him, naked, as she explored under his tuition the pleasures of sex.

Hurriedly he dragged his mind back to the social niceties. Took a step forward, attempting a friendly smile. '*Buongiorno*, Maria Lisa.' He deliberately used the version of her name he'd teased her with in childhood. '*Come stai?*'

She looked back at him then, and for the briefest instant he seemed to see in those long-lashed grey-green eyes such a glint of withering scorn that it stopped him dead. Then, next moment, she was responding quietly and politely to his greeting, even allowing him to take her hand, and he told himself that it must have been his imagination.

Because that was what his ego wanted him to think, he told himself bitterly. That it was an honour for this girl to have been chosen as a Santangeli bride, and if *he* had no objections, especially now that he had seen her again, it must follow that she could have none either.

Prompted sharply by her cousin, she accepted the party invitation, and agreed expressionlessly to his suggestion that he should return the next day to discuss the arrangements.

And although she knew—had obviously been told—that the real reason for his visit was to request her formally to become his wife, she gave no sign of either pleasure or dismay at the prospect.

And that in itself should have warned him, he thought in self-condemnation. Instead he'd attributed her lack of reaction to nervousness at the prospect of marriage.

In the past, his sexual partners had certainly not been chosen for their inexperience, but innocence was an essential quality for the girl who would one day bear the Santangeli heir. He had told himself the least he could do was offer her some reassurance about how their relationship would be conducted in its early days—and nights.

Therefore, he'd resolved to promise her that their honeymoon would be an opportunity for them to become properly reacquainted, even be friends, and that he would be prepared to wait patiently until she felt ready to take him as her husband in any true sense.

And he'd meant every word of it, he thought, remembering how she'd listened in silence, her head half-turned from him, her creamy skin tinged with colour as he spoke.

All the same, he knew he'd been hoping for some reaction—some slight encouragement for him to take her in his arms and kiss her gently to mark their engagement.

But there'd been nothing, then or later. She'd never signalled in any way that she wanted him to touch her, and by offering forbearance he'd fallen, he realised, annoyed, into a trap of his own making.

Because as time had passed, and their wedding day had approached, he'd found himself as awkward as a boy in her cool, unrevealing company, unable to make even the slightest approach to her—something which had never happened to him before.

But what he had not bargained for was losing his temper. And it was the guilt of that which still haunted him.

He sighed abruptly as he knotted a dry towel round his hips. Well, there was no point in torturing himself afresh over that. He ought to go to bed, he thought, and try to catch some sleep for what little remained of the night. But he knew he was far too restless to relax, and that the time could be used to better effect in planning the coming campaign.

He walked purposefully out of the bathroom, ignoring the invitation of the turned-down bed in the room beyond, and proceeded instead down the hallway to the *salotto*.

It was an impressive room, its size accentuated by the pale walls and a signal lack of clutter. He'd furnished it in light colours too, with deep, lavishly cushioned sofas in cream leather, and occasional tables in muted, ashy shades.

The only apparently discordant note in all this pastel restraint was the massive desk, which he loved because it had once belonged to his grandfather, and which now occupied a whole corner of the room in all its mahogany magnificence.

In banking circles he knew that he was viewed as a moderniser, a man with his sights firmly set on the future, alert to any changes in the market. But anyone seeing that desk, he'd always thought dryly, would have guessed immediately that underlying this was a strong respect for tradition and an awareness of what he owed to the past.

He went straight to the desk, extracted a file from one of its brass-handled drawers and, after pouring himself a generous Scotch, stretched out on one of the sofas and began to glance through the folder's contents. An update had been received the previous day, but he'd not had a chance to read it before, and now seemed an appropriate time.

He took a contemplative mouthful of whisky as his eyes scanned swiftly down the printed sheet, then sat up abruptly with a gasp, nearly choking as his drink went down the wrong way and he found himself in imminent danger of spilling the rest everywhere.

He recovered instantly, eyes watering, then set down the crystal tumbler carefully out of harm's way before, his face thunderous, he re-read the unwelcome information that the private surveillance company engaged for the protection of his absentee wife had provided.

'We must advise you,' it stated, 'that since our last report Signora Santangeli, using her maiden name, has obtained paid employment as a receptionist in a private art gallery in Carstairs Place, apparently taking the place of a young woman on maternity leave. In the past fortnight she has lunched twice in the company of the gallery's owner, Mr Corin Langford. She no longer wears her wedding ring. Photographic evidence can be provided if required.'

Renzo screwed the report into a ball and threw it across the room, cursing long and fluently.

He flung himself off the sofa and began to pace restlessly up and down. He did not need any photographs, he thought savagely. Too many of his own affairs had begun over leisurely lunches, so he knew all about satisfying one appetite while creating another—was totally familiar with the sharing of food and wine, eyes meeting across the table, fingers touching, then entwining.

What he did not—could not—recognise was the mental image of the girl on the other side of the table. Marisa smiling back, talking and laughing, the initial shyness in her eyes dancing into confidence and maybe even into desire.

The way she had never once behaved with him. Nor looked at him—or smiled.

Not, of course, that he was jealous, he hastened to remind himself.

Just—angrier than he'd ever been before. Everything that had happened between them in the past paled into insignificance under this—this insult to his manhood. To his status as her husband.

Well, if his reluctant bride thought she could place the horns on him, she was much mistaken, he vowed in grim silence. Tomorrow he would go to fetch her home, and once he had her back she would not get away from him again. Because he would make very sure that from then on she would think of no one—want no one—but him. That she would be his completely.

And, he told himself harshly, he would enjoy every minute of it.

CHAPTER TWO

'MARISA? My God, it is you. I can hardly believe it.'

The slender girl who'd been gazing abstractedly into a shop window swung round, her lips parting in astonishment as she recognised the tall, fair-haired young man standing behind her.

She said uncertainly, 'Alan—what are you doing here?'

'That should be my question. Why aren't you sipping cappuccino on the Via Veneto?'

The million-dollar question...

'Well, that can pall after a while,' she said lightly. 'And I began to fancy a cup of English tea instead.'

'Oh,' he said. 'And what does Lorenzo the Magnificent have to say about that?'

The note of bitterness in his voice was not lost on her. She said quickly, 'Alan—don't...'

'No,' he said. 'I know. I'm sorry.' He looked past her to the display of upmarket baby clothes she'd been contemplating and his mouth tightened. 'I gather congratulations must be in order?'

'God, no.' Marisa spoke more forcefully than she'd intended, and flushed when she saw his surprise. 'I—I mean not for me. A girl I was at school with, Dinah Newman, is expecting her first, and I want to buy her something special.'

'Well, you seem to have come to the right place,' Alan said, inspecting a couple of the price tickets with raised brows. 'You need to be the wife of a millionaire banker to shop here.' He smiled at her. 'She must be quite a friend.'

'Let's just say that I owe her,' Marisa said quietly.

I owe her for the fact that she recommended me to Corin Langford, so that I'm now gainfully employed instead of totally dependent on Renzo Santangeli. And for not asking too many awkward questions when I suddenly turned up in London alone.

'Do you have to do your buying right now?' Alan asked. 'I just can't believe I've run into you like this. I was wondering if we could have lunch together.'

She could hardly tell him that her lunch hour was coming to an end and it was time she went back to her desk at the Estrello Gallery. She had already instinctively slid her betrayingly ringless left hand into the pocket of her jacket.

Meeting Alan again was a surprise for her too, she thought, but tricky when she had so many things to conceal.

'Sorry.' Her smile was swift and genuinely apologetic. 'I have to be somewhere in about five minutes.

'At your husband's beck and call, no doubt.'

She hesitated. 'Actually, Renzo's—away at the moment.'

'Leaving you alone so soon?'

Marisa shrugged. 'Well, we're hardly joined at the hip.' She tried to sound jokey.

'No,' he said. 'I can imagine.' He paused. 'So, what do grass widows do? Count the hours until the errant husband returns?'

'Far from it,' she said crisply. 'They get on with their own lives. Go places and see people.'

'If that's true,' he said slowly, 'maybe you'd consider seeing me one more time.' His voice deepened urgently. 'Marisa—if lunch is impossible meet me for dinner instead—will you? Eight o'clock at Chez Dominique? For old times' sake?'

She wanted to tell him that the old times were over. That they'd died the day he had allowed himself to be shunted out of her life and off to Hong Kong, because he hadn't been prepared to fight for her against a man who was powerful enough to kill his career with a word.

Not that she could altogether blame him, she reminded herself. Their romance had been at far too early a stage to command the kind of loyalty and commitment that she'd needed. It had only amounted to a few kisses, for heaven's sake. And it was one of those kisses that had brought their relationship to a premature end—when Alan had been caught saying goodnight to her by Cousin Julia.

That tense, shocking night when she'd finally discovered what the future really had in store for her.

If Alan had really been my lover, she thought, *I wouldn't have been a virgin bride, and therefore there'd have been no marriage to Renzo. But I—I didn't realise that until it was too late. Alan had already left, and, anyway, did I ever truly care enough for him to give myself in that way?*

She concealed a shiver as unwanted memories stirred. Lingered disturbingly. 'Alan—about tonight—I don't know… And I really must go now.'

'I'll book the table,' he said. 'And wait. Everything else is up to you.'

She gave him an uncertain smile. 'Well, whatever happens, it's been good to see you again.' And hurried away.

She was back at the gallery right on time, but Corin was hovering anxiously nevertheless, the coming session with his lawyers clearly at the forefront of his mind.

'He's going through a difficult divorce,' Dinah had warned her. 'The major problem being that he's still in love with his wife, whereas her only interest is establishing how many of his assets she can take into her new relationship. So he occasionally needs a shoulder to cry on.' She'd paused delicately. 'Think you can manage that?'

'Of course,' Marisa had returned robustly. She might even be able to pick up a few pointers for her own divorce when it became legally viable, she'd thought wryly. Except she wanted nothing from her brief, ill-starred marriage except her freedom. A view that she hoped Lorenzo Santangeli would share.

'I'd better be off,' Corin said, then paused at the doorway. 'If Mrs Brooke rings about that watercolour…'

'The price remains exactly the same.' Marisa smiled at him. 'Don't worry—I won't let her argue me down. Now go, or you'll be late.'

'Yes,' he said, and sighed heavily. 'I suppose so.'

She watched him standing on the kerb, raking a worried hand through his hair as he hailed a cab. And he had every reason to appear harassed, she mused. The former Mrs Langford had not only demanded the marital home, but was also claiming a major share in the gallery too, on the grounds that her father had contributed much of the initial financial backing.

'My father and hers were friends,' Dinah had confided. 'And Dad says he'd be spinning in his grave if he knew what Janine was up to. If she gets her hands on the Estrello it will be closed, and Corin will be out by the end of the year.'

'But it's very successful,' Marisa pointed out, startled. 'He's a terrific businessman, and his clients obviously trust him.'

Dinah snorted. 'You think she cares about that? No way. All she can see is a valuable piece of real estate. As soon as her father died she was badgering Corin to sell, and when he wouldn't she decided to end the marriage—as soon as she found someone to take his place.' She added, 'He doesn't deserve it, of course. But—as the saying goes—nice guys finish last.'

Yes, Marisa had thought bitterly, and bastards like Lorenzo Santangeli spend their lives in pole position. There's no justice.

Feeling suddenly restive, she walked over to her desk and sat down, reaching determinedly for the small pile of paperwork that Corin had left for her. It might not be much, she thought wryly, but at least it would stop her mind straying down forbidden pathways.

The afternoon wasn't particularly busy, but it was profitable, as people came in to buy rather than simply browse. A young couple seeking a wedding present for friends bought a pair of modern miniatures, Mrs Brooke reluctantly agreed to buy the watercolour at full price, and an elderly man eventually decided to acquire a Lake District landscape for his wife's birthday.

'We went there on our honeymoon,' he confided to Marisa as she dealt with his credit card payment. 'However, I admit I was torn between that and the wonderful view of the Italian coastline by the same artist.' He sighed reminiscently. 'We've spent several holidays around Amalfi, and it would have brought back a lot of happy memories.' He paused. 'Do you know the area at all?'

For a moment Marisa's fingers froze, and she nearly bodged the transaction. But she forced herself to concentrate, smiling stiltedly as she handed him his card and receipt. 'I have been there, yes. Just once. It—it's incredibly beautiful.'

And I wish you had bought that painting instead, because then I would never—ever—have to look at it again.

She arranged a date and time for delivery of his purchase, and saw him to the door.

Back at her desk, entering the final details of the deal into the computer, she found herself stealing covert looks over her shoulder to the place on the wall where the Amalfi scene was still hanging.

It was as if, she thought, the artist had also visited the Casa Adriana and sat in its lush, overgrown garden on the stone bench in the shade of the lemon tree. As if he too had looked over the crumbling wall to where the rugged cliff tumbled headlong down to the exquisite azure ripple of the Gulf of Salerno far below.

From the moment she'd seen the painting she'd felt the breath catch painfully in her throat. Because it was altogether too potent a reminder of her hiding place—her sanctuary—during those seemingly endless, agonising weeks that had been her honeymoon. The place that, once found, she'd retreated to each morning, knowing that no one would be looking for her, or indeed would find her, and where she'd discovered that solitude did not have to mean loneliness as she shakily counted down the days that would decide her immediate fate.

The place that she'd left each evening as sunset approached, forcing her to return once more to the cold, taut silence of the Villa Santa Caterina and the reluctant company of the man she'd married, to dine with him in the warm darkness at a candlelit table on a flower-hung terrace, where every waft of scented air had seemed, in unconscious irony, to breathe a soft but powerful sexuality.

And where, when the meal had finally ended, she would wish him a quiet goodnight, formally returned, and go off to lie alone in the wide bed with its snowy sheets, praying that her bedroom door would not open because, in spite of everything, boredom or impatience might drive him to seek her out again.

But thankfully it had never happened, and now they were apart without even the most fleeting of contact between them any longer. Presumably, she thought, biting her lip, Renzo had taken the hint, and all that remained now was for him to take the necessary steps to bring their so-called marriage to an end.

I should never have agreed to it in the first place, she told herself bitterly. *I must have been mad. But whatever I thought of Cousin Julia I couldn't deliberately see her made homeless, especially with a sick husband on her hands.*

She'd been embarrassed when Julia had walked into the

drawing room that night and found her in Alan's arms, but embarrassment had soon turned to outrage when her cousin, with a smile as bleak as Antarctica, had insisted that he leave and, in spite of her protests, ushered Alan out of the drawing room and to the front door.

'How dared you do that?' Marisa had challenged, her voice shaking when Julia returned alone. 'I'm not a child any more, and I'm entitled to see anyone I wish.'

Julia had shaken her head. 'I'm afraid not, my dear—precisely because you're not a child any more.' She'd paused, her lips stretching into a thin smile. 'You see, your future husband doesn't want any other man poaching on his preserves—something that was made more than clear when I originally agreed to be your guardian. So we'll pretend this evening never happened—shall we? I promise you it will be much the best thing for both of us.'

There had been, Marisa remembered painfully, a long silence. Then her own voice saying, 'The best thing? What on earth are you talking about? I—I don't have any future husband. It's nonsense.'

'Oh, don't be naive,' her cousin tossed back at her contemptuously. 'You know as well as I do that you're expected to marry Lorenzo Santangeli. It was all arranged years ago.'

Marisa felt suddenly numb. 'Marry—Renzo? But that was never serious,' she managed through dry lips. 'It—it was just one of those silly things that people say.'

'On the contrary, my dear, it's about as serious as it can get.' Julia sat down. 'The glamorous Signor Santangeli has merely been waiting for you to reach an appropriate age before making you his bride.'

Marisa's throat tightened. She said curtly, 'Now, that I don't believe.'

'It is probably an exaggeration,' Julia agreed. 'I doubt if he's given you a thought from one year's end to another. But he's remembered you now, or had his memory jogged for him, so he's paying us a visit in a week or two in order to stake his claim.' She gave a mocking whistle. 'Rich, good-looking, and a tiger in the sack, by all accounts. Congratulations, my pet. You've won the jackpot.'

'I've won nothing.' Marisa's heart was hammering painfully. 'Because it's not going to happen. My God, I don't even *like* him.'

'Well, he's hardly cherishing a hidden passion for you either,' Julia Gratton said crushingly. 'It's an arranged marriage, you silly little bitch, not a love match. The Santangeli family need a young, healthy girl to provide them with the next generation, and you're their choice.'

'Then they'll have to look elsewhere.' Marisa's voice trembled. 'Because I'm not for sale.'

'My dear child,' Julia drawled. 'You were bought and paid for years ago.' She gestured around her. 'How do you imagine we can afford to live in this house, rather than the one-bedroom nightmare Harry and I were renting when your parents died? Where did your school fees come from? And who's been keeping the roof over our heads and feeding us all, as well as providing the money for your clothes, holidays and various amusements?'

'I thought—you…'

'Don't be a fool. Harry edits academic books. He's hardly coining it in. And now that he has multiple sclerosis he won't be able to work at all for much longer.'

Marisa flung back her head. She said hoarsely, 'I'll get a job. Pay them back every penny.'

'Doing what?' Julia demanded derisively. 'Apart from this part-time course in fine arts you're following at the moment, you're trained for nothing except the career that's already mapped out for you—as the wife of a multimillionaire and the mother of his children. It's payback time, and you're the only currency they'll accept.'

'I don't believe it. I won't.' Marisa's voice was urgent. 'Renzo can't have agreed to this. He—he doesn't want me either. I—I know that.'

Julia's laugh was cynical. 'He's a man, my dear, and you're an attractive, nubile girl. He won't find his role as bridegroom too arduous, believe me. He'll fulfil his obligations to his family, and enjoy them too.'

Marisa said slowly, 'That's—obscene.'

'It's the way of the world, my child.' Julia shrugged. 'And life with the future Marchese Santangeli will have other compensations, you know. Once you've given Lorenzo his heir and a spare, I don't imagine you'll see too much of him. He'll continue to amuse himself as he does now, but with rather more discretion, and you'll be left to your own devices.'

Marisa stared at her. She said huskily, 'You mean he's involved with someone? He—has a girlfriend?'

'Oh, she's rather more than that,' Julia said negligently. 'A beautiful Venetian, I understand, called Lucia Gallo, who works in television. They've been quite inseparable for several months.'

'I see.' Instinct told Marisa that her cousin was enjoying this, so she did her best to sound casual. 'Well, if that's the case, why doesn't he marry her instead?'

'Because she's a divorcee, and unsuitable in all kinds of ways.' She paused. 'I thought I'd already indicated that Santangeli brides are expected to come to their marriages as virgins.'

Marisa said coolly, 'But presumably the same rule doesn't apply to the men?'

Julia laughed. 'Hardly. And you'll be glad of that when the time comes, believe me.' Her tone changed, becoming a touch more conciliatory. 'Think about it, Marisa. This marriage won't be all bad news. You've always said you wanted to travel. Well, you'll be able to—and first-class all the way. Or, with Florence on your doorstep, you could always plunge back into the art world. Create your own life.'

'And *that* is supposed to make it all worthwhile?' Marisa queried incredulously. 'I allow myself to be—used—in return for a couple of visits to the Accademia? I won't do it.'

'I think you will,' her cousin said with grim emphasis. 'We're Santangeli pensioners, my pet, all of us. Yourself included. We owe our lifestyle to their goodwill. And once you're married to Lorenzo, that happy state of affairs will continue for Harry and myself. Because they've agreed that we can move out of London to a bungalow, specially adapted for a wheelchair, and employ full-time care when the need arises.' For a moment her voice wavered. 'Something we could never afford to do under normal circumstances.'

She rallied, her tone harsh again. 'But if you try and back out now, the whole thing will crash and burn. We'll lose this house—everything. And I won't see Harry's precarious future in jeopardy because a spoiled little brat who's spent the past few years grabbing everything going with both hands, has suddenly decided the price is too high for her delicate sensibilities. Well, there's no such thing as a free lunch, sweetie, so make the best of it.

'And remember, a lot of girls would kill to be in your shoes. So, if nothing else, learn to be civil to him in the daytime, co-operate at night, and don't ask awkward questions when he's away. Even you should be able to manage that.'

Except I didn't, Marisa thought wearily, shivering as she remembered the note of pure vitriol in her cousin's voice. I failed on every single count.

She sighed. She'd fought—of course she had—using every conceivable argument against the unwanted marriage. She'd also spent the next few days trying to contact Alan, who had been strangely unavailable.

And when at last she had managed to speak to him on the phone, over a week later, she'd learned that he'd been offered a transfer, with promotion, to Hong Kong, and would be leaving almost at once.

'It's a great opportunity,' he told her, his voice uncomfortable. 'And totally unexpected. I could have waited years for something like this.'

'I see.' Her mind was whirling, but she kept her tone light. 'I suppose you wouldn't consider taking me with you?'

There was a silence, then he said jerkily, 'Marisa—you know that isn't going to happen. Neither of us are free agents in this. I know that strings were pulled to get me this job because you're soon moving to a different league.' He paused. 'I don't think I'm really meant to be talking to you now.'

'No,' she said, past the shocked tightness in her throat. 'Probably not. And I—I quite understand. Well—good luck.'

After that it had been difficult to go on fighting, once her stunned mind had registered that she had no one to turn to, nowhere to go, and, as Julia had reminded her, barely enough academic qualifications to earn her a living wage.

But in the end she'd wearily capitulated because of Harry, the quiet, kind man who'd made Julia's reluctant guardianship of her so much more bearable, and who was going to need the Santangeli generosity so badly, and so soon.

But if Renzo Santangeli believed she was going to fall gratefully at his feet, he could think again, she had told herself with icy bitterness.

* * *

It was a stance she'd maintained throughout what she supposed had passed for his courtship of her. Admittedly, with the result a foregone conclusion, he hadn't had to try too hard, and she'd been glad of it, reflecting defiantly that the less she saw of him the better. But the fact remained that her avowed resolve had not actually been tested.

The only time she'd really been alone with him before the wedding, she thought, staring at the screensaver on her computer, was when he'd made that strange, almost diffident proposal of marriage, explaining that he wanted to make their difficult situation as easy as possible for her, and that he would force no physical intimacies on her until she'd become accustomed to her new circumstances and was ready to be his wife in every sense of the word.

And as far as their engagement went, he'd kept his word. She hadn't been subjected to any unwelcome advances from him.

No doubt he'd secretly believed he wouldn't have to wait too long, she decided, her mouth tightening. He'd been sure curiosity alone would undermine her determination to keep him at arm's length, or further.

Well, he'd learned better during the misery of their honeymoon, and their parting at the end of it had come as a relief to them both. And, although he'd made various dutiful attempts to maintain minimal contact with her once she'd moved back to London, he clearly hadn't seen any necessity to try and heal the rift between them in person. Not that she'd have allowed that, anyway, she assured herself hastily.

So, now he seemed to have tacitly accepted that, apart from the inevitable legal formalities, their brief, ill-starred marriage was permanently over. Soon he'd be free to seek a more willing lady to share the marital bed with him when he felt inclined—probably some doe-eyed Italian beauty with a talent for maternity.

Which would certainly please his old witch of a grandmother, who'd made no secret of her disapproval of his chosen match from the moment Marisa had arrived back in Italy under Julia's eagle-eyed escort. Harry had not accompanied them, having opted to spend the time quietly at his sister's home in Kent, but he'd announced his determination to fly out for the wedding in order to give the bride away.

But Renzo's next wooing would almost certainly be conducted in a very different manner.

She'd wondered sometimes if it had been obvious to everyone that he'd rarely touched her, apart from taking her hand when making introductions. And that he'd never kissed her in any way.

Except once…

It had been during the dinner his father had given at the house in Tuscany for her nineteenth birthday, with a large ebullient crowd of family and friends gathered round the long table in the sumptuous frescoed dining room. She'd been seated next to him in her pale cream dress, with its long sleeves and discreetly square neckline, the epitome of the demure *fidanzata*, with the lustrous pearls that had been his birthday gift to her clasped round her throat for everyone to see and admire.

'Pearls for purity,' had been Julia's acid comment when she saw them. 'And costing a fortune too. Clearly he'll be expecting his money's worth on his wedding night.'

Was that the message he was intending to convey to the world at large? Marisa had wondered, wincing. She'd been sorely tempted to put the gleaming string back in its velvet box, but eventually she'd steeled herself to wear it, along with the ring he'd given her to mark their engagement—a large and exquisite ruby surrounded by diamonds.

She could not, she'd thought, fault his generosity in material matters. In fact she'd been astonished when she'd discovered the allowance he proposed to make her when they were married, and could not imagine how she'd spend even a quarter of it.

But then, as she had reminded herself, he was buying her goodwill and, as Julia had so crudely indicated, her body.

It was a thought that had still had the ability to dry her mouth in panic, especially with the wedding drawing closer each day.

Because, in spite of his promised forbearance, there would come a night when she would have to undergo the ordeal of submission to him. 'Payback time', as Julia had called it, and it scared her.

He scared her…

She had turned her head, studying him covertly from under her lashes. He'd been talking to the people across the table, his hands moving incisively to underline a point, his dark face vivid with laughter, and it had occurred to her, as swiftly and shockingly as a thunderbolt crashing through the ceiling, that if she'd met him that night for the first time she might well have found him deeply and disturbingly attractive.

His lean good looks had been emphasised by the severe formality of dinner jacket and black tie. But then, she'd been forced to admit, he always dressed well, and his clothes were beautiful.

But fast on the heels of that reluctant admission had come another thought that she'd found even more unwelcome.

That, only too soon, she would know what Renzo looked like without any clothes at all.

The breath had caught in her throat, and she'd felt an odd wave of heat sweep up over her body and turn her face to flame.

And as if he'd picked up her sudden confusion on some secret male radar, Renzo had turned and looked at her, his brows lifting in enquiry as he observed her hectically flushed cheeks and startled eyes.

And for one brief moment they had seemed caught together within a cone of silence, totally cut off from the chatter and laughter around them, his gaze meshing with hers, only to sharpen into surprise and—oh, God—amused awareness.

Making her realise with utter mortification that he'd read her thoughts as easily as if she'd had *I wonder what he looks like naked?* tattooed across her forehead.

He had inclined his head slightly in acknowledgement, the golden eyes dancing, his mouth twisting in mocking appreciation, and reached for the hand that wore his ring, raising her fingers for the brush of his lips, then turning them so he could plant a more deliberate kiss in the softness of her palm.

Her colour had deepened helplessly as she'd heard the ripple of delighted approbation from round the table, and she had known his gesture had been noted.

And she had no one to blame for that but herself, she'd thought, her heart hammering within the prim confines of the cream bodice as she had removed her hand from his clasp with whatever dignity she could salvage. She had known, as she did so, that the guests would be approving of that too, respecting what they saw as her modesty and shyness, when in reality she wanted to grab the nearest wine bottle and break it over his head.

When the dinner had finally ended, an eternity later, she'd been thankful that courtesy kept Renzo with the departing guests, enabling her to escape upstairs without speaking to him.

Julia, however, had not been so easily evaded.

'So,' she said, following Marisa into her bedroom and draping herself over the arm of the little brocaded sofa by the window. 'You seem to be warming at last to your future husband.'

Marisa put the pearls carefully in their case. 'Appearances can be deceptive.'

'Then you're a fool,' her cousin said bluntly. 'He may be charming, but underneath there's one tough individual, and you can't afford to play games with him—blushing and sighing one minute, and becoming an ice maiden the next.'

'Thank you,' Marisa returned politely. 'I'll bear that in mind.'

She'd momentarily lost ground tonight, and she knew it, but it was only a temporary aberration. She'd find a way to make up for it—somehow.

And so I did, she thought now, *only to find myself reaping a bitter harvest as a consequence.*

Her reverie was interrupted by the return of Corin, looking woebegone.

'She wants her half-share in the gallery,' he announced without preamble. 'She says that I'm far too conventional, and she's planning to take an active part in the place—imposing some ideas of her own to widen the customer base. Which means she'll be working next to me every day as if nothing's happened. Well, it's impossible. I couldn't bear it.'

He sat down heavily at his desk. 'Besides, I know her ideas of old, and they just wouldn't work—not somewhere like this. But I can't afford to buy her out,' he added, sighing, 'so I'll just have to sell up and start again—perhaps in some country area where property isn't so expensive.'

Marisa brought him some strong black coffee. She said, 'Couldn't you find a white knight—someone who'd invest in the Estrello so you could pay your wife off?'

He pulled a face. 'If only. But times are bad, and getting harder, and luxury items like these are usually the first to be sacrificed, so I could struggle to find someone willing to take the risk. Anyway, investors generally want more of an instant return than I can offer.'

He savoured a mouthful of his coffee. 'I may close up early tonight,' he went on, giving her a hopeful look. 'Maybe we could have dinner together?'

I'm sorry, Corin, she thought. *But I'm not in the mood to provide a shoulder for you to cry on this evening—or whatever else you might have in mind. You're a nice guy, but it stops at lunch. And it stops now. Because I have issues of my own that I should deal with.*

Aloud, she said gently, 'I'm sorry, but I already have a date.'

She hadn't intended to meet Alan either, of course, but it had suddenly come to seem a better idea than sitting alone in her flat, brooding about the past.

That's a loser's game, she told herself with determination, *and I need to look to the future—and freedom.*

CHAPTER THREE

EVEN as she was getting dressed for her dinner date with Alan, Marisa was still unsure if she was doing the right thing.

It occurred to her, wryly, that even though it was barely a year since she'd actually contemplated running away with him her heart was not exactly beating faster as she contemplated the evening ahead.

And she hadn't promised to meet him, so ducking out would be an easy option.

On the other hand, going out to a restaurant appeared marginally more tempting than spending another solitary night in front of the television.

Yet solitary, she thought with a faint sigh, *is what I seem to do best.*

Up to now, having her own place for the first time in her life had felt a complete bonus. Admittedly, with only one bedroom, it wasn't the biggest flat in the world—in fact, it could have been slipped inside the Santangeli house in Tuscany and lost—but it was light, bright, well furnished, with a well-fitted kitchen and shower room, and was sited in a smart, modern block of similar apartments in an upmarket area of London.

Best of all, living there, as she often reminded herself, she answered to no one.

There was, naturally, a downside. She had to accept that her independence had its limits, because she didn't actually pay the rent. That was taken care of by a firm of lawyers, acting as agents for her husband.

After the divorce was finalised, she realised, she would no longer be able to afford anything like it.

Her life would also be subject to all kinds of other changes, not many of them negative. In spite of Julia's dismissive words, her academic results had been perfectly respectable, and she hadn't understood at the time why she'd received no encouragement to seek qualifications in some form of higher education, like her classmates.

How naive was it possible to get? she wondered, shaking her head in self-derision.

However, there was nothing to prevent her doing so in the future, with the help of a student loan. She could even look on the time she'd spent as Renzo's wife as a kind of 'gap year', she told herself, her mouth twisting.

And now she had the immediate future to deal with, in the shape of this evening, which might also have its tricky moments unless she was vigilant. After all, the last thing she wanted was for Alan to think she was a lonely wife in need of consolation.

Because nothing could be further from the truth.

She picked out her clothes with care—a pale blue denim wrap-around skirt topped by a white silk shirt—hoping her choice wouldn't look as if she was trying too hard. Then, proceeding along the same lines, she applied a simple dusting of powder to her face, and the lightest touch of colour on her mouth.

Lastly, and with reluctance, she retrieved her wedding ring from the box hidden in her dressing table and slid it on to her finger. She hadn't planned to wear it again, but its presence on her hand would be a tacit reminder to her companion that the evening was a one-off and she was certainly not available—by any stretch of the imagination.

Two hours later, she was ruefully aware that Alan's thinking had not grown any more elastic during his absence, and that, in spite of the romantic ambience that Chez Dominique had always cultivated, she was having a pretty dull evening.

A faintly baffling one, too, because he seemed to be in a nostalgic mood, talking about their past relationship as if it had been altogether deeper and more meaningful than she remembered.

Get a grip, she thought, irritated. *You may have been a few years older than I was, but we were still hardly more than boy and girl. I was certainly a virgin, and I suspect you probably were too, although that's almost certainly no longer true for either of us.*

He had far more confidence these days, smartly dressed in a

light suit, with a blue shirt that matched his eyes. And he seemed to have had his slightly crooked front teeth fixed too.

All in all, she decided, he was a nice guy. But that was definitely as far as it went.

However, the food at Chez Dominique was still excellent, and when she managed to steer him away from personal issues and on to his life in Hong Kong she became rather more interested in what he had to say, and was able to feel glad that he was doing well.

But even so, the fact that he had not gone there through choice clearly still rankled with him, and although he'd probably bypassed a rung or two on the corporate ladder as a result of his transfer, she detected that there was a note of resentment never far from the surface.

As the waiter brought his cheese and her *crème brûlée*, Alan said, 'Are you staying with your cousin while you're in London?'

'Oh, no,' Marisa returned, without thinking. 'Julia lives near Tonbridge Wells these days.'

'You mean you've actually been allowed off the leash without a minder?' His tone was barbed. 'Amazing.'

'Not particularly.' She ate some of her dessert. 'Perhaps—Lorenzo—' she stumbled slightly over the name '—trusts me.' *Or he simply doesn't care what I do...*

'So I suppose you must have a suite at the Ritz, or some other five-star palace?' He gave a small bitter laugh. 'How the other half live.'

'Nothing of the sort,' Marisa said tersely. 'I'm actually using someone's flat.' Which was, she thought, an approximation of the truth, and also a reminder of how very much she wanted to get back there and avoid answering any more of the questions that he was obviously formulating over his Port Salut.

She glanced at her watch and gave a controlled start. 'Heavens, is that really the time? I should be going.'

'Expecting a phone call from the absent husband?' There was a faintly petulant note in his voice.

'No,' she said. 'I have an early appointment tomorrow.' *At my desk in the Estrello, at nine o'clock sharp.*

At the same time she was aware that his remark had made her freeze inwardly. Because there'd been a time, she thought, when Renzo had called her nearly every day, coming up each time against the deliberate barrier of her answering machine, and leaving increasingly brief and stilted messages, which she had deleted as quickly as she'd torn up his unread letters.

Until the night when he'd said abruptly, an odd almost raw note in his voice, 'Tomorrow, Marisa, when I call you, please pick up the phone. There are things that need to be said.' He'd paused, then added, 'I beg you to do this.'

And when the phone had rung the following night she'd been shocked to find that she'd almost had to sit on her hands to prevent herself from lifting the receiver. That she'd had to repeat silently to herself over and over again, *There is nothing he can say that I could possibly want to hear.*

Then, in the silence of all the evenings that followed, she had come to realise that he was not going to call again, and that her intransigence had finally achieved the victory she wanted. And she had found she was wondering why her triumph suddenly seemed so sterile.

Something, she thought, she had still not managed to work out to her own satisfaction.

She had a polite tussle with Alan over her share of the bill, which he won, and walked out into the street with a feeling of release. She turned to say goodnight and found him at the kerb, hailing a taxi, which was thoughtful.

But she hadn't bargained for him clambering in after her.

She said coolly, 'Oh—may I drop you somewhere?'

He smiled at her. 'I was hoping you might offer me some coffee—or a nightcap.'

Her heart sank like a stone. 'It is getting late…'

'Not too late, surely—for old times' sake?'

He was over-fond of that phrase, Marisa decided irritably. And his 'old times' agenda clearly differed substantially from hers.

She said, not bothering to hide her reluctance, 'Well—a quick coffee, perhaps, and then you must go,' and watched with foreboding as his smile deepened into satisfaction.

She didn't doubt her ability to keep him at bay. She had, after all, done it before, with someone else, even though it had rebounded on her later in a way that still had the power to turn her cold all over at the memory.

But she told herself grimly, Alan was a totally different proposition. She'd make sure that when he'd drunk his coffee he would go away and stay away. There'd be no more meetings during this leave or any other.

As they went up in the lift to the second floor of the apartment block she was aware he'd moved marginally closer. She stepped back, deliberately distancing herself and hoping he'd take the hint.

But as she turned the key in the lock he was standing so close behind her that his breath was stirring her hair, and she flung the door open, almost jumping across the narrow hallway into the living room.

Where, she realised with shock, the light was on.

Also—the room was occupied.

She stopped so abruptly that Alan nearly cannoned into her as she saw with horror exactly who was waiting for her.

Lorenzo Santangeli was lounging full-length on the sofa, totally at ease, jacket and tie removed, with his white shirt unbuttoned almost to the waist, its sleeves turned back over his bronze forearms.

An opened bottle of red wine and two glasses, one half-filled, stood on the low table in front of the sofa.

As she stood, gaping at him, he smiled at her, tossed aside the book he was reading and swung his legs to the floor.

'Maria Lisa,' he said softly. '*Carissima*. You have returned at last. I was becoming worried about you.'

Throat dry with disbelief, she found a voice from somewhere. 'Renzo—I—I…' She gulped a breath, and formed words that made sense. 'What are you doing here?'

'I wished to surprise you, my sweet.' His voice was silky. 'And I see that I have done so.' He walked to her on bare feet, took her nerveless hand, and raised it briefly and formally to his lips before looking past her. With a feeling of total unreality she saw that he needed a shave.

He went on, 'Will you not introduce me to your escort, and allow me to thank him for bringing you safely to your door?'

In the ensuing silence she heard Alan swallow—deafeningly. Got herself somehow under control.

She said quietly, 'Of course. This is Alan Denison, an old friend, home on leave from Hong Kong.' *And he seems to have turned the most odd shade of green. I didn't know people really did that.*

For a moment she thought she saw a swift flicker of surprise in Renzo's astonishing golden eyes. Then he said smoothly, 'Ah, yes—I recall.'

'We just—happened to run into each other.' Alan spoke hoarsely. 'In the street. This morning. And I asked your—Signora Santangeli—to have dinner with me.'

'A kind thought,' Renzo returned. He was still, Marisa realised, holding her hand. And instinct warned her not to pull away. Not this time.

All the same, he was far too close for comfort. She was even aware of the faint, beguiling scent of the cologne he used, and her throat tightened at the unwanted memories it evoked.

Alan began to back towards the door. If she hadn't been in such turmoil, Marisa could almost have found it funny. As it was, she wanted to scream, *Don't go*.

He babbled on, 'But now I can safely leave her in your…' He paused.

Oh, God, Marisa thought hysterically, please don't say *capable hands*.

But to her relief, Alan only added lamely, 'In your care.'

Which was quite bad enough, given the circumstances.

'You are all consideration, *signore*. Permit me to wish you goodnight—on my wife's behalf as well as my own.' Keeping Marisa firmly at his side, Renzo watched expressionlessly as the younger man muttered something incomprehensible in reply, then fumbled his way out of the flat, closing the door behind him.

Once they were alone, she wrenched herself free and stepped back, distancing herself deliberately, her heart hammering against her ribcage.

As she made herself meet Renzo's enigmatic gaze, she said defensively, 'It's not what you think.'

The dark brows lifted. 'You have become a mind-reader during our separation, *mia cara*?'

'No.' It was her turn to swallow. 'But—but I know how it must look.'

'I know that he looked disappointed,' Renzo returned pleasantly. 'That told me all that was necessary. And you are far too young to claim a man as an old friend,' he added, clicking his tongue reprovingly. 'It lacks—credibility.'

She drew a deep breath. 'When I want your advice I'll ask for it. And Alan and I *were* friends—until you stepped in. Also,' she went on, defiantly bending the truth, 'he came back here this evening at my invitation—for coffee. That's all. So please don't judge other people by your own dubious standards.'

He looked at her with amusement. 'I see that absence has not sweetened your tongue, *mia bella*.'

'Well, you're not obliged to listen to it,' she said raggedly. 'And what the hell are you doing here, anyway? How dare you walk in and—make yourself at home like this?'

Renzo casually resumed his seat on the sofa, leaning back against its cushions as if he belonged there. He said gently, 'Not the warmest of welcomes, *mia cara*. And we are husband and wife, so your home is also mine. Where else should I be?'

Marisa lifted her chin. 'I'd say that was an open question.' A thought occurred to her. 'And how did you get in, may I ask?'

Renzo shrugged. 'The apartment is leased in my name, so naturally I have a key.'

There was a silence, then she said jerkily, 'I—I see. I suppose I should have realised that.'

He watched her, standing near the door, her white cotton jacket still draped across her shoulders. His mouth twisted. 'You look poised for flight, Maria Lisa,' he commented. 'Where are you planning to go?'

Her glance was mutinous. 'Somewhere that you won't find me.'

'You think there is such a place?' He shook his head slowly. 'I, on the other hand, think it is time for us to sit down and talk together like civilised people.'

'Hardly an accurate description of our relationship to date,' she said. 'And I'd actually prefer you to be the one to leave.' She marched to the door and flung it wide. 'You got rid of Alan, *signore*. I suggest you follow him.'

'A telling gesture,' he murmured. 'But sadly wasted. Because I am going nowhere. I came here because there are things to be said. So why don't you sit down and drink some wine with me?'

'Because I don't want any wine,' she said mutinously. 'And if there's any talking to be done it should be through lawyers. They can make all the necessary arrangements.'

He stretched indolently, making her tinglingly and indignantly aware of every lean inch of him. 'What arrangements are those?'

'Please don't play games,' she said shortly. 'Our divorce, naturally.'

'There has never been a divorce in the Santangeli family,' Renzo said quietly. 'And mine will not be the first. We are married, Maria Lisa, and that is how I intend us to remain.'

He paused, observing the angry colour draining from her face, then added, 'You surely cannot have believed that I intended this period of separation to be permanent?'

She looked at him defiantly. 'I certainly hoped so.'

'Then you will have to preserve your optimism until death parts us, *carissima*.' His tone held finality. 'This was a breathing space, no more than that.' He paused. 'As I made clear, though you may have chosen to think otherwise. But it makes no difference. You are still my wife, and you always will be.'

Her hands were clenched at her sides, the folds of her skirt concealing the fact that they were trembling.

'Is that what you've come here to tell me—that I can never be free of you, *signore*? But that's ridiculous. We can't go on living like this. You can't possibly want that any more than I do.'

'For once we are in agreement,' he said softly. 'Perhaps it is a good omen.'

'Don't count on it.'

His mouth twisted. 'With you, Maria Lisa, I count on nothing, believe me. *Tuttavia*, I am here to invite you to return to Italy and take your place beside me.'

For a moment she stared at him, appalled, and then she said, 'No! You can't. I—I won't.'

He poured more wine into his glass and drank. 'May I ask why not?'

She stared down at the carpet. She said huskily, 'I think you know the answer to that already.'

'Ah,' he said. 'You mean you are still not prepared to forgive me for the mistakes of our honeymoon. Yet even you must admit they were not completely one-sided, *mia cara*.'

'You can hardly blame me,' she flashed. 'After all, I promised you nothing.'

'Then you were entirely true to yourself, *mia bella*, because you gave nothing,' Renzo bit back at her. 'And you cannot pretend you did not know the terms of our marriage.'

'No, but I didn't expect they'd be exacted in that particular way.'

'And I did not expect my patience to be tried so sorely, or so soon.' His golden gaze met hers in open challenge. 'Maybe we have both learned something from that unhappy time.'

'Yes,' Marisa's voice was stony. 'I have discovered you can't be trusted, and that's why I won't be going with you to Italy, or anywhere else. I want out of this so-called marriage, *signore*, and nothing you can say or do will change my mind.'

'Not even,' he said slowly, 'when I tell you my father is sick and has been asking for you?'

She came forward slowly and sat down on the edge of the chair opposite, staring at him. She said shakily, 'Zio Guillermo—sick?' She shook her head. 'I don't believe you. He's never had a day's illness in his life.'

'Nevertheless, he suffered a heart attack two nights ago.' His tone was bleak. 'As you may imagine, it was a shock to both of us. And now to you also, perhaps.'

'Oh, God. Yes, of course. I can see…' Her voice tailed away in distress. She was silent for a moment, then moistened her dry lips with the tip of her tongue. 'Poor Zio Guillermo. Is it—very bad?'

'No,' he said. 'He has been very fortunate—this time. You see that I am being honest with you,' he added, his mouth curling sardonically. 'At the moment his life is not threatened. But he has to rest and avoid stress, which is not easy when our marriage continues to be a cause of such great concern to him.'

She'd been gazing downwards, but at that her head lifted sharply. She said, 'That's—blackmail.'

'If you wish to think so.' Renzo shrugged. 'Unfortunately, it is also the truth. Papa fears he will not live to see his grandchildren.' His eyes met hers. 'He does not deserve such a disappointment, Maria Lisa—from either of us. So I say it is time we fulfilled the terms of our agreement and made him a happy man.'

She stared back at him. She said, in a small, wrenched whisper, 'You mean you're going to—force me to have your child?'

He moved suddenly, restively. 'I shall enforce nothing.' His tone was harsh. 'I make you that promise. What I am asking is your forgiveness for the past, a chance to make amends to you—and begin our life together again. To see if we can at least become friends in this marriage, if nothing else.'

Marisa sank her teeth into her bottom lip. 'But you'll still want me to do—*that*.'

His mouth hardened. '*That*,' he said, 'is how babies are made.' He paused, then added quietly, 'It is also how love is made.'

'Not a word,' Marisa said, icily, 'that could ever be applied to our situation.'

He shrugged cynically. 'Yet a girl does not have to be in love with a man to enjoy what he does to her in bed. Did your charming cousin not mention that in her pre-marital advice?' He saw the colour mount in her face and nodded. 'I see that she did.'

She said curtly, 'It is not an opinion that I happen to share.'

'And were you hoping for a more romantic encounter tonight, which I have spoiled by my untimely arrival?' His smile did not reach his eyes. 'My poor Marisa, *ti devo delle scuse*. You have so much to forgive me for.'

Her glance held defiance. 'But not for this evening—which was a—mistake.' *One of so many I've made…*

'*Che sollievo*,' he said softly. 'I am relieved to hear it. He paused. 'I have reservations on the afternoon flight tomorrow. I hope you can be ready.'

'I haven't yet said I'll go with you!' There was alarm in her voice.

'True,' he agreed. 'But I hope you will give it serious consideration. However poorly you think of me, Maria Lisa, my father deserves your gratitude and your affection. Your return would give him the greatest pleasure. Can you really begrudge him that?'

She hesitated. 'I could come for a visit…'

He shook his head. 'No, *per sempre*. You stay for good.' His mouth twisted. 'You have to learn to be my wife, *mia bella*. To run the household, manage the servants, treat my father at all times with respect, entertain my friends, and appear beside me in public. This will all take time, although by now it should be as natural to you as breathing. I have waited long enough.'

He paused. 'Also, at some mutually convenient time, you will begin to share my bed. *Capisci?*'

She turned away, saying in a suffocated voice, 'Yes, I—I understand.' She took a deep breath. 'But I can't possibly leave tomorrow. You see—I—I have a job, and I need to give proper notice.'

'Your job at the Estrello Gallery is a temporary one,' Renzo said casually. 'And I am sure Signor Langford will make allowances once he understands the position.'

She swung back, staring at him in stunned silence. At last she said unevenly, 'You—already knew? About my work—everything?' Her voice rose. 'Are you telling me you've been having me *watched*?'

'Naturally,' he returned, shrugging. 'You are my wife, Marisa. I had to make sure that you came to no harm while we were apart.'

'By having me—*spied on*?' She took a quick breath. 'My God, that's despicable.'

'A precaution, no more.' He added softly, 'And with your best interests at heart, *mia cara,* whatever you may think. After all, when you would not answer my letters or return my calls I had to maintain some contact with you.'

She pushed her hair back from her face with a shaking hand. 'I only wish I'd thought of setting detectives on *you*. I bet I'd have all the evidence I need to be rid of this marriage by now.'

He said gently, 'Or perhaps you would find that I am not so easily disposed of.' He poured wine into the second glass and rose, bringing it to her. 'Let us drink a toast, *carissima*. To the future.'

'I can't.' Marisa put her hands behind her back defensively. 'Because I won't be a hypocrite. This is the last thing in the world I was expecting. You—must see that, and you have to give me more time—to think…'

'You have had months to think,' Renzo said. 'And to come to terms with the situation.'

'You make it sound so simple,' she said bitterly.

'You are my wife,' he said. 'I wish you to live with me. It is hardly complicated.'

'But there are so many other girls around.' She swallowed. 'If not a divorce, we could have an annulment. We could say that nothing happened—after all, it hardly did—and then you could choose someone you wanted—who'd want you in return.'

'There is no question of that.' His tone was harsh. 'I have come to take you home, Maria Lisa, and, whether it is given willingly or unwillingly, I shall require your agreement at breakfast tomorrow. No other answer will do.'

'Breakfast?' she repeated, at a loss. 'You mean—you wish me to come to your hotel?'

'You will not be put to so much trouble,' he said. 'I am spending the night here.'

'No!' The word burst from her. 'You—you can't. It's quite impossible.' She paused, swallowing. 'Even you must see that the flat's far too small.'

'You mean that there is only one bedroom and one bed?' he queried with faint amusement. 'I had already discovered that for myself. But it need not be an obstacle.'

She wrapped her arms defensively round her body. 'Oh, yes, it is,' she said, her voice shaking. 'Because I—I won't…' She flung her head back. 'Oh, God, I knew I couldn't trust you.'

'Calmati!' His voice bit. 'I am under no illusion, *mia bella*, that I am any more welcome in your bed now than I was on our wedding night. And for the time being I accept the situation. So believe that you are quite safe. *Inoltre*, your sofa seems comfortable enough, if you will spare me a pillow and a blanket.'

She stared at him almost blankly. 'You'll—sleep on the sofa?'

'I have just said so.' His brows lifted. 'Is there some law forbidding it?'

'Oh, no,' Marisa denied hastily. She sighed. 'Well, if—if you're determined to stay, I'll—get what you need. And a towel.'

'Grazie mille,' he acknowledged sardonically. 'I hope you will not be so grudging with your hospitality when you are called upon to entertain our guests.'

'Guests,' she said grittily, 'are usually invited. Also welcome.'

'And you cannot imagine that a day might come when you would be glad to see me?' he asked, apparently unfazed.

'Frankly, no.'

'Yet I can recall a time when your feelings for me were not quite so hostile.'

Pain twisted inside her as she remembered how hopelessly—helplessly—she'd once adored him, but she kept her voice icily level. 'The foolishness of adolescence, *signore*.' She shrugged. 'Fortunately it didn't last. Not once I realised what you really were.'

He said reflectively, 'Perhaps we should halt there. I think I would prefer not to enquire into the precise nature of your discovery.'

'Scared of the truth?' Marisa lifted her chin in challenge.

'Not at all,' he said. 'When it *is* the truth.' He looked at her steadily, his mouth hard. 'But I swore to myself on my mother's memory that I would not lose my temper with you again, whatever the provocation.' He paused significantly. 'Yet there are limits to my tolerance, Maria Lisa. I advise you to observe them, and not push me too far.'

'Why?' She looked down at the floor, aware of a sudden constriction in her breathing. 'What more can you possibly do to me?'

He said quietly, 'I suggest you do not find out,' and there was a note in his voice that sent a shiver the length of her spine. 'Now, perhaps you will fetch me that blanket—*per favore*.'

She was halfway to her room when she realised he was right behind her.

She said, 'You don't have to follow me. I can manage.'

'My travel bag is on your floor,' he said tersely. 'Also I wish to use the shower.'

'You have an answer to everything, don't you?'

He gave her an enigmatic glance. 'Not to you, *mia bella*. That is one of the few certainties in our situation,' he added, bending to retrieve the elegant black leather holdall standing just inside her bedroom door.

And he walked away before she could commit the fatal error of asking what the others might be.

Not that she would have done, of course, Marisa told herself as she extracted a dark red woollen blanket and a towel from the storage drawers under her bed, and took a pillow from a shelf in the fitted wardrobes. She would not give him the satisfaction, she thought, angry to discover that she was trembling inside, and still breathless from their encounter.

But then she was still suffering from shock at having come back and found him there, waiting for her. Waiting, moreover, to stake a claim that she had thought—hoped—had been tacitly forgotten.

She'd actually allowed herself to believe that she was free. To imagine that the respite she'd been offered had become a permanent separation and that, apart from a few legal formalities, their so-called marriage was over.

But she'd just been fooling herself, she thought wretchedly. It was never going to be that easy.

Because as she now realised, too late, they'd never been apart at all in any real sense. Had been, in fact, linked all the time by a kind of invisible rope. And it had only taken one brief, determined tug on Renzo's part to draw her inexorably—inevitably—back to him, to keep the promises she'd made one late August day in a crowded sunlit church.

And of course, to repay some small part of that enormous, suffocating debt to him and his family in the only currency available to her.

She shivered swiftly and uncontrollably.

She could, she supposed, refuse to go back to Italy with him. He was, after all, hardly likely to kidnap her. But even if they remained apart there was no guarantee that the marriage could ever be brought to a legal end. He had made it quite clear that she was his wife, and would continue to be so, and he had the money and the lawyers to enforce his will in this respect, to keep her tied to him with no prospect of release.

The alternative was to take Julia's unsavoury advice. To accede somehow to the resumption of Renzo's physical requirements of her and give him the son he needed. That accomplished, their relationship would presumably exist in name only, and she could then create a whole new life for herself, perhaps. Even find some form of happiness.

She carried the bedding down the hall to the living room, then stopped abruptly on the threshold, her startled gaze absorbing the totally unwelcome sight of Renzo, his shirt discarded, displaying altogether too much bronze skin as he casually unbuckled the belt of his pants.

She said glacially, 'I'd prefer you to change in the bathroom.'

'And I would prefer you to accustom yourself to the reality of having a husband, *mia bella*,' he retorted, with equal coolness. He looked her up and down slowly, his eyes lingering deliberately on the fastening of her skirt. 'Now, if you were to undress in front of me I should have no objection,' he added mockingly.

'Hell,' Marisa said, 'will freeze over first.' She put the armful of bedding down on the carpet and walked away without hurrying.

Yet once in the sanctuary of her bedroom she found herself leaning back against its panels, gasping for breath as if she'd just run a mile in record time.

Oh, why—*why*—did the lock on this damned door have no key? she wondered wildly. Something that would make her feel safe.

Except that would be a total self-delusion, and she knew it. Because there was no lock, bolt or chain yet invented that would keep Renzo Santangeli at bay if ever he decided that he wanted her.

Instead, she had to face the fact that it was only his indifference that would guarantee her privacy tonight.

A reflection that, to her own bewilderment, gave her no satisfaction at all.

CHAPTER FOUR

THE sofa, Renzo thought bleakly, was not at all as comfortable as he'd claimed.

But even if it had been as soft as a featherbed, and long enough to accommodate his tall frame without difficulty, he would still have found sleep no easier to come by.

Arms folded behind his head, he lay staring up at the faint white sheen of the ceiling, his mind jagged and restless.

He was enough of a realist to have accepted that he wouldn't find a subdued, compliant bride awaiting him in London, but neither had he anticipated quite such a level of intransigence. Had hoped, in fact, that allowing her this time away from him might have brought about a faint softening of her attitude. A basis for negotiation, at least.

But how wrong was it possible to be? he asked himself wryly. It seemed she had no wish either to forgive him—or forget—so any plans he'd been formulating for a fresh start between them were back in the melting pot.

The simplest solution to his problems, of course, would be to settle for the so-called annulment she had offered and walk away. Accept that their marriage had never had a chance of success.

Indeed, the days leading up to the wedding had been almost surreal, with Marisa, like a ghost, disappearing at his approach, and when forced to remain in his presence speaking only when spoken to.

Except once. When for one brief moment at that dinner party he'd discovered her looking at him with a speculation in her eyes there had been no mistaking. And for that moment his heart had lifted in frank jubilation.

He remembered how he hadn't been able to wait for their

dinner guests to leave in order to seek her out and invite her to go for a stroll with him in the moonlit privacy of the gardens, telling himself that maybe he was being given a belated opportunity for a little delicate wooing of his reluctant bride, and that, if so, he would take full advantage of it.

But once all the goodnights had been said, and he'd gone to find her, she had retreated to the sanctuary of her room and the chance had gone—especially as he'd had to return to Rome early the following morning.

But he hadn't been able to forget that just for an instant she had lowered her guard. That she had seen him—reacted to him as a man. And that when he'd kissed her hand she'd blushed helplessly.

Which suggested that, if there'd been one chink in her armour, surely he might somehow find another…

So, he was not yet ready to admit defeat, he told himself grimly. He would somehow persuade her to agree to erase the past and accept him as her husband. A resolve that had been hardened by his unwanted interview with his grandmother that very morning.

He had arrived to visit his father at the clinic just as she was leaving, and she had pounced instantly, commanding him to accompany her to an empty waiting room, obliging him, teeth gritted, to obey.

'Your father tells me you are flying to England today in an attempt to be reconciled with that foolish girl,' she commented acidly, as soon as the door was closed. 'A total waste of your time, my dear Lorenzo. I told my daughter a dozen times that her idea of a marriage between such an ill-assorted pair was wrong-headed and could only end in disaster. And so it has proved. The child has shown herself totally unworthy of the Santangeli family.

'My poor Maria would not pay attention to me, sadly, but you must listen now. Cut your losses and have the marriage dissolved immediately. As I have always suggested, find a good Italian wife who knows what is expected of her and who will devote herself to your comfort and convenience.'

'And naturally, Nonna Teresa, you have a candidate in mind?' His smile was deceptively charming. 'Or even more than one, perhaps? I seem to remember being presented to a positive array of young women whenever I was invited to dine with you.'

'I have given the matter deep thought,' his grandmother conceded graciously. 'And I feel that your eventual choice should be Dorotea Marcona. She is the daughter of an old friend, and a sweet, pious girl who will never give you a moment's uneasiness.'

'Dorotea?' Renzo mused. 'Is she the one who never stops talking, or the one with the squint?'

'A slight cast in one eye,' she reproved. 'Easily corrected by a simple surgical procedure, I understand.'

'For which I should no doubt be expected to pay—the Marcona family having no money.' Renzo shook his head. 'You are the one wasting your time, Nonna Teresa. Marisa is my wife, and I intend that she will remain so.'

'Hardly a wife,' his grandmother said tartly. 'When she lives on the other side of the continent. Your separation threatens to become a public scandal—especially after her mortifying behaviour at the wedding.' She drew her lips into a thin line. 'You cannot have forgotten how she humiliated you?'

'No,' Renzo said quietly. 'I—have not forgotten.'

In fact, thanks to Nonna Teresa, he'd found the memory grating on him all over again—not merely on his way to the airport, but throughout the flight, when it had constantly interfered with his attempts to work. So he'd reached London not in the best of moods, when he should have been conciliatory, only to find his wife missing when he reached the flat.

And when she did return, she was not alone, he thought with cold displeasure. Was with someone other than the Langford man whom he'd come prepared to deal with. Someone, in fact, who should have been history where Marisa was concerned.

And to set the seal on his annoyance, his bride had not been in the least disconcerted, nor shown any sign of guilt over being discovered entertaining a former boyfriend.

But then, attack had always been her favourite form of defence, he recalled grimly, as his mind went back to their wedding day.

He'd always regarded what had happened then as the start of his marital troubles, but now he was not so sure, he thought, twisting round on the sofa to give his unoffending pillow a vicious thump. Hadn't the problems been there from the very beginning? Even on the day when he'd asked Marisa to marry him, and felt the tension emanating from her like a cold hand on his skin, forcing him to realise for the first time just how much forbearance would be required from him in establishing any kind of physical relationship between them.

Nevertheless, the end of the wedding ceremony itself had certainly been the moment that had sounded the death knell of all his good intentions towards his new bride, he thought, his mouth tightening.

He could remember so vividly how she'd looked as she had joined him at the altar of the ancient parish church in Montecalento, almost ethereal in the exquisite drift of white wild silk that had clothed her, and so devastatingly young and lovely that the muscles in his chest had constricted at the sight of her—until he'd seen her pale, strained face, clearly visible under the filmy tulle of her billowing veil. Then that sudden surge of frankly carnal longing had been replaced by compassion, and a renewed determination that he would be patient, give her all the time she needed to accept her new circumstances.

He remembered too how her hand had trembled in his as he'd slid the plain gold wedding band into place, and how there'd been no answering pressure to the tiny comforting squeeze he'd given her fingers.

And how he'd thought at the time, troubled, that it almost seemed as if she was somewhere else—and a long way distant from him.

He'd heard the Bishop give the final blessing, then turned to her, slowly putting the veil back from her face.

She had been looking down, her long lashes curling on her cheeks, her slender body rigid under the fragile delicacy of her gown.

And he'd bent to kiss her quivering mouth, swiftly and very gently, in no more than a token caress, wanting to reassure her by his tender restraint that he would keep his word, that she would have nothing to fear when they were alone together that night.

But before his lips could touch hers Marisa had suddenly looked up at him, her eyes glittering with scorn, and turned her head away so abruptly that his mouth had skidded along her cheekbone to meet with just a mouthful of tulle and few silken strands of perfumed hair.

There had been an audible gasp from the Bishop, and a stir in the mass of the congregation like a wind blowing across barley, telling Renzo quite unequivocally, as he'd straightened, heated colour storming into his face, that his bride's very public rejection of his first kiss as her husband had been missed by no one present. And that she'd quite deliberately made him look a fool.

After which, of course, he'd had to walk the length of the long aisle, with Marisa's hand barely resting on his arm, forcing himself to seem smiling and relaxed, when in fact he had been furiously aware of the shocked and astonished glances being aimed at them from some directions—and the avid enjoyment from others.

Tenderness was a thing of the past, he had vowed angrily. His overriding wish was to be alone somewhere with his bride where he could put her across his knee and administer the spanking of her life.

But instead there had been the ordeal of the wedding breakfast, being held in the warm sunlight of the main square so that the whole town could share in the future Marchese's happiness with his new wife. Where there would be laughter, toasting, and sugared almonds to be handed out, before he and Marisa would be expected to open the dancing.

What would she do then? he had wondered grimly. Push him away? Stamp on his foot? God alone knew.

However, she must have undergone a partial change of heart, because she had gone through the required rituals with apparent docility—although Renzo had surmised bitterly that they must be the only newlyweds in the world to spend the first two hours of their marriage without addressing one word to each other.

It had only been when they were seated stiffly side by side, in the comparative privacy of the limousine returning them to the villa to change for their honeymoon trip, that he'd broken the silence.

'How dared you do such a thing?' His voice was molten steel. 'What possessed you to refuse my kiss—to shame me like that in front of everyone?'

She said huskily, 'But that was exactly why. You've never made any attempt to kiss me before, and, believe me, that's suited me just fine.' She took a breath. 'But now all of a sudden there's an audience present, so you have to play the part of the ardent bridegroom—make the token caring gesture in order to look good in the eyes of your friends and family. So that you might make them think it's a real marriage instead of the payment of a debt—a sordid business deal that neither of us wants.'

She shook her head. 'Well—I won't do that. I won't pretend for the sake of appearances. And you, *signore*,' she added with a little gasp, 'you won't make me.'

There was another silence, then Renzo said icily, 'I trust you have quite finished?' and saw her nod jerkily before she turned away to stare out of the car window.

Only it had not been finished at all, he thought bleakly as he pulled the blanket closer round him and turned awkwardly onto his side. On the contrary, it had been just the beginning of a chain of events from which the repercussions were still impacting on their lives. And God only knew how it might end.

She felt, Marisa thought, as if she'd swallowed a large lump of marble.

Curled into a ball in the middle of the bed, she tugged the coverlet over her head in an effort to shut out the ever-present hum of London traffic through the open window, just as if that was the only reason she couldn't sleep.

Yet who was she trying to fool? she asked herself ironically.

Renzo's unexpected reappearance in her life had set every nerve ending jangling, while her mind was occupied in an endless examination of everything he'd said to her.

Especially his galling assertion that it had been mistakes by them both that had caused the collapse of their marriage.

Because it was his fault—*all* his fault. That was what she'd told herself—the mantra she'd repeated almost obsessively during the endless nightmare of their honeymoon and since. Her determined and inflexible belief ever since.

Yet now, suddenly, she was not so sure.

She should have let him kiss her at the wedding and she knew it. Had always known it, if she was honest. Realised she should just have stood there and allowed it to happen. And if she hadn't responded—had refused to return the pressure of his lips—her point would have been made, but just between the two of them. No one else would ever have known.

Julia, in particular.

'Are you off your head?' her cousin had said furiously, cornering her in the pretence of straightening her veil. 'My God, he must be blazing. If you know what's good for you tonight you'll forget your little rebellion, lie on your back and pray that he puts you up the stick. Redeem yourself that way—by doing what you've been hired for.'

'Thank you for the unnecessary reminder,' Marisa threw back defiantly and moved away, her half-formed resolve to go to Renzo, to tell him she'd been overcome by nerves and obeyed an impulse that she'd instantly regretted, melting like ice in the hot sunlight.

Neither was her mood improved by their first exchange in the car, nor during the largely silent journey down to their honeymoon destination near Amalfi—the first time, she realised, that she'd been entirely alone with him since he proposed to her. A reflection she found disturbing.

It wasn't the first time he'd ignored her, of course, she thought ruefully, casting a wary glance at his stony profile, but that had been when she was younger, because he'd regarded her as something of a pest. Not because he was angry and humiliated.

And she knew with a kind of detachment that she would have to pay for what she'd done in one way or another.

It occurred to her too that she'd never been his passenger before—another first for her to add to all the others—and as the low, powerful car sped down the *autostrada* under his casually controlled expertise she remembered a jokey magazine article she'd once read, which had suggested a man's sexual performance could often be judged by the way he drove.

She observed the light touch of his lean fingers on the wheel and found herself suddenly wondering how they would feel on her skin, before deciding, with a swift churning sensation in the pit of her stomach as Julia's words came back to haunt her, that from now on she would do better to concentrate firmly on the scenery. However, as the silence between them became increasingly oppressive, she felt that a modest conversational overture might be called for.

She said, 'The villa—is it in Amalfi itself?'

'No, in a village farther along the coast.'

His tone was not particularly inviting, but she persevered.

'And you said it belongs to your godfather?'

'Yes, it is his holiday retreat.'

'It's—kind of him to offer it.'

He gave a faint shrug. 'It is quiet, and overlooks the sea, so he felt it would be a suitably romantic location for a newly married couple to begin their life together.' He added curtly, 'As he was at the wedding, I am sure he now realises his error.'

Marisa subsided, flushing. So much for trying to make conversation, she thought.

She looked down at her slim smooth legs, at the slender pink-tipped feet displayed by the elegant and expensive strappy sandals she was wearing—the same hyacinth-blue as her sleeveless dress.

Apart from having her hair cut, she'd not been a great frequenter of hair and beauty salons in the past, but that had all changed in the last few days, when she'd been taken to Florence and waxed, plucked, manicured and pedicured to within an inch of her life in some pastel, scented torture chamber.

She'd endured the ministrations of various beauticians in a state of mute rebellion, and as perfumed creams and lotions had been applied to the softness of her skin she'd found herself thinking that maybe the old joke about 'Have her stripped, washed and brought to my tent' wasn't so damned funny after all. That there was nothing faintly amusing in finding herself being deliberately prepared for the pleasure of a man.

The beautician had imagined, of course, that she rejoiced in all the intimate preparations because she was in love and wanted to be beautiful for her lover. She'd seen the hastily concealed envy in their faces when they realised the identity of her bridegroom.

What girl, after all, would not want to spend her nights in the arms of Lorenzo Santangeli?

If they only knew, she thought wryly, wondering what other women passed their time in similar salons, being pampered for his delight.

Even that morning two girls had arrived at the villa—one to do her hair, the other her make-up—and she'd been presented with a beauty case containing everything that had been used. Presumably so that she could keep up the good work while she was away, she thought, biting her lip.

Except that it was all a complete waste of time and effort. Renzo had married her by arrangement, not as an object for his romantic desires, but in order to provide himself with a mother for his heir, because she was young, healthy and suitably innocent.

Not the kind of fate she had ever envisaged for herself, she acknowledged with an inward pang. But this was the situation, and she would have to learn to make the best of it—eventually.

And it might indeed have been a step in the right direction if she'd made herself accept that token kiss in church earlier, she thought uneasily. At least they'd have commenced this so-called honeymoon on talking terms. Whereas now…

Even at this late stage, and if they hadn't been on a motorway, she might actually have been tempted to request him to pull over, so that she could follow her original plan and offer him some kind of apology. Try at least to improve matters between them.

But that clearly wasn't going to happen in the middle of the *autostrada*, and besides, she had a whole month ahead of her in which to make amends—if that was what she wanted, of course, she thought, her hands knotting together in her lap. At the moment she felt too unsettled to decide on any definite course of action.

In addition, Renzo might well have his own ideas on how their marriage should be conducted, she reminded herself dejectedly, stifling a sigh as she risked another wary glance at his unyielding expression.

But no amount of dejection could possibly have survived her first glimpse of the enchanting coastline around Amalfi.

Marisa leaned forward with an involuntary gasp of delight as she saw the first small town, its white buildings gleaming in the late-afternoon sunlight, clinging intrepidly to the precipitous rocky slopes above the restless sea which dashed itself endlessly against them in foam-edged shades of turquoise, azure and emerald.

The road itself, however, was an experience all its own, as it wound recklessly and almost blindly between high cliffs on one side and the toe-curling drop to the sea on the other. The rockface didn't seem very stable either, Marisa thought apprehensively, noting the signs warning of loose boulders, and the protective netting spread along the areas most at risk.

But Renzo seemed totally unconcerned as he skilfully negotiated one breath-stopping bend after another, so she sat back and tried to appear relaxed in her turn. She wasn't terribly successful, to judge by the swift and frankly sardonic glance she encountered from him at one point.

'If it's all the same to you, just keep your eyes on the damned road,' she muttered under her breath.

Yet, if she was honest, her nervousness wasn't entirely due to the vagaries of the *Costiera Amalfitana.* It was perfectly obvious that they would soon arrive at their destination, and she would find herself sharing a roof with him—no longer as his guest, but as his wife.

And that infinitely tricky moment seemed to have come, she thought, her fingers twisting together even more tightly as they turned inland and began to climb a steep narrow road. Marisa glimpsed a scattering of houses ahead of them, but before they were reached Renzo had turned the car between tall wrought-iron gates onto a winding gravel drive which led down to a large, sprawling single-storey house, roofed in faded terracotta, its white walls half-hidden by flowering vines and shrubs.

He said quietly and coldly, as he brought the car to a halt. '*Ecco*, La Villa Santa Caterina. And my godfather's people are waiting to welcome us, so let us observe the conventions and pretend we are glad to be here, if you please.'

Outside the air-conditioned car it was still very warm, but the faint breeze was scented with flowers, and Marisa paused, drawing a deep, grateful breath, before Renzo took her hand, guiding her forward to the beaming trio awaiting them.

'Marisa, this is Massimo, my godfather's major-domo.' He indicated a small thin man in a grey linen jacket and pinstripe trousers. 'Also his wife, Evangelina, who keeps house here and cooks, and Daniella, their daughter, who works as the maid.'

Evangelina must be very good at her job, Marisa thought, as she smiled and uttered a few shy words of greeting in halting Italian, because she was a large, comfortable woman with twinkling eyes, and twice the size of her husband. Daniella too verged towards plump.

Inside the house there were marble floors, walls washed in pastel colours, and the coolness of ceiling fans.

Marisa found herself conducted ceremoniously by Evangelina

to a large bedroom at the back of the house. It was mainly occupied by a vast bed, its white coverlet embroidered with golden flowers, heaped with snowy pillows on which tiny sprigs of sweet lavender had been placed.

It was like a stage setting, thought Marisa, aware of a coyly significant glance from Evangelina. But contrary to the good woman's expectations, the leading lady in this particular production would be sleeping there alone tonight, and for the foreseeable future.

The only other pieces of furniture were a long dressing table, with a stool upholstered in gold brocade, and a chaise longue covered in the same material, placed near the sliding glass doors which led onto the verandah.

On the opposite side of the room, a door opened into a bathroom tiled in misty green marble, with a shower that Marisa reckoned was as big as her cousin Julia's box room.

Another door led to a dressing room like a corridor, lined with drawer units and fitted wardrobes, and at the far end this, in turn, gave access to another bedroom of a similar size, furnished in the same way as the first one except that the coverlet was striped in gold and ivory.

Presumably this was the room which Renzo would be using—at least for the time being, she thought, her mouth suddenly dry. And she was relieved to see that it, too, had its own bathroom.

Turning away hurriedly, she managed to smile at Evangelina and tell her that everything was wonderful—magnificent—to the housekeeper's evident gratification.

Back in her own room, she began to open one of her suitcases but was immediately dissuaded by Evangelina, who indicated firmly that this was a job for Daniella, who would be overjoyed to wait upon the bride of Signor Lorenzo.

All this goodwill, Marisa thought with irony, as she followed the housekeeper to the *salotto*, where coffee was waiting. Yet how much of it would survive once it became clear to the household, as it surely would, that the bride of Signor Lorenzo was totally failing to live up to everyone's expectations?

She'd braced herself for another silent interlude, but Renzo was quietly civil, showing her the charming terrace where most of their meals would be taken, and explaining how the rocky local terrain had obliged the large gardens to be built on descending levels, connected by steps and pathways, with a swimming pool and a sunbathing area constructed at the very bottom.

'My godfather says the climb keeps him healthy,' Renzo said, adding with faint amusement, 'His wife has always claimed it is all part of a plot to kill her. But it does not, however, stop her using the pool every day.'

She looked over the balustrade down into the green depths. 'Do you have the same plan, perhaps?' It seemed worth carrying on the mild joke.

'Why, no,' Renzo drawled, his glance travelling over her. 'You, *mia bella*, I intend to keep very much alive.'

I suppose I led with my chin there, thought Marisa, crossly aware she was blushing a little. And if he's going to say things like that, I'd much rather he was silent again.

No one ate early in Italy, and she was used to that, but by the time dinner was eventually served the strain of the day was beginning to tell on her.

She was ruefully aware that she had not done justice to the excellence of Evangelina's cooking, especially the sea bream which had formed the main course, and her lack of appetite was not lost on her companion.

'You are not hungry? Or is there something you would prefer?'

'Oh, no,' she denied hurriedly. 'The fish is wonderful. I'm just very tired—and I think I'm getting a headache,' she added for good measure. 'Perhaps you'd apologise to Evangelina for me—and excuse me.'

'Of course.' He rose politely to his feet. *'Buona notte, mia cara.'*

She walked sedately to the door, trying hard not to appear as if she was running away, but knowing he wouldn't be fooled for a minute. But at least he'd let her go, and what conversation there'd been during the meal had been on general topics, avoiding the personal.

In her bedroom, she saw that the bed had been turned down on both sides, and that one of her trousseau nightgowns, a mere wisp of white crêpe de Chine, had been prettily arranged on the coverlet.

More scene-setting, she thought. But the day's drama was thankfully over.

She had a warm, scented bath, and then changed into the nightgown that Daniella had left for her because there was little to choose between any of them. In fact all her trousseau, she thought, had been chosen with Renzo's tastes in mind rather than hers.

Not that she knew his tastes—or wanted to—she amended quickly, but this diaphanous cobweb of a thing, with its narrow ribbon steps, would probably be considered to have general masculine appeal.

She climbed into the bed and sank back against the pillows, where the scent of lavender still lingered, aware of an odd sense of melancholy that she could neither dismiss or explain.

Sleep's what I need, she told herself. *Things will seem better in the morning. They always do.*

She was just turning on her side when an unexpected sound caught her attention, and she shot upright again, staring towards the dressing room as its door opened and Renzo came in.

'What are you doing here?' she demanded huskily.

'An odd question, *mia bella*, to put to your husband when he visits your bedroom on your wedding night.'

She sat rigidly against the pillows, watching him approach. He was wearing a black silk robe, but his bare chest, with its dark shadowing of hair, and his bare legs suggested that there was nothing beneath it.

She lifted her chin. 'I—I said I was tired. I thought you accepted that.'

'Also that you had a headache.' He nodded. 'And by now you have probably thought of a dozen other methods to keep me at a distance. I suggest you save them for the future. You will not, however, need them tonight,' he added, seating himself on the edge of the bed.

It was a wide bed, and there was a more than respectable space between them, but in spite of that Marisa still felt that he was too close for comfort. She wanted to move away a little, but knew that he would notice and draw his own conclusions. And she did not wish him to think she was in any way nervous, she thought defensively.

As for what he was wearing—well, she'd seen him in far less in the past, when she'd been swimming or sunbathing in his company, but that, somehow, was a very different matter.

She marshalled her defences. 'You still haven't said why you're here.'

He said, 'I have come to bid you goodnight.'

'You did that downstairs.'

'But I believe that there are things that remain to be said between us.'

He paused. 'We have not begun well, you and I, and these difficulties between us should be settled at once.'

'What—what do you mean?'

He traced the gold thread on the coverlet with a fingertip. 'Earlier today you implied that I had been less than ardent in my wooing of you. But if I stayed aloof it was only because I believed it was what you wanted.'

'And so it was,' she said. 'I said so.'

'Yet if that is true,' he said softly, 'why mention the matter at all?'

She said defiantly, 'I was simply letting you know what a hypocritical farce I find this entire arrangement. And that I won't play games in public just to satisfy some convention.'

'How principled,' he said, and shifted his position, moving deliberately closer to her. 'But we are no longer in public now, *mia cara*. We are in total privacy. So there is no one else to see or care what I ask from you.'

She swallowed. 'You—promised that you—wouldn't ask.' Her voice was thin. 'So I'd really like you to go—please.'

'In a moment,' he said. 'When I have what I came for.'

'I—I don't understand.'

'It is quite simple,' he said. 'I wish to kiss you goodnight, Maria Lisa. To take from your lovely mouth what you denied me this morning—nothing more.'

She stared at him. 'You said you'd wait…'

'And I will.' He leaned forward, brushing a strand of hair back from her face. 'But I think—don't you?—that when you come to me as my wife it will be easier for both of us if you have become even a little accustomed to my touch, and learned not to dread being in my arms.'

'What are you saying, *signore*?' Her voice sounded very young and breathless. 'That I'm going to find your kisses so irresistible that I'll want more and more of them? That eventually I'll want you?'

She shook her head. 'That's not going to happen. Because you can dress up what you've done any way you like, but the fact is you bought me. Anything you do to me will be little more than legalised rape.'

There was a terrible silence, then Renzo said, too quietly, too evenly, 'You will never use such a word to me again, Maria Lisa. Do you understand? I told you I would not force myself on you and I meant it. But you would be unwise to try my patience twice in twenty-four hours.'

She threw back her head. 'Your loss of temper doesn't seem much to set against the ruin of my life, Signor Santangeli. Whatever—I have no intention of kissing you. So please leave. Now.'

'And I think not.' Renzo took her by the shoulders, pulling her towards him, his purpose evident in his set face.

'Let me go.' She began to struggle against the strength of the hands that held her, scared now, but still determined. 'I won't do this—I won't.'

She pushed against his chest, fists clenched, her face averted.

'*Mia cara*, this is silly.' He spoke more gently, but there was a note in his voice that was almost amusement. 'Such a fuss about so little. One kiss and I'll go, I swear it.'

'You'll go to hell.' As she tried to wrench herself free one of the ribbon straps on her nightgown suddenly snapped, and the flimsy bodice slipped down, baring one rounded rose-tipped breast.

She froze in horror, and realised that Renzo too was very still, his dark face changing with a new and disturbing intensity as he looked at her. His hand slid slowly down from her shoulder to a more intimate objective, cupping her breast in lean fingers that shook a little. He brushed her nipple softly with the ball of his thumb, and as it hardened beneath his touch she felt sensation scorch through her like a naked flame against her flesh. Frightening her in a way she had never known before.

'No.' Her voice cracked wildly on the word. 'Don't touch me. Oh, God, you *bastard*.'

She flailed out wildly with her fists, and felt the jolt as one of them slammed into his face.

He gave a gasp of pain and reared back away from her, his hand going up to his eye. Then there was another silence.

She thought, the breath catching in her throat, *Oh, God, what have I done? And, even worse, what is he going to do?*

She tried to speak, to say his name—anything. To tell him she hadn't meant to hit him—or at least not as hard.

Only she didn't get the chance. Because he was lifting himself off the bed and striding away from her across the room without looking back. And as Marisa sank back, covering her own face with her hands, she heard first the slam of the dressing room door and then, like an echo, the bang of his own door closing.

And knew with total certainty that for tonight at least he would not be returning.

CHAPTER FIVE

EVEN after all this time Marisa found that the memory still had the power to crucify her.

I'd never behaved like that before in my entire life, she thought, shuddering. *Because I'm really not the violent type—or I thought I wasn't until that moment. Then—pow! Suddenly, the eagle landed. Only it wasn't funny.*

So completely not funny, in fact, that she'd immediately burst into a storm of tears, burying her face in the pillow to muffle the sobs that shook her entire body. Not that he could have heard her, of course. The dressing room and two intervening doors had made sure of that.

But why was I crying? she asked herself, moving restively across the mattress, trying to get comfortable. *After all, it was an appalling thing to do, and I freely admit as much, but it got him out of my bedroom, which was exactly what I wanted to happen.*

And he never came back. Not even after…

She swallowed, closing her eyes, wishing she could blank out all the inner visions that still tormented her. That remained there at the forefront of her mind, harsh and inescapable. Forcing her once again to recall everything that had happened that night—and, even more shamingly, on the day that had followed….

Once she was quite sure that he'd gone, her first priority was to wash the tearstains from her pale face and exchange her torn nightgown for a fresh one—although that, she soon discovered, did nothing to erase the remembered shock of his touch on her bare breast.

So much for his promise to leave her alone until she was ready, she thought, biting her lip savagely.

The way he'd looked at her, the delicate graze of his hand on her flesh, proved how little his word could be trusted.

Yet at the same time it had brought home to her with almost terrifying force how fatally easy it would be to allow her untutored senses to take control, and to forget the real reason—the only reason—they were together.

She'd agreed to this marriage only to repay a mountainous debt and to make life easier for a sick man who'd been good to her. Nothing else.

Lorenzo had accepted the arrangement solely out of duty to his family. And to keep a promise to a dying woman. That was all, too.

'Oh, Godmother,' she whispered under her breath. 'How could you do this to me? To both of us?'

She'd assumed Renzo's offer to postpone the consummation of their marriage was a sign of his basic indifference. Now she didn't now what to think.

Because it seemed that Julia's crude comments about his readiness to take full advantage of the situation might have some basis in truth, after all. That he might indeed find her innocence a novelty after the glamorous, experienced women he was used to, and would, therefore, be able to make the best of a bad job.

'But I can't do that,' she whispered to herself. And as for learning gradually to accustom herself to the idea of intimacy with him, as he'd suggested—well, that would never happen in a million years.

A tiger in the sack, she recalled, wincing. Although she'd tried hard not to consider the implications in Julia's crudity, the way Renzo had touched her had provided her with an unwanted inkling of the kind of demands he might make.

But then she'd known all along that spending her nights with her bridegroom would prove to be a hideous embarrassment at the very least. Or spending some of her nights, she amended hastily. Certainly not all of them. Maybe not very many, and hopefully never the entire night.

Because surely he would soon tire of her sexual naiveté?

In some ways she knew him too well, she thought. In others she didn't know him at all. But on both counts the prospect of sleeping with him scared her half to death.

Not, of course, that sleeping would actually be the problem, she thought, setting her teeth.

She'd tried to play down her fears—telling herself that all he required was a child, a son to inherit the Santangeli name and the power and wealth it represented—and had spent time before the wedding steeling herself to accept that part of their bargain, to endure whatever it took to achieve it, assuring herself that his innate good breeding would ensure that the…the practicalities of the situation would be conducted in a civilised manner.

Only to blow her resolution to the four winds when he'd attempted to kiss her for the first time and she'd panicked. Badly.

She had reason, she told herself defensively. The night of her nineteenth birthday had made her wonder uneasily if Renzo might not want more from her than unwilling submission. And the last half-hour had only confirmed her worst fears—which was why she'd lashed out at him like that.

Her relationship with him had always been a tricky one, she thought unhappily. Leading his own life, he'd figured in her existence, when he chose to appear there, as eternally glamorous and usually aloof. Casually kind to her when it suited him, even occasionally coaching her at tennis and swimming, although never with any great enthusiasm, and almost certainly at his mother's behest—as she'd realised later.

But all that had ended summarily when, longing for him just once to see her as a woman instead of a child, she'd made a disastrously misguided attempt to emulate one of the girls who'd stayed at the villa as his guest by 'losing' her bikini top when she was alone with him in the swimming pool—only to experience the full force of his icy displeasure.

'If you think to impress me by behaving like a slut, you have misjudged the matter, Maria Lisa.' His words and tone of voice had flayed the skin from her. 'You are too young and too green to be a temptress, my little stork, and you dishonour not only yourself, but my parents' roof with such ridiculous and juvenile antics.' He'd contemptuously tossed the scrap of sodden fabric to her. 'Now, cover yourself and go to your room.'

Overwhelmed by distress and humiliation, she had fled, despising herself for having revealed her fledgling emotions so openly, and agonising over the result.

She had felt only relief when her visits to Tuscany had gone into abeyance, and in time had even been able to reassure herself that any talk about her being Renzo's future bride had been simply sentimental chat between two mothers, and could not, thankfully, be taken seriously.

And if I never see him again, she'd thought defiantly, it will be altogether too soon.

Now, when she looked back, she could candidly admit that she must have been embarrassment on a stick even before the swimming pool incident.

But that being the case, why hadn't he fought tooth and nail not to have her foisted on him as a wife only a few years later?

Surely he must have recognised that there was no chance of their marriage working in any real sense?

On the other hand, perhaps he didn't actually require it to work in that way. Because for him it was simply a means to an end. A business arrangement whereby her body became just another commodity for him to purchase.

Something for his temporary amusement that could be discreetly discarded when its usefulness was finished.

When she'd had his baby.

This was the viewpoint she'd chosen to adopt, and so, in spite of Julia's insinuations, she hadn't really expected him to behave as if—as if he—wanted her…

Or was that just a conditioned reflex? Girl equals bed equals sex? Identity unimportant.

That, she thought with a little sigh, was the likeliest explanation.

For a moment she stood staring at herself in the mirror, studying the shape of her body under the thin fabric of her nightdress. Noticing the length of her legs and the way the shadows in the room starkly reduced the contours of her face, making her features stand out more prominently. Especially her nose…

The stork, she thought painfully, was alive and well once more. And certainly not likely to be the object of anyone's desire. Renzo's least of all.

She turned away, smothering a sigh, and made her slow, reluctant way back to the bed, lying there shivering in its vastness in spite of the warmth of the night.

Still listening intently, she realised, for the sound of his return, no matter how many times she promised herself that it wasn't going to happen. While at the same time, in her head, the events of the day kept unrolling before her in a seemingly endless loop of error and embarrassment.

It was several hours before she finally dropped into a troubled sleep. And for the first time in years there was no bedside alarm clock to summon her into a new morning, so she woke late to find Daniella at her bedside with a tray of coffee, her dark eyes sparking with ill-concealed interest and excitement as she studied Signor Lorenzo's new bride.

Looking to see how I survived the night, Marisa realised, sitting up self-consciously, aware that her tossing and turning had rumpled the bed sufficiently to make it appear that she hadn't slept alone.

My God, she thought, as she accepted the coffee with a stilted word of thanks. If she only knew…

And silently thanked heaven that she didn't. That no one knew, apart from Renzo and herself, what a total shambles her first twenty-four hours of marriage had been.

Daniella's grasp of English was limited, but Marisa managed to convince her gently but firmly that she could draw her own bath and choose her own clothing for the day without assistance, uttering a silent sigh of relief when the girl reluctantly withdrew, after informing her that breakfast would be served on the rear terrace.

Because she needed to be alone in order to think.

She'd made a few decisions before she'd eventually allowed herself to sleep, and rather to her surprise they still seemed good in daylight.

The first of them was that this time she must—*must*—apologise to Renzo without delay, and offer him some kind of explanation for her behaviour. She had no other choice.

But that would not be easy, she thought, cautiously sipping the dark, fragrant brew. Because if she simply told him that she'd been too scared to let him kiss her he would almost certainly want to know why.

And she could hardly admit that the angry words she'd hurled at him last night might in fact be only too true. That she'd feared she might indeed find the lure of his mouth on hers hard to resist.

No, she thought forcefully. And no again. That was a confession she dared not make. A painful return to adolescent fantasy land, as unwelcome as it was unexpected. Threatening to make her prey to the kind of dreams and desires she'd thought she'd banished for ever, and which she could not risk again. Not after they'd crashed in ruins the first time.

Oh, God, she thought, swallowing. I'm going to have to be so careful. I need to make him believe it was just a serious fit of bridal nerves.

From which I've now recovered…

Because that was important, she told herself, when considering the next huge obstacle she had to overcome. Which was, of course, the inevitable and unavoidable establishment of their marriage on as normal a footing as it was possible to achieve—given the circumstances.

She replaced her empty cup on the bedside table and drew up her knees, wrapping her arms around them. Frowning as she wondered how she could possibly tell him that she was now prepared to fulfil her side of their arrangement. While making it quite clear, at the same time, that she intended to regard any physical contact between them as solely part of a business deal and certainly not the beginning of any kind of—relationship.

He didn't require her for that, anyway, she thought. According to Julia his needs in that respect were already well catered for by—what was her name? Ah, yes, Lucia, she recalled stonily. Lucia Gallo.

And throwing aside the covers, she got out of bed and prepared to face the day.

She hadn't taken a great deal of interest in the purchase of her trousseau, except to veto her cousin's more elaborate choice of evening dresses. But here she was, on the first morning of her marriage, with a tricky confrontation ahead of her, so choosing something to wear from the array that Daniella had unpacked and hung in one of the dressing room closets, suddenly seemed to acquire an additional importance.

She finally decided on one of her simplest outfits, a square-necked, full-skirted dress in pale yellow cotton. She brushed her light brown hair into its usual style, curving softly on to her shoulders, and added a coating of mascara to her lashes, a coral-based colour to her lips.

Then, slipping on low-heeled tan leather sandals, she left the bedroom and went in reluctant search of Lorenzo.

She'd assumed he would be at the breakfast table, but when she walked out into the sunshine she saw that only a single place was set in the vine-shaded pergola.

She turned to Massimo in faint surprise. 'The *signore* has eaten already?'

'*Si, signora*. Early. Very early. He say you are not to be disturbed.' He paused, his face lugubrious. 'And then he goes out in the car. Maybe to see a doctor—for his accident.'

'Accident?' Marisa repeated uneasily.

Evangelina came surging out to join them, bearing a fresh pot of coffee and a plate of sweet rolls to add to the platter of ham and cheese already on the table.

'*Si, signora*,' she said. 'Last night, in the dark, Signor Lorenzo he walk into door.' Her reproachful glance suggested that the *signore* should have been safely in bed, engrossed with his new bride, rather than wandering around bumping into the fixtures and fittings.

Marisa felt her colour rise. 'Oh, that,' she said, trying to sound nonchalant. 'Surely it isn't that bad?'

Pursed lips and shrugs invited her to think again, and her heart sank like a stone as it occurred to her that Renzo might not be feeling particularly receptive to any overtures this morning, and that her apology might have to be extremely humble indeed if it was to cut any ice with him.

Which was not altogether what she'd planned.

She hung around the terrace most of the morning, waiting with trepidation for his return. And waiting…

Until Massimo came, clearly bewildered, to relay the *signore*'s telephone message that he would be lunching elsewhere.

Marisa, managing to hide her relief, murmured '*Che peccato*,' and set herself to the task of persuading Massimo that it was far too hot for the midday banquet Evangelina seemed to be planning and that, as she would be eating alone, clear soup and a vegetable risotto would be quite enough.

She still wasn't very hungry, but starving herself would do no good, so she did her best with the food, guessing that any lack of appetite would be ascribed to the fact that she was pining for Lorenzo.

She was already aware that glances were being exchanged over her head in concern for this new wife left to her own devices so soon after her bridal night.

If Renzo continued his absence they might start putting two and two together and making all kinds of numbers, she thought without pleasure.

Her meal finished, she rested for a while in her room with the shutters drawn, but she soon accepted that she was far too jittery to relax, so she changed into a black bikini, topping it with a pretty black and white voile overshirt, and went back into the sunshine to find the swimming pool.

As Renzo had indicated, it was quite a descent through tier upon tier of blossom-filled terraces. It was like climbing down into a vast bowl of flowers, Marisa thought, with the oval pool, a living aquamarine, at its base. The sun terrace surrounding the water was tiled in a mosaic pattern of ivory and gold, and sunbeds had been placed in readiness, cushioned in turquoise, each with its matching parasol.

At one end of the pool there was a small hexagonal pavilion, painted white, containing towels, together with extra cushions and a shelf holding an extensive range of sun protection products. It also contained a refrigerator stocked with bottled water and soft drinks.

The air was very still, and filled with the scent of the encircling flowers. The only sounds were the soft drone of bees searching for pollen and, farther away, the whisper of the sea.

Marisa took a deep breath. If she'd simply been visiting on holiday, by herself, she'd have thought she was in paradise. As it was…

But she wouldn't think about that now, she told herself firmly. For the present she was alone, and she would make the most of it. Even if it was only the calm before an almost inevitable storm.

She slipped off her shirt and walked to the side of the pool. She sat on the edge for a moment, testing the temperature of the water with a cautious foot, then slid in, gasping with pleasure as the exquisite coolness received her heated body.

She began to swim steadily and without haste, completing one length of the pool, then another, and a third, feeling relaxed for the first time in days.

Out of the water, and dried off, she was careful to apply a high-factor lotion to her exposed skin before stretching out to sunbathe.

Allowing herself to burn to a frazzle might be an effective way of postponing the inevitable, she thought ruefully, but it wouldn't do much to advance the cause of marital harmony. And she couldn't afford to let matters deteriorate any further—not now she'd made up her mind to yield herself to him.

She capped the bottle and lay back on the padded cushions of her shaded lounger, closing her eyes and letting her thoughts drift.

Dinner tonight, she supposed, would probably be the best time to tell him of her decision—and then she might well drink herself into oblivion for the first time in her life, which was not something she'd ever contemplated, or a prospect she particularly relished.

It was just a question of doing whatever was necessary to get her through this phase in her life relatively unscathed, she thought unhappily, and alcohol was the only available anaesthetic.

It occurred to her that Renzo would probably know exactly why she was drinking as if tomorrow had been cancelled, but why would he care as long as he got what he wanted? she asked herself defiantly.

Anyway, she'd deal with that when the time came, and in the meantime she should stop brooding and turn her thoughts to something else entirely.

She ought to have brought something to read, she told herself ruefully. But when she'd mentioned packing some books into her honeymoon luggage Julia had stared at her as if she was insane, then told her acidly that Renzo would make sure she had far better things to do with her time.

Which brought her right back to square one again, she thought with a sigh, sitting up and reaching for her shirt.

She'd noticed some magazines yesterday in the *salotto*, and although they seemed exclusively to feature high fashion and interior design, they'd at least be a diversion.

Also they were in Italian, and Zio Guillermo had suggested kindly, but with a certain firmness too, that it would be good for her to start improving her language skills as soon as possible. So she could kill two birds with one stone.

Because of the heat, she deliberately took the climb up to the terrace very easily, pausing frequently to stand in the shade, and look back over the view.

But as she reached the top of the last flight of steps she halted abruptly, her heart thumping out a warning tattoo against her ribcage.

Because Renzo was there, sitting at the table, his feet up on an adjacent chair, reading a newspaper, a glass of wine beside him. He was wearing brief white shorts, a pair of espadrilles and sunglasses. The rest of him was tanned skin.

There was no way to avoid him, of course, Marisa realised uneasily, because this was the only route to the house. She just wished she was wearing more clothes. Or that he was.

It was all too horribly reminiscent of the last time he'd seen her in a bikini, when she'd given way to an impulse she'd hardly understood and been left to weep at her own humiliation.

She swallowed. But that had been years ago, and she wasn't a child any longer—as he'd demonstrated last night.

And now there were things which had to be said, which couldn't be put off any longer. Three birds, she thought, for the price of two. And bit her lip.

As she stood, hesitating, Renzo glanced up and saw her. Immediately he put his paper aside and got politely to his feet. '*Buon pomeriggio.*' His greeting was unsmiling.

'Good afternoon,' she returned, dry-mouthed. *In some odd way, he seemed taller than ever.* 'I—I was hoping you'd be back.'

He said expressionlessly, 'I am flattered.'

His tone suggested the opposite, but Marisa ploughed on, trying to look anywhere but directly at him.

'Evangelina said you might need medical treatment. I—I was—concerned.'

'In case I had been blinded?' he questioned with faint derision. He shook his head. 'Evangelina exaggerates. As you see, no doctor was necessary,' he added, removing his dark glasses.

She had to look at him then, staring with horror at the dark bruising at the corner of his eye. It was even worse than she'd expected.

She said huskily, 'I—I'm truly sorry. Please believe that I didn't mean to do it—that it was a total accident.'

He shrugged. 'Then God help me if you ever intend to do it.'

Colour rose in her face. She said, 'I never would. I—I was startled, that's all.' She spread her hands defensively. 'All this—the strain of these last weeks—the wedding—it hasn't been easy for me.'

'And therefore my quite unreasonable wish to kiss you goodnight was the final straw?' he said softly. 'Is that what you are saying?'

She bit her lip. 'Yes—perhaps.' She looked down at the black and white marble tiles at her feet. 'Although I realise it's no excuse.'

'At least we agree on something.'

He was not making this very easy for her, she thought. But then why should he? He was the one with the black eye.

'Also,' she went on, 'I have to thank you for pretending that you walked into a door.'

'It is the usual excuse, I believe,' he said crisply. '*Inoltre*, I felt the truth would hardly be to the credit of either of us.' His mouth twisted. 'And Evangelina would have been most distressed. She is a romantic creature.'

She did not meet his gaze. 'Then we must already be a terrible disappointment to her.'

'No doubt,' he said. 'But we must all learn to live with our various disillusionments.' He shrugged again. 'And for some time to come, it seems, to judge by last night.'

The moment of truth had arrived. Earlier than she'd planned, but a few hours couldn't really matter. Anyway, there was no turning back now, she thought, taking a deep breath. But her voice faltered a little just the same. 'Well—perhaps not.'

There was an odd silence, then Renzo said slowly, 'Why, Maria Lisa, are you saying you want me to make love to you?'

She realised that he was looking at her, studying her, allowing his eyes to travel slowly down her half-naked body. Thought again of a time when she would have responded with eager joy to the caress of his gaze, and how her pathetic attempt to lure him had met with rejection instead.

A small, cold stone seemed to settle in the middle of her chest.

She said, lifting her chin, 'Shall we save the pretence for the staff, *signore*? You don't want me any more than I want you. Julia told me you already have this Lucia Gallo in your life, so we both know exactly why we're here, and what's expected of us, and it has nothing to do with love.'

She stared rigidly past him. 'You said last night that you wanted me not to—not to dread being with you, but that's not going to happen. It—can't. Because, however long you wait, I'm never going to be—ready in the way you wish.'

He was utterly still, she realised, and completely silent. In fact, she could have been addressing a statue. A man of bronze.

Oh, God, she thought. This would have been so much less complicated over dinner. And she wasn't explaining it all in the way she'd rehearsed down at the pool either. In fact, she seemed to be saying all kinds of things she hadn't intended. But she'd started, and she had to go stumbling on. She had no choice now.

'You bought me for a purpose.' Her voice quivered a little. 'So you're entitled to use me—in that way. I—I realise that, and I accepted it when I agreed to marry you. Truly I did. I also accept that you were trying to be kind when you said you'd be patient and—and wait in order to make…sex with you…easier for me. Except, it hasn't worked. Because waiting has just made everything a hundred times worse. It's like this huge black cloud hanging over me—a sentence that's been passed but not carried out.'

She swallowed. 'It's been this way ever since we became engaged, and I can't bear it any longer. So I'd prefer it—over and done with, and as soon as possible.'

She slid a glance at him, and for a brief instant she had the strangest impression that it wasn't only the corner of his eye but his entire face that was bruised.

Some trick of the light, she thought, her throat closing as she hurried on with a kind of desperation.

'So I need to tell you that it's all right—for you to come to my room tonight. I'll do whatever you want, and—I—I promise that I won't fight you this time.' And stopped, at last, with a little nervous gasp.

The silence and stillness remained, but the quality of it seemed to have changed in some subtle way she did not understand.

But all the same it worried her, and she needed it to be broken. To obtain some reaction from him.

She drew a breath. 'Perhaps I haven't explained properly…'

'*Al contrario*, you have been more than clear, *signora*.' His voice reached her at last, cool and level. 'Even eloquent. My congratulations. I am only sorry that my attempt at behaving towards you with consideration has failed so badly. Forgive me, please, and believe I did not intend to cause you stress by delaying the consummation of our marriage. However, that can soon be put right. And we do not have to wait until tonight.'

Two long strides brought him to her. He picked her up in his arms and carried her towards the open French windows of the *salotto*.

She said, in a voice she did not recognise. 'Renzo—what are you doing?' She began to struggle. 'Put me down—do you hear? Put me down at once.'

'I intend to.' He crossed the room to the empty fireplace, setting her down on the enormous fur rug that fronted it and kneeling over her. He said softly, 'You said you would not fight me, Marisa. I recommend that you keep your promise.'

She looked up at him—at the livid bruising and the hard set of his mouth. At the cold purpose in his eyes.

'Oh, God, no.' Her voice cracked. 'Not like this—please.'

'Do not distress yourself.' His voice was harsh. 'Your ordeal will be brief—far more so than it would have been tonight. And that is my promise to you.'

He reached down almost negligently, stripping her of the bottom half of her bikini and tossing it aside, before unzipping his shorts.

He did not hold her down, nor use any kind of force. Shocked as she was, she could recognise that. But then he did not have to, she thought numbly, because she'd told him that she wouldn't resist.

And he was, quite literally, taking her at her word.

Nor did he attempt to kiss her. And the hand that parted her thighs was brisk rather than caressing.

She tried to say no again, because every untried female instinct she possessed was screaming that it should not be like this.

That, whatever she'd said, this wasn't what she'd intended. That she'd been nervous and muddled it all. And somehow she had to let him know this, and ask him, in spite of everything, to be kind.

But no sound came from her dry, paralysed throat, and anyway it was all too late—because Renzo was already guiding himself slowly into her, pausing to give her bewildered face a swift glance, then taking total possession of her stunned body with one long, controlled thrust.

Arching himself above her, his weight on his arms, his clenched fists buried in the softness of the rug on either side of her, he began to move, strongly and rhythmically.

Marisa had braced herself instinctively against the onset of a pain she'd imagined would be inevitable, even if she'd been taken with any kind of tenderness.

But if there'd been any discomfort it had been so slight and so fleeting that she'd barely registered the fact.

It was the astonishing sensation of his body sheathed in hers that was totally controlling her awareness. The amazing reality of all that potent, silken hardness, driving ever more deeply into her aroused and yielding heat, slowly at first, then much faster, that was sending her mind suddenly into free fall. Alerting her to possibilities she had not known existed. Offering her something almost akin to—hope.

And then, with equal suddenness, it was over. She heard Renzo cry out hoarsely, almost achingly, and felt his body shuddering into hers in one scalding spasm after another.

For what seemed an eternity he remained poised above her, his breathing ragged as he fought to regain his control. Then he lifted himself out of her, away from her, dragging his clothing back into place with frankly unsteady hands before getting to his feet and looking down at her, his dark face expressionless.

'So, *signora*.' His voice was quiet, almost courteous. 'You have nothing more to fear. Our distasteful duty has at last been done, and I trust without too much inconvenience to you.'

He paused, adding more harshly, 'Let us also hope that it has achieved its purpose, and that you are never forced to suffer my attentions again. And that I am not made to endure any further outrage to my own feelings.'

He walked to the door without sparing her one backward glance. Leaving her where she was lying, shaken, but in some strange way feeling almost—bereft without him.

And at that moment, when it was so very much too late, she heard herself whisper his name.

CHAPTER SIX

EVEN now Marisa could remember with total clarity that she hadn't wanted to move.

That it had seemed somehow so much easier to remain where she was, like a small animal cowering in long grass, shivering with resentment, shame and—yes—misery too, than to pull herself together and restore some kind of basic decency to her appearance as she tried to come to terms with what had just happened.

Eventually the fear of being found by one of the staff had forced her to struggle back into her bikini briefs and, huddling her crumpled shirt defensively around her, make her way to her room.

There, she'd stripped completely, before standing under a shower that had been almost too hot to be bearable. As if that could in any way erase the events of the past half-hour.

How could he? she'd asked herself wretchedly as the water had pounded its way over her body. *Oh, God, how could he treat me like that—as if I had no feelings—as if I hardly existed for him?*

Well, I know the answer to that now, Marisa thought, turning over in her search for a cool spot on her pillow. *If I'm honest, I probably knew it then too, but couldn't let myself admit it.*

It happened because that's what I asked for. Because I added insult to the injury I'd already inflicted by telling him to his face that he didn't matter. That sex with him would only ever be a 'distasteful duty'—the words he threw at me afterwards.

She'd sensed the anger in him, like a damped-down fire that could rage out of control at any moment, in the way he'd barely touched her. In the way that the lovemaking he'd offered her only moments before had been transformed into a brief, soulless act accomplished with stark and icy efficiency. And perhaps most of all in his subsequent dismissal of her before he walked away.

Yet, anger had not made him brutal, she reflected broodingly. He had not behaved well, perhaps. After all, she had still been his new bride, and a virgin, but he had not forced her—merely used her confused and unwilling assent against her. And he most certainly hadn't hurt her.

Or not physically, at least.

Which made it difficult to blame or hate him as much as she wanted to do, she realised, aggrieved.

An important stone that would for ever be missing from the wall of indifference she'd deliberately constructed between them.

And it was a wall that she was determined to maintain at all costs, Marisa told herself, now that Renzo had so unexpectedly come back into her life, it seemed with every intention of remaining there, totally regardless of her own wishes.

Which surely constituted just cause for resentment, however you looked at it?

Suddenly restive, she pushed the coverlet aside and got out of bed, moving soundlessly to the small easy chair by the window.

If ever she'd needed a good night's sleep to ensure that she was fresh, with all her wits about her for the morning, it was now. And it just wasn't going to happen—thanks to the man occupying her living room sofa and the memories his arrival had forced back into her consciousness.

Memories of leaning slumped against the shower's tiled wall, a hand pressed against her abdomen as she realised it would be nearly three weeks before she knew for certain whether Renzo's 'purpose', as he'd so bleakly expressed it, had been achieved, and his child was growing in her body.

Of trying desperately to formulate some credible excuse to avoid having to face him at dinner in a few hours' time—or ever again, for that matter—and knowing there was none. She would have to pretend that she didn't care how he'd treated her. That she'd neither anticipated nor wanted anything more from him, and was simply thankful that the matter had been dealt with and need not be referred to again.

Of eventually dressing in a pretty swirl of turquoise silk—not white, because it was no longer appropriate, and not black because it might suggest she was in some kind of mourning—and joining him with an assumption of calmness in the *salotto*.

Of accepting his coolly civil offer of a drink with equal politeness, realising he had no more wish to speak of the afternoon's events than she did. And then of sitting opposite him in silence, during an interminable meal.

A pattern, she had soon discovered, that would be repeated each evening.

Not that he'd planned to spend time with her during the day either, as she had found out when she joined him for breakfast the following morning, at his request, conveyed by Daniella.

'This is a very beautiful part of the world, Marisa, and you will no doubt wish to go sightseeing—to explore Amalfi itself, of course, and then discover the delights of Ravello and Positano.'

Was he offering to escort her? she wondered in sudden alarm, her lips already parting to deny, mendaciously, that she had any such ambition. To say she was quite content to stay within the precincts of the villa while he went off to Ravello, or wherever, and stayed there.

But before she could speak, he added smoothly, 'I have therefore arranged to have a car placed at your disposal. The driver's name is Paolo. He is a cousin of Evangelina and completely reliable. He will make himself available each day to drive you anywhere you want to go.'

So I don't have to...

The unspoken words seemed to hover in the air between them.

'I see.' She should have been dancing with relief. Instead, she felt oddly—blank. She hesitated. 'That's—very kind of you.'

He shrugged. 'It's nothing.'

And that she could believe, she thought bleakly. It was his way of dealing with an awkward and disagreeable situation—by simply ridding himself of the source of annoyance.

After all, he'd done it not that long ago—with Alan.

Renzo paused too. He went on more slowly, 'I have also ordered a box of books to be delivered here for you—a selection from the bestseller lists in Britain and America. I recall you used to like thrillers, but perhaps your tastes have changed?'

Marisa found she was biting her lip—hard.

'No,' she said. 'Not really. And I'm very grateful.' Adding stiffly, '*Grazie*.'

'*Prego*.' His mouth curled slightly. 'After all, *mia bella*, I would not wish you to be bored.'

A comment, she thought stonily, that removed any further need for appreciation on her part.

For the next few days it suited her to play the tourist—if only because it got her away from the villa and Renzo's chillingly aloof courtesy. To her endless embarrassment he continued to treat her with quite astonishing generosity, and as a result she found herself in possession of more money in cash than she'd ever dreamed of in her life, plus a selection of credit cards with no apparent upper limit.

She'd often wondered what it might be like to have access to unrestricted spending, only to find there was very little she actually wanted to buy.

Maybe I'm not the type to shop till I drop, she thought, sighing. *What a waste.*

But she did make one important purchase. In Positano she bought herself three *maillots*—one in black, another in a deep olive-green, and the third in dark red—to wear for her solitary late-afternoon swim, and to replace the bikinis she never wanted to see again, let alone wear.

In Amalfi she visited an outlet selling the handmade paper for which the region was famous, and dutifully bought some to send back to England to Julia and Harry. She also sent her cousin a postcard, with some deliberately neutral comments on the weather and scenery. After all, she thought wryly, she could hardly write *Having a wonderful time*.

She was particularly enchanted by Ravello, its narrow streets seemingly caught in a medieval time warp, and thought wistfully how much she would like to attend one of the open-air concerts held in the moonlit splendour of the gardens at the Villa Rufulo. But she acknowledged with a sigh, it was hardly the kind of event she could attend alone, without inviting even more speculation than already existed.

Paolo was a pleasant, middle-aged man who spoke good English and was eager to guide her round his amazing native landscape and share his extensive knowledge of its history. But Marisa was conscious that, like the staff at the villa, he was bemused at this bride who seemed never to be in her husband's company, and she was growing tired of being asked if the *signore* was quite well.

Eventually she decided she had visited enough churches, admired enough Renaissance artefacts, and gaped at sufficient pictures. Also, she felt disinclined to give any more assurances about Renzo's health—especially as the bruise on his eye was fading at last.

Her main danger was in eating far too many of the delicious almond and lemon cakes served in the cafés in Amalfi's Piazza del Duomo, as she sat at a table in the sunlight and watched the crowds as they milled about in the ancient square.

So many families strolling with children. So very many couples, too, meeting with smiling eyes, a touch of hands, an embrace. No one, she thought, had ever greeted her like that, as if she was their whole world. Not even Alan. But their relationship hadn't had a chance, being over almost as soon as it had begun.

And then, in her mind, she saw a sudden image of Renzo, standing at the altar only a week before, as if transfixed, an expression that was almost wonder on his dark face as she walked towards him.

And what on earth had made her think of *that*? she thought, startled, as she finished her coffee and signalled for the bill.

Not that it meant anything—except that the sight of her had probably brought it home to him that his head was now firmly in the noose.

All the same, the buzz of talk and laughter in the air around her only served to emphasise her own sense of isolation.

She thought, with a pang, *I have no one. Unless, of course…* And her hand strayed almost unconsciously to the flatness of her stomach.

The next morning, when Evangelina enquired at what hour the *signora* would require Paolo to call for her, Marisa said politely that she did not wish to do any more sightseeing for a while.

'Ah.' Something like hope dawned in the plump face. 'No doubt you will be joining the *signore* by the pool?'

'No,' Marisa returned coolly. 'I thought I would go up to the village for a stroll.'

'The village is small,' said Evangelina. 'It has little to see, *signora*. Better to stay here and relax.' She gave a winning smile. 'Is quiet by the pool. No disturb there.'

In other words, Marisa thought, caught between annoyance and a kind of reluctant amusement, no one would go blundering down there in case the *signore* decided to take full advantage of his wife's company by enjoying his marital rights in such secluded and romantic surroundings.

She shrugged. 'I'll swim later, as usual,' she said casually. 'After I've been for my walk.' And she turned away, pretending not to notice the housekeeper's disappointment.

Fifteen minutes later, trim in a pair of white cut-offs topped by a silky russet tee shirt, with her pretty straw bag slung across her shoulder, Marisa passed through Villa Santa Caterina's wide gateway and set off up the hill.

Evangelina, she soon discovered, had been perfectly correct in her assessment. The village *was* small, and no tourist trap, its main street lined with houses shuttered against the morning sun, interspersed with a few shops providing life's practicalities, among them a café with two tables outside under an awning.

Maybe on the way back she'd stop there for a while and have a cold drink. Enjoy the shade. Read some of the book she'd brought with her. Anything to delay the moment when she would have to return to Villa Santa Caterina and the probability of Evangelina's further attempts to throw her into Renzo's arms.

At the same time she became aware that every few yards, between the houses and their neat gardens, she could catch a glimpse of the sparkling azure that was the sea.

The view from the villa garden was spectacular enough, she thought, but up here it would be magical, and in her bag she'd also brought the small sketching block and pencils that she'd acquired on yesterday's trip to Amalfi.

She was standing, craning her neck at one point, when she realised the lady of the house in question had emerged and was watching her.

Marisa stepped back, flushing. '*Perdono*,' she apologised awkwardly. 'I was looking at the view—*il bel mare*,' she added for good measure.

Immediately the other's face broke into a beaming smile. '*Si—si,*' she nodded vigorously. She marched over to Marisa and took her arm, propelling her up the village street while chattering at a great and largely incomprehensible rate—apart from the words '*una vista fantastica*', which pretty much explained themselves.

At the end of the street the houses stopped and a high wall began, which effectively blocked everything. Marisa's self-appointed guide halted, pointing at it.

'Casa Adriana,' she announced. '*Che bella vista.*' She kissed her fingertips as she urged Marisa forward, adding with a gusty sigh, '*Che tragedia.*'

A fantastic view, I can handle, Marisa thought as she moved off obediently. But do I really need a tragedy to go with it?

However, a glance over her shoulder showed that her new friend was still watching and smiling, so she gave a slight wave in return and trudged on.

As she got closer she saw that the wall's white paintwork was dingy and peeling, and that the actual structure was crumbling in places, indicating that some serious attention was needed.

It also seemed to go on for ever, but eventually she realised she was approaching a narrow, rusting wrought-iron gate, and that this was standing ajar in a kind of mute invitation.

Beyond it, a weed-infested gravel path wound its way between a mass of rioting bushes and shrubs, and at its end, beckoning like a siren, was the glitter of blue that announced the promised view.

The breath caught in Marisa's throat, and she pushed the gate wider so that she could walk through. She'd expected an outraged squeal from the ancient metal hinges, but there wasn't a sound. Someone, she saw, had clearly been busy with an oil can.

This is what happens in late night thrillers on television, she told herself. *And I'm always the one with her hands over her face, screaming* Don't do it! *So it will serve me right if that gate swings shut behind me and traps me in here with some nameless horror lurking in the undergrowth.*

But the gate, fortunately, displayed no desire to move, and the nameless horror probably had business elsewhere, so she walked briskly forward, avoiding the overhanging shrubs and bushes with their pollen-heavy blossoms that tried to impede her way.

There was a scent of jasmine in the air, and there were roses too, crowding everywhere in a rampant glory of pink, white and yellow. Marisa was no expert—her parents' garden had been little more than a grass patch, while Julia had opted for a courtyard with designer tubs—but from her vacations in Tuscany she recognised oleanders mingling with masses of asters, pelargoniums, and clumps of tall graceful daisies, all wildly out of control.

Halfway down, the path forked abruptly to the right, and there, half-eclipsed by the bougainvillaea climbing all over it, was all that remained of a once pretty house. Its walls were still standing, but even from a distance Marisa could see that many of the roof tiles were missing, and that behind the screen of pink and purple flowers shutters were hanging loose from broken windows.

But there'd been attempts elsewhere to restore order. The grass had been cut in places, and over-intrusive branches cut down and stacked, presumably for burning.

In the centre of one cleared patch stood a fountain, where a naked nymph on tiptoe sadly tilted an urn which had not flowed with water for a very long time.

And straight ahead, at the end of the path, a lemon tree heavy with fruit stood like a sentinel, watching by the low wall that overlooked the bay.

Rather too low a wall, Marisa thought, when she took a wary peep over its edge and discovered a stomach-churning drop down the sheer and rocky cliff to the tumbling sea far below.

She stepped back hastily, and found herself colliding with an ancient wooden seat, which had been placed at a safe distance in the shade of the tree, suggesting that the garden's owner might not have had much of a head for heights either.

That was probably the tragedy that her friend in the village had mentioned, she thought. An inadvertent stumble after too much *limoncello* by some unlucky soul, and a headlong dive into eternity.

She seated herself gingerly, wondering if the bench was still capable of bearing even her slight weight, but there was no imminent sign of collapse, so she allowed herself to lean back and take her first proper look at the panorama laid out in front of her.

One glance told her that 'fantastic' was indeed the word, and she silently blessed the woman who'd sent her here.

Over to her left she could see the cream, gold and terracotta of Amalfi town, looking as if it had grown like some sprawling rock plant out of the tall cliffs that sheltered it. The towering stone facades themselves gleamed like silver and amethyst in the morning sun under a dark green canopy of cypresses. And below the town the deep cerulean sea turned to jade and turquoise edged with foam as it spilled itself endlessly on the shingle shore.

She could even see the rooftop swimming pools of the hotels overlooking the port, and the sturdy outline of the medieval watchtower, which no longer scanned the horizon for pirates or enemies from neighbouring city states, but served food in its elegant restaurant instead. Beyond it lay Ravello, and if she turned to glance the other way she could see the dizzying tumble of Positano, and in the far distance a smudge that might even be Capri.

The horizon was barely visible, sky and sea merging seamlessly in an azure blur.

It was also very quiet. The sound of traffic along the ribbon of coast road was barely audible at this distance, and for the first time in weeks Marisa felt the tension within her—like the heaviness of unshed tears—beginning to ease, and something like peace take its place.

So good, she thought. So good to be truly alone and leave behind the pressure of other people's expectations. To be free of the necessity of changing into yet another charming and expensive dress just to make occasional and stilted conversation across a dinner table with a young man whose smile never reached his eyes.

To be, just for a while, Marisa Brendon again and nothing more, with no apology for a marriage to haunt her.

She looked down at her hand, then slowly slid off her wedding ring, and buried it deep in her pocket.

There, she thought. Now I can pretend that I'm simply here on vacation, with my whole life ahead of me, free to enjoy no one's company but my own.

Only to hear from behind her a small, mild cough which announced that she was not alone after all. That someone else was there, sharing her supposed solitude.

Startled, she jumped to her feet and turned, to find herself confronted by a small woman with rimless glasses and wisps of grey hair escaping from under a floppy linen sun hat. Her khaki trousers and shirt were smeared with earth and green stains, and she carried a small pair of pruning shears in one hand and a flat wicker basket full of trimmings in the other.

Oh, God, Marisa thought, embarrassed colour flooding her face. *That house can't be as derelict as I thought.*

Aloud, she said, in halting and woefully incorrect Italian, 'Please forgive me. I was not told that anyone lived here. I will leave at once.'

The newcomer's brows lifted. 'Another Englishwoman,' said a gentle voice. 'How very nice. And I'm afraid we're both trespassers, my dear. I also came here one day to look at the view, but I saw a potentially beautiful space going to rack and ruin and I couldn't resist the challenge. No one has ever objected,' she added. 'Probably because they think I'm mad to try.'

Her smile was kind. 'So please don't run away on my account. And I'm sorry if I startled you. You were a shock to me too, appearing so quietly. For a moment I thought Adriana had returned, and then I realised you were totally twenty-first century. Quite a relief, I have to say.'

She tugged off her thick gardening gloves and held out her hand. 'I'm Dorothy Morton.'

'Marisa Brendon.' *Well, I've done it now,* Marisa thought as she returned the smile and the handshake. *Crossed my own small Rubicon back to being single again.*

'Marisa,' the older woman repeated thoughtfully. 'Such a charming name. And Italian too, I believe?'

'After my late godmother.'

'Ah,' said Mrs Morton. 'And did she live locally? Are you familiar with the area?'

Marisa shook her head. 'No, this is my first visit.' *And almost certainly my last.* 'I'm staying with—some people.'

'My husband and I were fortunate enough to be able to retire here.' Mrs Morton looked out at the bay with an expression of utter contentment. 'We have an apartment nearby, but it only has a balcony, and I do miss my gardening. So I come here most days and do what I can.' She sighed. 'But as you see, it's an uphill struggle.'

'It must be tiring too.' Marisa gestured towards the bench. 'Shall we sit down—if you have time?'

'My time is very much my own.' Mrs Morton took a seat at the other end of the bench. 'I have a most understanding husband.'

'That's—lovely for you.' Marisa was suddenly conscious of the ring buried in her pocket. She added hurriedly, 'But why has the garden been allowed to get into such a state?' She glanced around her. 'Doesn't the owner—this Adriana—care?'

'I think she would care very much if she was alive to see it, but she died a long time ago—over fifty years, I gather—and ownership of the property is no longer established.'

'She didn't have an heir?' Marisa asked with a certain constraint. Another topic, she thought, she'd have preferred to avoid.

'She and her husband were still newlyweds,' Mrs Morton explained. 'According to the local stories they made wills leaving everything to each other. And when he pre-deceased her she refused to make another.'

She shrugged. 'Relatives on both sides have made legal claims to the estate over the years, but I suspect that most of them have died too by now, so the whole thing is in abeyance.'

'Oh.' Marisa drew a deep breath. 'So that's the tragedy. This wonderful place just left to—moulder away.' She shook her head. 'But why on earth didn't this Adriana change her will?'

'Oh, that's quite simple,' Mrs Morton said quietly. 'You see, she never actually believed that her husband was dead.'

Marisa frowned. 'But surely there must have been a death certificate at some point?' she objected.

'Under normal circumstances,' the other woman said. 'But sadly there was no real proof of death. Filippo Barzoni was sailing back from Ischia—he was a keen and experienced sailor, and had made the trip many times before—when a sudden violent squall blew up. Neither he nor his boat were ever seen again.

'Some wreckage was washed up near Sorrento, but it was considered inconclusive as the storm had produced other casualties. However, no one but his widow believed that Filippo could possibly have survived. They were passionately in love, you see, and Adriana always claimed she would know, in her heart, if her husband were no longer alive. She felt most strongly that he was still with her, and that one day he would return.'

She sighed. 'That's why she had this bench placed here, so

she could sit and watch the bay for a blue boat with maroon sails. She came every day to keep her vigil, summer and winter, and she refused to listen to any arguments against it. "One day, he will come back to me," she used to say. "And he will find me waiting."'

'How awful,' Marisa said softly. 'Poor woman.'

Mrs Morton smiled again. 'She didn't see herself at all in that way, by all accounts. She was very calm, very steadfast, and doing what she believed in. As well as love, you see, she had faith and hope, so maybe she was one of the lucky ones.'

'What happened in the end?' Marisa asked.

'She caught a chill, which she neglected, and which turned to pneumonia. She was taken to hospital, much against her will, and died a few days later.' She added with faint dryness, 'It's said her last words were "Tell him I waited," which one can believe or not.'

She put on her gloves and rose. 'But this is far too lovely a day, and you're much too young and pretty for any more sad stories about lost love. And I must get on with some work.' She looked again at the sea. 'However, this is a wonderful spot—especially to sit and think—and I hope I haven't depressed you so much that you never come back.'

'No,' Marisa said. 'I'd love to come and sit here—as long as I won't be in the way.'

'On the contrary, I think we can peacefully co-exist.'

'And I have to say that it doesn't actually feel sad at all.'

'Nor to me,' Mrs Morton agreed. 'But I know some of the local people tend to avoid it.'

Marisa said slowly, 'You said, when you saw me, that you thought for a moment Adriana had come back. Is that what people think?'

Behind her spectacles, Mrs Morton's eyes twinkled. 'Not out loud. The parish priest is very against superstition.' She paused. 'But I was surprised to see you, because so very few visitors come here. In fact, I always think of it as the village's best-kept secret.'

'Yet they told me?' Marisa said, half to herself.

'Well, perhaps you seemed like someone who needed a quiet place to think in the sunshine.' As she moved away Mrs Morton glanced back over her shoulder. 'But that, my dear, is entirely your own business.'

* * *

And co-exist, we did, Marisa thought, looking back with a pang of gratitude.

It had been late afternoon when she'd finally returned to Villa Santa Caterina, and she had fully expected to be cross-examined about her absence—by Evangelina if no one else, particularly as she'd failed to return to the villa for lunch. But not a word was said.

And no questions had been asked when she'd announced the following day that she was going for another walk, or any of the days that followed, when she'd climbed the hill to the house, passing her hours quietly on Adriana's bench. She read, and sketched, and tried to make sense of what had happened to her and where it might lead.

Keeping, she realised now, a vigil of her own.

She'd invariably been aware of Mrs Morton's relaxed presence elsewhere in the garden, and sometimes they had chatted, when the older woman took a break from her endeavours, having kindly but firmly refused Marisa's diffident offer of help.

Conversation between them had been restricted to general topics, although Marisa had been aware that sometimes her companion watched her in a faintly puzzled way, as if wondering why she should choose to spend so much time alone.

Once, indeed, she'd asked, 'Do your friends not mind seeing so little of you, my dear?'

'No, not at all.' Marisa looked down at her bare hand. 'We're not—close.'

And then, in the final week of the honeymoon, all her silent questioning was ended when she woke with stomach cramps and realised there would be no baby.

Realised, too, that she would somehow have to go to Renzo and tell him. And then, on some future occasion, steel herself to have sex with him again.

Both of those being prospects that filled her with dread.

She took some painkillers and spent most of the morning in bed, informing Evangelina that she had a headache, probably through too much sun.

'Perhaps you would tell the *signore*,' she added, hoping that Renzo would read between the lines of the message and guess the truth. That as a result she might be spared the embarrassment of a personal interview with him. But Evangelina looked surprised.

'He is not here, *signora*. He has business in Naples and will not return before dinner. Did he not say?'

'I expect so.' Marisa kept her tone light. *Let's keep up the pretence,* she thought, *that this is a normal marriage, where people talk to each other. After all, in a few more days we'll be leaving.* 'I—probably forgot.'

In a way she was relieved at his absence, but knew that her reprieve was only temporary, and that eventually she would have to confront him with the unwelcome truth.

By which time, she told herself unhappily, she might have thought of something to say.

The business in Naples must have taken longer than Renzo had bargained for, because for the first time Marisa was down to dinner ahead of him. And when he did join her he was clearly preoccupied.

She sat quietly, forcing herself to eat and making no attempt to break the silence between them.

But when the coffee arrived and he rose, quietly excusing himself on the grounds that he had phone calls to make, she knew she couldn't delay any longer.

She said, 'Can they wait for a few moments, please? I—I'd like to talk to you.'

'An unexpected honour.' His voice was cool, but he stood, waiting.

She flushed. 'Not really. I—I'm afraid I have—bad news for you. I found out this morning that I'm—not pregnant after all.' She added stiltedly, 'I'm—sorry.'

'Are you?' His tone was expressionless. 'Well, that is understandable.'

She wanted to tell him that wasn't what she meant. That, however it had been conceived, during the weeks of waiting to her own astonishment the baby had somehow become very real to her—and in some strange way precious.

And that this had come home to her most forcefully today, when she'd had to face the fact that his child had never actually existed, and had found herself in the extremity of a different kind of pain.

She said with difficulty, 'You must be very disappointed.'

His faint smile was as bleak as winter. 'I think I am beyond disappointment, Marisa. Perhaps we should discuss this—and other matters—in the morning. Now, you must excuse me.'

When he had gone, Marisa sat staring at the candle-flame, sipping her coffee and feeling it turn to bitterness in her throat. Then she pushed the cup away from her, so violently that some of its contents spilled across the white cloth, and went to her bedroom.

She undressed, cleaned her teeth, and put on her nightgown, moving like an automaton. She got into bed and drew the covers around her as if the night was cold. The cramps had subsided long ago, and in their place was a great hollowness.

It's gone, she thought. *My little boy. My little girl. Someone to love, who'd have loved me in return. Who'd have belonged to me.*

Except it was only a figment of my imagination. And I'm left with nothing. No one.

Until the next time, if he can ever bring himself to touch me again.

Suddenly all the pent-up hurt and loneliness of her situation overwhelmed her, and she began to cry, softly at first, and then in hard, choking sobs that threatened to tear her apart.

Leaving her, at last, drained and shivering in the total isolation of that enormous bed.

CHAPTER SEVEN

AND the following morning she had found that her honeymoon had come to an abrupt end.

Her confrontation with Renzo had taken place, to her discomfort, in the *salotto*—a room she'd tried to avoid ever since…since that day, and where she'd managed never to be alone with him again.

She had sat. He had stood, his face bleak, almost haggard. The golden eyes sombre.

He'd spoken quietly, but with finality, while she had stared down at her hands, gripped together in her lap.

As they were now, she noticed, while her memory was recreating once again everything he'd said to her.

He had wasted no time getting to the point. 'I feel strongly, Marisa, that we need to reconsider the whole question of our marriage. I therefore suggest that we leave Villa Santa Caterina either later today or tomorrow, as no useful purpose can be served by our remaining here. Do you agree?'

She hadn't wholly trusted her voice, so it had seemed safer just to nod.

When he had resumed, his voice had been harder. 'I also propose that we spend some time apart from each other, in order to examine our future as husband and wife. Clearly things cannot continue as they are. Decisions will need to be made, and some consensus reached.'

He'd paused. 'You may, of course, take as much time as you need. You need not fear that I shall pressure you in any way. Therefore I am quite willing to stay at my apartment in Rome, and make our home in Tuscany available to you for your sole occupation.'

'No!' She had seen his head go back, and realised how vehement her negation had been. 'I mean—thank you. But under the circumstances that's impossible. Your father will expect to see us together.' She took a deep breath. 'So, I would very much prefer to go back to London. If that can be arranged.'

'London?' he'd repeated. He had looked at her, his eyes narrowing in faint disbelief. 'You mean you wish to rejoin your cousin?'

All hell, Marisa had thought, would freeze over first. But she'd glimpsed a chance of escape, and had known a more moderate answer might achieve a better result.

She'd shaken her head. 'She's moving to Kent very soon, so the question doesn't arise.' She'd paused. 'What I really want, *signore*, is a place of my own. Somewhere just for myself,' she'd added with emphasis. 'With no one else involved.'

There had been a silence, then Renzo had said carefully, 'I see. But—in London? Do you think that is wise?'

'Why not?' Marisa had lifted her chin. 'After all, I'm not a child any more.' *Or your tame virgin, who has to be protected from all predators but you,* her eyes had said, and she'd watched faint colour burn along his cheekbones.

'Besides,' she'd added, her voice challenging. 'If you have an apartment in Rome, why shouldn't I have a flat in London?'

Renzo had spread his hands. He'd said, almost ruefully, 'I can think of a string of reasons, although I doubt you would find any of them acceptable.'

'Nevertheless, that is my choice.' She'd looked down at her hands again. 'And as we'll be living apart anyway, I don't see what difference it can make.'

There had been another pause, then he'd said quietly, 'Very well. Let it be as you wish.'

For a moment she'd felt stunned. She had certainly not expected so easy a victory.

Unless, of course, he simply wanted her out of sight—and out of mind—and as quickly as possible…

For a moment, her feeling of triumph had seemed to ebb, and she'd felt oddly forlorn.

Yet wasn't that exactly what she wanted too? she'd rallied herself. So why should she care?

She had looked at him. Forced a smile. '*Grazie*.'

'*Prego*.' He had not returned the smile. 'Now, if you will excuse me, there are arrangements to be made.' And he'd gone.

After that, Marisa recalled, things had seemed to happen very fast.

Renzo, it appeared, only had to snap his fingers and a first-class flight to London became available. Arrangements were made for a chauffeur and limousine to meet her at the airport, together with a representative from the Santangelis' UK lawyers. He or she would be responsible for escorting her to a suite at a top hotel, which had been reserved for her as a temporary residence, before providing her with a list of suitable properties and smoothing her path through the various viewings. Money, of course, being no object.

In fact, she found herself thinking with a pang, as her plane took off and she waved away the offered champagne, what wouldn't Renzo pay to be rid of the girl who'd so signally failed him as a wife?

Because this had to be the beginning of the end of their marriage, and his lawyers would soon be receiving other, more personal instructions concerning her.

And she would be free—able for the first time to make a life for herself as Marisa Brendon. Answerable, she told herself, to no one. Least of all to her erstwhile husband, now breathing a sigh of relief in Rome.

Her only regret was that she hadn't had time to pay a final visit to Casa Adriana and say goodbye to Mrs Morton. But perhaps it was better this way.

Those warm, quiet days in the garden had begun to assume a dreamlike quality all their own. Even when she had been entirely alone there, she thought, in some strange way she had never felt lonely.

She did not believe that Adriana's ghost had ever returned, but perhaps love and hope still lingered somehow. And they'd been her comfort.

Once established in London, she had not expected to hear from Renzo again, so his phone calls and letters had come as a distinct shock. A courteous gesture, she'd told herself, that she needed like a hole in the head and could safely ignore.

And now here he was in person, suddenly and without warning. Back in her life, she thought with anger, because in reality he'd never had the slightest intention of letting her go.

Her 'breathing space' was over and there was nothing she could do about it.

Because he clearly had no intention of giving her the divorce she'd been counting on, and she had no resources for a long legal battle.

The first of many bitter pills she would probably have to swallow.

Besides—she owed him, she told herself unhappily. There was no getting away from that. Morally, as well as fiscally, she was obligated to him.

And now, however belatedly, it was indeed payback time.

Was this the so-called consensus he'd offered that day at Villa Santa Caterina? she asked herself bitterly, then paused, knowing that she was banging her head against a wall.

What was the point of going back over all this old ground and reliving former unhappiness?

It was the here and now that mattered.

And she couldn't escape the fact that she'd gone into their marriage with her eyes open, knowing that he did not love her and recognising exactly what was expected of her.

So, in that way, nothing had changed.

This was the life she'd accepted, and somehow she had to live it. And on his terms.

But now she desperately needed to sleep, before tomorrow became today and she was too tired to deal with all the difficulties and demands she didn't even want to contemplate.

And this chair was hardly the right place for that.

With a sigh, she rose and crossed to the bed. As she slipped back under the covers it occurred to her that this might be one of the last nights she would spend alone for some time.

Something else, she told herself grimly, that she did not need to contemplate. Yet.

And she turned over, burying her face in the pillow, seeking for oblivion and discovering gratefully that, in spite of everything, it was waiting for her.

She awoke as usual, a few moments before her alarm clock sounded, reaching out a drowsy hand to silence it in advance. Then paused, suddenly aware that there was something not quite right about this wakening.

Her heart pounding, Marisa lifted her head and turned slowly and with infinite caution to look at the bed beside her. And paused, stifling an instinctive gasp of shock, when she saw she was no longer alone.

Because Renzo was there, lying on his side, facing away from her and fast asleep, his breathing deep and even, the covers pushed down to reveal every graceful line of his naked back.

Oh, God, Marisa thought, swallowing. *Oh, God, I don't believe this. When did he arrive, and how could I not know about it?*

And why didn't I spend the night in that bloody chair after all?

A fraction of an inch at a time, she began to move towards the edge of the bed, desperate to make her escape before he woke too.

But it was too late, she realised, freezing. Because he was already stirring and stretching, making her vividly conscious of the play of muscle under his smooth tanned skin, before turning towards her.

He propped himself casually on one elbow and studied her, his eyes quizzical. *'Buon giorno.'*

'Good morning be damned.' She found her voice. 'What the hell are you doing here?'

He had the gall to look faintly surprised. 'Getting some rest, *mia cara*. What else?'

'But you said—you promised that you'd sleep on the sofa.'

'Sadly, the sofa had other ideas,' Renzo drawled. 'And I decided that I valued my spine too much to argue any longer.'

'Well, you had no right,' she said hoarsely. 'No right at all to—to march in here like this and—and—help yourself!'

His brows lifted. 'I did not march, *mia bella*. I moved very quietly so I would not disturb you. And I did not, as you continued to sleep soundly.'

He paused. 'Besides, as a good wife, surely you do not begrudge me a little comfort, *carissima*?' He added softly, 'After all, despite considerable temptation, I made no attempt to take anything more.'

'I am not a good wife.' Totally unnerved by the tone of his voice, and the look in his eyes, she uttered the stupid, *stupid* words before she could stop herself, and saw his smile widen hatefully into a grin of sheer delight.

'Not yet, perhaps,' he agreed, unforgivably. 'But I live in hope that when you discover how good a husband I intend to be your attitude may change.'

Marisa realised his eyes were now lingering disturbingly on her shoulders, bare under the narrow straps of her nightdress, and then moving down to the slight curve of her breasts revealed by its demure cotton bodice.

Her throat tightened. *I have to get him out of here,* she thought. *Not just out of this bed, but this room too. Before I make an even bigger fool of myself.*

'But as we are here together,' he went on musingly. 'It occurs to me that maybe I should teach you what a man most desires when he wakes in the morning with his wife beside him.'

He reached out, brushing the strap down from her shoulder, letting his fingertips caress the faint mark it had left on her skin. It was the lightest of touches, but she felt it blaze like wildfire through her blood, sending her every sense quivering.

Suddenly she found herself remembering their wedding night, and that devastating, electrifying moment when she'd experienced the first stroke of his hand on her naked breast.

Dry-mouthed, she said, 'No, Renzo—please.' And despised herself for the note of entreaty in her voice.

'But I must, *mia bella*,' he murmured. 'Don't you think I have waited quite long enough to instruct you in my needs? What I like—and how I like it?'

She tried to think of something to say and failed completely. She was aware that he'd moved close, and knew she should draw back—distance herself before it was too late.

'Because it is quite simple,' the softly compelling voice went on. 'I require it to be very hot, very black, and very strong—without sugar. Even you can manage that, I think.'

Marisa shot bolt upright, glaring at him. 'Coffee,' she said, her voice almost choking on the word. 'You're saying you want me to—make you—coffee?' She drew a stormy breath. 'Well, in your dreams, *signore*. I don't know what your last slave died of, but you know where the kitchen is, so make your own damned drink.'

Renzo lay back against the pillows, watching her from under lowered lids. 'Not the response I had hoped for, *carissima*.' His drawl held amusement. He glanced past her at the clock. 'However, I see it is still early, so maybe I will forgo the coffee and persuade you to join me in a little gentle exercise instead. Would you prefer that?' Another pause. 'Or has the kitchen suddenly become more attractive to you after all?'

She said thickly, 'Bastard,' and scrambled out of bed with more haste than dignity, grabbing at her robe. She was followed to the door by the sound of his laughter.

Once in the kitchen, she closed the door and leaned against it while she steadied her breathing.

Renzo had been winding her up, she thought incredulously, subjecting her to some light-hearted sexual teasing, and it was a side of him she hadn't seen before.

Or not since the night of her birthday dinner, she amended, swallowing, when his eyes and the touch of his mouth on her hand had asked questions she'd been too scared to answer and once again she'd run away.

A girl does not have to be in love with a man to enjoy what he does to her in bed. His own words, and he clearly believed them.

But it isn't true, she thought, her throat tightening. *Not for me. Simply wanting someone isn't enough, and never could be. I'd have to be in love to in order to give myself, and even then there'd have to be trust—and respect as well.*

Things that Renzo had probably never heard of as he swanned his way through life from bed to bed.

Besides, he didn't really want her. She was simply a means to an end. But what happened on their honeymoon obviously still rankled with him. For once his seduction routine hadn't worked, and with his wife of all people.

His pride had been damaged, and he couldn't allow that, so now he didn't only want a son from her, but an addition to his list of conquests. To have her panting to fall into his arms each time he walked through the door.

Well, I don't need this, she thought fiercely. *I've no interest in his technique as a lover, and I won't let myself be beguiled into wanting him. It's not going to happen.*

I'm going to be the one that got away. The one that proves to him, as well as myself, that there is life after Lorenzo Santangeli.

She filled the kettle and set it to boil, noting with rebellious satisfaction that there was no fresh coffee. So he'd have to drink instant and like it.

She spooned granules into a beaker, then glanced around her, wondering what would happen to her little domain when she returned to Italy. It was hardly likely she'd be able to retain it as a bolthole when her role as Santangeli wife and future mother became too much to bear.

Although she supposed she could always ask. Because she'd need somewhere eventually, after she'd given Renzo his heir and became surplus to requirements.

In fact, she could impose a few conditions of her own on her return to him, she thought. Let him know that her acquiescence to his wishes now, and later, was still open to negotiation.

Not just a place to live, she told herself, but a purpose in life, too. For afterwards…

In painful retrospect, she'd worked out that any plans she might have for her eventual child—the bond she'd once envisaged—would be little more than fantasy.

She'd seen the stately nurseries at the Santangeli family home, and knew that once she'd given birth her work would be over. There'd be no breastfeeding or nappy-changing for Signora Santangeli. The baby would be handed over to a hierarchy of doting staff who would answer its cries, be the recipients of its first smile, supervise the tooth-cutting and the initial wobbly steps, with herself little more than a bystander.

So she'd be left to her own devices, she thought bleakly, in Julia's classic phrase. And would need something to fill her time and assuage the ache in her heart.

And quite suddenly she knew what it could be, what she would ask in return for her wifely compliance.

Simple, she thought. Neat and beautiful. Now all she required was Renzo's agreement, which could be trickier.

The coffee made, she carried the brimming beaker back to the bedroom. But it was empty, the covers on the bed thrown back.

He was in the adjoining bathroom, standing at the basin, shaving, a towel knotted round his hips and his dark hair still damp from the shower.

'You haven't wasted any time.' Self-consciously she stepped forward, and put the beaker within his reach.

'I wish I could say the same of you, *mia cara*.' His tone was dry. 'I thought you had gone to pick the beans.' He tasted the brew and winced slightly. 'But clearly not.'

'I'm sorry if it doesn't meet your exacting standards.'

Damn, she thought. In view of what she was about to ask, a more conciliatory note might be an improvement.

He rinsed his razor and laid it aside. 'Well, it is hot,' he said. 'And I am grateful for that, at least. *Grazie, carissima.*'

And before she could read his intention, or take evading action, his arm snaked out, drawing her swiftly against him, and he was kissing her startled mouth, his lips warm and delicately sensuous as they moved on hers.

The scent of his skin, the fragrance of the soap he'd used, were suddenly all around her, and she felt as if she was breathing him, absorbing him through every pore, as he held her in the strong curve of his arm.

And she waited, her heart hammering, for his kiss to deepen. To demand…

Then, with equal suddenness, she was free again. She took an instinctive step backwards on legs that were not entirely steady, the colour storming into her face as she met his ironic gaze.

'So,' he said. 'We make progress, *mia bella*. We have not only shared a bed, but I have kissed you at last.' He collected his razor and toothbrush, and put them in his wash-bag, then walked to the door, where he paused.

He said gently, 'You were worth waiting for, Maria Lisa,' and went out, leaving her staring after him.

If there had to be only one door in the flat with a bolt on it, she was glad it was the bathroom.

Not that she would be interrupted. Instinct told her that Renzo would not try to make immediate capital out of what had just happened, but would leave her to wait—and wonder.

Which, of course, she would, she thought, gritting her teeth.

She'd always known it would be dangerous to allow him too close, and she could see now that her wariness had been fully justified.

He was—lethal, she thought helplessly.

Yet even she could see it was ridiculous to be so profoundly disturbed by something that had lasted only a few seconds at most.

Her only comfort was that she had not kissed him back, but had stayed true to her convictions by remaining passive in his embrace.

But he was the one who stopped, a small, niggling voice in her head reminded her. *So don't congratulate yourself too soon.*

Showered and dressed in her working clothes, with her hair drawn back from her face and secured at the nape of her neck with a silver clip, she emerged from the bathroom, mentally steeling herself for the next encounter.

Cool unresponsiveness would seem to be the answer, she thought, but a lot might depend on how the question was asked.

A reflection that sent an odd shiver tingling through her body.

But it seemed there was to be no immediate confrontation because, to her surprise, Renzo wasn't there. The only sign of his presence was the neatly folded blanket, topped by the pillow, on the sofa.

She stood looking round her in bewilderment, wondering if by some miracle he'd suddenly decided to cut his losses and leave for Italy alone.

But it wasn't a day for miracles, because his travel bag was still there, standing in the hall.

On the other hand, she thought, she could always fling a few things together herself, and vanish before he returned. There had to be places where the Santangeli influence didn't reach—although she couldn't call any of them to mind.

And with that she heard the sound of a key in the flat door and Renzo came in, dangling a bulging plastic carrier bag from one lean hand.

Marisa stared at it, then him. 'You've been shopping?'

'Evidently. I found the contents of your refrigerator singularly uninspiring, *mia bella*.'

'But there's nowhere open,' she protested. 'It's too early.'

'Shops are always glad of customers. This one was no exception.' He held up the bag, emblazoned with the name of a local delicatessen. 'I saw a light on and knocked. They were perfectly willing to serve me.'

'Oh, naturally,' Marisa said grittily. 'How could anyone refuse the great Lorenzo Santangeli?'

'That,' he said gently, 'is a question that you can answer better than anyone, *carissima*.' He paused. 'Now, shall we have breakfast?'

She wanted to refuse haughtily, furious at having been caught leading with her chin yet again, but she could smell the enticing aroma of warm bread and realised that she was starving.

He'd bought ham, cheese, sausage and fresh rolls, she found, plus a pack of rich aromatic coffee.

They ate at the small breakfast bar in the kitchen, and in spite of everything Marisa discovered it was one of the few meals she'd enjoyed in his company.

Renzo poured himself some more coffee and glanced at his watch. 'It is almost time we were leaving. There are a number of things to be attended to before we leave for the airport, and you have yet to pack.'

'That won't take very long,' she said. 'I haven't many clothes.'

'No?' he asked dryly. 'You forget, *mia cara*, that I remember how many cases you brought with you to England.'

She bit her lip. 'Actually,' she said, trying to sound casual, 'I don't have those things any more.'

'You had better explain.'

'I gave all my trousseau away,' she admitted uncomfortably. 'To various charity shops. And the luggage too.'

'In the name of God, why?' He looked at her as if she had grown a second head.

'Because I didn't think I'd need clothes like that any more,' she said defiantly. 'So I'll just have one bag.'

'Very well.' His voice held a touch of grimness. 'Then let us start by going to this place where you have been working. Handing in your notice will take the least time.'

It wasn't the ideal moment after her last revelation, Marisa thought, but it was still now or never.

She cleared her throat. 'Actually, the visit may take rather longer than that. You see, there's something I need to—discuss with you first.'

'About the gallery?' Renzo put the knife he'd been using back on his plate with almost studied care. 'Or its owner?'

'Well—both,' she said, slightly taken aback.

'I am listening,' he said harshly. 'But are you sure you want me to hear?'

'Yes, of course. Because it's important.' She took a deep breath. 'I want—I mean I would really like you to buy me—a half-share in the Estrello.'

There was a silence, then he said, almost grimly. 'You dare ask me that? You really believe I would be willing to give money to your lover?'

Marisa gasped. 'Lover?' she echoed in disbelief. 'You think that Corin—and I…? Oh, God, that's so absurd.' She faced him, eyes sparking with anger. 'He's a decent man having a bad time, that's all.'

She paused, then added very deliberately. 'I don't have a lover, *signore*, and I never have done. As no one should know better than yourself.'

Renzo looked away, and for the second time in her life she saw him flush. 'Then what is your interest in this place?'

'Corin's wife is divorcing him, and she wants a financial stake in the gallery. She's not interested in artists or pictures, just in the Estrello's potential as a redevelopment site. She's even planning to work there after they're divorced, so she can pressure him into selling up altogether.'

'And he will do this?' Renzo asked. 'Why does he not fight back?'

'Because he still loves her,' Marisa said fiercely. 'I don't suppose you can imagine what it would be like for him, being forced to see her each day under those circumstances.'

'Perhaps I am not as unimaginative as you believe,' Renzo said, after another pause. 'However, I still do not understand why you should wish to involve yourself—or me.'

'For one thing it's successful,' she said. 'So it would be a good investment.' She hesitated. 'For another, being part-owner will provide me with an interest—even a future career, which I'm going to need some day.'

His brows lifted sardonically. 'It does not occur to you that some wives seem to find a satisfactory career in their marriages—their families?'

'But not,' she said, 'when they know the position is on a strictly temporary basis.' She paused. 'Shall I go on?'

'Please do. I assure you I am fascinated.'

'Thirdly,' she said, 'Corin really needs the money. He would be so thankful for help.' She looked away, biting her lip. 'And I would be grateful too, of course.'

'Ah,' he said softly. 'And what form would this gratitude take? Or is it indelicate to ask?'

It was her turn to flush. 'I think it's a little late for delicacy.'

'Then tell me.'

She stared down fixedly at her empty plate. 'I'll go back to Italy with you—as your wife. And give you—whatever you want.'

'However reluctantly,' he said softly. 'A new feast day should be proclaimed. The martyrdom of Santa Marisa.'

'That's unfair.'

'Is it?' His mouth twisted. 'As to that, we shall both have to wait and see.' He paused. 'But this is the price of your—willing return to me?'

She lifted her chin. Met his gaze unflinchingly. 'Yes.'

'And your uncomplaining presence in my bed when I require it?'

'Yes.' She forced herself to say it.

'*Incredibile*,' he said mockingly. 'Then naturally I accept. If I can agree to terms with this Corin, who needs another man's wife to fight his battles for him.'

She was about to protest that that was unfair too. That it was not just for Corin, but herself, and her life after marriage, but she realised it would be wiser to keep quiet. So she contented herself with a stilted, 'Thank you.'

Renzo got to his feet, and she rose too. As she went past him to the door he took her arm, swinging her round to face him.

He said unsmilingly, 'You set a high price on your favours, *mia bella*. So this is a bargain you will keep. *Capisci?*'

She nodded silently, and he released her with a swift, harsh sigh.

But as she followed him out of the room she realised that she was trembling inside, and she thought, *What have I done? Oh, dear God, what have I done?*

CHAPTER EIGHT

'DEAR child.' Guillermo Santangeli kissed Marisa on both cheeks, then stood back to regard her fondly. 'You look beautiful, although a little thin. I hope you are not on some silly diet.'

'No, I'm fine,' she returned awkwardly, embarrassed by the open affection in his greeting. It was as if the last painful months had never happened, she thought, bewildered, and she was simply returning home, a radiant wife, from her honeymoon. 'But Renzo told me what happened to you, and I was—worried.'

Her father-in-law shrugged expansively. 'A small inconvenience, no more. But it made me feel my age, and that was not good.' His arm round her shoulders, he took her into the *salotto*. Renzo followed, his face expressionless. 'Now that you are here I shall recover completely, *figlia mia*.

'You remember Signora Alesconi, I hope?' he added, as a tall, beautiful woman rose from one of the deep armchairs.

'That is hardly likely, Guillermo.' The older woman's handshake was as warm as her smile. 'I attended your wedding, Signora Santangeli, but I do not expect you to recall one person among so many. So let us count this as our true meeting.' She turned, her expression becoming more formal. 'It is also a pleasure to see you again, Signor Lorenzo,' she added, as he bowed over her hand.

'And I, *signora*, am glad to have this opportunity to thank you for acting so quickly when my father became ill,' Renzo returned. 'Please believe that I shall always be grateful.' He smiled at her. 'And that it is good to see you here.'

'We are indeed a family party,' his father remarked, studying an apparent fleck on his fingernail. 'Nonna Teresa arrived this afternoon. She is resting in her room at present, but will join us for dinner.'

There was a pause, then Renzo said expressionlessly, 'Now, that is a joy I did not anticipate.'

'Nor I,' said Guillermo, and father and son exchanged level looks.

Marisa felt her heart plummet. Of all the Santangeli connections, Renzo's grandmother had always been the least friendly, dismissing the proposed marriage as 'insupportable sentiment' and 'dangerous nonsense'.

And although Marisa had privately agreed with her views, it had still not been pleasant hearing her total unsuitability voiced aloud—and with such venom.

And now the *signora* was here—apparently uninvited—on what promised to be the most difficult night of her entire life.

Following, as it did, one of the most difficult days.

But for the emotional turmoil that had had her in its grip, the events at the Estrello Gallery that morning might almost have been amusing, she thought, as she took a seat and accepted the cup of coffee that Signora Alesconi poured for her.

Corin's face had been a study when she'd broken the news that she was leaving, and why. And when finally, with trepidation, she had introduced an unsmiling Renzo as her husband, explaining that the problem of the gallery's future might have a solution, the whole encounter had almost tipped over into farce.

Almost, she thought, swallowing, but not quite.

She'd been thankful to leave the pair of them to talk business in Corin's cubbyhole of an office while she cleared her few personal items from her desk.

But her feelings had been mixed when Corin had emerged, clearly pole-axed, to tell her the deal was done and it was now down to the lawyers.

Because it had not simply been a matter of legalities, and she had known that. And so had the man who'd stood behind Corin, watching her, his dark face uncompromising. The husband who would seek recompense by claiming his right to her body that night.

'So—partner.' Corin had given her a wavering smile. 'I guess it's hail and farewell—for a while, anyway.' He shook his head. 'God, I can hardly believe it. I—I don't know how to thank you. Both of you,' he added, sending a faintly apprehensive glance back at Renzo.

Then he brightened. 'Perhaps you'll let me give you something to mark the occasion—a combined wedding present and goodbye gift, eh?'

And before Marisa could stop him he went over to the wall and lifted down the Amalfi picture.

'I've often seen you looking at this,' he confided cheerfully. 'I realise now that it may have been reviving some happy memories.'

'A most generous thought,' Renzo interposed smoothly as Marisa's lips parted in instinctive protest. 'My wife and I will treasure it.'

'Treasure it?' Marisa queried almost hoarsely a little later, as the picture, well cushioned by bubble-wrap and brown paper, shared the opulent rear of the limousine that was taking them to Renzo's next appointment at the London branch of the Santangeli Bank. 'I'd like to put my fist through it.' She shook her head. 'God, how could you say such a thing? Tell such a downright lie?'

His brows lifted. 'Did you wish me to tell him the unhappy truth?' he enquired coolly. 'Besides, it is a beautiful scene, very well painted. I have no objection to owning it. However, if you prefer, I will hang it where you are unlikely to see it.' He paused, adding sardonically, 'In my bedroom, perhaps.'

She sat back, bright spots of colour blazing in her cheeks, unable to think of a riposte that wouldn't lead to worse embarrassment.

After a pause, Renzo went on, 'So, Marisa, as you wished, you now have a half-share in a London gallery.'

She did not look at him. 'And you have me.'

'Do I?' His tone was reflective. 'I think that has yet to be proved, *mia bella*.'

He added, more briskly, 'If there is anything you wish to take from the flat apart from your clothes then you should make a list. I will have them sent on to us. After our departure the place will be cleared for re-letting.'

'Oh.' She bit her lip. 'I hoped I—we—might keep it. Maybe as a *pied à terre* for visits to London.' She paused. 'It could be useful, don't you think?'

'I am sure, in time, you will prefer less cramped surroundings.'

And that, she realised resentfully, was that. Renzo had made his final concession. From now on it would be her turn. And she shivered.

Later, he watched while she packed, and she saw his mouth tighten when he observed the few basic items that her wardrobe contained, but he made no further comment.

Possibly, she thought, because for once he was lost for words. Or calculating how much it would cost him to re-equip her for her unwanted role.

No! Her self-reproach was instant and whole-hearted. That was totally unfair. If money was all it took to make her happy, then by now she'd be ecstatic, because in material ways she'd lacked for nothing from the very beginning.

Kept in the lap of luxury, she told herself derisively. And knew she would not be the first to discover how lonely and unrewarding that could be.

As she sat beside him on the way to the airport, trying to present at least an appearance of calm, he was the first to break the silence between them.

'Our flight is booked to Pisa, but I am wondering whether Rome would not be a better option.' He paused, glancing at her. 'A transfer is easily arranged. We could spend a few days at my apartment and then travel to Tuscany at the weekend.'

A few days, she thought, her throat tightening. And a few nights—alone with him.

A situation which bore all the hallmarks of a second honeymoon, but the same propensity for disaster as the first. In an apartment that she'd never seen, and which might not have the separate bedrooms which offered at least a semblance of privacy at the Villa Proserpina.

And then, with dizzying abruptness, she found herself remembering those few brief moments earlier that day, when his arms had held her and his lips had touched hers for the first time.

When she'd experienced the hard, lean warmth of his body against hers and realised, in a blazing instant of self-knowledge, that she didn't want him to let her go…

And she wondered if he had known it too.

Shock jolted her like a charge of electricity. *No*, she protested in silent horror. *Oh, please, no. That didn't happen. It couldn't happen. I'm just uptight, that's all. And the kiss took me by surprise.*

She said, too quickly, 'But your father's expecting us. He'll be disappointed if we break our journey like that.'

'You are all consideration, *mia bella*. *Tuttavia*, I think, given the circumstances, he would completely understand.' He added with faint amusement, '*In effetti*, he could even be pleased.'

Her heart missed a beat. 'But I would still worry,' she said. 'After all, he's been ill. And I want to see him. So maybe we should stick to the original arrangement.'

There was a brief silence before he said quietly, 'Then let it be as you wish.'

As I wish? she thought, with a mixture of bewilderment and desperation, as new tensions—new forebodings—began to twist themselves into a knot in her mind. *Dear God, suddenly I don't know what I wish—not any more. And that really scares me.*

Because nothing had changed. That kiss had simply been to prove a point. Unfinished business, that was all. Because he'd made no attempt to put a hand on her since. Even sitting side by side in the back of the car like this, he was making sure there was a distinct space between them.

But, she thought, swallowing, all that would change tonight. There was no escaping that harsh reality. And she'd had that softly arousing brush of his mouth on hers to warn her what she might expect.

She was trembling inside again, bleak with an apprehension she couldn't dismiss, and in spite of the comfort of the flight, and the assiduous attentions of the cabin staff, she found herself developing a headache.

However, as she reminded herself tautly, it would hardly be politic, in the current situation, to mention the fact—even if he believed her. Better, indeed, to suffer in silence than to be treated with icy mockery. Or anger again.

No, she thought, please—not anger.

And she closed her eyes, wincing.

They were met at Galileo Galilei airport by her father-in-law's own sumptuous limousine and its chauffeur, who, with due deference, handed Renzo a briefcase as he took his seat.

'You will excuse me, *mia cara*?' He spoke, she thought, as if the flight had been an endless exchange of sweet nothings, instead of several more edgy hours almost totally lacking in conversation. 'There are some urgent messages I must read.'

Huddled in her corner, Marisa observed some of the most exquisite scenery in Europe with eyes that saw nothing. Maybe one of the messages would summon him immediately to the other side of the globe, she thought, without particular hope.

But he went through the sheaf of papers swiftly, scribbling notes in the margins as he went, then returned them to the briefcase just as the car turned in between the tall stone pillars and took the long avenue lined with cypresses leading to the gracious mass of pinkish-grey stone that formed the Villa Proserpina.

All too soon they'd arrived at what would be her home for the foreseeable future, and as if things weren't quite bad enough Teresa Barzati had to be waiting for them, like a thin, autocratic spider that had invaded and occupied a neighbouring web.

But we could have been elsewhere, of course, Marisa reminded herself bitterly, sitting on the edge of her chair, tension in every line of her body. *Renzo offered me an alternative, and in retrospect Rome seems marginally the better choice, no matter what I thought at the time. Because no change of location is going to make the obligation of going into his arms—his bed—any easier.*

But it's too late now. Everything's much too late.

Wearily, she pushed her hair back from her face, aware that her head was throbbing badly now, and she was almost grateful when her untouched cup was taken from her hand and Renzo said quietly, 'You have had a long day, Marisa. Perhaps you might like to follow Nonna Teresa's example and relax for a while in your room?'

Yes, she thought longingly. *Oh, yes!* Some time and space to herself, however brief.

Renzo stepped to the long bell-pull beside the fireplace, and gave succinct instructions in his own language to the uniformed maid who answered its summons.

As a result, only a few minutes later Marisa found herself lying under the silk canopy of the large four-poster bed that dominated her bedroom, divested of her outer clothing and covered by a thin embroidered quilt.

In addition, a cloth soaked in some soothing herbal essence had been placed on her forehead, and she'd been offered two anonymous white tablets and a glass of water to swallow them with.

Even while she was telling herself that relaxation under the circumstances was totally impossible, she went out like a light.

* * *

He had never, Renzo thought, felt so nervous. Not even on his wedding day.

He dried his face and applied a little aftershave, reflecting as he did so that his hand had shaken so much while he was carefully removing even the tiniest vestige of stubble from his chin that it was a miracle he'd not cut himself to ribbons.

Like some adolescent, he thought in self-derision, with his first love. Except he was no longer a boy, but a man and a husband, wanting everything to be perfect on this, his real wedding night, with the girl he planned to make his own at last. Somehow…

Yet he was afraid at the same time that it might already be too late for the errors of the past to be forgotten. Or forgiven.

Especially that first disastrous time, which it still shamed him to remember.

Are you saying you want me to make love to you?

He recalled the faint flicker of hope in his question.

Say—yes, he'd prayed silently. *Ah,* Dio, *say yes,* carissima mia, *and let me take us both to heaven.*

Instead, stunned by anger and disappointment, and wounded by her declared indifference, he'd simply taken her without any of the gentleness and respect he'd promised himself he would bring to her initiation, forcing himself to remain grimly oblivious to anything but his own physical necessity.

To appease by that brief and selfish act the aching desire that had tormented him since that moment at her cousin's house when he'd first seen her as a woman. And which had only increased throughout the weeks of self-imposed denial that had followed their engagement.

With hindsight, he knew that in spite of what he'd said afterwards he should have swallowed his pride and gone to her that night, and for both their sakes put matters right between them. That he should have told her that since her acceptance of his proposal there'd been no other girl in his life, that Lucia Gallo was history, and then convinced her that he did indeed want her by devoting himself exclusively to her pleasure until she slept, fulfilled and sated, in his arms.

One small sign—one—over dinner that night that she too had regrets was all it would have taken. But there'd been nothing except that quiet, nervous politeness that had chilled him to the soul.

Leaving him to wonder in anguish whether that afternoon's quick, soulless episode was all she would ever want from him—as much intimacy as she would ever permit. Whether she neither expected nor required any joy or warmth from the uniting of their flesh. Whether her real hope was that pregnancy would release her from any further demands by him.

Forcing him to realise too that she had no more wish to spend her days with him than she did her nights. That she seemed to prefer total solitude to even a moment of his company. Which was perhaps the most hurtful thing of all.

And that was why, when she'd told him in that small, stony voice that after all there would be no baby, it had seemed like a reprieve. As if he'd been given another chance to redeem himself and their marriage, he'd thought, hiding his instinctive thankfulness.

A God-given opportunity to try again.

Evangelina had told him, brow furrowed, that 'the little one' had spent an uncomfortable day, which had given him the excuse he needed to go to her at last. To share her bed, he'd told himself dryly, without even a suspicion of an ulterior motive, and prove to her that he could be capable of real tenderness.

And in doing so accustom her by degrees to his continued presence beside her at night. So that he could tell her gently, at some point, that he wanted their baby made in mutual happiness and delight. Perhaps more.

He'd shaved again that night too, he recalled ironically, before walking resolutely down the length of the dressing room corridor to her door, where he'd paused to knock.

The first time that he'd ever hesitated to enter a woman's bedroom.

And then, as he'd raised his hand, he'd heard her weeping—listened, frozen in shock, to the harsh, agonised sobs reaching him all too clearly through the thick wooden panels—and every thought, wish, desire that had accompanied him from his room to hers had vanished. Leaving in its place a sick, empty void.

Because she couldn't have been crying over a child that had never existed—a child she hadn't even wanted.

No, it was the realisation that eventually she would have to submit to him again—allow her body to be used a second time—

that must have released such a terrible storm of grief. Grief, he'd recognised painfully, and revulsion. It could be nothing else.

His worst fears had been horribly justified.

Yet who was to say that anything had changed now—tonight? Renzo asked himself broodingly as he dropped the towel he'd been wearing and put on his robe. What if the morning's bravado suddenly deserted her, and when the time came for her to redeem her promise he found her in tears again?

What would he do then?

Last time he'd returned silently to his room and spent a wretched night sleepless with his regrets, knowing, as dawn approached, that he had to let her go for a while. That he simply did not trust himself to live any longer as they had been doing.

Because there would come a night, he'd told himself with brutal candour, when his need for her might overwhelm him. And he could not risk that.

Of course any separation would be purely temporary. He would make that clear. Then gradually he would resume contact between them, and begin courting her as he should have done from the first.

A laudable ambition, Renzo thought wryly, as he combed his damp hair, but doomed from the moment she'd announced her defiant determination to leave Italy.

He'd accepted that his fight to win her would be conducted from a distance, at least at the start, but he'd never for a moment anticipated crashing headlong into the implacable wall of silence she'd proceeded to build between them from London.

Leaving him struggling a second time against that lethal combination of damaged pride and sheer bad temper that had been his downfall previously.

And proving, he told himself bitterly, that he'd learned precisely nothing in the intervening period.

Because he should, of course, have followed her, preferably on the next flight, and courted her properly. Sweeping away her resentment and resistance until he found her again.

Found Maria Lisa—the girl who'd once looked at him as if he was the sun that warmed her own particular universe.

Every instinct he possessed told him that she had to be there, somewhere, if only he could reach her.

So what had stopped him? The fear, perhaps, that she might still elude him and he could fail?

He did not, after all, take rejection well. So when all his overtures had been ignored he'd looked deliberately for the most practical form of consolation he could find.

And now he was back at the beginning, trying to construct a whole new marriage from the ruins of the old.

The only certainty being that she would not make it easy for him.

She hadn't even trusted him enough to tell him that she'd been in pain on the journey, but he'd seen the strain in her eyes, the way her hand had gone fleetingly to her forehead when she'd thought he wasn't looking, and had taken appropriate action once they'd reached the villa.

But that was the simple part, he thought wryly. Now, somehow, he had to win her.

And for the first time in his life he had no idea how to begin.

Marisa awoke slowly and lay for a moment, feeling totally disorientated. Then, as her head cleared, she remembered where she was. And more importantly, why.

Swallowing, she sat up, pushing the hair back from her face as she stared around her, feeling once more as if she'd been caught in some time warp.

She was again the nervous bride-to-be of the previous year, being shown her future domain by the man who would share these rooms with her. And too embarrassed at the prospect to allow herself more than a fleeting overall glance.

But some details had remained locked in her memory. This huge bed, for instance, with its tapestried canopy and curtains, where eventually she'd be obliged to submit to whatever Renzo asked of her. And those two doors—one leading into the palatial white-and-silver bathroom which they would share, and the other the communicating door into the adjoining room, his room. At present, mercifully closed.

She became aware of other things too. That the shutters over the long windows leading out to the *loggia* were fastened, and their concealing drapes drawn over them. That the pair of deeply shaded lamps that flanked the bed had been lit by someone, too. And all this while she'd slept.

But how long had she been there? She reached for her watch, which had been placed on the night table, but was instantly distracted by the unwelcome sight of the communicating door swinging open and Renzo walking into the room.

Stifling a gasp of dismay, she slid hastily back under the shelter of the coverlet and saw him halt, his brows lifting cynically at the manoeuvre.

Beautifully cut charcoal pants clung to his lean hips and accentuated the length of his legs, and his white shirt hung negligently open, revealing far too much of his muscular brown chest.

In spite of herself Marisa felt her mouth dry, and her heart beginning to thud. She said with faint breathlessness, 'Good—good evening. Did you want something?'

'Certainly not what you seem to expect,' he returned crisply. He looked her over, the golden eyes assimilating the slender shape of her under the concealing coverlet. 'Unless, of course, you insist?'

'I don't!' The denial seemed choked out of her.

He smiled faintly. 'I believe you. But for the present I wish only to speak to you.' He walked over to the bed and stood at its foot, his golden gaze examining her. 'Are you feeling better?'

'Yes—thank you.' Her recent headache seemed to have vanished completely, she realised with surprise. But no doubt there would be many more to take its place. And this interview could be the first.

'I am delighted to hear it.' His tone was silky. 'And I hope you will please my father too, by joining him for dinner.' He paused. 'He wished to make it a black tie celebration in your honour, but has now consented to a less formal affair. I trust that is agreeable to you?'

'Yes,' Marisa said in a hollow voice, reflecting on the deficiencies of her wardrobe. 'Of course.'

He nodded. 'Also the meal will be earlier than usual, as it is considered unwise for Papa to stay up too late. Can you be ready in an hour?'

She fastened her watch back on her wrist. 'I could probably be ready in five minutes. After all, I'm hardly going to be spoiled for choice over what to wear.'

'One of the reasons I suggested a stopover in Rome,' he said softly. 'So that you could go shopping.' He paused. 'Although not the only reason, of course.'

'No.' She made a slight adjustment to the watch's bracelet, not looking at him. 'I—appreciate that.'

'And we would also have been spared the reception committee,' he went on. 'For which I apologise.'

She did glance up then. In the days leading up to the wedding, in spite of her own inner turmoil, she'd been aware there were other tensions in the household.

She bit her lip. 'Do you no longer mind so much about Signora Alesconi?' she asked in a low voice.

'Ottavia?' There was genuine surprise in his voice. 'No, how could I? What right have I of all people to begrudge my father another chance to be happy?' He paused, then added dryly, 'I did not mean her.'

Marisa took a breath. 'Oh—your grandmother.' She hesitated. 'Considering how little she likes me, I'm surprised she chose to be here.'

Renzo shrugged. 'No doubt she has her reasons. I regret her presence, but you must not allow it to disturb you.'

Your grandmother, signore, she told him silently, *is the least of my worries.*

Aloud, she said tautly, 'She clearly thought I wasn't worthy to be your wife. I expect she thinks so still. And that she's quite right.'

'Not a view I have ever shared.' He hesitated. 'Which is one of the things I came to say to you. We did not begin our marriage well, Maria Lisa, but all that could so easily change—with a little…goodwill, perhaps.'

She stared unseeingly at the embroidery on the coverlet. 'How can it? We're still the same people, after all. Both pushed into this situation by our families,' she added bitterly.

'No one pushed me,' Renzo said quietly. 'It is true that the mothers who loved us both believed that we could be happy together, but that would have counted for nothing if I had wished to choose elsewhere. But—I did not.'

He paused again. '*Tuttavia*, I am aware that for you the choice was not so easy,' he added ruefully. 'That there was—pressure. But if you truly found the idea of our marriage so repulsive then you should have said so—and to me.'

Marisa's lips parted in a gasp of sheer indignation. 'In my dreams,' she said stormily. She propped herself on an elbow, uncaring that the coverlet had slipped down below her lace-cupped breasts. 'And you know it, *signore*. How could I *choose* when I'd been bought and paid for, like any other commodity? And when my cousin's husband's future wellbeing depended on me doing exactly as I was told?'

She drew a breath. 'That was the clincher. Because Harry's sweet and decent in a way you couldn't appreciate, and it was impossible for me to let him down. So I had to consent to being… handed over—untouched—to the great Lorenzo Santangeli. Someone who'd never given me a second glance until he was reminded of his dynastic obligations and suddenly required a willing virgin.' She added furiously, 'Not many of those to draw on in your social circle, I dare say. So my life had to be wrecked to provide one for you.' She shook her head. 'What a pity I wasn't the slut you once called me.

'At least I'd have been spared…all this.'

There was a silence, then Renzo said slowly, 'That was quite a speech, *mia bella*. How strange that you only speak from the heart when saying things you know I will not wish to hear. But at least now I understand that your resentment of me goes back much further than this past year alone.'

He stood up and walked slowly round the bed to her side.

'You were only fifteen, were you not, when you decided to test my self-control that day in the pool?' He spoke softly. 'And while I do not aspire to your Harry's level of sanctity, I am occasionally capable of a spark of decency—such as not taking advantage of the heedless innocence of a girl hardly out of childhood. If I was harsh with you, it was because I wished to ensure that you would not be lured into making a similar offer to any other man.'

His voice slowed to a husky drawl. 'But do not ever think, Maria Lisa, that I was not tempted. And if I had succumbed to your enticement I would not have merely looked, believe me. Not with a second or even a third glance.'

He sat down on the edge of the bed, and as she tried to move away from him, leaned across to place a hand squarely on the other side of her, trapping her where she lay.

'So what would you have done, *carissima?*' he queried softly, looking into her dilating eyes. 'If you had suddenly found yourself naked with me in the water? And if I had taken you in my arms…?'

'As it didn't happen,' Marisa said curtly, aware that she was trembling, 'this is a totally pointless discussion. And now please let me up.'

'In my own good time,' he said, and had the gall to smile at her. 'Because it is quite clear to me, *mia bella*, that my dismissal of you that day still rankles with you. Therefore it is time I made reparation.'

He bent towards her, his purpose evident, and Marisa reacted, gasping, her hands braced, to her dismay, against the warmth of his bare chest.

'Renzo—please—you can't.'

'Why not?' he countered, shrugging. 'You are no longer a child to be protected from herself, my lovely wife.' He paused significantly. '*Inoltre*, you promised me only this morning that I would find you willing.'

'Well—yes. But not—not like this.' She swallowed desperately, realising that by some totally unscrupulous means he'd altered his position and was now lying beside her. Holding her. 'You seem to have forgotten that we—we're having dinner with your father,' she went on, improvising wildly. Realising, too, how absurd she must sound. 'I—I have to—get ready.'

'I have forgotten nothing, *carissima*.' Renzo's smile widened disgracefully into a grin of pure enjoyment at her stumbling words. 'Particularly your assurance that it will take you only five minutes to dress.'

He lifted a hand and brushed a strand of hair back from her flushed face. Ran an exploring finger down the curve of her cheek and across the moist heat of her startled, parted lips.

'So, at long last,' he added softly, 'we are together—and with all the time we need.'

CHAPTER NINE

MARISA stared up into the dark face poised above her, unable to think coherently. Scarcely able, she realised, to breathe. Shatteringly conscious of the heat of his lean body and the beguiling, never-forgotten scent of his skin: the clean tang of the soap he used overlaid with the faint musky fragrance of his cologne.

The almost hypnotic beat of his heart was imprinting itself on her spread hands, still trapped against the hair-roughened wall of his chest, and finding an echo throughout her entire bloodstream.

Then Renzo bent his head, and for only the second time in her life she felt the warmth of his mouth on hers. But not in the way she'd experienced in that brief contact this morning, she thought, her brain reeling. No—it was not like that at all.

Because this was an unhurried and totally deliberate exploration of the contours of her mouth, unlike anything she'd ever encountered before or expected to meet with. And although his lips were still gentle, they were also offering a frank enticement which she could not ignore. Or, it seemed, resist.

Not this time…

Then, in one dizzy, shaking moment, Marisa knew that her instincts had been entirely accurate. Understood completely why she'd been so right all this time to keep him at arm's length and further.

Why she'd reacted so violently to his touch on her wedding night—and later, when she'd been offered the chance of escape, why she'd fled across Europe, telling herself it was over.

Determined to make it so by doing her utmost to cut him completely out of her memory, her life.

And, God help me, she thought with anguish, *my heart.*

Renzo lifted his head and looked down at her for a long

moment, before leaning down again to brush small kisses on her forehead, her half-closed eyes and along the betraying hectic flush that she could feel heating her cheekbones.

Then his mouth returned to hers with renewed urgency, and involuntarily, devastatingly, her lips were parting under his insistence, allowing the silken glide of his tongue to invade the inner moist heat that he sought.

She found too that she was no longer trying to push him away. That in fact she was not simply yielding to his kiss, but slowly and shyly offering him a response.

And that as a result his demand was deepening—turning to undisguised and passionate hunger.

When he lifted his head, they were both breathless. His lambent gaze holding hers, Renzo ran a caressing finger along the curve of her lower lip.

'You are trembling, *mia bella*.' His voice was soft. 'Am I truly such an object of terror to you still?'

She stared back at him, wordlessly shaking her head. Not terror, she thought, but excitement and the promise of unimagined delight.

Everything that she most feared from him. Everything that she most desired.

He said, half to himself, 'And I came here only to talk…'

He drew her back to him. His lips touched her throat, dwelt for an instant on the leaping, uneven pulse, then found her ear, caressing its inner whorls with the tip of his tongue and allowing his teeth to graze softly at its small pink lobe, forcing a gasp from her.

His mouth moved downward, planting kisses on the delicate line of her neck before lingering in the fragrant hollow at its base.

She didn't even know when he'd slipped her bra straps from her shoulders, but they were certainly bare when he traced their slenderness with his lips, touching her skin as if it was fragile silk.

At the same time his fingertips began to glide gently over the exposed curves of her breasts, where they rose above the scalloped edge of her bra, and she felt her nipples swell and harden against their lace confinement in a response to his touch, which was as stark as it was involuntary.

His hand slid under her back, releasing the metal clasp so that he could slip the tiny garment from her body completely and allow his fingers to cup her breasts instead, stroking them gently, almost reverently, while his lips captured hers again, caressing them with an explicit insistence she was unable to refuse.

More than that, as she returned his kisses Marisa found she was touching him in turn, pushing his shirt from his shoulders in clumsy haste so that her eager, untutored hands could begin to learn his body. Could seek the muscled planes and angles of his shoulders and the supple length of his spine under the satiny skin.

Could turn his kiss, too, into a sigh of longing.

Renzo reached down and threw the shrouding coverlet aside, his hands drifting slowly and sweetly down the length of her body before returning to her tumescent breasts, taking them in the palms of his hands and offering them to the candid adoration of his mouth.

His lips gently possessed first one scented mound and then the other, his tongue teasing the puckered rosy peaks with lingering sensual expertise.

Her body was alive, quivering with the sensations he was provoking, and fierce shafts of delight were running through her like a flame in the blood as she arched towards him, stifling a little sob. Wanting more.

And—as his questing hand slid down over her ribcage and her stomach to the flimsy barrier of her briefs—wanting everything…

Only to feel his whole body grow suddenly tense, and to realise that he was lifting himself away from her, looking across the room at the door, his brows snapping together.

Reality came storming back as she heard it too—the sound of knocking, followed by a woman's voice.

'What—who is it?' Her voice was unrecognisable.

Renzo called sharply in his own language, 'A moment, if you please.' He turned back to Marisa. 'It is Rosalia,' he told her ruefully, shrugging. 'The maid who attended you earlier. She has come to prepare your bath and assist you to change.' He added dryly, 'My father's orders, you understand.'

He paused, looking down at her. 'So, does she come in, *carissima*?' he asked softly. 'Or shall I send her away in order that I may bathe and dress you myself—later?'

But the spell was broken, and the flush that warmed her face was suddenly one of embarrassment—not just at the unexpected interruption, but at the intimate picture his words had conjured up.

Also at the realisation of how close she had come to absolute surrender. And not just of her body, but her mind and will too.

She said, stumbling a little, 'But if you tell her to go then she'll know that we're—together. And why…'

'As we are married,' he said levelly, 'it will hardly come as any great surprise to her.'

'Yes.' Her blush deepened. 'But she might—say something—to other people.'

'It could happen.' Renzo studied her wryly. 'I think, *mia bella*, you must accustom yourself to a little curiosity from the staff. They too have waited a long time to see you here.'

'I understand that.' She snatched up her bra and fumbled it back into place, avoiding his gaze as she struggled with the hook. Telling herself to be thankful that matters had gone no further. 'But it's all too soon for me. I can't deal with it yet—this living under a spotlight. Knowing that everything that happens is going to be under scrutiny.'

Including, no doubt, the moment I become pregnant…

'Ah,' he said quietly. 'Then the answer to my question is no.'

He moved her hands aside, dealing briskly and deftly with the recalcitrant clip on her bra, then he lifted the soft mass of hair and dropped a kiss on the nape of her neck.

It was the lightest caress, but it made her burn and shiver all over again.

He said, 'I will leave you to your maid, Maria Lisa. But we still have to talk, *carissima*.' There was an odd note in his voice—almost strained. 'There are things that have to be said—things I think you must know—before we begin our real marriage.'

Retrieving his crumpled shirt, he swung himself off the bed and strode off towards his own room, leaving Marisa frantically hauling the coverlet back into place and straightening the pillows in an attempt to eliminate any indication of recent events.

Renzo paused in the doorway, sending her a final, frankly sardonic glance as he observed her efforts.

'Save yourself the trouble, *carissima*,' he advised. 'You would not deceive a blind woman.'

He called, '*Avanti*, Rosalia,' and disappeared, closing the door behind him.

The last thing in the world Marisa wanted was a personal maid, but Rosalia seemed quiet, and eager to please, discreetly ignoring her young employer's state of flushed dishevelment. But she was clearly distressed that the *signora* did not have a suitable dress in which to grace her father-in-law's celebration dinner table.

She listened with open astonishment to Marisa's halting explanation of mislaid luggage, her expression saying clearly that heads would roll at any airline foolish enough to mislay so much as a paper bag belonging to the Santangeli family.

In the end, it had to be the wrap-around skirt from the previous evening, teamed this time with a high-necked Victorian-style blouse in broderie anglaise. Not ideal, but the best she could do under the circumstances.

The circumstances…

She had to admit it was pleasant having a scented bath drawn and waiting for her, but the size of the deep, wide tub she was lying in, together with the twin washbasins and another of those king-size walk-in showers, its glass panels etched with flowers, all served to remind her that this bathroom had been specifically designed for dual occupation.

And that sharing this space with Renzo was yet another intimacy of marriage she would have to learn. And quickly.

What was more, she reflected as she dried herself, it was a space that had too many mirrors for her taste, with far too many naked Marisas reflected in them.

She gave the nearest image a fleeting glance, a hand straying to the curve of her breast as she remembered the other fingers that had touched it—the sensuous mouth that had brought the nipple to vibrant, aching life.

Recalled too the brief force of his body inside her own all those months ago. The moment when she'd realised she did not want his possession of her, however curt and perfunctory, to stop.

Acknowledged, without pride, that even the thought of it had caused her unfulfilled body to burn—to scald—with need ever since.

Which had always been an excellent reason for not thinking of it, she thought wryly as she rubbed body lotion in her favourite scent into her skin and put on fresh underwear.

But now, once again, as the events of the past half-hour had taught her, she had no choice. Because, as he'd proved in one succinct lesson, she could no longer pretend indifference to him.

It was not simply a matter of keeping the strictly conditional promise she'd made him in London that morning. Not any more.

No longer a granting of permission to take what he wanted, but no more.

Nor a private but steely resolve that, no matter what he did, she would somehow maintain her stance of indifference. Hold herself aloof from any possibility of genuine intimacy between them.

That was no longer possible.

Because, for good or ill, she'd been brought here to live with him as his wife. And this time it was the whole package.

Although nothing had fundamentally changed, she reminded herself painfully. Renzo might have proved beyond doubt that he could arouse her to the point of no return—but then, after their past encounters, his pride would demand no less.

Our real marriage. Renzo's own words, she thought. But without love they were meaningless. Nothing more than an invitation to sexual satisfaction.

But it wasn't just his lovemaking that would hold her in thrall to him. It was this enforced proximity of everyday living that was the actual danger to her heart, just as it always had been.

Because she'd already undergone a crash course in the subject of Renzo Santangeli during her earlier time in this house, and she hadn't forgotten a thing.

Even before she'd discovered desire she'd learned to crave his company, judge his moods, bask in his kindness—and to feel only half-alive when he wasn't there.

The sound of his voice in the distance had always been enough to set her heart racing. But apart from that moment of supreme lunacy in the swimming pool, she'd always managed to hide all the myriad feelings she had for him. Even, for a long time, to pretend they did not exist.

But now she had to share these admittedly spacious rooms with him, when, apart from sex, all he'd ever offered her was friendship.

So she would have to be careful never to hint by word or gesture that she might want much more, because that could lead to another rejection. And that would be—unendurable.

These are the circumstances, she told herself. And somehow I have to abide by them.

And sighing, she walked back into her bedroom.

She'd planned to wear her hair loose, as usual, but the waiting Rosalia was quite adamant about transforming it into a skilfully casual topknot, with a few soft strands to frame the face.

It provided a distinct touch of elegance, she discovered when it was done, and Rosalia was smiling and nodding.

And heaven knows, Marisa thought, as she applied a touch of soft pink to her mouth, *I'm going to need all the help I can get this evening.*

She found herself wondering a little shyly if Renzo would like her new style, but when he came to escort her downstairs, himself resplendent in a dark grey suit, his pristine white shirt set off by a deep crimson tie, he made no comment, seeming lost in his own thoughts. Nor were they particularly happy ones, if the grim set of his mouth was to be believed.

But what was wrong? Surely he couldn't be annoyed because she'd failed to send Rosalia away earlier? He must know that her surrender had only been postponed, not denied.

Perhaps he, too, was simply dreading tonight's dinner party.

Her premonition that this could be a seriously tricky occasion was reinforced into bleak certainty when she entered the *salotto* at his side and met Teresa Barzati's inimical gaze, directed at her from a high-backed chair at the side of the fireplace.

Impenetrably dark eyes swept her from head to foot, taking in every inch of the chainstore clothing, and the thin mouth pursed itself in open disapproval.

But what did it matter if she was inappropriately dressed when it came in the wake of so many other flaws? Marisa asked herself resignedly.

The *signora* herself clearly didn't do informal. Her own dress was black silk, its sombre magnificence relieved only by the matching emerald bracelets that adorned each bony wrist.

They were undoubtedly beautiful, and probably priceless, but Marisa found their brilliance oddly barbaric, and totally at odds with the general severity of the older woman's appearance.

'So you have decided to come back, Marisa,' was Nonna Teresa's eventual greeting, accompanied by a faint sniff. 'I suppose we must be gratified that you have at last remembered where your duty lies. And hope that you do not forget again.'

There was an appalled silence. As Marisa gasped, her face reddening with mingled indignation and embarrassment, Renzo's hand closed over hers.

He said softly, 'But my grandmother forgot to say, Maria Lisa, how delighted she is to see you again.' He looked at the older woman. 'Is that not so, Nonna?'

There was a pause, then Signora Barzati gave an abrupt jerk of the head that might have been interpreted as a nod.

Guillermo came surging forward at this juncture, offering Marisa an *aperitivo* and telling her pointedly how pretty she looked.

She was grateful, but hardly reassured, as she took a seat on one of the long sofas beside Ottavia Alesconi, chic in amethyst linen.

She'd hardly expected a full-frontal attack, she thought shakily. But clearly Renzo knew that his grandmother would be unable to resist some biting remark, and had been prepared for it.

Well, she'd done her worst, and now it was over, so perhaps they could all relax. Perhaps…

Yet when Emilio, her father-in-law's stately major-domo, eventually announced dinner, and although the food was delicious, as always, the atmosphere in the dining room was far from celebratory.

On the contrary, everyone seemed on edge still. Apart, that was, from Signora Barzati, who had commandeered the hostess's chair at the foot of the table—to Guillermo's open but silent annoyance—and was conducting a series of majestic monologues on the political situation, the iniquities of the taxation structure, plus the continued and unnecessary influx of foreign residents.

And no prizes for guessing who falls into that category, Marisa thought, trying to feel amused but not succeeding. She glanced across at Renzo, seated opposite, and realised he was already watching her, his mouth still unsmiling, but the golden eyes heavy with hunger. And something more. Something altogether less easy to define, she thought, as swift, shy heat invaded her face.

She would almost have said he was anxious—uncertain. But that was absurd, she told herself. After all, only a few hours before she'd betrayed herself utterly in his arms. And now she had nowhere left to hide. No more excuses to deny him the complete physical response he would soon demand from her.

When dinner ended, they were about to move back to the *salotto* for coffee, but Guillermo, who was looking tired, made his apologies and announced his intention to retire.

'Forgive me, my child.' He kissed Marisa on the forehead. 'We will talk together tomorrow.' He turned to Renzo. 'A word with you, my son? I promise I will not detain you too long from your wife's company.'

'My dear Guillermo.' Signora Barzati's tone was acid. 'You are joking, of course. After the events of the past year, that can hardly be an issue.'

'Basta!' He gave her a look of hauteur. 'I believed we had agreed to leave the past alone and look only to the future. I ask you, my dear mother-in-law, to remember that.'

She shrugged and turned away, walking into the *salotto* ahead of Marisa and Signora Alesconi, and resuming the seat she had occupied before the meal.

There was an awkward silence, rendered even more difficult when the coffee was brought in and the tray placed almost pointedly on a table beside Marisa. A move the *signora* observed with raised eyebrows and tightly compressed lips.

Then the door closed behind Emilio, and the three women were left alone.

By some miracle Marisa managed to pour coffee from the heavy pot without spillage or any other accident, and once they were all served Ottavia Alesconi immediately embarked on a flow of light, almost nervous chat, talking of a book she had just read, the coming opera season at Verona, and a new young designer who had taken Milan's fashion world by storm.

'Perhaps we should engage his services for Marisa,' said Nonna Teresa coldly, when the younger woman paused. 'She is clearly in need of someone's guidance. Someone to explain to her that Santangeli wives do not dress like penniless schoolgirls.'

Ottavia Alesconi bit her lip. 'I think Signora Santangeli looks charming,' she said quietly.

'Charming?' The older woman gave a grating laugh. 'She will need much more than charm if she is to sustain Lorenzo's interest long enough for him to render her *incinta*.'

'Signora Barzati,' Ottavia protested, casting a shocked glance at Marisa's burning face. 'That is hardly a topic for discussion amongst us.'

'Because it is a matter that should be kept within the family?' The *signora* moved her hands and her bracelets glinted in the lamplight like the eyes of malevolent cats. 'But surely we can have no secrets from you, my dear Signora Alesconi? Now that my son-in-law has apparently installed you here in my late daughter's place. And while I cannot be expected to approve of such a situation,' she added silkily, 'at least you are a widow, with no husband in the background to create a scandal—unlike Lorenzo's present mistress.'

It was suddenly difficult to breathe. Marisa found that the lamplit room seemed to have receded suddenly to some immense distance. She put her coffee cup back on the table with extreme care, as if it might dissolve at her touch.

The only reality was the cold, scornful voice, speaking with perfect clarity as it flayed the skin from her bones.

'No doubt Doria Venucci's beauty, and other attributes, have convinced my grandson that their affair is worth the risk.' Her smile was pure acid. 'Small wonder, too, *cara* Marisa, that he has been in no hurry to recall you from England. It is only his pressing need for an heir that has restored you to us at all—as I am sure you know.'

'Yes,' Marisa said, in a voice she did not recognise. 'I—know.'

'But what I must ask myself,' Nonna Teresa went on softly, 'is if it is likely that a girl already more trouble than she is worth can prevent Lorenzo from pursuing this disgraceful liaison which could be the ruin of us all. For myself, I think not.'

Ottavia Alesconi was on her feet. 'Signora Barzati,' she said in a choked voice. 'I—I must protest.'

'You do not agree with me, Signora Alesconi?' The older woman sounded mildly interested. 'You are, of course, very much a woman of the world. Perhaps you can use your…experience in pleasing men to give Marisa some tips—advise her on ways to ensure that Lorenzo does his duty and spends his nights in her bed, where he belongs.

'Something she has signally failed to accomplish so far,' she added with contempt. 'And I hold out little hope for the future.'

'This is unpardonable, *signora*.' Ottavia Alesconi's voice was ice. 'I overlook your insults to me—they are no more than I expected. But to turn your venom on an innocent girl—and at such a time—is beyond forgiveness.'

'Venom?' Nonna Teresa repeated. 'But you misunderstand, *signora*. I merely wish her to be under no illusion about the task ahead of her. To appreciate that once she is no longer a novelty for Lorenzo he will quickly become bored and look for other entertainment. If she is prepared for his—diversions, surely she is less likely to be hurt.'

'You are the one who does not understand, *signora*.'

She was dying inside, but somehow Marisa got to her feet and faced her adversary, her head high.

'You speak as if this was a love-match. As if Renzo and I—care for each other. But we do not, as everyone must be aware. You pointed out yourself that he married me only so that he could have a child—an heir.' She lifted her chin. 'It is a strictly limited commitment that suits us both perfectly. Therefore I do not need illusions, Signora Barzati. Nor do I expect fidelity. The fact that Renzo has other women does not matter to me. Why should it, when I don't love him?

'And once Renzo has his son, he is at liberty to choose any bed in the world—just so long as it isn't mine.'

She turned to the door and saw him standing there, silent and motionless, his face that of a stranger, carved from stone. The golden eyes blank with disbelief.

She had no idea how long he'd been in the doorway. How much he'd heard. But it had surely been enough.

A slow knife turned inside her, and she could have screamed with the pain of it. Could have stormed and wept and begged him to pretend—to lie that there was no one else. That for this one brief time he would be hers alone.

But she could not embarrass him—or herself—in such a way. Could not betray her inner agony.

Instead, keeping her voice cool and level, she said, 'Perhaps you would confirm for your grandmother, *signore*, the practicalities of our arrangement, and assure her that her kind advice, however well meant, is quite unnecessary?'

She added quietly, 'Forgive me if I do not stay, but it has been a long and tiring day. I would therefore prefer not to be disturbed—under the circumstances. I am sure you understand.'

And she went past him, her bright tearless eyes staring into space. Back to the lonely rooms and the empty bed waiting for her upstairs.

CHAPTER TEN

MARISA had not known it was possible to hurt so much and feel so empty at the same time. As if she'd been hollowed out and left to bleed.

She'd claimed tiredness, but she turned back at her bedroom door, knowing that she couldn't yet lie down on the bed where only a few hours ago she'd been held in Renzo's arms, her whole body alive and eager with the promise of joy.

But that was the illusion, she thought, shivering. Imagining even for a moment that she could exist on sex alone. Or his offer of friendship. That she could somehow make them enough when she wanted so much more. When she wanted—everything.

And now, in a few corrosive, malignant minutes, the impossibility of that had been spelled out to her in terms that left no room for hope.

That told her she was worse than a fool to think that Renzo's love-making could be prompted by anything but expediency. That he'd decided having her warm and responsive in his bed would simply make his task easier. And then, his duty accomplished, he would return to the glamorous forbidden mistress who'd kept him in Rome all this time, his marriage sidelined once again—for her sake.

So, for a while, she thought with pain, she didn't want to go back to that room—that bed. She needed quite badly to be…somewhere else.

Slowly, her arms wrapped round her body, she went along to the room at the end of the passage. On her previous visit it had been turned into another *salotto*—their own private sitting room. With a television, and a sophisticated sound system for Renzo's music collection and an alcove for dining.

Now it was long finished, the walls painted a restful colour between pale gold and apricot, and the shuttered windows that gave access to the *loggia* overlooking the garden hung with curtains in plain bleached linen.

The same fabric had been used to upholster the large, thickly cushioned sofa in front of the fireplace, and after lighting one of the tall lamps Marisa curled herself into one capacious corner, feeling the quiet comfort of the place close round her and wishing it could absorb her completely. That she could just…vanish, and never be seen again.

Never have to face anyone or try to deal with the wasteland her life had become.

Now, too late, she could understand the strange atmosphere she'd sensed in the house. It had been the uneasy calm before the storm. Because they must all have feared that Teresa Barzati had come there only to cause trouble.

I was the only one who didn't realise, she thought.

And while Zio Guillermo's reproof to the *signora* had provided a momentary respite, it had failed to silence her in the real mischief she planned to make. But then nothing could have done that.

Zia Maria, she thought bleakly, remembering her godmother's laughing eyes and the warm, comforting arms. Always there for her. How could all that gentleness possibly have been born from such hating and bitterness? From a hostility that had chilled her from the first?

Not that she'd been the only target tonight, she reminded herself. Ottavia Alesconi had also suffered from the *signora*'s malice. But in the scale of things Ottavia had got off lightly.

The real, lasting brutality had been aimed unerringly at herself.

Doria Venucci. She tried the name under her breath. A woman beautiful—experienced—and married. Everything she'd needed to know in one smiling, destructive sentence.

And everything that she was not, she thought, remembering those endless mirrors in the bathroom.

Because she was nothing special and never had been. Her sole venture into allure had been a disaster, whatever Renzo might have told her earlier, when he was trying to seduce her.

Although I have novelty value, she thought, digging her nails into the palms of her hands. *Let's not forget that.*

Or that for a few brief moments he almost made me forget something—the reason I'm here. The only reason…

She would not, however, allow herself to cry. That was definitely not an option. Because she needed to stay calm and rational in order to prepare for the moment when she would have to face Renzo again. When all her skill at self-protection would be brought into play once more.

Because wasn't that what the whole of the past year had really been about? Mounting guard on her emotions—her needs? Denying every instinct—every desire?

Nothing but an endless, futile attempt to convince herself that the war going on inside her was really fuelled by hate, she told herself broodingly. At the same time armouring herself against the possibility that one day he might come back.

And what good had it done her? she asked herself with despair. It had only taken a few kisses—the stroke of his hand on her breast—to bring her conquered and whimpering into his arms.

But for Rosalia's intervention she would have committed the worst mistake of her life—would have given herself completely—and she knew it. And in her surrender could have betrayed herself irretrievably. Could have sobbed out her pathetic yearnings against his skin.

Might even have broken the ultimate taboo and said the 'love' word, she thought in self-derision. At least she'd been spared that.

Otherwise, after tonight's bombshell had exploded, she'd have been forced to live, humiliated beyond belief, with the consequences of her own folly.

But now she needed to be strong. So a tear-stained face would simply be a sign of weakness she could not afford.

She moved restlessly, wondering what was happening in the other part of the house. What kind of recriminations were being aired.

No doubt she would find out tomorrow, she thought, then realised, with a startled glance at her watch, that it was nearly the next day already.

And that, in spite of her reluctance, it was time she went to bed.

I need to do the rational—the conventional thing, she told herself. As if it had been just another evening, and the *signora* had only been giving her some kindly but misguided advice.

A little tactless, maybe, but no lasting damage done.

Yes, that would be the way to handle it in the morning. As if the older woman's poisonous revelations really didn't matter.

With never a hint that she was falling to pieces and might never be whole again.

Rosalia seemed to have been busy again, because Marisa found her bed had been turned down—on both sides—and her nightgown arranged prettily on the coverlet.

She's clearly an optimist, Marisa thought ironically as she undressed quickly and slipped the white voile folds over her head. *Or maybe, if there's any kind of furore going on downstairs, it hasn't reached the servants' quarters yet.*

She went through the routine of removing her make-up, before finally unpinning her hair and brushing it loose into a silky cloud on her shoulders.

Then she walked reluctantly over to the bed, climbed in, and turned to switch off the lamp.

Only to realise with sudden, frozen shock that she was no longer alone. That Renzo was there, standing silently in the open doorway of his room.

'So,' he said at last, 'you are not asleep, after all.'

'But I plan to be,' she said tautly. 'In about two minutes.'

He was wearing, she noticed, one of the white towelling robes hanging in the bathroom and almost certainly nothing else. She felt her mouth go dry.

'And I thought I asked to be left in peace,' she added with hauteur.

'Is that how you see the present situation?' he asked. 'As peaceful?' His mouth twisted. 'You astonish me, *mia cara*.'

She bit her lip. 'But then in some ways it's been quite an astonishing evening all round, *signore*.' She made a business of arranging her pillows. 'Now, perhaps you'll excuse me?'

'There is nothing to excuse.' He came across to the bed and sat down on its edge, looking at her. 'You have taken down your hair,' he commented meditatively. 'I had hoped to do that for myself.' He smiled at her. 'Before, of course, I removed the charming concealment of that blouse, and everything else you were wearing tonight.'

'You—hoped?' Marisa echoed, her throat tightening to choking point.

She mustered her resources. 'How—how dare you? Just—get out of here.'

He smiled faintly. 'I grieve to disappoint you, Maria Lisa, but I am going nowhere.'

She stared at him. 'Is this some kind of sick joke?' she asked unsteadily. 'Because, arrogant as you are, you can't possibly imagine you're going to stay here. That I would allow you to—to…'

'But it has always been my intention to share your bed, *mia cara sposa*.' His gaze was steady. 'To make this the wedding night we never had. And nothing has happened to change my mind.'

'Nothing?' Marisa queried hoarsely. 'My God, didn't I make it clear enough that you wouldn't be welcome?'

'As always, you were a model of clarity, *mia bella*. Even my grandmother was left with nothing to say. And that does not happen very often,' he added reflectively.

He paused. 'You may be relieved to learn that she will be leaving after breakfast, and that any future visits will be—discouraged.'

'Why? Because she told the truth?' She took a quick harsh breath. 'Or are you now going to deny that you've been having an affair?'

'Deny it?' His brows lifted. 'Why should I?'

She stared at him defiantly. 'That underworked sense of decency you once mentioned, perhaps?'

'But I prefer to begin our marriage with honesty, Maria Lisa, rather than a convenient lie,' Renzo retorted. 'In spite of my efforts you were clearly determined to prolong your absence from me. To behave, in fact, as if I had ceased to exist for you.'

'I hoped you had,' she threw back recklessly.

'I do not doubt it.' His voice hardened. 'But did you really expect me to live like a eunuch until you chose or were forced to return?'

She gasped. 'You really have no sense of shame, do you?'

'An overrated virtue, I think.' He shrugged. 'Although I admit I deeply regret that I was stupid enough to seek consolation when you shut me out of your life, rather than take a more effective course of action. I must learn to curb my temper.'

He went on flatly, 'I also wish very much that I had done as I planned this evening and told you about the affair myself, before anyone else had a chance to do so.'

She stared at him. 'You—planned?' Her voice sounded dazed.

'*Sì.* I told you when I visited you earlier that there were things that needed to be said between us. But then I allowed myself to be—most exquisitely—diverted from my purpose,' he added ruefully. 'I hoped there would be time later, but unfortunately my grandmother always likes to be the first with bad news, so I had no chance to talk to you…to explain, perhaps, how—why—it happened.

'In that Nonna Teresa bears a certain resemblance to your cousin Julia,' he added coldly. 'We are neither of us blessed with our relatives, *carissima*.'

'You may think that.' Marisa lifted her chin. 'On the other hand, I shall always be grateful to them both, for reminding me what you're really like—and the kind of life I might expect with you.' She took a breath. 'Besides, what was there for you to explain—apart from the fact that you're a—a serial womaniser who can't keep his zip fastened?'

There was a tingling silence.

'Never a problem when I was near you, my little saint,' Renzo returned eventually, and too courteously. 'Although even you are not immune to the temptations of the flesh with other men, it seems.'

She gasped. 'What the hell do you mean?'

'Those intimate lunches with the unhappy husband,' he came back at her. 'Where might they ultimately have led, if he had asked for more than sympathy? Also the unfortunate Alan, who accompanied you back to your cosy flat with its one bed only last night, *mia sposa*.' The golden eyes narrowed. 'What would have happened, I wonder, if I had not been so tactlessly waiting?'

'Nothing,' she said curtly.

'How can you be so sure?'

Because I've never loved anyone but you, she thought, staring down at the coverlet. *Never loved or wanted any other man. That's the truth I've had to hide ever since you walked back into my life and asked me to marry you. That's the truth I've been trying to hide from myself all this time.*

Because you don't feel the same, and you never will. You only want someone to give you a child and turn a blind eye to your other women.

And I—I want all the things you can't give me. I want all of you, and that's what makes any real honesty between us impossible.

Because I couldn't bear it—I'd die before I let you find out how I really feel and embarrass you or have you feel sorry for me.

Aloud, she said shortly, 'Alan blew his chances when he took the money and ran off to Hong Kong.' She swallowed. 'But even if I had planned to take a lover, what possible right would you have to object when you have a mistress?'

'I have whatever rights I choose,' Renzo retorted crisply. 'And one is to ensure that I have you first, *carissima*. So that I can be certain that any child in your body will be mine and no other's.'

As she gasped in outrage, he paused. 'Also, my grandmother is out of date. The affair with Doria Venucci is already over,' he added, with a touch of grimness. 'And for that you have my word.'

'To spare my feelings?' she asked defiantly. 'Or to avoid the scandal your grandmother was predicting tonight?'

'Oh, the scandal, *naturalamente*.' His voice bit. 'I was not aware you had any feelings about our marriage—apart from resentment and distaste. But the gossipmongers were at work long before I met Signora Venucci—theorising on the reasons for our prolonged separation,' he added broodingly. 'Do not imagine I found their speculation pleasant.'

'Oh, how terrible for you,' she flung back at him. 'I never realised you were so sensitive, *signore*.'

'No,' he said harshly. 'That I can also believe.' He paused. 'Tell me something, *mia cara*, *per favore*. Just as you never returned any of my phone calls, did you ever read even one of the letters I wrote to you?'

She hadn't been expecting that. Had tried to put out of her mind the airmail envelopes, which had arrived so regularly, only to be torn up and binned, unopened.

She didn't particularly want to confess the awkward truth, but realised she couldn't sustain a lie either. He would be bound to ask questions about their contents that she'd be unable to answer.

She played with the edge of the embroidered sheet. 'No,' she admitted eventually. 'No, I didn't.'

'Che peccato,' he said. 'What a pity. You might have found them—instructive.'

She said defiantly, 'Or perhaps I felt I'd already learned what I needed to know about you, *signore*.'

He said silkily, 'But as you discovered in this room a few hours ago, *signora*, your lessons are only just beginning.' And he began to loosen the belt of his robe.

Marisa hurled herself on to her side, turning her back to him. Because she couldn't see him naked—she *dared* not…

'No,' she said hoarsely. 'Do you think saying your affair is over makes everything all right? Signora Venucci wasn't the first, *signore*, and she won't be the last. Knowing that, do you really think I'm going to allow you anywhere near me again?'

She felt the mattress dip slightly as he joined her in the bed, and her whole body tensed.

'Why, yes.' His voice reached her softly. 'Because that is what you agreed to do. In return, if you remember, for living the rest of your life in whatever way you wish. The agreement we reached only this morning. And also because you don't love me, Maria Lisa,' he went on. 'Nor are you in the least concerned if there are other women in my life, because you are only here to have my baby.'

He paused. 'You said so yourself, if you remember. Not long ago, and in front of witnesses too.'

His hand touched her bare shoulder. Stroked its soft skin with heart-stopping gentleness. 'So, if you don't care what I do, *mia cara*, if you are so supremely indifferent to the way I live my life and how I amuse myself when you are not there, why should it matter to you whether Doria Venucci goes or stays? Or who might take her place?

'Therefore what possible excuse do you have to withhold yourself from me any longer. To refuse to behave as my wife—and the future mother of my son? When this, on your own admission, is your sole consideration.'

Marisa could not speak or move. It occurred to her suddenly that this was how a hunted animal must feel when the trap closed around it. But this was a trap entirely of her own making.

But I do care, she cried out soundlessly. *Oh, God, I care so much. Just the thought of you with another woman is like a giant claw ripping into me. Tearing me apart. Making me only half a human being. Only I can never tell you so. I have to go on pretending.*

Aloud, she said very quietly, 'I suppose—logically—I have no excuse.'

'*Bene*,' Renzo approved, his tone ironic. 'At last we have reached an understanding. Tonight we will put the past behind us for ever, and you will learn to belong to me completely. And do not think to escape by telling me to do my worst,' he added mockingly. 'We have already trodden that path, and I found it—unrewarding.'

She said unevenly, 'You—bastard.'

'And no insult will stop me either,' Renzo retorted. 'You see, my reluctant wife, there was something about your latest piece of candour that intrigued me. While you were proclaiming your indifference you may have denied love, but you failed to mention—desire.'

His voice sank to a whisper. 'You never said, *carissima*, that you did not want me. Maybe because you knew it was not true, as you proved earlier right here in this room. Or did you think I had forgotten how sweet you were—how yielding?'

He allowed his words to settle into a tingling silence, then his hands closed on her, turning her inexorably to face him.

'So, for tonight at least, Maria Lisa, listen to your body, not your mind.'

Oh, God, he only has to touch me and I'm trembling inside—going to pieces…

'I'll give you nothing.' Her voice shook.

'You intend to break your word to me?' Renzo tutted in faint reproof as he tossed the covers away to the foot of the bed. 'I do not recommend it, *mia bella*.' He added meditatively, 'Also, I wonder if you can.'

He looked at the thin layer of voile that masked her body and smiled slowly. 'And now it seems that I have the privilege of undressing you just a little after all.'

'No.' She pushed at the hands that were drawing the straps of her nightgown down from her shoulders. 'I—I'll keep my promise—but…don't…please…'

'You wish to do it for me?' he asked, and his smile became a teasing, almost wicked grin. 'Even better. Having you strip for me has always been one of my favourite fantasies,' he added huskily. 'I am sure you remember why.'

Marisa turned her head away, her face warming helplessly, aware that just one unwanted glimpse of his lean, burnished body stretched against the snowy bedlinen had prompted the unwelcome resurrection of some of her own fantasies.

She said tautly, 'Do you have to—humiliate me like this?'

Reminding me how long I've loved you, how much I've always wanted to be yours—even when I could only guess…imagine… what that might mean?

'That is not my intention,' he said, with a sudden touch of harshness.

'But for once in our lives, Maria Lisa, I want there to be nothing to separate us from each other. Not clothing, not lies, not silence. Just a man with his wife.'

Her voice pleaded. 'Then will you at least let me turn out the light?'

'No,' he said. 'I will not.' He added more gently, '*Carissima*, I have waited so very long to see you—to hold you like this.'

She closed her eyes, trying to shut him out of her consciousness. To deny what was happening between them. But her other senses were still only too alive, and she felt the fabric whisper against her skin as he discarded it. And in the silence that followed she heard him sigh quietly, and with undisguised satisfaction.

Then he reached for her, drawing her into his arms, making her aware of every inch of his undisguisedly urgent body against her nakedness as his lips took hers.

And while she could never accuse him of using force, nevertheless his kiss was deep—and, she discovered, also implacably, unrelentingly thorough. Sparing her nothing as it possessed her.

A declaration, she realised dazedly, of intent.

A challenge to her powers of resistance, stating silently but potently that it was useless for her to pretend she was unmoved by what he was doing to her.

And perhaps it was. But that didn't mean she had to add to her earlier mistakes by making it easy for him, or by adding her name to the list of eagerly compliant women who'd shared his bed, she told herself with a kind of ragged determination, keeping her eyes so tightly shut they began to ache.

But Renzo wasn't making it easy for her either, as his mouth continued to move achingly, intensely on hers.

As she was made to discover the heated excitement that the deliberately sensuous brush of his bare skin against hers could generate. And was reminded, as he pulled her even closer to his hard loins, exactly how it had once felt to have all that aroused male potency and strength sheathed deep inside her.

And how, for one brief second of time, she had wanted it to last for ever.

Yet giving herself now would make her all too vulnerable to discovery, she thought, clinging to her last shreds of reason. Could lure her into betraying that she had more at stake from this encounter than any mere initiation into the deep waters of sensuality.

And if pride, maybe, and an atom of self-respect might be all she could salvage from this welter of confusion and unhappiness that was threatening to overwhelm her, then she would settle for that.

Yet how could she battle her own needs when his hands were renewing their lingering, pleasurable exploration of her body, tracing her bone structure as if he wished to commit it to memory and gently moulding every delicate curve and hollow?

When, wherever she felt his touch, her skin warmed and blossomed in helpless pleasure, making her senses swim?

She felt him lift his head and knew that he was looking down at her. She was glad that he could not see her eyes as his fingertips stroked her breasts, coaxing the rosy nipples to aching, unresisting life, making them stand proud for the homage of his lips.

And as they touched her—as she found herself pierced by a pleasure that bordered pain—Marisa turned her head away, pressing a clenched fist against the swollen contours of her mouth, biting at the knuckle.

This isn't making love, she thought desperately. *He's just testing your will—your capacity for endurance. So, fight. Fight, damn you. Don't let him know—don't ever let him see. You can't...*

Renzo's mouth enclosed each tumescent peak in turn, suckling them languorously, teasing them softly, exquisitely with his tongue. His fingers slowly traversed the flatness of her stomach, to outline the angle of one slender hip and close on it in a gesture so frankly proprietorial that she almost flinched.

Again she felt him pause, as if sensing—even gauging—her resistance, and his hand came up to capture her averted chin, compelling her to face him again.

She felt him smooth the hair back from her forehead, then brush a soft caress across her inimically closed eyelids, before returning to her mouth. And as he kissed her Marisa could taste the scent of her own skin on his lips.

His hands were moving again, sliding round to her back, his fingertips unhurriedly stroking the shivering skin up to her shoulderblades, then back down the graceful length of her spine to the sensitive area at its base, massaging it gently, before slipping down to caress the slight swell of her buttocks, his touch gentle, but deliberately inciting.

And for a shocked instant, in spite of herself, Marisa found her body arching towards him in shivering response, feeling his dark chest hair graze her swollen nipples in a torment that was as delicious as it was calculated.

'*Carissima.*' She could feel his smile whispering the words against her mouth. '*Tesoro mio.*'

He shifted his position slightly, putting her back against the heaped pillows as he bent to her, kissing her throat, her shoulders and slender arms, while his fingers travelled down to the hollow of her hipbone and lingered there.

Marisa could feel the dark headlong rush of desire scalding her body as his hand descended slowly to seek the silky mound at the junction of her thighs, his touch like gossamer against the downy flesh. Persuading her, she realised, to open herself to the ultimate intimacies.

Realised too that her resistance was ebbing under the insidious pressure of this skilful, studied arousal.

That all the deep, hot places of her womanhood were melting in this musky, wanton surge of passion, yearning to offer up their secrets to his possession. And that Renzo would already know this.

Would know exactly—oh, God—how to slide his hand between her slackened thighs and caress her moist inner flesh. How to find that tiny hidden nub that was somehow the centre of all delight and coax it to swell and harden under the delicate, practised play of his fingers as they stroked, circled and tantalised, just as her nipples were doing under the renewed cajolery of his tongue.

And Marisa was lost. She couldn't think or reason any more. Nothing seemed to exist but the sweet, terrifying anguish of this assault on her senses. The response that was being wrung from her shaken, defenceless body.

Her body was beginning to writhe, her hips lifting against his questing hand in mute pleading for—what?

For him to stop—to somehow end this shameful pleasure? To release her from this rack of delicious sensuality?

Or for him never to stop?

Her head turned restlessly on the pillows as she tried to stifle the moan of longing rising in her throat. The sound that would betray her utterly—telling him without words how desperately she needed to feel him inside her again. To feel him filling her, and offering the completion that had been denied when he'd taken her before.

And Renzo was whispering to her, his breath fanning her ear, his voice slurred and heavy as he told her that she was beautiful—that she was all the sweetness of the world—and, yes, it would be soon. It would be everything…

And in that moment she felt it, that first faint stirring deep within her, as if she was being drawn out of herself towards some distant unknown peak, with every nerve ending, every drop of blood concentrated, blindly focussed on that small, rapturous centre of sensation, aching and erect under the subtle, relentless glide of his fingertips.

Then, between one breath and the next, Marisa found herself overtaken, her shuddering, gasping body consumed by pulsations of pleasure spreading through every vein, every bone, every inch of her heated, shivering skin, each one more intense than the last. Until at their highest and fiercest pitch she thought she might faint or die, and heard herself cry out, her voice ragged with fear and wonder.

And when the hot, incredible trembling at last began to subside, she found herself wrapped closely in Renzo's arms, her sweat-dampened face buried in his shoulder and his lips against her hair.

Ashamed that, after all, she'd rendered him such an easy victory, but knowing that even if she wanted to she did not possess the strength to move away.

And that she did not want to…

CHAPTER ELEVEN

BUT at last it was Renzo who moved, reaching over the edge of the bed for his discarded robe.

Her body still quivering softly, Marisa opened weighted eyelids and stared at him, feeling suddenly bereft. Surely, surely that could not be all? a voice inside her begged. There must be more. There *had* to be…

Aloud, she said huskily, 'Where are you going?'

'Nowhere, *dolcezza mia.*' The reply was soft—almost soothing. When he turned back to her she realised he was tearing open a small packet taken from his pocket, and swiftly and deftly making use of its contents.

And in some dazed corner of her mind she thought, *But that can't happen. He shouldn't be doing that. Not if we're going to…*

Then he was drawing her once again into his arms, his mouth opening hers to admit the heated glide of his tongue. His hands stroked the length of her glowing body, then slid beneath her, lifting her towards the hardness of him that had already parted her unresisting thighs. He entered her with one sure, powerful thrust.

And all thought of protest died for her. Because, defying logic, reason and even common sense, this glorious and all-consuming sensation was what she'd been living for all these long, sterile months.

In spite of its comparative inexperience, her body, still blissfully euphoric in the wake of her first orgasm, was too relaxed to offer any impediment to his possession and she accepted him—welcomed him into her with joy.

It was so different, she thought, her mind reeling. So utterly—wonderfully different from that first time. Yet how could it possibly seem so right when everything between them was still so terribly wrong? And always would be…

And then, as Renzo began to move inside her, she abandoned all pretence at rationality and let her body think for her instead.

'I don't hurt you?' The question seemed torn from him as he looked down at her, the golden eyes searching hers. 'Maria Lisa—tell me—promise me that I do not…'

'No.' She breathed her answer, an instinct she'd not known she possessed prompting her to raise her hands and clasp his shoulders, to move her hips in slow, deliberate allurement. The ultimate physical reassurance—the candid offering of her entire self for his enjoyment.

At his instant, fervent reaction she closed on him hungrily, drawing him into her without reserve, holding him, then giving him release so that he could drive forward again, slowly and rhythmically, each time penetrating her more deeply, and surprising her into a gasp of raw pleasure.

Oh, God, he felt so amazing—so incredibly, dangerously beautiful…

At the same time her intuition told her that Renzo had himself well under control, patiently reining back his own needs in order to allow their bodies to became fully attuned to each other.

Until she realised her own responses, her own demands, should fully match his own, and they were finally joined in a harmony as old as the stars.

And even though she told herself it was—it must be—too soon, she could already feel within her, like a ripple on a tranquil sea, the renewed, irresistible build of helpless sexual excitement.

Felt it, reached for it, strained after it, half ashamed of her own greed, a tiny, frantic sob rising in her throat.

And in the next instant she found herself totally overwhelmed once more, her body throbbing in the harsh, almost feral throes of ecstasy as she moaned her pleasure aloud.

She became aware of Renzo rearing up above her, his head thrown back, throat muscles taut, as he gave a hoarse cry of rapture and his body shuddered into hers with the force of his own fulfilment.

Afterwards they lay motionless, still entwined, the only sound their ragged breathing as they struggled to return it to normality.

Marisa lay, eyes half-closed, her body still lost in its exquisite lassitude. She thought drowsily, *I'm not the same person, not any more. I've been transformed.*

She looked down tenderly at the dark head pillowed on her breasts, longing to hold him there for ever, to stroke his dishevelled hair, to kiss his eyes and mouth and whisper everything that her heart was crying out to tell him.

But she did not dare.

Because her mind was slowly and gradually beginning once more to deal with reality. Making her face a few essential truths.

Because nothing had changed at all. Not herself. And certainly not the situation that she was in.

Because sex, however magical, made no actual difference. And she must never fool herself into believing that it might.

So she did not try to stop him when eventually he eased himself away from her and left the bed to cross to the bathroom, but lay quietly, staring into space.

Asking herself how many more nights like this she could possibly endure. How deeply enmeshed in this web of passion and desire he'd spun round her might she become before she committed the cardinal sin of telling him that she loved him?

Might he even become so essential to her that there would come a time when she would not want to leave? A time when she would sacrifice every hope for the future and choose instead to remain here in his house, the obedient, docile wife, performing the domestic duties he'd outlined so succinctly to her only last night?

Careful never to be too curious about his absences. Scrupulous about ignoring the inevitable gossip that would reach her whenever he strayed too openly. And grateful for the occasional night when he would turn to her for his amusement.

Was it worth submitting to that kind of heartbreak? she asked herself wretchedly. Could she bear to watch herself slowly disintegrate in hurt and loneliness in this half-life he'd offered her?

No, she thought, shivering. *I—I can't do that. I won't...*

She made herself move, retrieve the covers from the foot of the bed and pull them into place, sheltering under them just before Renzo, yawning, came sauntering back into the room.

His brows lifted when he saw the straightened bed, but he made no comment as he slid in beside her, pulling her into his arms.

'Why don't we get a little sleep, *carissima*?' he suggested softly. 'Then see what the rest of the night brings.'

Novelty value…

The words seemed to beat in her head.

'No,' she said, taking a deep breath. 'I'd prefer not to.'

'You don't need to sleep?' Renzo whistled softly. 'You have miraculous powers of resilience, *mia cara*. I wish I shared them, but being only a man,' he added ruefully, 'I need a little time to recover.'

'I meant,' she said thickly, 'I'd rather be alone.'

There was a fractional pause, then he said gently, 'But sleeping and waking together is all part of marriage, Maria Lisa.'

'For other people, perhaps. Not for us.'

Renzo released her, lifting himself on to an elbow as he stared down at her. 'What are you saying? Have I displeased you in some way?'

'I want to know why you did that,' she said hoarsely. 'Why you used—that thing when you're supposed to be making me pregnant.'

'Ah,' Renzo said softly. 'I understand. But there is plenty of time ahead of us for that, *cara mia*.' He stroked the curve of her cheek. 'And maybe we should learn to be husband and wife before we attempt to become father and mother.' He grinned reminiscently. 'My grandfather, Nonno Santangeli, had a saying—*First the pleasure in bed, later the joy in the cradle.*' He added softly, 'After what we have just shared I thought you might agree with him.'

'But I don't. My recollection of the agreement between us is quite different.' She swallowed past the unbearable tightness in her throat. 'You seem to have forgotten that I'm here for one purpose only, *signore*, and not as your—plaything.' She added flatly, 'You have—someone else for that.'

'*Dio mio*, not that again.' His mouth tightened. 'I have told you—it is over. And it should never have begun, except…' He paused. 'Well, that does not matter. My concern is that you should believe me—and try, if you can, to forgive.' He added wryly, 'Or do you mean to punish me for the rest of our lives?'

'Signora Venucci may have been sidelined,' Marisa returned icily. 'But I'm sure there are plenty of other candidates waiting to take her place. Only I'm not one of them. I'm looking forward to my independence, and I won't be cheated out of it for a day longer than necessary just so that you can change the terms of our deal and use me as a substitute mistress.'

I can't believe I'm doing this—that I'm lying to him, saying these vile things, when every word is like sticking a knife into my own flesh.

'You believe that is what has happened here?' His voice changed—became harsh, almost derisive. 'My recollection is rather different. I think we *used* each other, Maria Lisa, and perhaps you cannot forgive me for that either. For showing you at last what your body was made for.'

'Mille grazie,' she said. 'It's always good to be taught by an expert.' She paused. 'No matter how that expertise was obtained. And by demonstrating that you can make me—amenable, you've mended your damaged pride in the process. Congratulations, *signore*. Everything's worked out for you.'

'I am glad you think so.' There was a silence, then he added with a kind of terrible weariness, 'How can this be? How can I be apart from you for minutes, no more, yet find a different girl—this stranger—on my return?' He shook his head in bitter disbelief. '*Santa Madonna*, how can I be in heaven at one moment and hell the next?'

'Because you forgot why you married me,' she said, struggling to keep her voice level. Unemotional. 'Why you forced me to come back to you. But I haven't. And until you remember the terms of our agreement and decide to follow them, maybe you should spend your nights in your own room.'

'I have an even better suggestion,' he said with icy savagery. 'Why, *signora*, do you not simply provide me with a list of the days each month when you are most likely to conceive, so that I can restrict my visits to those occasions only?' He paused. 'In that way we will both be saved time and trouble.'

He flung back the covers and got up, reaching for his robe and shrugging it on.

As he fastened the belt, he looked down at her. 'You accused me of cheating you, Maria Lisa,' he said quietly. 'But I say you are the cheat—because you are deliberately denying yourself warmth and passion. Turning your back on the sweetness we could make together.'

She looked past him. Kept her voice cool. 'I'll survive.'

Will I? Can I? When I already feel as if I'm fragmenting—breaking into tiny pieces. That I'll never be whole and entire again without you…

'And so shall I,' he said. 'As you say, there are plenty of other women in the world. Maybe I will find one who does not drive quite so hard a bargain. Who may even wish to be with me for myself.' His mouth twisted. 'But no doubt I am asking for the moon.'

And he turned away, walking across to his own room and closing the door behind him.

She nearly went after him. Nearly followed to tell him that she hadn't meant it—any of it. To beg him to come back. To hold her close and keep her safe. And to be there—at her side always.

Except that wasn't on offer.

There was sex, of course. The master with his latest pupil. He'd probably been sufficiently intrigued by the frenzy of her response to continue her lessons if she asked.

But how could she settle for a single course when she wanted an entire meal? A feast…?

And eventually there would be compensation, she thought achingly. A permissible focus for all the love dammed up in her heart, and one that she could even acknowledge, as she'd recognised that far-off day in the *piazza* at Amalfi.

There would be his baby…

So she could hope—live for that instead. Because, she thought, as she turned over, burying her unhappy face in the pillow that he'd used, trying to find some faint trace of him, because she had no other choice.

The Puccini aria with its theme of doomed love came to its plangent end.

She should, Marisa thought, get up and choose another CD—one, maybe, without quite so many resonances. But she remained where she was, curled up once more in the corner of the sofa in her private *salotto*.

Since she'd first arrived at the Villa Proserpina, three weeks earlier, the weather had remained unsettled, a mixture of sun and showers, with an occasional hint of thunder.

More in tune with her mood than brilliant heat, but hardly conducive to spending her afternoons in the garden or by the pool, so she was glad of this room as a kind of sanctuary.

At first she'd taken care to spend part of every day with her father-in-law, but now he'd begun to work in his study again, with his consultant's wary permission, preparing to pick up the reins at the bank once more.

'I hope he isn't overdoing things,' Marisa had said anxiously one evening after dinner, finding herself alone with Ottavia Alesconi, whose answering smile had been reassuring.

'Better, I think, that he should work a little than chafe at his restrictions.' She'd added meditatively, 'Also, it is necessary for him to take an interest as Lorenzo is away so much.'

Leaving Marisa to murmur an embarrassed, 'Yes—of course,' and hastily change the subject.

Because the truth was he was never there. In fact, she'd hardly set eyes on him since the night of their quarrel, she acknowledged wretchedly.

When she'd ventured downstairs the following morning, after a miserably restless night, it had been to discover that he'd already left for an appointment in Siena.

'You could have gone with him, dear child, but he insisted you should be left to sleep,' Guillermo had added, smiling, totally misinterpreting both Renzo's apparent solicitude and the deep shadows under her eyes.

He sees what he wants to see, Marisa had thought, stifling a sigh.

And when she and Renzo had met at dinner, the cool polite stranger of their honeymoon had returned. So much so that Marisa had wondered whether she'd only dreamed the events of the previous night. Because there was surely no way in which she could ever have sobbed the rapture of her climax in this man's arms.

Later, she had waited tensely in her bedroom until she saw the light come on under the communicating door, then made herself go and knock.

It had opened instantly to reveal Renzo, his shirt already half-unbuttoned and his expression wary.

'Sì?' His brusque tone did not encourage her either, nor the fact that he didn't seem to notice she was once again wearing only a nightgown.

Marisa held out a folded piece of paper. She said stiltedly, 'I—I wrote down that—information that you wanted.'

He took it from her, his face expressionless as he scanned the brief list of dates she'd provided.

Then, *'Grazie tante,'* he drawled, slipping it into his pants pocket. 'You are all consideration, *mia cara*, and I shall try to follow your example. But to my sorrow, I shall not be able to keep our first appointment. I have to go to Boston on business.' He paused, his wintry smile not reaching his eyes. 'Unless, of course, you wish to accompany me, *mia sposa*, in order that the opportunity is not wasted?'

'I hardly think so.' She looked down at the floor, aware that this was not going as she'd dared to hope. 'Emilio is still showing me the house—explaining my new responsibilities, how everything works. Besides, I really do need to buy some clothes before I go on any trips, and Ottavia has offered to take me shopping in Firenze.'

'Then I shall count the hours until the next occasion,' Renzo said too gently. 'I must tell my secretary to mark it in my diary.'

'Don't,' she whispered, still not looking at him. 'Please—don't.'

'I think perhaps that should be my line, not yours,' he said, and shrugged. *'Tuttavia—non importa. Buona notte*, Maria Lisa. Sleep well.'

He'd stepped back, and the door had closed between them.

But it wasn't just the door, Marisa thought now, sighing as she picked up the book she was struggling to read. All other lines of communication had been shut off too. No phone calls this time. And no letters either.

I miss him, she told herself, the breath catching in her throat. *I miss him so terribly.*

After all, it was in this house that she'd first started to fall in love with him, even when she had been too young to know what love meant.

But she knew now—knew it in all its aspects. And while she could stay busy by day, learning to be the mistress of the Villa Proserpina, her nights, whether she was awake or dreaming, were a continuing torment, her body on fire for an appeasement that never came.

Her imagination tortured with the thought that by now he would have taken her at her word and be sharing his bed with another woman.

Restlessly, she rose and walked across to the long windows, pushing them open and stepping out on to the *loggia*. The earlier rain had stopped, leaving the air filled with the scent of wet blossoms, and she stood, leaning on the balustrade, as she drew the fragrance deeply into her lungs.

I could be so happy here, she thought. *Whereas the most I can hope for is—acceptance.*

And she paused, tensing, as she heard in the distance the sound of a car approaching down the avenue.

Oh, God, she thought, her throat tightening in mingled fear and longing. Renzo—it must be Renzo. No one else was due.

She glanced down at her black cotton trousers and their matching shirt, her hand going to the clip confining her scraped-back hair at the nape of her neck. She was not going to meet him like this—not when she had cupboards full of new clothes, thanks to the good offices of Ottavia Arlesconi.

She was pulling off her things as she ran to the bedroom. Seconds later she was in the shower, emerging breathlessly after a couple of minutes to dry herself and apply scented lotion to her skin, spraying the matching perfume on her throat, her breasts and thighs.

She scrambled into her newest and prettiest white lace underwear and put on a straight linen dress, beautifully cut, in a soft misty green, sliding her feet into low-heeled pumps.

She brushed her hair until it crackled, then applied a coating of mascara to her lashes and some soft colour to her mouth.

It occurred to her that she'd not heard Renzo come up to the suite, or go into his room. No doubt he had stayed to talk to his father.

She wanted to run, but she made herself walk calmly and sedately downstairs. There would be time later to demonstrate how eager she was to see him again, she thought, her pulses hammering.

As she reached the entrance hall, Emilio was coming towards the stairs, carrying a travel bag and a briefcase.

She took a breath. Tried to sound casual. 'I thought I heard a car, Emilio. Has someone arrived?'

'*Sì, signora*.' He beamed, indicating the door of the *salotto*.

Try and play it cool, Marisa adjured herself as she pushed open the door. *But make sure you let him see that you're—pleased.*

She walked forward and halted, her throat closing with shock and disappointment. For the room's only occupant was Ottavia Arlesconi, seated on a sofa and glancing through a fashion magazine.

She glanced up with her usual calm friendliness. '*Ciao*, Marisa. *Come sta?*'

'Ottavia—how lovely.' She forced herself to smile. 'I didn't know you'd be here this weekend.'

'A last-minute decision.' The other woman spread her hands. 'Guillermo called me, and I could not refuse.' She studied Marisa with a faint frown. 'Are you quite well? You look a little pale.'

'I'm fine.' She took a seat, smoothing her skirt with nervous hands. 'I—I thought it might be Renzo's car.'

The *signora* put down her magazine. 'Renzo—here?' She shook her head. 'I don't think he is expected.' She paused. 'But you have received a different message, perhaps?'

There was a silence, then Marisa said quietly, 'No. No message.'

'Ah,' said the *signora*. There was another, longer silence, then Ottavia said, 'Marisa, you have no mother. I—I have no daughter, and maybe I am not qualified to speak, but I cannot stay silent when I see how unhappy you are.' She hesitated. 'It is no secret that your marriage has been troubled from the first. But when you returned here with Lorenzo we all hoped that you might find a life together.'

'Not quite all.' Marisa's hands gripped together in her lap.

'The woman is a witch,' Ottavia said calmly. 'We need not regard her. My concern is the words you spoke to her, and which Lorenzo heard. I saw him at breakfast the next morning and he looked grey—like a ghost. And when he left the following day he was alone.' She looked steadily at Marisa. 'As he has been, I think, since your marriage.'

She paused. 'I do not count the foolishness with the Venucci woman,' she went on, and held up a placatory hand as Marisa stiffened. 'Nor do I condone it, believe me. But when a man is hurt and lonely he will sometimes find comfort in the wrong place. And you were hardly around to object,' she added dryly.

Marisa bent her head. 'No,' she said with constraint. 'I stayed away because it's never been a real marriage. Renzo never wanted a wife—and he wanted me least of all.'

'Perhaps he was reluctant at first,' Ottavia said slowly. 'But after you became engaged that changed. He was quiet, thoughtful, when he returned from London, making plans for the wedding and where you would live. He wished everything to be perfect for you. He was also nervous, which I had never seen before.' She smiled suddenly. 'It made me like him better. And also think that he wished to be married to you very much.'

'Because he needed someone to give him a son and not make demands on his time and attention that he could not fulfil,' Marisa said tonelessly. 'I—fitted the template.'

'Is that why you are so determined not to love him?' Ottavia asked gently. 'Why you demonstrate to the world that he means nothing to you by leaving him for months on end? Why you even proclaim it aloud in front of him—treating him without kindness or respect?'

She shook her head. '*Dio mio*, is it any wonder that he stays away?'

Marisa said with difficulty, 'There might be another reason. Something I practically pushed him into.' She paused. 'Ottavia—has he got another woman?'

'I do not know,' the older woman returned. 'And if I knew, my dear child, I would not tell you. But I will say this,' she added more robustly. 'If I was a girl in love with a man as attractive as Lorenzo, I would not make the mistake of turning him out of my bed a second time. I would make sure I was always the one at his side when he slept.'

'Because you'd know you couldn't trust him?' It hurt to say it.

'No,' Ottavia said with emphasis. 'Because I could not bear to be apart from him. But if you cannot forgive his past errors with your whole heart, there is no more to be said.'

Marisa said in a low voice, 'Suppose he doesn't want to be forgiven? That he's had enough?'

Ottavia shrugged. 'That, *cara*, is a risk you will have to take. But in your shoes I would fight—and fight again.'

I already did that, Marisa thought as she left the room. *But it turned out to be the wrong battle. And now, heaven help me, I may never get another chance.*

CHAPTER TWELVE

SHE could, she supposed, follow Renzo to Rome, Marisa thought as she trailed slowly upstairs, her mind whirling. Try and talk to him.

But what on earth was she going to say? And anyway, after everything that had happened between them would he even be prepared to listen?

And suppose he wasn't alone…

Fight, Ottavia had said. But if it came down to that what kind of fight would it be? A stand-up, knock-down, hair-pulling, eye-scratching brawl with some glamorous Roman beauty, and Renzo as referee? That was a hideous prospect, she thought, shuddering inwardly. Besides, there was no guarantee she'd win.

She walked back into the *salotto* and closed the door. Late-afternoon sun was pouring in, filling the room with real warmth. Maybe it was a good omen, she thought. Or perhaps she was going a little crazy in the head, looking for signs and portents in the weather. Because at this time of the year storms were never far away.

She put on some more music—not Puccini, this time; not more love lost, love betrayed—but some lilting guitar and harp concertos.

Curling back into the corner of her sofa, she looked down at her hands, twisting her wedding ring on her finger. Something Ottavia had said was forcing itself back into her mind. 'When a man is hurt and lonely…'

Hurt, she thought, trying the words for herself, as if she was learning a foreign language. *Lonely?*

Hardly a description to apply to Lorenzo the Magnificent, who stalked through life, taking from it exactly what he wanted, making his own rules and expecting to be obeyed with one crook of his little finger.

And the last man in the world that she should ever have fallen in love with, she acknowledged with a swift, unhappy sigh. Or tried to live without…

She leaned back against the cushions, closing her eyes, letting the music soothe her, and the gentle golden heat permeate to the marrow of her bones, feeling relaxed for the first time in a long while.

Maybe she should spend her nights here on the sofa, she thought wryly, rather than in that big bed with all its memories. All its bitter regrets.

Perhaps, too, she would sleep without dreams she didn't want to remember in the morning. Or even no dreams at all.

And yet, as the weariness engendered by so many restless nights finally overcame her and she slept, she dreamed she was sinking down into a field of golden flowers, stretching around her as far as the eye could see. And as she turned her head, trying to capture a breath of their faint, elusive scent, she felt the blossoms brush her hair and the curve of her cheek.

The next instant the field had gone, transformed into an ordinary sofa again, and she was sitting up, eyes wide open and her heart pounding, wondering what had woken her.

She heard, not too far away, the soft sound of a closing door.

Rosalia, she thought. Coming as usual to ask what the *signora* wished to wear for dinner. Except it was much too early for that, as one startled glance at her watch confirmed.

It might have been Ottavia, of course, checking that their conversation earlier had not upset her. But the older woman would never visit this part of the house without an invitation, and neither would Guillermo, she was sure. They would both regard it as an invasion of privacy, whether Renzo was there or not.

Renzo…

With sudden shock, she remembered the subtle fragrance she'd encountered in her dream, and knew why it had seemed so strangely familiar—and so enticing.

It was his cologne, she thought, the one he always used, understated and expensive. As much a part of him as the colour of his eyes and the texture of his skin.

And it could only mean that he was here—somewhere. And that, however briefly, he'd been close to her. Maybe—touched her.

But it also meant that he'd found her asleep, slumped inelegantly, and, in a worst-case ever scenario, possibly even snoring—with her mouth open.

'Oh, God,' she muttered as she scrambled off the sofa, pushing back her dishevelled hair from her face, trying to straighten her creased dress, searching for and then abandoning her kicked-off shoes. 'Not that—please.'

She flew barefoot along the passage to her bedroom, but it was empty. She halted, a hand going to her mouth like a disappointed child.

Only to realise that the communicating door was standing half-open for the first time in weeks, and someone was moving around in the adjoining room.

Marisa walked across and pushed the door wide.

Renzo was there, crossing with an armful of shirts to the leather suitcase lying open on the bed.

She said his name quietly, almost tentatively, and he turned immediately, his brows lifting.

'Marisa.' He might be casually dressed, in blue pants and a matching half-buttoned shirt, but that was where the informality ended, because his tone was polite to the point of bleakness. 'I disturbed you. *La prego di accettare le mie scuse.*'

'There's no need to apologise,' she said quickly. 'I was just dozing in the sunshine.' She swallowed. 'I thought—I understood you wouldn't be here today.'

'I did not intend to be.' He began to put the shirts into the case. 'But I find I now have to go to Stockholm, then on to Brussels, and I need some extra things for the trip.' He paused. 'But you need not worry,' he added coolly. 'As soon as my packing is done I shall be returning to Rome.'

'You mean—tonight?'

'I mean in the next half-hour.' His tone was brusque.

'But you haven't been home—to stay—for quite some time.' *Which I could itemise in days, hours, and minutes.*

'And that is a problem?' His mouth twisted. 'I thought it would be a relief.'

'But not for your father, certainly. He—must miss you very much.'

'If so, it is strange that he did not mention it when I spoke to him on the telephone this morning. As I do each day.'

But you've never asked to talk to me, she thought, pain slashing at her anew. *Or even sent me a message…*

She said slowly, 'I—didn't know that.'

'Certo che no. Obviously not. However, there is no need for you to concern yourself on his behalf. He understands the situation.'

'Then perhaps you'd explain it to me.' Marisa lifted her chin. 'I thought I would see you—at least sometimes.'

'Ah,' he said softly. 'On the occasions you were good enough to list for me, no doubt?' He shrugged. 'Unfortunately I have quite enough meetings and agendas in my working day, *mia cara.* I find, therefore, I have no wish for them to invade my private life.' And he resumed his task.

Marisa could feel her throat tightening. Was aware that she was beginning to tremble inside once more.

She said, 'And if I—asked you to stay?'

He turned slowly, his face expressionless.

He said quietly, 'Give me one good reason why I should do so.'

She looked back at him—at the hooded watchful eyes and the firm mouth that seemed as if they would never smile again. At the lean body that had taught her with gentleness and skill such an infinity of pleasure. And she could sense tension flowing like an electrical current between them.

Hurt, she thought. *Lonely…*

And her mind became suddenly and quite magically clear.

She said, softly and simply, 'Because I want you.'

She waited for him to come to her—to take her in his arms—but he stayed where he was, putting the last shirt almost too carefully into place.

And when he spoke his voice was harsh. 'Prove it.'

For a moment she stood, frozen, as she realised what he was asking. As all her insecurities threatened to come flooding back to defeat her.

She thought, *I can't…*

Only to recognise, once again, that she had no choice. That this could be her last chance, and she had to make it work—had to…

And if this is all he'll ever require from me, she thought, *then—so be it.*

Without haste, she began to release the first of the buttons that fastened the green dress from neckline to hem, holding his eyes with hers.

When she'd undone them all, she shrugged the dress from her shoulders, unhooked her bra and let it drop, cupping her breasts with her fingers, watching the flare of colour along his cheekbones. She allowed her hands to drift down to the edge of her lace briefs, and pause teasingly as she smiled at him, touching her parted lips with the tip of her tongue.

As she uncovered herself completely for the intensity of his gaze.

She moved slowly across the space that divided them until she was within touching distance, then, remembering what she'd believed was a dream, she put up a hand to stroke his hair, before running her fingers, delicate as the petals of a flower, down the strong line of his face to the faint roughness of his chin.

Her hands slid down, freeing the remaining buttons on his shirt, pushing its edges wide apart so that her fingers had the liberty to roam over his shoulders and bare chest. To feel the clench of his muscles and experience the sudden unsteadiness of his heartbeat as she deliberately tantalised the flat male nipples, feeling them harden as she moved closer to brush them with the aroused peaks of her own breasts.

She began to touch him with her lips, planting tiny fugitive kisses all over the warm skin as her hands slid down to deal with the waistband of his trousers, pausing, the breath catching in her throat, as her fingers flickered on the iron-hardness beneath the fabric and heard his soft groan of response.

She tugged at his zip, then dragged the heavy fabric over his hips and down to the floor, so that he could step free of it. Then her fingers returned to release his powerfully aroused shaft from the cling of his silk shorts and, shyly at first, to caress him.

She felt his hand move in its turn, tangling in the soft fall of her hair, holding her still as his mouth came down on hers, his kiss hard and deep, his tongue probing all her inner sweetness.

Then, still kissing her, he lifted her into his arms and carried her into the other room and across to their bed.

There was no gentle wooing this time. No slow ascent to pleasure. Their mutual hunger was too strong, too urgent for that. Instead, he stripped off his shorts and sank into her, filling her, as he gasped his need against her parted lips. And Marisa arched against him, her body surging in a reply as rapturous as it was uncontrollable.

Almost before they knew it they had reached the agonised extremity of desire. Marisa sobbed into his mouth as she felt the first quivers of sensual delight ripple through her innermost being, then deepen voluptuously until her entire body was shaken, torn apart by a series of harsh, exquisite convulsions bordering on savagery. She called his name, half in fear, half in exultation, as the sensations reached their peak, and heard in the next instant his hoarse cry of pleasure as his body found its own scalding, shuddering release in hers.

Afterwards they lay wrapped together, exchanging slow, sweet kisses.

'Was that proof enough?' Marisa asked at last, nibbling softly at his lower lip.

'Let us say a beginning, perhaps. No more,' Renzo returned lazily, his fingers curving round her breast. 'You may, however, become more convincing in Stockholm,' he added musingly. 'And by the time we reach Brussels I may even start to believe that I have a wife.'

Her eyes widened. 'You're taking me with you?'

'I have no intention of leaving you behind, *carissima*. Not again. Rosalia can pack for you while we're having dinner.'

'But I thought you wanted to leave straight away.'

'I have changed my mind,' he said. 'I expect to be far too exhausted to drive anywhere tonight.' He moved deliberately. Significantly. 'With your co-operation, of course, *signora*.'

'I'll try to be of assistance, *signore*,' Marisa whispered, and lifted her smiling mouth to his.

But later, when he'd fallen into a light sleep, and she lay in his arms, her head pillowed on his shoulder, Marisa found the echoing tremors of delight were being replaced by an odd sadness.

Wife, she thought. At last she was his wife. But for how long would he want her? Until she'd justified her presence in his life—when he would have no further cause to play the passionate husband?

That was the uneasy possibility that was now suggesting itself.

Because her insistence on leading an independent life once she'd given him an heir might well turn out to be a two-edged sword.

The purpose of their marriage achieved, Renzo, too, would be free to live as he wished—even to renew the bachelor existence that had caused so much trouble between them in the past.

She knew herself better now, she thought wryly, so she could recognise that it was not dislike or indifference which had created the rift at the start of their marriage, but plain old-fashioned jealousy.

Julia's reference to Lucia Gallo had quietly gnawed away at her throughout her engagement, freezing her emotions and convincing her she would rather do without him altogether than share his attentions with another girl.

Her heart told her that she would feel no differently if there was a similar situation in the future. Indeed, it would be worse now that she had learned the meaning of delight in his arms.

And she thought painfully, there would be nothing she could do about it next time but accept—and suffer.

And remember that once, for a little while, he'd belonged to her completely.

'My dear Signora Santangeli,' Dr Fabiano said gently. 'I am sure that you are allowing yourself to worry without necessity over this matter.' He put down his pen and smiled at her. He was a tall, rather stooped man with a goatee beard and kind eyes behind rimless glasses. 'You have only been married for just over a year, I think.'

'Yes,' Marisa admitted. 'But I thought—by now—it might have happened.'

Especially, she thought, as she and Renzo had spent the past three months in the passionate and uninhibited enjoyment of each other's bodies, without any precautions whatsoever.

He'd said nothing more about learning to be man and wife. The imperative now was the continuation of the Santangeli name.

'And we both want a child so much,' she added.

Renzo needs his heir, she thought, *and I—I just wish him to have his heart's desire. To please him in this special way because I love him so desperately. And because if I give him the son he wants then I might begin to mean more to him than just the girl currently in his bed.*

He—he might start to—love me in return. Because he's never said that he does, or even hinted it.

Not before. Not when we've been going half-crazy in each other's arms. And not afterwards when he holds me as we sleep. When perhaps I need to hear it most.

'Sometimes nature likes to take its own time,' the doctor said easily. 'Also, *signora*, your husband may not wish to share you just yet.' He paused. 'Or does he share your anxieties?'

'We haven't really discussed it,' Marisa said. In fact, if she was completely honest, she admitted silently, the subject hadn't been mentioned at all. Or not out loud, anyway.

However physically attuned she and Renzo might have become, there were still no-go areas in the marriage. Subjects they walked around rather than introduced as topics into the conversation.

But she was aware that Renzo watched her quite often, as if he was—waiting for something.

She took a breath, 'I expect it's all my imagination, *dottore*, but as the weeks pass I do find myself wondering if everything's all right. With me, that is.'

He looked surprised. 'I have your notes from your doctor in England. Your general health seems excellent, and at the moment, Signora Santangeli, I would say you were glowing.'

'I feel fine,' she said, flushing a little. 'I suppose I'm just looking for—reassurance.'

'Because this would be a precious child.' He smiled at her. 'Perhaps a future Marchese Santangeli. I understand, of course.'

He paused thoughtfully. 'There are, of course, tests we can do—examinations that can be carried out. Usually I would not recommend them after so short a marriage—but if they put your mind at rest they could be useful. What do you think?'

She said, 'I think they could be exactly what I need.'

'Then I will make the necessary arrangements.' He pulled a pad towards him and began to scribble something on it. 'You will naturally tell your husband what you are planning?'

'Of course,' she said.

When it's all over and done with, and I know that it's just a question of patience and perseverance, because everything's fine. I'll tell him then, and we'll laugh about it.

* * *

Marisa was thoughtful as she drove home later. Uneasy too.

But she had to believe she'd just made a positive move. One that could change her life for the better.

As if it hadn't already altered in innumerable ways, she thought wryly. The fact that she had a driving licence and a car of her own now was only one of them. Yet she couldn't help remembering Renzo's quiet words as he had put the keys in her hand. 'A step towards your freedom, *mia cara*.'

Had he been reminding her that, despite the passion they shared, their present intimacy was only transient, and that one day their paths would permanently diverge?

No, she told herself, keep being positive. Apart from anything else, she was now the accepted mistress of the Villa Proserpina. If the staff had looked at her askance in the days of her estrangement from Renzo, she now basked in their approval.

And she had Zio Guillermo's whole-hearted support too. She could still see the expression of joyful incredulity on his face when she'd entered the *salotto* that first evening, shy but radiant, with Renzo's arm around her and his hand resting on her hip in a gesture of unmistakable possession.

And she had heard his muttered, 'At last—may the good God be praised.'

Later, when they could not be overheard, Ottavia too had whispered teasingly, 'I see the fight is over, *cara*, but I will not ask who won.'

And she'd started to travel too. Whenever possible Renzo insisted on taking her with him on his business trips, and gradually, with his encouragement, she'd begun to feel less gauche on the inevitable social occasions, was able to hold her own at cocktail parties and formal dinners, even once overhearing herself described as 'charming'.

When she'd repeated this to Renzo later, he'd merely grinned wickedly and drawled, 'I am glad that they cannot know precisely how charming you are at this moment, *mia bella*,' letting his mouth drift slowly and sensuously down her naked body.

The apartment in Rome was no longer unknown territory for her either. But her initial visit had almost sparked off a quarrel between them. Because that first night there, when he'd taken her in his arms, she'd found it difficult to relax, her imagination going haywire as she wondered, despite herself, who else had shared this particular bed with him.

'Is something wrong?' His hand had captured her chin, making her look at him.

'It's nothing,' she'd said, too quickly. 'Really—I'm fine.'

His mouth had tightened. 'Then remain so by avoiding unwise speculation,' he'd advised coldly. 'Because no other woman has ever stayed here. Not on moral grounds,' he'd added cynically. 'But because in the past I have always valued my privacy too highly. Perhaps I was wise.' And he'd turned over and gone to sleep.

He'd woken her around dawn, offering reconciliation with the ardour of his lovemaking, and it had never been mentioned again.

But Marisa had seen it as a warning that references to his past were now strictly taboo. And presumably the same sanction would apply to any future *amours* he might engage in.

He would be discreet, and would expect her, in turn, to be blind. Probably dumb too, she thought, and sighed.

But whatever happened she would still be his wife, with all the courtesies her status demanded. She would wear his ring, and manage his homes and raise their children.

Those were her rights, she told herself. No one could take them away from her.

And in spite of the heat of the day, she felt herself shivering.

'You are going where?' Ottavia asked, her brows lifting in astonishment.

'To the Clinica San Francesco,' Marisa said, her throat tightening. 'Just for a day—overnight, perhaps. Apparently Dr Fabiano wants me to have another more detailed examination.'

She looked down at her hands. 'And as I may not feel like driving immediately afterwards, I wondered if you'd be good enough to take me there in your car—and bring me back.'

'But this should be for Lorenzo to do,' the *signora* protested. 'He should not be in Zurich, but here with you. I am astonished that he should absent himself at such a time.'

Marisa was silent for a moment, then she said reluctantly, 'Renzo doesn't know.'

Ottavia's jaw dropped. 'You have not told him?'

Marisa shook her head. 'Not about the initial tests, or this—new development.' She paused. 'I cried off from Zurich—told him I had a tummy upset because I didn't want to worry him.'

'I think you should worry for yourself,' Ottavia told her grimly. 'When he finds out he will be very angry.' She groaned. 'Guillermo too, I think.' She took Marisa's hands in hers. 'Be advised, *cara*. You know where Renzo can be contacted. Ask him to come home and tell him everything.'

'But there may not be anything to tell,' Marisa said. 'In which case I'll have brought him back from an important round of meetings for no reason.' She tried to smile. 'He might not be very pleased about that either.'

'Another risk you should take.'

'I'd much rather deal with it by myself. There are so many problems in the financial markets these days that I don't want to burden him with anything else. Especially if it turns out to be some kind of—glitch.'

She looked appealingly at the other woman. 'So, will you do this for me? I—I have no one else I can ask.'

Ottavia sighed. 'When you put it like that—yes.' She hesitated. 'But understand this, Marisa, I will not lie for you on this matter. If Renzo returns and asks where you are, or Guillermo comes back early from Milano with the same question, then I shall tell them. *Capisce?*'

'Yes,' Marisa said steadily. 'I do understand. But I'm sure it won't be necessary, and I shall be back here long before either of them.' She took a deep breath. 'No harm done.'

She was praying wordlessly, as she'd done every day since the first tests, that it would be no more than the truth.

CHAPTER THIRTEEN

SHE couldn't stop crying. Ever since she'd looked at the grave, concerned faces at the foot of her bed, and realised that her inexplicable uneasiness was fully justified after all, tears had never been far away.

And now they were there, possessing, destroying her. Eyes blinded, throat raw with the long choking sobs, she could not… stop.

Although she'd been icily, deadly calm when they'd told her what she'd insisted on knowing, dismissing their protests that she should not be alone—that her husband, that Signor Lorenzo must be sent for while she heard what the tests and examinations had actually revealed.

When they had admitted with the utmost reluctance that there was something—not a simple matter of infertility alone, which could be treated, but a malformation of some kind—which, in the unlikely event that she ever conceived, would not allow her to carry the child full-term.

She'd said, in a voice she had not recognised, 'But there must be something to rectify the condition.' She'd bitten her lip until she tasted blood. 'Surely some kind of operation…?'

And had listened to the gentle, lengthy explanations, full of medical terms that she did not fully comprehend. But then she didn't have to. Because she understood only too well that beneath the compassion and the technicalities they were telling her no. There was nothing. Nothing…

As somehow she had already known, with some strange, inexplicable female instinct. She'd felt that strange fear like a black shadow in the corner of her life, getting closer with every day that passed, until it blotted out the sun and left her in the cold dark.

But at least now, she could be alone with her misery—her aching, uncontrollable despair.

The nursing staff, so hideously well-meaning as they fluttered around her with offers of water to drink, to wash her face, to help swallow a sedative, had finally been persuaded to leave. And they'd clearly been glad to go, hardly knowing what to do for this patient—this girl—this wife, *Santa Madonna*, of such an important man. So powerful, so attractive, so virile. Yet doomed, it seemed, through no one's fault, to be the last of his ancient name.

Small wonder that she felt such grief, they agreed as they left, glancing back at the slim, hunched shape in the bed. For who would wish to disappoint such a husband?

He had been sent for, of course. The Director had intervened personally, horrified that such information should have been given to Signor Santangeli's young wife in his absence. And now he was on his way.

But in the meantime the *signora* needed comfort, and who better than an older woman, a member of the family—her husband's own grandmother, no less—who was at the Clinica, the Director had learned, visiting a friend.

Which was why Marisa, having wept herself hollow, looked up from her soaking pillow as her door opened and saw Teresa Barzati advancing into the room.

She said in a small, cracked voice, 'What are you doing here?'

'I came to visit the Contessa Morico, who is recovering from a hip replacement. And now I find I have another errand of mercy.' The *signora* deposited herself in the room's solitary armchair, her thin lips stretched in an unpleasant smile. 'To bring you the consolation of a grandmother. Or should I keep that for Lorenzo, when he arrives from Zurich?'

Marisa made herself sit up and push the damp strands of hair back from her white face. Made herself look stonily back at the last person in the world she wanted to see. 'I don't think Renzo will wish to see you any more than I do,' she said. 'After the trouble you tried to make for us.'

The *signora*'s smile widened. 'I doubt you have the right to speak for my grandson,' she said. 'Not any longer. And the trouble you find yourself in at this moment has quite eclipsed anything I could do. Because you have failed, *signora.* According to the rumours all over the hospital you are incapable of bearing children.' She paused. 'Or, by some miracle, are these whispers wrong?'

Marisa thought with an odd detachment, as the older woman's eyes bored remorselessly into her, that it was like being mesmerised by a cobra. That even though you knew the death blow would be delivered at any moment you still could not look away. Or move to safety.

The stranger's voice she'd heard earlier said, 'No, they're—not wrong.'

Nonna Teresa nodded with a kind of terrible satisfaction. 'And what a heavy blow that will be for the Santangeli pride.' She paused. 'For a while, anyway. Until they acknowledge the mistake they have made with you and move on.'

She sighed. 'Poor Guillermo. I almost pity him. This alliance—planned for so long, arranged with such care—totally in ruins. The delicate path that he and Lorenzo must now tread, so that they do not appear too heartless when they bring the marriage to its end.'

'What are you talking about?'

'About you, Marisa. What else? About how Lorenzo will set you aside so that he can marry again. And next time, if he has sense,' she added cuttingly, 'he will choose some strong, fertile Italian bride who will do his bidding and know her place.'

'That won't happen.' She'd thought that she was quite empty, devoid of all emotion. But she had not allowed for the power of a different kind of pain. The kind that cut so deeply that you felt you might bleed to death, slowly and endlessly. She rallied herself. 'Lorenzo doesn't believe in divorce. He's always said so.'

'Divorce, no. That would indeed be too shocking,' Nonna Teresa said smoothly. 'But there are always grounds for annulment to be found, if you have influence in the right places. And Lorenzo and his father are supremely influential.' Her laugh was melodious. 'A barren wife will prove small obstacle to their plans for the future, believe me.'

Marisa stared at her in a kind of awful fascination. She said, 'How can you do this, *signora*? How can you come here at a time like this and say these things to me.'

'Because I almost feel sorry for you,' Signora Barzati returned. 'You were bought for a purpose, as you admitted yourself. And like most items that are damaged or otherwise unsuitable, you are about to be returned. But your departure will be cushioned,' she added negligently. 'You will not be dismissed as a pauper. Guillermo will make sure of that. In spite of this unsuitable liaison with the Alesconi woman, he still has sufficient respect for my late daughter's memory to adhere to her wishes in that regard.'

'I don't believe one word of this.' Marisa's voice was shaking. She reached up to the bell beside her bed. 'I won't believe it. Now I'd like you to get out.'

The *signora* stayed where she was. 'But I am trying to be your friend, Marisa. To explain frankly what lies ahead for you. I thought you would be grateful.'

'Grateful to be told that I'm going to be thrown aside by my husband like a piece of junk?' Marisa asked hoarsely.

'Hardly,' Nonna Teresa said reprovingly. 'That is not the Santangeli way. I am certain he will be kind to you. As long as you understand you no longer have any part in his life and accept your departure with grace.'

She played with the ring on her hand.

Another emerald, Marisa thought, her eyes drawn against her will to the green flash of the stone. And for the rest of my life I shall always hate emeralds.

'Besides, this should be good news for you,' the *Signora* went on musingly. 'You never wished to be Lorenzo's wife, and made your indifference to him quite clear. In front of him, too, as I recall. Now you will be single again, and he can find another wife, more to his taste.' She smiled, her glance raking the tearstained face and slender body. 'It should not be difficult. And then everyone will have what they want, is that not so?'

The questioning silence seemed endless. Then she said softly, 'Or perhaps not. Is it possible, my dear Marisa, that you have had a change of heart? Can you have mistaken my grandson's performance of his marital duties for something warmer and been foolish enough to fall in love with him?'

She laughed again, contemptuously. 'I do believe it is so. What a truly pathetic child you are if you imagine you have ever been more to Lorenzo than a willing body in his bed. One of so many.' She examined a nail. 'And although he may have been assiduous in his attentions while he thought you might provide the Santangeli heir, now that he knows the truth he will no longer have to pretend. And how will you like that?'

Marisa felt naked under the scorn in those inimical eyes. The fact that her heart was breaking was not enough for this monstrous woman, she thought, fighting sudden nausea. Every last shred of pride and dignity had to be stripped from her too.

She said slowly, 'You've always hated me. And you didn't like my mother. I can remember things you said when I was small, and Zia Maria being upset about them.'

'You are quite right,' the older woman agreed. 'I detested your mother, and wished my daughter had never met her. My husband was a fool, and worse than a fool to insist that she should go to a school where she could make such friends—betray me and all I held dear. I never forgave him for it. However, I made sure that my child, my beloved Maria, married well—only to find she intended to contaminate the Santangeli blood with that of an outsider, an enemy.' She brought a clenched fist down on the arm of her chair. '*Dio mio*—that she could do such a thing.'

'But I never wished to be your enemy, *signora*.' Marisa was shaken by the older woman's furious vehemence. 'And nor did my parents.'

'You? You think I ever cared about you? It was what you were—you and all your family.' Signora Barzati's voice rose. 'You were British—part of the cursed nation that caused my most beloved brother, noble in every way, to die as a prisoner of war in North Africa and to be buried in some unmarked grave in the desert. To know that you were destined for my grandson was an insult to his glorious memory.'

Oh, God, Marisa thought, dry-mouthed. *This is crazy. The war's been over for more than sixty years. Teresa was little more than a child when it happened. And yet to carry such a grudge—to hate all this time. It beggars belief. But it explains so much, too.*

She said quietly, 'But there has been peace for a long time, *signora*. And forgiveness.'

'Virtues you admire, perhaps?' Signora Barzati had herself

under control again, leaning back in her chair. 'And soon you will have a chance to practise them, if you choose. Will you do so, Marisa? Will you let Lorenzo think that you spoke nothing but the truth when you said you did not love him and did not care about your marriage? Will you sign the annulment papers and leave peacefully, taking your sad little secret with you?

'And when you are living alone in England, without even the illusion of Lorenzo's love to comfort you, will you forgive him for not caring for you in return—and for letting you go so easily? You could do all that and earn some goodwill on your departure, if you wished. Even a little respect.'

She paused. 'Or you could make more trouble by attempting to remain where you are not wanted—and of no further use. By embarrassing Lorenzo with your protestations of devotion. Nothing will prevent you being sent away. But you have a choice in the way it is done.' She smiled. 'In your shoes I would go of my own accord. I would jump, as they say, before I was pushed. But the decision, *naturalamente*, is yours.'

She rose, smoothing the skirt of her dark dress. 'I say this for your own good, you understand. There is no sense in making a bad situation worse, and I am sure you see that. That you are not such a fool as to…hope. Because the Santangeli family will do as it must, and you can either survive—or be crushed.'

She walked to the door, then turned, her voice throbbing with sudden emotion. 'And if you think I have been cruel, imagine how you would feel, holding out your arms to the man you desire more than all the world and watching him turn away. Knowing that he will never want you again. If you still do not believe me, try it when Lorenzo comes here. Reach for him—if you dare.'

And she was gone.

By the time she heard the faint hubbub in the corridor signalling that Renzo had arrived, Marisa had prepared herself. Made sure she was under control. That she would not weep. Would not beg.

And that she would not take the risk of reaching for him and being rejected. That most of all.

After the *signora* had left she had lain, staring into space, with eyes that burned and saw nothing.

With a mind that had heard only the ugly, corrosive words that had told her what she'd already known in her heart. That the doctors' verdict had not simply passed sentence on her hope of a baby, but also on her marriage.

That Teresa Barzati, however uncaring and malign, had spoken only the truth. If she could not fulfil the purpose for which she'd been married she would have to step aside. She would have no choice.

Therefore she must try not to think of these last rapturous months with Renzo. Must remember only that he would have seen them ultimately as a means to an end. That an eager and co-operative wife was much to be preferred to a girl who received his advances with sullen resentment.

But that sexual passion, however skilful and generous, did not equate with the kind of love that could weather all the storms that life sent.

It would be so much easier for me now, she thought with dull weariness, *if I'd let myself go on thinking that I hated him. That I didn't want any part of marriage to him.*

If I hadn't let myself love him, and hope that one day he would tell me that he loved me in return.

Yet he never did. Even in our most intimate moments he never said the words I longed to hear. And now he never will. And that, somehow, will be the worst thing I have to bear.

Because I need his arms round me. Need to feel the shelter of his warmth and strength.

But it wasn't only the loss of his lovemaking—those moments when he lifted her up to touch the stars—that she would mourn. There were all the small things—her hand in his when they walked together, the private smiles across a table or a room. The conversations about everything and nothing as they shared the sofa in the *salotto*, or lay wrapped in each other's arms, all passion spent.

Learning, she'd thought, to be husband and wife, just as he'd once suggested. Forging a bond that could never be broken.

And now, because of nature's cruellest trick, her dreams of the future lay in pieces.

And somehow she had to find the strength to walk away and build a different kind of life. Without him.

A withdrawal that would have to begin as soon as he came through that door.

She had done what she could to look calm and in control, even if her emotions were like shards of broken glass. She'd washed her face, and put drops in her eyes to conceal the worst ravages. She'd changed into a fresh nightgown and brushed her hair. Even added a touch of lipstick to her pale mouth.

He came slowly into the room, closed the door and leaned against it, staring at her, his eyes shadowed, his mouth a bleak line.

Marisa realised she'd been holding her breath, praying silently that he would come across the room and take her in his arms. That he would somehow do the unthinkable—the impossible—and make it all right.

But her prayer was not answered, and instead she heard herself say quietly, 'Have the doctors told you?'

'Yes,' he said. 'I now know everything.'

She looked down at the edge of the crisp white sheet. 'I—I'm so sorry.'

'And I am sorry too,' he said. 'That you did not tell me of your concerns. That you chose instead to bear this alone, so that I had to be…summoned to hear these things. Why did you do this?'

'Because I didn't want to worry you,' she said. 'Not if it was all in my imagination, as Dr Fabiano originally thought.'

'But later,' he said. 'When it became more than a suspicion. You still let me walk away—leave for Zurich without you.'

'It might still have been just a glitch.' She could hear the pleading note in her voice and suppressed it. 'Something easily put right. And life goes on.'

But not life inside me—life that you put there…

'Yes,' he said. 'Life goes on.' He was very still for a moment, then he sighed, and straightened. 'I have been told that I must not stay too long. That more than anything you need rest. Accordingly, the consultant has recommended that you remain here for another day. So I will come for you tomorrow, after I have spoken with my father, and then we must talk, you and I.'

'Couldn't you do that now?' she said. 'Say what you have to say?'

'It is too soon,' he said. 'I have to clear my mind—to think. But tomorrow it will be different. And then we will speak.'

'Until tomorrow, then.' With a superhuman effort she managed to say the words without her voice cracking in the middle.

He looked at her, and for a moment she saw the faint ghost of his old smile. 'Until then,' he said. 'Maria Lisa.'

She watched the door close behind him, and the breath left her body in a shaking sob.

Yes, she thought, tomorrow would indeed be different…

Amalfi looked even more beautiful with the approach of autumn, although Marisa still wasn't sure why she'd decided to return there, when the obvious course had been to fly straight back to England. After all, she was co-owner of a gallery in London, so there was work waiting for her. And everyone said that work was a solace—didn't they? So if she worked hard enough and long enough the pain might begin to subside.

Except that she wasn't working. She was sitting under a lemon tree in a garden, looking at the sea. The wheel had turned full circle, and she was back at the beginning, more alone than ever.

Leaving the Clinica had been much easier than she'd expected. After all, she'd hardly been a patient needing medical sanction to be discharged. So she had simply woken after a sedative-induced night's sleep, dressed and walked out, moving confidently, her head high. Bearing, she'd hoped, no resemblance to the broken, weeping girl of yesterday.

She'd taken a taxi to the Villa Proserpina—a quick phone call having ascertained that Signor Lorenzo had left very early that morning to visit his father the Marchese in Milano, and that therefore the coast was clear.

No one at the house had seemed anxious about her absence, probably because they thought she'd decided to follow Renzo to Zurich after all.

Once in their suite it had been the work of minutes to pack a bag and retrieve her passport. And a second's pause to leave the letter she had struggled to write the previous evening on the mantelpiece in the *salotto* for Renzo to find on his return.

She had kept it brief, stating only that it was impossible, under the changed circumstances, for their marriage to continue, and that she would sign whatever was necessary to obtain their mutual freedom as soon as her lawyers received the papers. Adding that she wished him well.

Then she'd gone downstairs, walked out into the sunshine, got into her car and driven away.

It was better this way. Better to take the initiative, as she kept telling herself, even though leaving like that, without a proper word to anyone, like a thief in the night, had torn her apart. But it had been infinitely preferable to the anguish of an interview with Renzo—hearing from his own lips that her brief shining happiness had to end.

And Signora Barzati had said he would be generous, therefore he would hardly begrudge her the car he'd given her, or the money she would need to spend in order to remove herself from his life.

Not that she'd spent that much. Just petrol, her meals, and payment for the past three nights in a simple room above the *trattoria* in the village. No five-star luxury for this trip, she thought. Not that it had ever mattered to her. For her, the greatest luxury of all had always been the man she loved, lying beside her in the night.

But she wouldn't be staying long in this place where she'd once found a kind of peace, because, to her astonishment, the Casa Adriana had been sold.

She'd learned this from Mrs Morton, who was still fighting the good fight in the garden, even though her days there were numbered, because, as she said, the new owners were bound to have their own outside staff.

'The builders move in next week,' she'd told Marisa. 'I'm almost sorry, although it's good that such a lovely place will realise its full potential at last.' She smiled. 'Someone else must have fallen in love with the view, my dear.'

Marisa made herself smile back. 'Well, I hope Adriana approves of them, that's all.'

'Ah,' Mrs Morton said softly. 'So it was that old story that drew you back?' She paused. 'Will you tell me something, my dear? Because I've often wondered. When you were here before, there was a young man who used to come and stand at the gate each day and watch you. Tall and very attractive. Did you ever meet him?'

The breath caught in Marisa's throat. 'Someone at the gate?' she managed. 'I never knew…'

'He would never come in,' said Mrs Morton. 'Which made me

sorry, because it seemed to me that he was just as sad as you were alone, and I hoped that somehow you might find each other.'

Hurt, Marisa thought, *and lonely*. Ottavia had apparently been right. She looked at the kind face and forced a smile. 'We did—for a while,' she said. 'But it didn't last.'

'Because you were already married, perhaps? I don't judge, my dear, but I can't help notice you're wearing a ring now.'

'Yes,' Marisa said quietly. 'Exactly because I was…married.'

Mrs Morton had completed her tasks and left, returning to her apartment, her husband, the waiting drink on the terrace and the comfortable discussion of the day's events. Her marriage, in fact.

And I should leave too, Marisa thought, sighing. *In fact, I should never have come back to this place, with all its resonances. Because there's no comfort or peace here for me any more, and I was a fool to expect it.*

I don't have faith and hope to sustain me, as Adriana did, and I can't sit here, letting my life drift by, eternally waiting for something that reality and my own common sense tells me will never happen.

She thought again of what Mrs Morton had said. That Renzo—*Renzo*—had followed her here each day and never said anything—then or later…

If I'd only known, she thought, and stopped with a little gasp. Because, she realised suddenly, she had known. She'd been aware, so many times, of something—some presence—that had made her feel less lonely but which she'd dismissed, telling herself that she was simply letting Adriana's legend get to her rather too much.

She lifted her head and stared at the restless sea, her eyes stinging with the tears she'd refused to let herself shed since she'd left Tuscany.

Oh, darling, she whispered silently. *Why didn't you come in? Why didn't you walk down the garden and sit beside me?*

Not that it would have made any real difference, she reminded herself in anguish. Their story would still be ending, like that of Adriana and Filippo, in separation and loss. But at least they would have had all those other wasted months together. Another store of memories for her to draw on in the utter blankness ahead.

'Maria Lisa.' She might have imagined his voice, born out of her own desperate yearning, but not the hand on her shoulder.

'Renzo!' She turned to face him, acutely aware of the blurred eyes and trembling mouth she hadn't allowed him to see at their last meeting. 'What are you doing here?'

'Following my wife,' he said. He came round the bench and sat beside her. 'And I would have been here much sooner if I had not seen your passport was gone and wasted time looking for you in England.' The dark, haggard face tried to smile. 'Your business partner now thinks I am insane, bursting in on him like a wild man and demanding you back.'

He paused. 'And then I remembered this place, and I wondered.'

'Oh, God,' she said hoarsely. 'Couldn't you have shown a little mercy and just—let me go?'

'Never,' he said. 'Not while I have life. How could you not know that?'

'But I can't be your wife. Not any longer,' she whispered. 'For your family's sake you have to have an heir, and I can't have children. You know that. So you have to find someone else to marry, who won't fail you. Someone you can love—' She broke off, swallowing. 'And I can't— I won't stand in your way.'

'But you do stand in the way, Maria Lisa,' he said gently. 'And you always will, *mi amore*. Because all the love that I have is for you. I see no one else, hear no other voice, want only you.'

His shaking hands framed her face as he kissed her wet eyes, her cheeks and parted, unhappy lips.

'Believe me,' he whispered between kisses. 'My love, my sweet one, believe me, and come back to me.'

'But when you came to see me in hospital,' she said huskily, 'you were so cold—like a stranger.'

'They told me that you were heartbroken,' he said. 'That it had been impossible to calm you. Therefore it was impressed upon me that I could not give way. That, as your husband, I had to be strong for us both or your emotional recovery might be impeded. So I dared not come near you. Dared not touch you or kiss you, *carissima*, or I too would have been lost. Because I knew that all I wanted was to lie beside you, put my head on your breasts and weep. I told myself—tomorrow will be different. Tomorrow we can find comfort in our love for each other.' He gave a shuddering sigh. 'And then I came back from Zurich with Papa and you were gone, leaving just that little note. And then I did weep, Maria Lisa, sitting alone in the room we'd shared. Because I thought that maybe I was wrong, and that you had not begun to love me during these last happy weeks together. That, after all, your independence mattered more to you than I did.'

He shook his head. 'But I also remembered all your warmth and sweetness—how Zurich had been hell without you. And I told myself that I would get you back, no matter how long it took or whatever obstacles were in the way.'

She touched his cheek with hesitant fingertips. 'I was so unhappy I just wanted to die,' she said. 'But it makes no difference.' She paused. 'Darling, your grandmother came to see me, and even though I hated everything she said I knew she was right. That if I loved you I would have to give you up.'

'She telephoned me,' he said grimly. 'Telling me that she grieved for me but hoped, once you had gone, I would be sensible and do my duty.'

'But don't you see?' she said in a low voice. 'If you hadn't wanted a child you wouldn't have married me or anyone else.'

'That may have been true once,' Renzo admitted wryly. 'But when you came to stand beside me in church, and I put my ring on your finger, I knew I would not have changed places with anyone on earth. And that somehow I had to persuade you to feel the same.' He shook his head. 'But that was my failure, and I can never forgive myself for it, or for what followed. Those weeks of our honeymoon were a living nightmare, *carissima*. I wanted so badly to put things right between us, but I did not know how to begin.'

'Was that why you used to follow me, but never let me know?'

'I needed to find out what drew you here every day,' Renzo said simply. 'And as you seemed contented I could not intrude and spoil it for you.'

'But if you felt like that,' she said shakily, 'why—why did you send me away?'

He said roughly, 'Because I heard you crying and I thought you could not face the prospect of having to live with me as my wife. That I had scared and disgusted you too much.'

'No,' she said softly. 'I was crying because I knew I'd really wanted our baby so that there would be someone in my life I could love without reservation.'

'And I wanted you to love me,' he said. 'To give me another chance to make you happy. That was what I tried to say in all those letters you did not read.'

He slipped off the bench and knelt beside her, his head in her lap.

'So will you take me now, Maria Lisa?' he asked, his voice uneven. 'Will you believe that our marriage means more to me than anything in the world, and love me as I love you, *mi adorata*, and even after this sadness live with me, let us build our future together?'

'Yes,' she said, stroking his hair. 'Oh, my dearest love, yes.'

Perhaps Adriana was right, she thought, as later they walked from the garden, hand in hand, knowing they would never come back there. That they had all they needed.

Perhaps faith and hope would always prevail. And then healing could begin.

Or that was what she would believe.

And Maria Lisa Santangeli smiled up at her husband.

CPSIA information can be obtained at www.ICGtesting.com
Printed in the USA
LVOW13s2120300414
383887LV00008BA/1062/P

Lowertown

also by Richard A. Thompson

Fiddle Game
Frag Box
Big Wheat

Lowertown

A Herman Jackson Mystery

Richard A. Thompson

This book is a work of fiction. The names, characters, and incidents are products of the writer's imagination or have been used fictitiously and are not to be construed as real. Any resemblance to persons, living or dead, actual events, or organizations is entirely coincidental.

Lowertown: A Herman Jackson Mystery

Cover photo: Michael Thomson
Design: John Toren

Forty Press, LLC
427 Van Buren Street
Anoka, MN 55303
www.fortypress.com

ISBN 978-1-938473-09-8

Library of Congress Cataloging-in-Publications Data
Library of Congress Control Number: 2013943028
Thomson, Richard
Lowertown/Richard A. Thompson
First Edition: October 2013
10 9 8 7 6 5 4 3 2 1

For Andrea

Chapter One

The Tenacity of Bad Judgment

Public defenders don't believe in evil. Not the ones who keep at it, anyway. Their clients, they say, are all just victims of circumstance and bad luck, poor souls caught up in the cosmic equivalent of a bad hair day.

Maybe they have to think that way, just to keep their sanity. They are, after all, highly overworked and underpaid. Even when they are skilled and dedicated, they seldom win a case. In fact, they seldom even get a compliment on one. And they never, ever get to choose their clients.

I don't have any of those problems. I'm a bail bondsman. My name is Herman Jackson, and I work with whomever I damn well please. And if some of them are evil from the ground up, at least I have no illusions about it.

"Herman, all I'm asking is that you talk to him. How bad could that be?"

The woman making the plea was a public defender named Trish Hanover. She was a tallish, thin-faced blond whose rather ordinary features were made attractive by her perpetual look of eagerness and energy. She wore her hair pulled back in a French roll, and she wore a severely tailored gray suit with an electric blue silk blouse. Considering her budget, I figured it was probably her best outfit, put on just to charm me, as was the radiant smile. And I was charmed. At the moment, she wore a tiny gold stud on one nostril. It matched her earrings, and I took it to be an act of mild rebellion at the severe dress

code of the court, where she would not be allowed any such tribal baubles. If so, it was a little forced.

We were having a late breakfast at the last of the downtown Saint Paul greasy spoons. The plastic-laminated menu said they served breakfast any time, so I ordered steak and eggs in the Middle Ages. The waitress was not amused. Trish at least pretended to be. She beamed an intense, approving smile at me and locked her eyes with mine. Again the charm. Though I liked her well enough, I had never thought of her in any way but professionally, and I didn't know how to react. I looked down at my coffee and pretended I had just noticed the secret of life floating around on top of the oily black liquid.

"What about it, Herman?" she said.

"Look, Trish, from what I hear, the DA has an iron-clad cinch on a conviction here, and your guy has to be smart enough to know that. If I bond him out, he's guaranteed to skip, and I'm out a very large chunk of change. I can't believe you're asking me to do that."

"I only asked you to talk to him, Herman."

"Yeah, right." I took a sip of the coffee and found that I had been wrong; the secret of life was not there.

"How much money can you lose talking to somebody?" she said.

"Ask anybody who has a stock broker."

The smile was still there, but her lips thinned. I could see she was getting very frustrated with me but was trying hard to stay sweet.

"Anyway," I said, "if I talk to him—not that I'm saying I will—then what?"

Her face brightened a notch.

"Maybe you'll see he's not such a bad guy."

"I'm so sure."

"And the DA's case isn't half as good as he thinks it is. A lot, and I mean an *awful* lot, of the evidence was obtained illegally."

"Inadmissible is not the same as invalid, Trish. People can be totally railroaded and still be guilty, you know."

"You're a legal scholar now?"

"The best."

"Give me an example, then."

"Sacco and Vanzetti. Julius and Ethel Rosenberg. They were as guilty as unoriginal sin, but the cases against them were completely bogus."

"That was a long time ago, a whole other era."

"Charles Manson."

"Also another era."

"All right then, in our era. Bad cops or bad prosecutors can taint every shred of evidence they touch or even allude to, and that still doesn't make the suspect innocent."

"This isn't L.A., Herman."

"No. But are you seriously telling me you think this guy is innocent?"

"I don't know, Herman. I really don't. You know, there's some set of circumstances that can make you, me, or anybody else into a vicious killer. Or make us look like one, anyway."

"I've never bought that."

"Oh, all right. But even so, there's something about him, some…"

Her words trailed off, and she got a look like a person remembering some deep secret from early childhood, something wonderful but also slightly disturbing. Had this guy charmed the sense right out of her? If the cops and the newspapers were right, that's what he typically did to his victims. If Trish had fallen under his spell, I felt sad about it. I liked and respected her, and I hated to see her being made into a patsy. Which was all the more reason for distancing myself from this case.

"The man is evil, Trish. From what I hear, he practically has a tattoo on his forehead advertising it. Do you really want to be a party to letting him flee the jurisdiction?"

"If you want to use that kind of talk, Herman, everybody is evil."

I rolled my eyes.

"Martin Luther said so."

"I'm a Neo-Buddhist Skeptic," I said.

"So did Robert Penn Warren. 'Man is conceived in evil and proceeds from the stench of the diaper bag to the stench of the shroud.'" She waved her hand. "Or something like that."

"But some are way more evil than others, including, as I recall, the character you just quoted. The answer is no."

"Aw come on, Herman. One little talk, and then you do whatever you want. Please? I'll make it worth your while." Again the take-no-prisoners smile, and again I was charmed.

"Come over to my apartment tomorrow night, and I'll make you a nice home-cooked dinner." She wrote her address on the back of one of her cards. "How long has it been?"

"One year, two months, and three days, but who's counting?" We both knew what she was referring to. That was the length of time since Anne Packard had gone east, to write for the *New York Times*. We thought our relationship had more to it than old-fashioned jungle lust, but emails and long-distance phone calls had proved insufficient to hold it together.

"I know how you feel, Herman. I really do. A blind person could see it. But hasn't it been long enough?"

"Has it? I'm new at this game. I don't know the rules yet, much less how the smart money bets."

"Come and have a nice dinner with me. No strings. She would want you to."

I had to admit, that was probably true. Anne would wish me happiness, whatever that meant. Trish put her hand over mine and gave me a different kind of intense look, one that radiated more genuine good will and concern than I thought any one person had a right to.

"Tomorrow night, Herman. Seven-ish?"

"If I talk to Valento," I said.

"Please?"

With or without the dinner, you couldn't turn down a please that looked like that. I couldn't, anyway.

⁂

Ray Valento was on the other side of the Mississippi, in the Hennepin County jail. But they didn't put him in the new, enlightened facility, where the arrestees are allowed to check themselves in, get their orange coveralls and sandals, and find their assigned wards by reading prompts from video monitors. Instead, they held him across the street in the old dungeon-like jail, with windowless stone walls, small cells, and high, intimidating security. The spaces there were reserved for violent criminals, suspects with blatant attitude problems, and people who had just pissed off the staff in one way or another. A uniformed cop escorted me through a tunnel under the street, then up in a sterile-looking elevator to a series of dim corridors with mauve-colored stone walls. The place managed to smell damp and musty at the same time. *Dust on the Dismal Swamp* flashed into my mind. Our footsteps rang on the old terrazzo floors, and our voices echoed.

"You going to bond this piece of shit?" The cop was young, big, and serious looking, as was most of the guard staff. Every Minneapolis cop begins his or her career doing a year as a jail guard. Few find that they want to stay with it.

"I don't know yet. I promised a friend I'd talk to him, is all."

"The Minneapolis bondsmen all turned him down, you know."

"Really?" I didn't know. "Why is that?"

"Maybe because we asked them to. You want to keep being welcome over here, maybe you'll do the same."

"I don't come over to this side of the river much. I don't get the scuttlebutt. Tell me what I'm missing."

"He's a bad actor, is what you're missing."

"Well, there's never been any shortage of them."

"Not like this guy. I don't know if the DA can make this case or not," he said, "but if he gets back on the street while we're waiting to find out, something bad is going to happen, if you get my meaning. And that could get a good cop in a lot of trouble."

I didn't think for a minute that he merely meant the perp might hurt somebody else. What he was telling me was that if this guy walked, some cop was definitely going to waste him.

"Got it," I said.

"But of course you didn't hear that from me."

"Hear what?"

"Good man. You still want to see him?"

"I promised I would."

"Okay, then. Just remember how things stand." We stopped at a metal-clad door that looked like it belonged on a firewall on a battleship. The cop peeked into the spy hole and then picked out a key from the ring on his belt.

"The door stays open." He inserted the key and turned it. "And I stay right behind you in the corridor. You talk through the phone set. I hear it all, and it's all recorded. You want to pass something to the prisoner, you give it to me. He is not allowed to pass anything to you. Nothing. Are we clear?"

I said we were. He swung the heavy door out into the corridor. Inside, there was an alcove maybe three feet deep and eight wide, with a window that looked into a tiny cell. In front of the glass were a narrow counter, a chair, and a wall-hung phone receiver. I didn't know how they got the prisoner into the cell, but the door we had just opened obviously wasn't it.

He was tallish, maybe six feet, and fairly fit-looking. His orange jail jumpsuit did not bulge at the belly, but it did at the shoulders and chest. I knew from his booking sheet that he was forty-two, but he looked younger. He had a boyish face with fierce, clear blue eyes and curly, very short blonde hair. His nose had a bit of a hook to it and looked as if it

had been broken at least once, but I suspected most women would find him attractive anyway, or at least interesting. I did not. To me he looked like a dangerous smartass, one of those characters who invade somebody else's space just to show that they can. He smiled slightly when he saw me, a crooked, arrogant smirk. I knew that smirk and the kind of person who wore it. He would smile like that and look you right in the eye while he stuck a knife in your guts. And that would just be the beginning.

He walked over to the chair on his side of the glass. Even his walk radiated menace. We picked up our phones.

"About time," he said.

"You think it's a good idea to start our conversation by bitching at me?"

"Like I give a rat's ass what you think. You just write me a bond. You want to get kissed, go someplace else."

"When you put it so charmingly, how can I refuse?"

"They said you like to think you're cute, Jackson. Am I supposed to giggle now? Is that what my lawyer does? Does she do that before she fucks you?"

"That wouldn't be any of your business, would it?"

"Don't try to tell me you're not getting any off her."

"I wouldn't waste my time trying to tell you anything. How much is your bail set for?"

"A hundred and fifty big ones, okay? That's an easy fifteen gees for you, and no hassle."

"Oh, I can see how little hassle there is, all right. You own anything that's worth a hundred and fifty thousand? Come to think of it, do you even own anything that's worth fifteen?"

"Information."

"I'm not looking for any information."

"I think you are."

"You think wrong," I said. "Try the DA."

"Yeah, I'm so sure. The DA hates me. Take my car, then, if you have to show you got something. See here?" He produced

a glossy photo and pressed it up against the glass. "I've got a cherry sixty-eight Shelby Mustang GT. It's a classic." In the middle of the colored picture was a white rectangle, probably a post-it note. I bent closer to read it, my body hiding it from the view of the guard behind me. Then I sat down again. The hair on the back of my neck was standing up.

"I'm not a collector," I said. "And even if I were, cars are no good for security. They take up too much room to store, and the value fluctuates worse than sowbelly futures. No dice."

"You're kidding."

"Do I look amused?"

"Hey, this is the genuine goods, the real shit."

"Unless it isn't. See you around, okay?"

"Not okay. But you'll be back, after you think it over. You won't get what I've got any other way."

"We'll see." I stood up and told the guard I was ready to leave. As we were walking back down the corridor to the elevator, he asked again if I was going to bond his least favorite prisoner. I didn't answer him. My shrink would say I was too busy being conflicted.

According to the cops, Ray Valento was a garden-variety sociopath who sometimes ran complicated con games but more often talked his way into women's homes and then tortured, raped and robbed them. Sometimes he killed them too, but not always.

The cops had caught him by sheer luck. His last victim was in the middle of a phone call when she answered her door. Her friend on the other end listened long enough to hear that something very wrong was happening and had called 911. So the guy was not very smart. The fact that he had a PD for an attorney meant he was not connected, either. Could he have something I needed anyway, or did he merely know enough about me to think I'd be interested? I tried to think of another way to find out.

The note on Valento's car photo had been in pencil, in

simple block printing and all caps, so it could be read from a couple feet away. It had said, simply: I KNOW WHO ATTACKED YOUR WIFE.

The problem with that, of course, was that I didn't have a wife.

Chapter Two

Eight Ball and Bad Vibes

"I hate January." I was back in my office the next day, looking out the storefront window to where it was as bright as high noon on the Gobi Desert and as cold as a bookie's heart. I ought to know. I used to have one. Now I'm a bondsman instead of a bookie, and the weather is crueler than I am. I suppose that's a positive change.

"Only January?" said Agnes, my secretary, from behind me.

Agnes has been with me since I first started the business, which is a long time now. She was originally one of those wholesome farm girls from the western part of the state who came to the Twin Cities to go to Hamline University on a scholarship. After that, she went to William Mitchell for a couple years, but the more she studied law, the less she liked it. She finally decided she would rather make her living doing "honest work." That's how she sees her job, and I don't argue with her. She also sees herself as the big sister I never had, and she wastes a lot of energy trying to reinvent me.

"No, I pretty much hate all of winter." I answered without turning around. "It's front-loaded with holidays that are supposed to make us feel good, but when they're over, there's still three months of misery left to go."

"Why don't you move someplace warm? They need bail bondsmen in Florida, too, you know." She gets sick of my bitching, and she's within her rights.

"It's too hot in Florida."

"Well, make up your mind."

"And it's full of trigger-happy drug thugs and fat old retired broads with frenetic little dogs."

"Go west. Go to Texas."

"Nothing in Texas but big mouths and big hats with tiny brains under them."

"Farther west."

"I'm scared of people who would elect Bonzo's dad and the Terminator."

"Then stay here and shut up about it, okay?"

"I hate January." I surveyed the sheet ice outside.

Wabasha Street had shrunk to less than forty feet wide, on account of the huge piles of snow covering the curbs. People parked there anyway, brazenly poking out into the traffic lanes and ignoring the half-buried sticks with numbers on them that have replaced the traditional parking meters. But being a scofflaw would still cost you. The meters as such were gone, but meter readers were on the job, only now they wore high boots. I wondered what you call a meter maid who's a guy. We have a lot of them. I've never seen "Lovely Rita."

I had come into the office that day partly to call Anne, in New York. My office phone has a re-dial feature that my home phone doesn't, and with Anne, I knew I would need to use it. On the very outside chance that Ray Valento really did know something bad and merely had the logistics of our relationship wrong, I wanted to find out if she was all right. On her office phone and her cell phone, I got a recording. I didn't have a home number for her, which says something about what had become of our affair. I gave Agnes both the numbers I had for Anne and asked her to call New York again, every fifteen minutes or so. Even if she was okay, it was possible that Anne needed a warning. Maybe the attack hadn't happened yet.

There was nothing that needed my attention in the office at the moment, so I put on my coat and headed for the door. "I'm going to go shoot some pool at Lefty's."

"What happened to, 'I hate January?'"

"Some things are worth a little pain. Call me there if you get ahold of Anne, okay?"

"If you carried a cell phone, I could call you wherever you were."

"If we had some ham, we could have some ham and eggs, if we had some eggs."

"What is that? Is that some kind of Zen answer?"

"No, it's a Luddite answer. I don't want a cell phone."

She made a big show of sighing. We'd had this conversation before, many times. In fact, it was the main reason I was seeing a shrink. Agnes had talked me into doing something about my "irrational fear of technology." So far, I had learned a lot about the residual guilt from my wasted youth and all the reasons I didn't screw Pamela Brown back in the eleventh grade, but nothing about my feelings toward machines.

⁂

The afternoon sun was streaming through the high windows at Lefty's, making distinct beams in the dusty air that somehow managed to look brown. The air in Lefty's is always dusty despite several ceiling fans and a perfectly good forced-air heating system. I've never figured that out. It makes the place look like one of the sets for *Blade Runner*. I like it.

Wide Track Wilkie, my sometime friend and bounty hunter, was at a table near the back, practicing his nine ball game. He looked like a bear playing with a small green card table. He nodded to me through a sunbeam, and I strolled over to him.

"You'll make a lot more money if you play with a real person, Wide."

"You won't. Rack them up, sucker."

I racked all fifteen balls and picked out a cue. Wilkie is better at nine ball than I am, and he knows it, so he's not surprised when I refuse to play it. My game is really straight pool,

but he says that always takes too long. Sure. So we compromised on shooting eight ball at twenty bucks a game, and the money passed back and forth more or less evenly.

Three tables away, four kids with buzz cuts and athletic jerseys were clowning around, pretending to shoot snooker while they competed to see who could tell the loudest, stupidest jokes and guzzle beer the fastest.

I made a slick two-ball combination in the side pocket, putting me up on Wilkie by one ball. But then one of the kids yelled even louder than usual, and I missed an easy bank into the corner. I glared at the kid while Wilkie chalked his cue and looked over the new arrangement.

"Herman, my man, even when you screw up, you don't leave much. That's really a crappy setup." He took a sip of beer. It had gone flat a long time ago, but then, we weren't there for the beer.

"Oh, good. I was afraid I gave you a shot."

"Well, they say the great ones create their own shots, but I gotta say, I'm not seeing it."

"You're allowed to miss, you know."

"Hmm." He bent down to sight a possible line, then stood back up when the snooker players had another loud goof fest. One of them was pretending to masturbate a pool stick while two others jumped up and down, hooting.

"College pukes, you think?"

I shook my head. "Jocks."

"Same difference."

"No, it isn't," I said. "I don't hate college kids who aren't free-ride dumbshit athletes."

"I guess maybe I don't, either. Excuse me a minute."

Wilkie put his cue stick on his shoulder like a baseball bat and walked over to the other table. He stopped motionless for long enough to fix each one of them in his gaze in turn, and they stopped their yelling and looked at him. "Listen up, assholes," he said. "This is a place where grownups shoot pool.

And distracting them is not a good idea. Ever. If your folks didn't teach you how to behave in public, go back to the day care center. Otherwise, start thinking about what you're going to say in the emergency room when they ask how you got a pool cue shoved up your nose."

One of them started to say something but thought better of it when Wilkie held up a hand, palm facing out, and studied his fingernails. It was easy to see that the hand was big enough to cover the kid's entire face and still have fingertips left over.

"Don't make me come over here again." He walked back to our table, leaving the jocks staring nervously at the floor. As well they should. Wilkie has an unshakable sense of right and wrong, but putting somebody in the hospital just for being an obnoxious twit wasn't on his "wrong" list at all.

"That was a nice, intellectual discussion."

"I'm good at them."

"I've noticed."

"Makes you wish we still had the draft, doesn't it? I'd really love to see those guys in boot camp."

"Paris Island?"

He nodded. "Changes your whole outlook on life."

"You ever kill anybody, Wide?"

"What? In boot?"

"Anywhere."

"In Iraq, sure. Hard to get out of there without killing somebody. Why? You looking for a favor?" He looked away from the table now and gave me a puzzled frown.

"I want to know how it affects you."

"Me personally, or just anybody?"

"Anybody, I guess."

"It hits different people different ways."

"Tell me one."

"Some guys like it. They usually don't know that right away, but every time they do it, they like it more. And after every

time, they get a little crazier. I wouldn't go in a bar with any of them."

"What kind of crazy?"

"Like they don't see reality the way you and I do, man. They don't think anything matters. I mean, anything."

"Can you see it on them?"

"From across the street. Like tattoos on their foreheads, if you know what to look for."

"What else?"

He took an indifferent shot at the thirteen ball in the center of the table, then put the cue down, no longer interested in the game.

"We had one guy, after his first kill, you'd have thought he just invented sex or something. Couldn't calm down and couldn't shut up about how great it was. Didn't even go to sleep that night, just paced around, talking to himself and giggling."

"How long did that last?"

"We never knew. Next day, we went out on checkpoint duty, and the loot wouldn't let him go because he was still too wired. When we came back, he was asleep. And damned if he didn't sleep the whole rest of his life."

"You lost me."

"He couldn't stay awake after that. He'd open his eyes long enough to eat part of an MRE or go to the latrine, but then he'd zonk out again, wherever he happened to be. He'd sleep standing up and on guard and on patrol, and even when we were taking fire. He couldn't do anything else anymore. The CO was going to ship him out to a loony bin someplace stateside, but some raghead came along and shot him first. Damndest thing I ever saw."

"What about you?"

"What about me?"

"How did you react to killing?"

He heaved a huge sigh and put his chin on his hands, which

were folded over the top of his cue stick.

"I tried not to, you know? I tried not to feel anything, either when I did it or afterwards. They have you shoot watermelons now days, you know?"

"Who does?"

"In boot. You don't shoot at paper targets with bullseyes anymore. You shoot at stuff that looks like real soldiers. And in the last week, you get to shoot watermelons and plastic bags full of red paint, so you get used to red stuff splattering all over when you make a hit."

"I never heard that before. Does it work?"

"For some people, maybe. I didn't like it much. Afterwards, I started insulating myself. If I had a gut reaction to anything in that world, I shut it off, right now. Always. So I'm not so sure about how I felt about the real killing, even now. You know, in some primitive tribes, they think when you kill a big animal or a man, you take its power or its manna, or some such shit. I don't buy it. I think every time you kill somebody, you lose a little piece of yourself. I used to wonder what happens when you lose it all."

"But you never found out?"

"No." He studied me. "You looking to kill somebody, Herman?"

"No, but yesterday I think I talked to somebody who has done it a lot. He looked scary as hell."

"That's probably one of the snuff junkies, the guys who like it. I'd stay away from him, if I were you."

"I'd say that's good advice." Now if I could only get Trish Hanover to believe it. But of course, she didn't have any choice about dealing with the guy. Or so I thought.

Chapter Three

Meatloaf and Worse Vibes

Agnes did not call me at Lefty's. By seven o'clock, she would have gone home for the day, and I decided it was time to quit putting off giving Trish the bad news. I was down two games to Wilkie, so I knew he wouldn't mind me walking away.

"Got to go, Wide."

"Hot date?"

"I wish."

"You really ought to start seeing somebody, you know. It doesn't sound to me like your woman Anne, is coming back from the Crappy Apple."

"Maybe not. But in case you hadn't noticed, there aren't a lot of hot little numbers hanging around here. And even if there were, they probably wouldn't be crazy with desire for either pool shooters or bondsmen."

"You should try an online dating service."

"Jesus, you too?"

"Me too, what?"

"You and Agnes, with the idea that anything worth doing is better if you run it through a computer."

"Hey, I don't think like that. But I do online dating, and I meet some nice broads that way. Well, one, anyway. You got to be sure to put a photo with your questionnaire, though. Otherwise people will think you're fat, you know? Or married."

I was too stunned to think of a reply. Wilkie was absolutely

fearless in the face of any adversary, but he has always been almost pathologically shy with women. "You want to tell me about this nice broad of yours?"

"Absolutely not."

"Just as well. If I knew more about her, maybe I'd get the silly notion that I needed to buy a computer and try a dating service, too. Anyway, I do not have a hot date. I've got to go tell a PD that I'm not going to bond somebody out, some client."

"Is this client the same guy you were talking about, with murder written all over him?"

"That's the one."

"Well, break it to her gently, but don't back down, okay?"

"That's the plan." I put my cue back in the rack and took my coat off the chair I had draped it over. I wondered briefly how Wilkie had known the PD I was going to see was a woman, but it didn't seem important enough to bother asking.

Outside, it was still colder than the proverbial witch's teat, and now pitch dark, as well. It wasn't all that far to Trish's building, but it was past the end of the downtown skyway system, and I hunched down inside my collar and walked as fast as I could. I remembered that Trish had promised to make dinner, and even though I figured she would probably withdraw the offer when I gave her the news, I found a place along the way to buy a bottle of wine. It was from a California vintner, but it had a sexy French bicycle poster for a label. I had no idea if it was any good or not, but I liked that label. Pathetic little creatures, aren't we?

Trish lived in a loft-type condo in a brick building in an area that had once been industrial. It had also once been the wino district, and there were times not all that long ago when you didn't go there alone after dark, unless you were carrying some firepower. That was then. But as my sometime friend The Prophet likes to say, everything changes except the stuff that stays the same. Lowertown was gentrified now.

On the ground floor of the building, an upscale restaurant

was just getting into the evening rush. I breezed past the maitre d' and headed for the interior, but he called me back, making irritated gestures as he pointed to his guest ledger.

"Are you joining a party that's already seated, sir?"

"No, I'm joining a party that's upstairs. Well, maybe it's a party."

"Then you should use the condo entrance, on the east side of the building."

"I'll remember that. But I'm not going back outside just because you don't like people walking through your fine restaurant."

"I'm not going to need to have you removed, am I, sir?"

"I don't think so. I'll remove myself. If I were going to make some trouble, I'd be sure to let you know first." He glowered at me and I pretended not to notice. I continued through the restaurant to where a glass-sided elevator went up through a big atrium to the residential units above. On the ground floor, it opened onto a secure glassed-in foyer. Trish was on the fifth floor. I threw the paper bag from my sexy wine bottle into a trashcan and rang the bell for her unit. The foyer door buzzed open almost instantly, without me needing to talk into the intercom.

Up on the fifth floor, the door to her unit opened just as quickly.

"God, I was afraid something happened and I would—oh." She froze in mid-sentence and gaped. "Herman. Um, I wasn't…" She was wearing jeans and a baggy sweatshirt. She definitely did not look as if she was expecting company, though I could smell cooking in the background. Maybe it just wasn't me she was expecting. I suddenly wished her foyer had a trap door I could fall into.

"I'm really sorry, Trish." I handed her the bottle of wine. "I must have misunderstood you completely. Keep the wine. I'll be on my way."

"You didn't misunderstand, I just, um—"

"I can see it's inconvenient. I'll go."

"No, no. It's okay, really. It's just that it's been one of those days when Chicken Little was right, and the sky really did fall. I forgot about our dinner. We're still good, but I need to make a quick phone call, okay?"

"I am not going to let you cancel a date on my behalf, Trish."

"No, it's not that. It's something else. Let me just make that call."

"You're sure?"

"A quick one, that's all." She nodded, a bit too enthusiastically.

"I'll wait out in the corridor." Her unit was very artsy-trendy, with high wood ceilings and a sleeping loft, but it wasn't very big. There was no place I could stand in it and not be able to overhear her conversation. So I went back out on the balcony that circled the central atrium, leaned on the fancy wrought iron rail, and watched the elevator go past the huge timber beams and columns for a while. And for one of the first times in my life, I actually wished I had a cell phone, so I could pretend to get a call on it, demanding that I dash off to take care of urgent business. I also wished I had a note pad, so I could fold a sheet from it into a paper airplane and see if I could hit the maitre d' down below.

Trish's quick phone call was more like ten minutes, but I could see she was in some kind of awkward situation, and I didn't begrudge her. When she opened the door again, she was more composed than the first time, but still a bit breathless.

"I'm making my famous sunshine meatloaf. I hope that's all right."

"How does a meatloaf get to be sunshiny?" *And who was it really for?*

"It has an unbroken egg yolk somewhere inside it. It's good luck for whoever gets it."

That's not going to be you, Trish, I thought. Aloud, I said, "What fun."

We stood around in the kitchen below the sleeping loft and

made small talk and drank wine while she assembled the meal. I decided I might as well drop the depth bomb and get it over with.

"I saw your man Valento."

"Who?"

"Ray Valento, remember? The psychopath you wanted me to bond? The short take on it is I'm not going to. Sorry." *But not very.*

"Oh, that's okay."

"It is?"

"Sure. I've decided he's a loser. Don't worry about him." She really did sound quite unconcerned. That left me totally baffled, but I decided to leave well enough alone.

"Consider me not worried." And I had thought she was such a simple and vulnerable soul, lawful prey for her own clients. Silly me.

Dinner was a bit of a strain. She had obviously been planning to entertain somebody else, and I wanted to get out of there and leave her to her own affairs as fast as was gracefully possible. The wine helped.

The side dishes were mostly forgettable, but the meatloaf, as promised, deserved to be famous. She told me her secret was using Rice Krispies instead of breadcrumbs. Neither of us got the egg yolk, which turned out to be more prophetic than I could possibly have imagined.

"About the rest of the evening—" she began.

"There is no rest of the evening, Trish. You have somebody you have to see, and I'm going to get out of here and let you do it. Thanks for a lovely meal."

"Aw, Herman, that is so sweet."

Actually, it sucked, but I didn't say so. She gave me the world's hastiest hug at the door, and I was on my way.

Back downstairs, I made a point of walking through the restaurant dining room again, instead of using the handier rear

exit. The maitre d' glowered at me and I gave him a cheery wave.

The frigid air immediately drove off all the glow from the wine. I put my collar up and my head down and set out. Across the street, a large figure was half-hiding behind an ornate lamppost. Had he been there when I first came to the building? That was a long damn time to be stalking out in the cold, if that's what he was doing. I decided to stroll over and have a chat with him, or maybe a confrontation. But then my eye caught another figure, a block ahead of me. Shorter and lighter than Mr. Lamppost, he was coming toward me with a swagger that was all too familiar. Jesus Christ, could it be? The man looked up and saw me, and he immediately spun on his heel and ran off. Before I had time to muster up some better sense, I ran after him.

He went south at first, toward the river, then headed west into an alley between some gentrified industrial buildings. I lost him once, picked him up again a block farther away, then lost him again down by the old parking ramp that used to be under the rail yard at the Union Depot. And as I was peering into that ramp, trying to make some pattern out of the shadows, I lost not only him but everything else. My world went totally black.

Chapter Four

The Morning After the Night Before

My dentist has Impressionist prints on his ceilings. They leave you with the feeling that besides needing your teeth cleaned, you also need to get glasses. But I suppose that makes them a good distraction, like an impossible crossword puzzle. The ceiling that I just woke up to, by contrast, had no pictures at all, but instead a huge array of incomprehensible machinery, like tune-up equipment for an android.

I supposed that meant I was in an emergency room, rather than a regular hospital room or a hotel. I didn't care for the place. It looked cold and I felt cold, despite about a hundred blankets heaped on top of me. I tried lifting my head, and I cared for that even less. Given a choice, I would definitely have preferred remaining unconscious.

Eventually a pretty Asian woman with a crisp white lab coat and a stethoscope came into my field of vision. She took my blood pressure and pulse and shined a little flashlight into my eyes, one at a time.

"I'm Doctor Yang. How are you feeling?"

"Oh, I'm so glad you didn't say, 'we.'"

"I'm glad you're glad. What's your answer?"

"My head feels like the sole object of God's wrath. Maybe you ought to amputate it. I haven't tried any of my other parts yet. I'm in some kind of fuzzy sandwich press here."

"You were borderline hypothermic when they brought you in, so you have a lot of blankets. We can take them off now if you like."

"No, leave them for a while."

"Do you know your name?"

"Sure I do. I know it as well as I know my own name."

"Well?"

"Not very trusting, are you?'

"No."

"I'm Jimmy Hoffa. A lot of people are looking for me." It was, after all, a silly damn question, and I didn't want to admit to her that I couldn't quite seem to answer it.

"We'll get back to that one, okay? You are at Regions Hospital. Do you know where that is?"

"Next to the wye-duct. Down by the winney-gar woiks. Somebody told me that once, I think." Maybe the wine wasn't all worn off, at that. That made perfect sense to me.

"Hmm. Listen, I don't see anything alarming on your head x-rays, but I'm going to bring in an expert to look at them. I can't do that until morning."

"What time is it now?"

"Two a.m. How about if I give you something to put you back to sleep?"

"When I wake up again, will I feel like keeping my head?"

"One can hope." She gave me the gentle smile that was a good doctor's best asset.

"Doctor, you are definitely on."

"I don't want to give you anything very strong, in case we have a brain damage problem here. But this should do the job for you."

She gave me two pills and a glass of water. Maybe it wasn't all that strong, but I was back in la-la land before I finished putting the glass down. Nice stuff, whatever it was.

The next time I woke up, I was in a different room. This one had a very ordinary ceiling, with no pictures but no weird machinery, either. And this time, I did know my name, and the ceiling stayed in focus and didn't move. Things were definitely

looking up. Then another face floated into my field of vision.

"Oh, Herman, I'm so glad to see you open your eyes."

"Agnes? How on earth did you know I was here? I mean, I didn't even know I was here."

"Somebody from the hospital called the office, wanting to know your next of kin."

"How did they know who to call?"

"I don't know. I suppose you must have had a business card on you."

"Well, I hope you haven't been here for a long time."

"Why? Don't you think you're worth it?"

"No. Do you realize how humiliating this is? First I let some asshole blindside me, and then instead of shaking it off, I wind up in a hospital with somebody keeping a deathwatch on me. I go to the movies, Aggie. I know how the tough-guy hero is supposed to act. He's not supposed to need hospitals."

"I've never thought of you as a tough guy, Herman."

"God, it just gets better and better, doesn't it?" I noticed she didn't say she didn't think of me as a hero, though. I settled for that. "What are you doing, Aggie?"

"Pushing your call button. Your doctor said to call when you woke up."

"Ah yes, Doctor Yang. What did you think of her?"

"I thought *he* was kind of cute."

He? The watch changeth, apparently. I was wrong; things weren't looking up at all.

My new doctor was the renowned expert on the interpretation of head shots, it seemed. He showed me a big, complicated picture of the inside of my head on a computer screen, complete with a little white arrow pointing to where I had been hit. Then he pronounced my skull seamless and my brain unscrambled. Any other problems I had were strictly my own, and he didn't want to hear about them. He said I could leave anytime after I paid my bill, but first there was somebody else who wanted to talk to me. Swell. I love

interviewing people when I'm flat on my back and wearing a dopy gown that the frumpiest grandma wouldn't be caught dead in.

The other person turned out to be a plainclothes cop. He dressed better than most of them and didn't have a doughnut belly, but he definitely had that cheerful-predator look that I associate with enforcement pros. A small, fit-looking man with quick movements, he had a ferret-like face and black hair that he combed straight back. He pulled open the lapel of his sharp dark blue suit and let me have a look at the gold badge on the back of it.

"Armstrong. Robbery-homicide." He shook my hand. "The hospital says you got mugged. You want to tell me about that?"

"Personally I missed most of it, but I'll tell you what I can." And I did. I didn't know if my wallet had been stolen or not, so Detective Armstrong retrieved my clothes from the tiny closet for me. My wallet was still in my pants pocket, and it appeared to have all its credit cards in it.

"So much for robbery," I said.

"I could make it work anyway, if I had a suspect." He shrugged. "But it doesn't look like I do. You say you didn't see your assailant at all?"

"Never saw him or heard him coming." Unless, of course, it turned out to be the guy I had been chasing, in which case I *really* felt stupid.

"And where were you coming from, Mr. Jackson?"

"The loft condos, two blocks north of where I got hit. I was having dinner with a friend."

"At the restaurant?"

"No, in her condo."

"What's her name?"

"Trish Hanover."

The hand that had been writing in his notebook froze.

"Tell me about your relationship with Trish Hanover."

"There is no relationship. She's a lawyer, I'm a bail bondsman."

"But you had dinner in her condo?" The hand went back to scribbling.

"Yes. I'm allowed to do that."

"And exactly what time did you last see her?"

"A little after eight last night. I was—"

"I seriously doubt that, Mr. Jackson."

"Really? Why?"

"At eight o'clock last night, Trish Hanover had already been dead for several hours."

"*What*? That's insane! What day is this?"

"Thursday."

"Good God, I've been off-world for a day and a half." I took back what I had thought about the ceiling not moving.

"Can you prove that?"

"It's not like I chatted up the desk clerk when I checked in, you know? But somebody here has got to have a record of it."

"For your sake, I hope so.

"Don't you have anything important to do?"

For the next forty-five minutes, he didn't.

Chapter Five

Gone

Agnes insisted on driving me away in her meticulously preserved antique Toyota. And she was adamant that I should not go back to work for a while, as if what I did was anything resembling vigorous. I thought about telling her to drop me at the Athletic Club, but she would approve of that even less.

"How did poor Miss Hanover die, Hermie?"

"The cop, Armstrong, wouldn't tell me, except to say she was murdered in her condo sometime in the middle of the day yesterday and it was about as nasty as it gets."

"What a terrible shock for you."

"Tell me about it. And it gets worse. He thinks I might have done it, or had it done."

"But you have the best alibi in the world. You were unconscious in a hospital."

"If you think like a cop, then I might have left and come back again."

"That's just dumb."

"Well, he didn't arrest me, did he? But I can see where he's coming from. When you don't have any apples at all, you shake any tree you can find."

"He ought to have better manners. Where am I taking you, by the way?"

"The Victory Ramp. I have to get my Beemer."

"Herman, you are *not* going to drive yourself."

"Well, I can't very well go home and whistle for it to follow me, can I?"

"I'll call Mr. Wilkie and have him pick it up."

"Why do you always call him *Mister* Wilkie?"

"He's a nice man. Give me your keys this very minute."

"Okay, Mom. I hope he doesn't break the springs."

She dropped me off at my townhouse and watched me intently while I fished my spare key out of the mailbox and let myself inside. I suppose I ought to be grateful she didn't insist on coming in and tucking me into bed. Was she always this possessive? How could I not have noticed?

About an hour later, my 328i pulled up at the curb. I could tell Wilkie was driving, because the left front corner sagged. I put on my coat and went out to meet him.

"I heard what happened, Herman. Major not good."

"Are you going to tell me I can't drive, too?"

"You know I never tell you what to do." He handed me my keys.

"Not much, you don't. Where can I drop you?"

"Lefty's. I got an unfinished game there."

"What are you going to tell Agnes?"

"I'll tell her I dropped the car and took the bus, what do you think?"

"The bus is good." We got in and headed back downtown. I was surprised that the steering didn't pull more to the passenger side.

"You got any idea who nailed you, Herman?"

"No. But it wasn't a pro, I'm sure of that much."

"How do you figure?"

"I've seen you use a sap, Wide. If you want to put somebody out for an hour, you do not put him out for two hours. Crude as a sap is, there can be a certain finesse to the thing. This was somebody who didn't know what he was doing."

"Or somebody who wanted to kill you."

"Now there's a cheery thought."

"Who found you?"

"Nobody knows. Anonymous call to nine-one-one."

"So it could even be the guy who slugged you, having second thoughts."

"Yes, it could. It would be nice to get a listen to the tape of that call."

"Wouldn't it, though?"

"Do you know how to do that?"

"No."

"Me neither."

I dropped Wilkie at the front door to Lefty's and headed north to I-94, and then west, across the river and into Minneapolis and back to the Hennepin County Jail. The guy I had chased down in Lowertown had borne a damned uncomfortable resemblance to Ray Valento, and I didn't want merely to hear that he was still tucked safely away where he was supposed to be, I wanted to see it.

The desk sergeant wasn't having it.

"You got a lot of goddamn nerve coming back here, Jackson."

"Excuse me?"

"We thought it was made very clear to you that you shouldn't bond out that asshole, Valento."

"Crystal clear. That's why I didn't do it."

"That would be a very nice story, except that in the middle of the afternoon Tuesday, somebody delivered a properly signed and executed form 702, and we were obliged to spring the little jerk."

"Well, I sure as hell didn't deliver it. Were you here at the time?"

"Just like you see."

"Who brought the bond in?"

"Some guy in a FedEx uniform."

"*What*? Nobody uses FedEx to deliver bail bonds."

"Except you."

"I do not. What does—"

"Take a look." He put a thick ledger on the counter, flipped to the appropriate page, and stuck it in my face. And there, bigger than sin, was my name and my license number.

"I don't suppose I could take a look at the actual 702, itself?"

"No, I don't suppose you could. Why don't you go look at your own copy?"

"Would it help if I said there's been a terrible mistake?"

"There sure has. And you made it."

"Mother of chaos."

"Now, who are you here to see today, Jackson? Jack the Ripper?"

"Nobody. But I would like to get a look at Valento's jacket. You know, to see where he's likely to go when he skips, which he certainly will."

"I don't have that. Try the guy's PD, across the street."

"But she's—"

"Chris Parker is the guy's name."

"That's impossible. Trish Hanover told me—"

"You got a lot of impossibles, for a guy that ain't even welcome here. It's Chris Parker, always has been. But if any other cop asks, I made you find that out on your own."

I was starting to think that I didn't just get bonked on the head, I got knocked into a completely different universe.

Chapter Six

Empty Nest

I never did get a look at Valento's bond, but I checked with the court clerk to be sure that one really did exist and that it had my name on it. He did not, of course, agree to tell me who had bought and paid for it. None of it should have been possible at all, but it had happened. Until I could find out who did it and how, I had to act as if I really had bonded the guy. And if I didn't find him, I could be out one very large chunk of money. Hell, I was already out the basic bond fee.

Technically, Valento wouldn't be jumping bail until his trial date came up, which is not quick, in a major felony case. I usually tell my customers to check in with me before they leave town, even though their bonds don't usually have any domestic travel restrictions on them. But the court can set any kind of special conditions it wants, and in this case it had decided that our boy should not be allowed to go off to a hot lunch date in Timbuktu. If he tried to leave the jurisdiction any time before the end of his trial, a bounty hunter could legally apprehend him. And with extreme prejudice, in fact. Bounty hunters don't have all the civilized restraints that cops do.

The PD Chris Parker said he had always had the Valento case, from day one, even before the cops had successfully arrested the guy. He didn't mention poor Trish, and neither did I. He gave me the copy of his file on Valento, but it wasn't a whole lot of help. It had a lot of pages detailing a

string of really sickening, bloody crimes, but very little about the man's friends, family, hangouts, or interests. Personal interests can be especially useful. Wilkie once nailed a skip at a stamp collectors' convention. But this guy didn't have anything of the sort in his dossier. I knew he was into old muscle cars, of course, but in the middle of the winter, that didn't lead me in any useful directions.

I wanted Wilkie along on the search for this guy, right off the bat. Despite letting myself be blindsided in Lowertown, I like to pretend I can handle myself with most hostile natives in most parts of the jungle. But somebody who has killed always has a built-in advantage over somebody who hasn't, and I wanted the extra muscle and the extra edge, too.

Valento's last known address was an apartment in the Midway area of St. Paul, in Ramsey County. Normally, when the court says "jurisdiction," it means the county where the crime was committed and where the trial would therefore be held, which would be Hennepin. In this case, the area the court said he had to stay in was expanded to include Ramsey County as well as Hennepin. But that was okay. If we had to, Wilkie and I could find a way to get him out of both places. And then he would be fair game.

We headed over to the address in Wilkie's Ford Explorer, which had beefed up springs for him and a wire cage in the back, like a cop car, for his occasional customers. We weren't really expecting to find Valento at his digs. He had a two-day lead on us already, and if he hadn't made use of it, he was dumber than a brick. But we had to start somewhere.

"What do you want to do if we actually find this guy, Herman?"

"Legally, we can't do anything. If he's here, he's legit."

"Is that why you've got your nine millimeter stuck in your belt? He ain't been legit since the day he was born."

"Well, I did hope to have a little heart-to-heart talk with him about that bond."

"Heart-to-heart. That's the best kind."

"I thought you'd like it."

The apartment turned out to be on the top floor of a two-story building that looked like it belonged in an Edward Hopper painting. It was very old but had never been very elegant. Dark, crumbling brick flanked a storefront with fluted cast iron columns and dirty glass. A sign above the window said AUNTIE KEW'S ANTIQUES, and a smaller one below read BUY AND SELL. It was not the kind of place where professional interior decorators shop. The folks from "Pawn Stars" could spend a whole day there and never find anything worth ten bucks on the open market. Small as the building was, it had two upstairs apartments, each with its own stair from street level. The stair to Valento's unit opened onto the side street.

Wilkie parked in the alley behind the store, and we got out and tried the door to the side stairs. There was a beat up mailbox next to the door that was stuffed and locked. The door was also locked. There was a doorbell button, but we didn't push it.

"Now what, Sherlock?"

"Stay where you can watch the back fire escape." I took out my set of picks.

"Do you really know how to do that?"

"I'm a little out of practice, but it's not exactly Fort Knox. Standard Schlage deadbolt. Five pins. Walk in the park." I put the tension bar in the key slot and followed it with the first pick.

"If you get in any trouble, I've got a crowbar in the truck."

"Oh, that would be a big help. Then it becomes breaking and entering."

"What is it now?"

"Open to interpretation."

The lock hadn't been oiled in decades, and that actually made it easier to work. Once I found the break point in any pin, it would stay put, just from the side tension on it. After

two minutes of scowling and biting my tongue, the cylinder spun free, and we were in.

"How do you want to play it?" I said.

"Well, you said it: somebody's got to watch the back."

"That should probably be you, Wide. You're better than me at stopping somebody without shooting him, and we don't want to be flashing any guns around out in public."

"Yet."

"Yet." I pulled the Beretta out of my belt and started up the narrow staircase. "Give me five minutes before you move." There was a wall sconce light fixture at the top of the shaft, but it was out, and the place was as dark as a vice cop's thoughts. It reminded me of an old gangster movie, where Robert De Niro had unscrewed a hallway light bulb so he could shoot the guy who tried to screw it back in. It worked very well, which made me even more nervous. I opened my eyes as wide as they would go and pointed my gun wherever they looked. The safety was off.

At the top of the stairs there was a hallway no more than three by five feet with a scarred-up wood panel door at the end. It had two locks, and neither one was any tougher than the one down below. I found to my surprise that it's easier to pick a lock in the dark. Maybe next time I did it, I would close my eyes. Not in front of Wilkie, though. He'd think I was praying.

The second lock opened with a clunk that was a lot louder than I would have liked. I put my picks back in their little case and stuffed it in my hip pocket. Then I pulled on a pair of disposable vinyl gloves, raised the Beretta 9 mm to high port, took a deep breath, and turned the knob.

The door opened to my left, so I dove into the room to the right and rolled to a low squat. I needn't have bothered. There was nobody home.

There were only three rooms—living/sleeping, kitchen, and bathroom—and they were all empty. I put the safety back on

the Beretta and put it back in my belt.

If the outside of the building was a work by Hopper, the inside was probably by the Three Stooges. With so little furniture and so few possessions, it was hard to see how somebody could have made such a mess. It didn't look like a home, it looked like a hideout. I thought of all the movies I've seen where cops go to a crime scene to look for something that's been disturbed. The script writers never seem to realize that for some people, disturbed is the normal state of affairs. In a corner of the kitchen, a mouse looked up at me from atop a dusty pizza carton.

"Brazen little bastard, aren't you?" He had been chewing on the corner of the box, and I wondered if the reason he didn't run was that he thought I might open it for him. Instead, I opened the refrigerator. It contained two bottles of beer, another pizza box, some hot dogs covered in fuzzy mold, and a package of sixty-watt light bulbs. I opened up the box and found that they really were just light bulbs. Go figure. I heard somebody stomping around on the rear fire escape landing, and I opened the door and let Wilkie in.

"No joy?"

I shook my head. "I don't think our boy's been here for some time. Wide, you ever notice how the mice get bolder when nobody's been chasing them for a while?"

"I can't say as I have a lot of personal experience with mice, Herman."

"Take my word for it. They practically come up and shake your hand."

"They try it with me, they'll wind up decorating the bottom of my shoe."

"Have you ever talked to anybody about all that bottled up aggression?"

"Not lately, but I'm always ready to. What's with the mattress over there?" He nodded at the middle of the living room, where a bare mattress and pillow lay partly ripped or slashed

apart. There were short pieces of rope on the floor nearby and a lot of nasty dark stains all over the place. I didn't know for a fact that it was blood, of course, but that was what my gut was telling me.

"Not a very pretty piece of work, is it? Looks like he had a fold-up bed in the wall for sleeping, but he kept this sorry mess for…well, messier stuff."

"I think this is one sick son of a bitch we're chasing, Herman."

"I think you're right. That's pretty much what the Minneapolis cops said, too."

"Have you checked the bed yet?"

"No." I pulled out my gun again and pointed it at the big cupboard door in the living room wall. "Give it a try."

Wilkie pulled on the handle, and a bed came rolling into the room on casters. It had a gray comforter on it and was made up, if not too neatly. Sitting in the middle of it, gleaming dully and just begging to be picked up, was a black Dell laptop.

"Time to go, Wide." I put my gun away again, tucked the computer under my arm, and headed for the door.

"Is this open to interpretation, too, Herman?"

"No, this is simple theft."

"Oh, good."

"Good?"

"I like to know where I stand."

Since he liked the situation so much, I stopped on the way back to the vehicle and picked the mailbox lock, too.

"Is there any kind of lock you don't know how to pick?"

"I can't do combination locks. Nickel Pete spent a whole afternoon once, trying to teach me how to open a simple gym locker padlock, with no luck. I just couldn't get a feel for the thing."

"Hell, padlocks are easy. You just take a bolt cutters to them."

That may have defined the differences in our entire life philosophies.

Chapter Seven

Social Work

"I know what you're going to say, Herman. Don't, okay? Because I'm not going to do it." He put the pedal down on the Explorer and threw a little gravel going out of the alley.

"I can't imagine what you're talking about, Wide."

"The hell you can't. I'm not going to go see the crazy Prophet."

"I never said anything of the sort."

"You were going to."

"Maybe, maybe not. Let's see what we can find out on our own first." I started sorting through Valento's mail. He had only been in jail for a little over a week, but he hadn't paid his phone or electric bills for two months. Excel Energy, in particular, was getting really pissed. A pornography-of-the-month club thought his credit was just fine, though, and his subscriptions to two hot rod magazines were all paid up.

"Where am I going, Herman?"

"Someplace that has free wi-fi. Valento's place didn't have cable, and his phone bill doesn't say anything about Internet service, so I figure that's where he went to do email and whatever."

"I can't believe I heard that out of you. You're actually going to use something electronic?"

"I'm not a total techno-idiot, you know."

"You fooled me."

Wilkie doesn't like what he calls chi-chi demitasse joints, so we went to a coffee house up in the Cathedral Hill area that has rough wood tables, no elevator music, and nice, substantial-feeling coffee mugs. And free wi-fi. It also had a cute little brunette at the counter who rendered Wilkie nearly speechless. I had to order for him. I got him a dark coffee and a cookie that was actually bigger than his hand and had every kind of fruit and nut known to mankind in it.

"I think it's backpacker's food," I said.

"Looks good." He took a bite without waiting to get to a table, and suddenly the thing was only half as big as his hand. "Get me another one, will you?"

Armed with two more cookies, we took a table back in a corner and fired up the Dell. We looked at the usual array of Bill Gates' promo images and then settled down to a display that was as cluttered as Valento's apartment. Most of the icons turned out to be pornography of one kind or another that had been copied from websites. Lots of kinds, in fact. There was everything from simple T and A to bondage, to rape, and even torture. No kiddy porn, though. This guy was definitely a sick son of a bitch, but he wasn't *every* kind of sick. He also had a lot of stuff on his screen about cars and some stuff that was muscle cars and porn, all in one.

"That's some kind of sexy Barracuda," said Wilkie.

"I think you call that a cougar."

"I meant the car."

"Oh, that."

There was also a file folder labeled JOBS. We opened it and found a bunch of files that may have been lifted off Facebook or Match-dot-com. Profiles of women.

"Are you thinking what I'm thinking, Herman?"

I nodded. "This is his trophy file, his list of past victims."

"Or future ones."

"Some of each, maybe." I looked over the table of contents, and my heart sank. Trish Hanover was on the list. And so, I

was sorry to note, was Doctor Margaret Yang, though that was a file he had constructed from scratch, not lifted from some social site.

"We're going to have to give this computer to the cops, aren't we?" said Wilkie. "I mean, I'm no lawyer, but this is industrial-strength evidence if I've ever seen it."

"When we're done, they get a turn. Let's see what else we've got."

There were icons for three web browsers and two email servers. Two of the browsers and one of the emails opened with no fuss, but they had almost nothing in the "History" file or the "Bookmarks". The other browser, a version of Google, had a lot of stuff in its recent history.

"Looks like our boy was at his digs more recently than we thought, Wide."

"How's that?"

"He was looking at Map Quest the day before yesterday."

"Oh yeah? It'd be nice to see where he quested, wouldn't it?"

"Ask and ye shall be enlightened." I clicked on the site listing. But instead of opening it, the machine flashed me a huge window.

"It says you gotta have a login name and a password, Herman."

"I see that, Wide. I picked right up on it."

"Well, it's a crock. I mean, who the hell puts password protection on a web browser?"

"This guy. Let's see what his email gives us." I opened the email server and got exactly the same result. I could look at a list of saved messages, but I couldn't open any of them or get any new mail without a password.

"Shit," I said.

"Bat shit."

"Sour bat shit. We've got to have those keys."

Wilkie sighed.

"What's the sigh for?"

"We're going to see The Prophet after all, aren't we?"

"Just for you, we'll try a little social engineering first."

We went to a Best Buy on the north end of the metro area and went straight to the extensive computer section. I picked out the youngest clerk I could see and gave him a look that said I trusted him completely. I don't know if clerks work on commission or not, but I do know that everybody likes to be made to feel they look competent. He brightened up and headed straight over to me. Wilkie hung around by the end of the display case with the cash register on it, made no eye contact with anybody, and looked totally disinterested. The clerk's nametag said he was Jeff.

"Hey, Jeff, how are things with you today?"

"Just great, sir. What can I help you find?"

"How are you liking it, working for Best Buy?"

"Um, fine, I guess. I mean, look at all the nifty stuff I get to play with. And they have—"

"The reason I ask is that I have a nephew who's a major techno-geek, and he's looking for a job. I was wondering if I ought to tell him to try here."

"Oh, like that. Sure. If he's really good, he might even get to work in the Geek Squad. You know, where people bring in their computers that don't work or they don't know how to run? They always want people for there."

"And where is that, exactly?"

He pointed to another part of the store. "But he can start by talking to any manager."

"Great. I'll tell him. Thanks. And you charge people for going there, is that how it works?"

"Well, if you have one of our extended service contracts, it's free."

"I see. And I can get one of these contracts for any device?"

"Any computer, sure."

"Is it, like, a piece of paper? Can I hold it in my hand? I don't trust all that electronic stuff."

"Sure. It's like this, see?" He pulled a multi-carbon form out from some cubbyhole and put it on the counter. I pretended to look it over, then passed it to Wilkie.

"Is it good on all that stuff?" I pointed to a computer display as far away from us as I could find, and Jeff followed my lead and moved over that way. The service contract immediately went in Wilkie's pocket. I babbled a bit about how competent he seemed to be, and then we went back to where we started.

"Actually, it's on account of that same nephew that I'm here. I want to get him a birthday present, but I really don't know anything about this stuff. So I need to be sure I get all the right paperwork, so he can exchange whatever I get, if I guess wrong.

"He can always do that, if he saves the receipt. How about a notebook, does he have one of them?

"I never heard him say so. What are they?"

"They're like a stripped-down laptop. We've got a good sale on the HP Touch Pad III, Wi Fi series right now." He showed me a little black box about the size of a large paperback novel, only not as thick. He did something with it, and the screen turned deep blue and came to life.

"That's nice, I guess. What's that go for?"

"Special this week only, $475."

I grabbed my throat and pretended to scream. "He's not *that* nice a nephew. What have you got for under a hundred?"

"Seriously?"

"Very."

"A plain vanilla cell phone?"

"I hate cell phones."

"But it's not for you, you said."

"I hate anybody's cell phones. What else?"

"Maybe a camera, then. There's a big range in cameras. Does he have a girlfriend?"

"Why would that make a difference?"

"Sometimes a couple that's really tight will keep an extra

camera, to pass back and forth between them."

"And they say there's no passion in electronics. I love it."

I wound up buying a fifty-dollar camera that had a sexy shape and a candy apple red paint job. I paid in cash, and Wilkie and I headed for the door.

"Did you get any extras?" I asked, when we were back in the Explorer.

"Does the Phony Express deliver?" He opened up his coat and gave me three blank copies of all the papers good old Jeff had shown me. I immediately started using the Dell for what it claimed to be, a laptop desk, and filled in all the blanks. I used Jeff's full name and his "secret sales ID number," which he had been proud to point out to me when I asked. And of course, I filled in the name and serial number of the laptop and Ray Valento's name and address as the purchaser.

"How old would you guess this thing is, Wide?"

"Open it up. Hmm. The keyboard's not very dirty at all. I'd say it's pretty new."

"We'll make it a year, exactly. That way I don't have to alter quite as much of the sales slip." I crumpled the sales slip from the camera a bit, spat on it a few times, and smeared the light ink with my fingers. Then I dried it out by holding it over the windshield defroster of the Explorer and penciled in the numbers that were "missing." The date became a year earlier, and the price became the exact price of the camera, plus an extra eleven hundred. The Best Buy stock number, I just smeared beyond all recognition.

"That's pretty good, Herman."

"A little coffee would be a nice touch."

We got a cup of coffee at a fast food drive-through, plus a few burgers for Wilkie, "just so we don't look like cheapskates." I added some stains to my doctored little piece of paper, dried it out again, and we were set for street theater.

"Shall we go back to the same store?"

"I don't think so. I definitely would not like to run into our

buddy Jeff again."

We went east instead, and half an hour later we were at the Geek Squad area of yet another Best Buy. I put the computer on the counter in front of a young blond woman with the biggest glasses I've ever seen and a nametag that said she was Cherri. I gave her my best look of utter helplessness.

"Look, I was out of town for a while, and I didn't have my laptop with me. And now I find I can't remember the login name and password I added for email and Google. Can you help me out, here, Cherri? What an interesting name, by the way." *What a total affectation.*

"Oh, thanks. It took me a long time to come up with it. You bought the computer here, sir?"

"One of your other stores. Here's all the papers on it."

"Well, the service contract papers look okay, Mr.…um… Valento. Wow, you just brought it back in time, didn't you? This is a one-year contract. That's okay, but this sales slip is a real mess."

"Yeah, I know. I spilled coffee on it, and then my wife crumpled it up and tried to throw it away. Some of it, you just about couldn't read anymore, so I touched it up with a pencil. I hope that's okay."

"I guess it's not all that bad. Could I see some ID, please?"

"Well that's the other problem, I'm afraid. I had my license taken away for a while, too. That's why this guy is driving me around." I jerked a thumb at Wilkie and made a helpless gesture. "But I brought a recent phone bill and electric bill. Can you make that work?"

She hesitated for a while, I raised my eyebrows in my "Only you can help me, Obi-Wan" expression, and she finally smiled and said, "Sure,"

She did some utterly incomprehensible things with the machine, consulted another machine a few times, and finally wrote down two non-words for me on the back of one of her cards.

"Can I give you a tip, sir? Put these two items in a file on your computer. Label it something nobody would ever open, like 'old lottery numbers' or 'tax laws.' Then when you need to use them, or if you ever lose them again, you can just copy the characters out of the file and paste them into the engine, without broadcasting the keystrokes to anybody who might be eavesdropping.

"Wow, that's really clever." I had no idea what she'd just said.

"One other little tip? You might want to change these sometime soon."

"Why is that?"

"Well, mainly to come up with something that's easier for you to remember. But sometimes you need to let somebody else have your passwords, too. Then it might be nice to have some that weren't quite so likely to offend anybody."

"Like who?"

"Like me?"

"Oh." I looked at the card again. Valento's username was "fuckyou2," and the password was "biteme69."

"Believe it or not, those are both really common, too."

So Valento was just as predictable as all the other dimwitted lowlifes. I had no illusions about him being a scumbag, but I had somehow imagined he was a little brighter than that. Oh, well.

"Point taken," I said. And suddenly it occurred to me that there could be all sorts of good reasons why I would like to be the only one in the world who could access his email. The more I thought about it, the more I liked the idea.

"How many characters should they be?"

"Eight is usually good, sir, with at least two of them numbers. You can go as high as twenty."

"Can you make the change for me?"

"Sure, nothing to it. But I can teach you to do it, too. You just—"

"I'll never remember what you tell me. Just change it." I thought for a minute about what I might be capable of remembering for a password. I decided the place where somebody tried to bash my brains in would be good. I wrote L0wert0wn, with zeroes instead of O's, on the same card as the old ones and handed it to her.

"You want the same one for everything, Sir?"

"It'll definitely be easier to remember."

Ten minutes later I gathered up all my bogus papers and valid passwords, told Cherri one last time what a sweetheart she was, and left. She blushed. I love it when they blush.

Chapter Eight

Detour

The place Valento had been looking at on Map Quest turned out to be a small island in Lake Superior. It was called Madeline Island, and it was offshore of the little town of Bayfield, Wisconsin, at the end of a chain of islands called the Apostles. From the town, you could take a ferry to the island in the summer. There was no indication of how you got there in the winter.

Then we opened the email, and things got dark and weird. There were several messages to and from Trish Hanover, and the content of them was very strange indeed. I wasn't sure if he was trying to lure her into some kind of trap, or she was trying to lure him. Quite possibly both. Whatever she thought she was doing, though, I was becoming very certain it had been fatal for her.

There was also a lot of email to what you might call an electronic soul buddy, somebody who signed himself Alfie. Valento would send Trish a message telling her about a lot of nice things he wanted to do for her and then he would almost immediately email Alfie and tell him what he really had in mind. Sometimes they would trade tips on ways to keep victims conscious longer while they cut or beat them. There were also ways to inflict maximum pain and combinations of drugs that would produce horrible hallucinations. I was starting to genuinely hate this guy.

"We have to turn this over to the cops, Herman." Wilkie was looking over my shoulder. "If any of those messages

includes the way Trish was killed, this gives them a lock on nailing the guy."

"You know what, Wide? This asshole is already up for murder in Minneapolis, and the cops there said they were going to nail his ass if he ever got out. But I don't think I'm going to wait for them, or the St. Paul cops, either."

"Are you thinking we're going to get bloody on this one?"

"Count on it."

"I'm good with that."

"I thought back at Lefty's, you were telling me you—"

"I'm good."

There were a lot more emails I hadn't read, but as I was maneuvering that crappy substitute for a mouse over to one, I got a sudden window telling me that I was almost out of power.

"What kind of batteries do we put in this thing, Wide? Double-A's?"

"You can't be serious. Where's the AC adapter?"

"There's supposed to be an AC adapter?"

"Suffering Job, Herman, are you seriously telling me you stole a computer and didn't get anything to charge it with?"

"Well, I didn't see it. You were there, why didn't you get it?"

"Oh, maaan!" He tilted his head back and glared at the ceiling. Apparently he had already forgotten about all those cookies and Burgers I bought him.

"I guess we need to go back to Best Buy, huh?"

He turned his back and headed for the door without another word. I followed him to his Explorer.

On the way back to the store, the lights went out again.

This time the machinery on the ceiling was familiar, and so was the pretty face hovering above me.

"Hello, Dr. Yang. I wish I could say it's nice to see you again."

"We get more repeat customers in Emergency than you might expect, Mr. Jackson, but usually not so soon. How have you been feeling?"

"Until I blacked out, I felt fine. Come to think of it, I feel fine now. Want to go to dinner with me?"

"That's too bad."

"No it's not. I know some very nice places."

"I meant it's too bad you had no symptoms before you blacked out. That means it could happen again anytime—driving, using some kind of tool, crossing the street—"

"Beneath the Twelve Mile Reef?"

"Excuse me?"

"Never mind."

"What does that mean?"

"It means I'm a lot older than you."

"I'll take your word for it. We've done you a great disservice, I'm afraid, sending you out without more tests."

"You're excused. Now, about that dinner—"

"No, it really is quite inexcusable. We're going to have to get an MRI on you as soon as possible, and no casual interpretations this time."

"I'm afraid I can't accommodate you, doc. I have things to see and people to do, and they won't keep."

"I'll see what I can schedule."

"Try next summer. I've really got to go."

"You really can't, Mr. Jackson. You could be in great danger."

"Only could be? That's not so bad. I've been past that, lots of times."

"One of these days, you won't get past it. Have you talked to anybody about that death wish of yours?" She headed for the door.

"I talk to a shrink about a lot of things, but she hasn't mentioned that yet."

"Trust me, she'll get around to it." But she smiled as she said it. I thought that was nice.

"Look, where's the guy who brought me in? Maybe I can delegate some things."

She gave me a blank look.

"Big guy? Looks like half of a rugby team, only with more attitude?"

"I'm afraid he must have gone. I didn't see anybody like that. Wait here, okay?" She checked something on her clipboard and was out the door before I had a chance to give her any more grief.

I figured if I talked to the good doctor again, I was a goner. Or rather, a stayer. She would have a hundred good reasons why I had to hang around for the MRI and I wouldn't have any good reasons why I shouldn't. Or no reasons she would buy, anyway. And meanwhile, Valento would just be getting farther and farther away. I decided it would be best all around if I simply joined the ranks of the missing.

They hadn't deprived me of my clothes this time, but I had to look around a lot for my shoes. For some reason, it was hard to focus on things down at floor level.

There was a long corridor outside the room, and I took a wild guess about which way would lead out. At one end of the corridor was a drinking fountain, and it reminded me of a story Wilkie once told me about getting his vaccinations in boot camp. They got lots of them, whether they needed them or not. Maybe they even got a few phony ones, just to keep them feeling properly intimidated. One in particular was known as "the water cooler shot," and it was supposed to be a real killer. As the story goes, the recruits lined up in a long corridor to wait for their turn at the needle. Behind them, near the door to the outside, there was a water cooler. Being mere E-1 recruits and therefore lower than squid shit, they were not allowed to use the cooler, of course, but everybody was aware of it. As each man came out of the chamber of horrors, rolling his sleeve back down, he would smile and say something to the effect that there was really nothing to the dreaded shot, after all. It was the most nearly painless one of them all. Then he would get to the end of the corridor by the cooler, and the real pain of the shot would catch up with him. Some of the guys

would scream and a few would even pass out.

Wilkie thought it was a funny story, and so did I. But now I found myself wondering if I had a "water cooler concussion." Or whatever the hell it was. As it turned out, I didn't get as far as the drinking fountain. Ten paces from it, I thought I had been stabbed in the back of the head with an ice pick. The pain was so intense, it took my breath away. I grabbed the wall to keep from falling over. As my knees turned to rubber and I slid down the wall, I was dimly aware of a lot of legs in greenish-blue hospital scrubs, all running toward me. Somewhere far, far away, I heard a pleasant woman's voice say, "Get his wallet. The MRI will erase his license and all his credit cards if he keeps them. Stat, people, stat. This one's going down fast."

⁂

Horizontal turned out to be a much better way to be, and I really didn't mind the closeness of the machine. But the technician who ran it turned out to be the end product of about six generations of people who mated with vegetables. He liked hard-lard, cornball country-western background music, and I think he piped it directly into the MRI chamber.

"Will you for chrissakes cut that shit out?"

"Are you feeling a little claustrophobic, sir? Do you want something to help you to relax?"

"Yes. It's called silence."

"Oh, you mean the music is too loud?"

"I haven't heard any music. All I've heard is some ignorant hillbilly blowing his nose at an out-of-tune guitar."

"Hey, that's real down home grit. Most people like it."

"You're really lucky I'm not armed, you know that? But you keep playing that shit and I'll figure something out anyway."

The noise stopped.

"You moved your head, you know, arguing with me. Now we have to start all over."

"Break my heart."

"What do you want to hear?"

"Machinery."

"You have a real attitude problem, sir."

"Talk to mom."

The rest of the scan went smoothly enough. The big machine spat me back out, and nurses who were a lot stronger than they looked picked me up, dumped me on a gurney, and wheeled me straight into an operating room.

"I really don't think—" And somebody put my lights out again. I was getting very tired of that.

If the MRI was something from the original *Star Trek*, what they did next was straight out of *The Matrix*. They bored a hole in the back of my skull and inserted some kind of smart electronic worm with a laser in its mouth. And faster than I could have believed, I was back in an ordinary hospital room, talking with Doctor Yang.

"That was lucky." She looked at her clipboard again. She looked at her clipboard a lot. I decided it was a poise thing.

"Oh, it definitely felt lucky, all right. That was the first thing I thought."

"I mean it was lucky you were still in the hospital. We took a blood clot out of your brain, or rather vaporized it."

"You vaporized my brain? Wow, I hardly noticed."

"I see you're not wearing a wedding ring, Mr. Jackson. But you must be a real joy to your girlfriend." Despite the put-down, she smiled that same quiet, half-smirk of hers, which I thought was nice.

"My girlfriend is in New York, probably for good."

"That's too bad. I suppose it would be pointless to tell you that you really ought to stay here for a day or two?"

"That's what it would be, yes."

"Well, for the next several days, you shouldn't be by yourself. You had a serious concussion and who knows what else. Traumatic brain injuries can be insidious things. Sometimes it

seems as if the brain continues to re-injure itself well after the event, even though it appears to be in fine shape. And if you get another clot or a secondary concussion, you want to have somebody with you, to get help."

"Would you like to volunteer for that job? I'm still open for dinner."

"You are irrepressible, Mr. Jackson."

"Thank you. Call me Herman. Are you sure you don't know where my friend is?"

"Good day, Herman."

Chapter Nine

Body English

Lacking the company of the good doctor, I settled for a late dinner of takeout Chinese, with a bottle of the same sexy-label wine I had bought to give Trish. I ate it in front of my TV while I watched a DVD of *Anatomy of a Murder*. Amazing, how well that film has aged. My shrink would probably say that's because I think I'm Jimmy Stewart. Or maybe I'm still in love with Eve Arden. She looks pretty good for somebody who's probably pushing 100 by now.

The next morning, being all out of other options, I went back to my office. Agnes said she hadn't seen Wilkie. So, it followed that he hadn't left the Dell laptop there, with or without a new charging device. He also hadn't told her where he was going, and he wasn't answering his cell phone. And people think those damn things just solve all your problems.

Much as I hate talking to machines, I left him a message. "Wide, this is me, and if you don't call back and tell me where the hell you are, *tout suite*, I'm going to tell everybody down at Lefty's that your new girlfriend turned out to be a lesbian. With a drug problem." That ought to do it, I thought, unless he was up to something really heavy, in which case nothing I said would make any difference.

"There's a '*de*' in there, Herman."

"In where?"

"It's really '*tout de suite*'. Lots of people get that wrong."

"Trust me, Wilkie won't notice."

Had he convinced himself he needed to go to Madeline

Island, to apprehend our wayward boy before he morphed into an anonymous ice fisherman? If I followed and was wrong, it would be not just a wild goose chase, but also a damn long one.

"What did the doctor say about your head, Herman?"

"She said she's seen better, but it will do. It's not cute enough to make her want to go out to dinner with me, though."

"Someday I'm going to get a straight answer out of you."

"Not today." I headed for the door, but a stray thought stopped me in my tracks.

"Aggie, how did you know there was a problem with my head?"

"Um. Well. I was at the hospital, remember?"

"Not this time, you weren't."

"How do you know? You were unconscious, so you didn't see me. And I left so I wouldn't embarrass you again."

"It won't wash, Aggie. You weren't there. But Wilkie was. After he left me, he came to see you, didn't he? And you and he are hiding something from me."

"Oh, Herman, that's so silly."

"Why is it silly?"

"Because if I'm hiding something, then clearly I'm not going to tell you about it. And if I'm not, then there's nothing to tell." She gave me a palms-up gesture that said, "Is this obvious to the meanest intelligence, or what?"

I couldn't think of anything to say to that, so I headed for the door again.

"Where are you going, Herman?"

"I have to see a man about a very disturbing email." And he was the last man I ever expected to want to see.

⁂

To the best of my knowledge, the cops on opposite sides of the river do not talk to each other. So unlike the desk sergeant in Minneapolis, the one at St. Paul Police Headquarters had

no reason to be pissed at me. He settled for weary indifference and directed me to an interview room, where my man Armstrong, the detective who had talked to me in the emergency ward, joined me after ten minutes or so. If he was happy to see me again, he did a good job of hiding it. But he had brought some files, as I had requested. He threw them on the bare steel table and sat down.

"What's the story, Jackson, your conscience bothering you?"

"Are you offering to play father confessor?"

"Any time, any place. Father John of the Strong Arm, bridge over troubled water and former missionary to the lost. Save your soul and clean up your record, all in the same trip. What've you got for me?"

"I'm not sure if I have anything. But let me ask you this: if an ordinary citizen, somebody who has no official ties to the police at all, somehow gets his hands on a piece of evidence that—"

"Gets his hands on? Is that otherwise known as 'steals'?"

"Let's leave it at 'gets his hands on' for the moment, okay? He gets this evidence that the cops *can't* legally get, okay? And he gives it to them. Just gives it, with no coercion of any kind. Can they use it?"

"I assume you mean can they use it to prosecute, versus just using it to find some bad guy?"

"Correct."

"But this is all totally hypothetical, right?"

"Totally."

He sucked on his teeth a moment and then let out a deep sigh. "It's not good. Not good at all. In fact, it's totally fucked. Theoretically, the damning goods should be admissible, since the police didn't violate any protocol getting them. Theoretically. But a defense lawyer with any moxie at all is going to argue that your *ordinary citizen* was a *de facto* officer of the court, whether he knew it or not, and anything he snatched without probable cause is tainted as hell."

"No way around that?"

"A legal way, you mean?"

"Not necessarily."

"Well since we're talking totally hypothetically here, I'll give you an imaginary scenario that would be illegal as hell to tell you about, but more likely to work. Our theoretical public-spirited citizen puts the evidence back wherever the hell he found it and gives us an anonymous phone call with enough hard information in it to get us a search warrant. Then we go find this smoking gun or whatever the fuck it is, and we're just as surprised and happy as a little kid hunting Easter eggs in the park. We put the bad guy away for a long time and the DA actually loves us for a change. Then we all go out together and get falling down drunk. Only you don't get to go along, because you're just an anonymous phone caller."

"Not me. I'm merely the one telling a hypothetical story here."

"Yeah? Well, tell me the rest of it, will you? I'm dying to put it in my memoirs."

"Absolutely, maybe. First I want to see Trish Hanover's body."

"Speaking of things that are totally illegal." He leaned back in his chair and folded his hands behind his head, probably thinking over which of many fine ways he was going to tell me to go straight to hell. "Why would you want to do that?" I decided to let him have him a bit more paydirt than I really wanted to.

"Suppose I saw some emails that I wasn't supposed to see? Nobody was supposed to see them. And in them, one very sick individual describes some very depraved things he's going to do to an unnamed young woman."

"Suppose, huh? Sounds like you're already guilty of with-holding important evidence."

"If a crime was actually committed, I could be. But if this guy was just indulging his taste for twisted fantasies, it could

all be innocent nonsense. Still sick, but innocent. I want to see—"

"You want to see if he did the things to the Hanover woman that he said he was going to do to *somebody*."

"That's about it."

"There's some other link between her and him that you're not telling me. Otherwise we wouldn't be having this conversation."

"Yes there is. And I have no doubt that, fine detective that you are, you will find it."

"Spare me the ego grease."

"Okay, I will. But before I tell you any deep secrets, I want to see if there's a more blatant link than what I already have."

"Uh huh. You know, I kind of like you, Jackson. I'm really going to be sorry to arrest you."

"For what?"

"Withholding evidence? How about obstruction of justice? That might work. Or just being too lazy to do things the right way."

"I can make bail, you know."

"Hmm." He sat forward again, put his hands on his desktop, and knitted his brows more elaborately than was called for. "You ever hear the Chinese proverb about the crow?"

"I don't think so."

"The crow is lazy, is the thing. So it flies up the pig's ass, thinking it can get at the meat faster that way."

"That's very profound."

"Don't you want to know what happens?"

"Can I see the body or not?"

"Settle for looking at the photos?"

"Depends on how thorough they are."

"They're Medical Examiner's photos and crime scene photos. They're thorough."

"Are they real?"

"What the hell do you mean, 'real'?"

"I mean printed on real paper, not just flashed on some stupid little screen."

"We have them both ways. You like paper, I got paper."

"Okay."

"First, though, you tell me who this guy is who *might* just be innocently sicko."

"His name is Ray Valento. They nailed him in Minneapolis for multiple robbery, aggravated assault, and rape. They also like him for a few kidnap-slash-murders they haven't quite figured out yet. But he managed to get out of jail on a phony bond, and now he's—"

"How the hell does somebody get a phony bond?"

"That's what I'd like to know. Are you going to show me the photos now?"

He pulled a manila folder out of his stack and tossed it toward me. Then he pulled several dozen glossy photos out of it. I immediately wanted to cry for the poor hacked and battered soul in the pictures. But I also felt a pang of surprise and relief.

"You pulled the wrong file."

"No, I didn't. I was at the crime scene, remember? That's what she looked like, in every grisly detail. Just like that."

"Okay, I believe you."

"So are those the right, um, *injuries*?"

"The wounds here," I said, pointing. "Could they have been made with an ice pick?"

"Could have been and probably were. Does that fit?"

"The damage is right, but the body isn't."

"What are you telling me?"

"That's not Trish Hanover."

Chapter Ten

The Scene of the Seen

Now that I knew for sure that somebody did more than just fantasize about inflicting his horrors upon people, I didn't necessarily disagree with Armstrong about putting the laptop back where I found it and letting the cops discover it. But the simple fact was that I didn't have it anymore. Quite probably, Wilkie did, but I didn't know where he was, so that was no help. And in any case, I wasn't about to admit that we had stolen the thing. The detective and I left the interview room and went to his office. I think that was supposed to make me feel as if he was my buddy. It didn't, but nevertheless, I told him about the emails I could remember and the Map Quest item. I did not tell him about Trish claiming to be Valento's defender. If she was still out there somewhere, playing her own strange hide-and-seek game, I didn't necessarily want to mess it up for her. Not until I knew more, anyway. I returned to the topic of Map Quest.

"You have any cop friends in Northern Wisconsin?"

"Not really, but I'm sure the local sheriff will give us a hand. Do we know what this guy drives?"

"He once showed me a photo of a sixty-eight Shelby Mustang, black with gold racing stripes. But whether he really has one or merely dreams about it, I don't know."

"DMV can tell us, if it really is registered to him. I'll make a call, see what I can find out. What else you got?"

"High blood pressure and a recurring concussion."

"We all have our problems, don't we? You were going to tell

me the other connection between Trish Hanover and this Ray Valento character, I believe."

"I want to see Trish's apartment. I want to see the crime scene."

"You know, for a guy who's already in extreme danger of being charged with obstruction of justice, you've got a lot of damned conditions and demands."

"That's my deep, penetrating curiosity. Some people think it's an asset."

"Some people collect old bottle caps."

"Can we go, or not?"

"Jesus, the things I do for a lousy thirty-year pension." He took his nine-millimeter semiauto out of his desk and put it in his shoulder holster, and we headed for the door.

⁂

IT WAS NICE, going to Lowertown in a vehicle that we could park anywhere with impunity. That was about the only nice thing about the trip. We went in the front door, just as I had, three days earlier. I was going to waive to the maitre d' again, but I didn't see him this time. Over at the elevator lobby, Armstrong took a key out of his pocket and used it to open a small, red wall-mounted box that said FIRE on it. He took two more keys out of the box and used them to open the elevator lobby and, five floors later, Trish's door. That was some kind of nifty key he had in his pocket. I assumed there was no point in asking him where I could get one like it.

The inside of the condo was utter chaos, and I knew that, unlike the mess in Valento's joint, that was not the normal state.

"Whoever this woman was, looks like she managed to put up one hell of a fight," I said. There were broken dishes, smashed lamps, and kitchen knives all over the place.

"It didn't help her, in the end. But yeah, sometimes you have

to feel glad that the victim didn't meekly give in, you know?"

"Maybe that means she knew what to expect from this guy. How do we find out who she was?"

"Autopsy has prints by now. We didn't rush checking on them because we were so sure we already knew who she was."

"What if she's never been printed before?"

"What if the stock market collapses and we get invaded by Martians? Take the problems as they come up, not as you imagine them, will you? Then maybe you won't have such high blood pressure. Don't touch anything, by the way."

"Hasn't the place already been dusted?"

"It has, but that's no excuse for knowingly contaminating it."

"I think you're conning me, Armstrong. I think what you really mean is that if there are already some of my prints here, you don't want to give me a chance to say they didn't get here until just now."

"You're in the wrong profession, you know that?"

"If only you knew. There will already be some of my prints here, you know, from when I had dinner with Trish."

"Yeah, you told me. Are there any in the sleeping loft?"

"No, I've never been up there."

"Just wasn't a good night for you at all, was it?"

"Go fuck yourself, Armstrong."

"Oh, thank you. I was afraid I was losing my touch at pissing people off."

Right. And pissed off people say things they didn't mean to, don't they? This guy is really not bad.

If I was looking for some dazzling insight from looking at the scene, my damaged brain let me down completely. Up in the sleeping loft, I nearly lost my lunch. The cops don't outline the body with tape or chalk anymore. But in this case, it didn't matter, because the place the body had been was outlined in blood. A lot of blood.

"Holy slaughterhouse, Batman."

"That would be the mild version, I believe. Watch where you step."

"Trish must have thought it was really nifty, having an antique four-poster bed."

"Probably so. The victim sure didn't think so, though."

"No. How did the perp restrain her?"

"Very old school. Ordinary rope. Not very professional-looking knots, though. Our guy was not a former Boy Scout."

"Well put. What did he do about the screams? There had to be screams."

"He gagged her with a rubber ball and plastic tape."

Something about that tripped a circuit far, far back in the archives of my brain, but I couldn't quite dredge up a memory to go with it yet. I left the loft and went into the bathroom, which was the only area that wasn't in complete chaos. Armstrong stood in the doorway behind me. I opened the medicine cabinet and looked in. I saw ibuprofen, rubbing alcohol, q-tips, antacid tablets, multi-vitamins, and a tube of anti-wrinkle cream.

"What's wrong with this scene?" I said.

"Nothing I can see."

"That's right, there's nothing here to see. How many people do you know who don't have any prescription medications?"

"I don't know. Not me or my wife, that's for sure."

"Not me, either. But here's a medicine cabinet, the only one in the place, with nothing in it that can't be bought over the counter anywhere. And while we're at it, where's her toothbrush? And her signature dark lipstick?"

"What are you saying, Jackson, that our perp collects toothbrushes as trophies?"

"No. I'm saying that when Trish left here, she knew she wasn't coming back."

"That would fit, yes."

"Now are you going to tell me who the dead woman is?"

"I told you, we—"

"You didn't find a purse?"

He stuck his hands deep in his pockets and scowled. "Yeah, okay then. We found one and we shrugged it off because we thought we already knew the victim was Trish."

"But you looked at it. You didn't throw it away. And being a cop, you remember whose ID was in it, too. Jesus, Armstrong, you're not *that* sloppy."

"No. I'm not. In fact, I'm not sloppy at all. To tell the truth, I was waiting to see if you already knew her name."

"Well, I don't."

"Well, until I'm sure of that, you're not going to hear it out of my mouth."

"Asshole."

"Maybe. We cops have a saying."

"Wonderful. First a stupid Chinese proverb and now a saying. You're a very deep fellow, for a cop. All right, lay it on me."

"Policemen and soldiers are society's sheep dogs. Everybody else is either a lamb or a wolf."

"Okay. So?"

"So you don't strike me as a lamb, Jackson."

"So maybe you ought to make some kind of temporary alliance with me. Deputize me or something."

"Or watch you, damn carefully. Yes, I think that's exactly what I'll do."

"I take that to mean you're not going to show me the dossier on the dead woman."

"You're a quick study, Jackson, I'll give you that."

Chapter Eleven

The Pursuit of Enlightenment

Without Wilkie around to bitch about it, I was free to talk to the rather strange person who called himself The Prophet. What he was the prophet of varied from time to time, as did what he was busy saving the world from, or for, or whatever. He answered his door and his phone by saying "Praise Yah!," but sometimes he called himself a high priest of Babism and simultaneously of the Cargo Cult of the Great God John Frum, which seemed to have neither a philosophy nor any institutions. Occasionally he also had a lot to write about Tetragrammaton, but nothing to say, since that's forbidden. The last time I saw him, he had finally lost interest in aluminum siding as a disharmonic bad-joss resonator and was concentrating on institutional greed as being mass suicide by monetary chocolate. It left him spending a lot of time looking for something called "ashe," or something like that. I try not to listen to any more of his ideas than I have to. It can all get very mentally exhausting. But in addition to his other, stranger roles, he was also the most accomplished illegal hacker I had ever seen or heard of. And I was definitely in need of his skills.

The Prophet lived and worked in a former railroad maintenance building on the far East Side. The building itself violated every building and safety code known to humankind. Not that the Prophet had any legal right to be there in the first place. And almost everything he did when he was there was also illegal. For some reason, that made me like him a lot.

I didn't go to his lair. I didn't know if Armstrong's threat about watching me included any actual surveillance or not. Until I found out, it would be a huge betrayal of trust to risk leading anybody to that spot.

He's probably also a certifiable nut case, but for most purposes, that doesn't matter.

I went to the electronics department of a Target store, looked around to make sure nobody I knew was watching, and bought a prepaid cell phone. The clerk contacted the cell company for me, and we spent half an hour setting it up, getting a number assigned to it, and assuring the company that no matter how good a deal it was, I did not want to buy an extra century or two of air time. No wonder they call the damn things burners.

I drove to a park by a containerized freight transfer terminal on Pierce Butler Road, where there's a lot of background noise and not much cover. But before I called the Proph, I made a call to the Ramsey County Morgue. A young-sounding woman answered.

"Yes, hello?" I said. "My name is Harper, Lew Harper, and I'm calling about a body you have?"

"I'm afraid autopsy results are not public information, sir."

She was afraid, she said. How nice. "Oh, I don't need that. And I don't need to see the body or its possessions, either. I simply wanted to know if the body had been released for the funeral yet? I was a very good friend of the—um—dead person, and I want to be sure and go to the funeral? And I hate to bother her family about it? They're pretty shook up, as you might expect." People are a lot more likely to help you if you make all your statements sound like questions. Better yet, very sorrowful questions. Still better, if you imply that the person you're talking to is your last hope in the whole world.

"What is the name, sir?"

"Trish Hanover?"

"One moment, sir."

She really had a good phone set. I could hear her talking to other people in the background quite nicely. She was back almost at once.

"Sir? We have no body here with that name."

"Oh dear. I really think you must be mistaken. She would have been brought in last Wednesday? She was murdered at her condo, down in Lowertown? It was terrible."

"How did you come by that information, sir?"

"One of her neighbors, at the condos, called me."

"Hold on."

Far, far in the background, I could hear another, older woman's voice. *Oh, that one? We thought it was a Trish Hanover at first, but it turned out to be the Watkins woman. You can't tell your caller that, though.*

"Sir? Are you still with me?"

"Yes I am."

"I've checked again, sir. There's nobody here by that name. The neighbors must have made some kind of mistake."

"So you're saying Trish is still alive?"

"I have no information about her at all, sir."

"Oh. Thank you anyway." *Yes, thank you a lot*. I disconnected, wrote "Watkins" in my pocket notebook, and then punched a number into the phone that very few people have, a number I have sworn never to write down.

"Praise Yah!" said the phone. Well it would, wouldn't it? "Neither your exotic phone nor the machine you are listening to will provide a window into your soul, but if you leave a name and number, I will ponder whether I wish to take on that task."

He had to be there, for real. In warm weather, he likes to play ersatz street preacher and shepherd to "the wandering souls who have neither a home nor an identity, nor a reality to put them in." But when winter comes, he's in his brick and byte fortress just about all the time. So I talked to the machine,

but I fully expected him to pick up. That's unless my karma had gone bad, of course.

"This is Herman, Prophet. I need you to—"

There were a couple of loud clunks and then a deep, booming voice. "Pilgrim! I can't believe you, of all people, would come to me over the electron-laden airways instead of as a physical manifestation. 'The world has lost its youth, and the times begin to wax old.'"

"No, they don't. Somebody may be following me right now, and I didn't want to risk leading them to you."

"What kind of 'them,' Pilgrim?"

"Cops."

"Good thinking. 'The hearing ear and the seeing eye, The Lord hath made even both of them.' Yeah, verily. But if they belong to the barbarians in blue, they can mind their own damn business. What kind of phone are you calling on?"

"I think you call it a burner."

"What do you call it?"

"A throwaway."

"Hmm. Anybody hanging around within parabolic earshot?"

"No. Nobody around, period."

"I can make that work. What is it that your soul thirsts for, pilgrim?"

"Information, of course."

"Not knowledge?"

"No, just information."

"A great tragedy. I'm better at knowledge. At wisdom, I am better yet."

"No offense, Prophet, but you're better at information."

"Only you, do I allow to say that. Anybody else, it'll cost them."

"I appreciate that."

"So, what are we hunting?"

"People." I gave him Ray Valento's name and home address. "I already have his official criminal history," I said. "What I

want is all his current personal stuff—credit card numbers and where they've been used in the last month, phone calls, vehicles licensed to him, anything that might tell me where he could be right now. Oh, and see if Mom is alive, and if so, where." The bonding business would fold in a fortnight if moms went away. Skips go right to them.

"Are we concerned about ethics as the square world defines them?"

"That's a trick question, right?"

"It is good to be with a kindred spirit, Pilgrim. What else?"

"A murder victim last Wednesday in St. Paul. All I know is that it's a thirtyish woman with the last name Watkins. I want her full name and her background, as much as you can get. The SPPD detective working the case is named John Armstrong, if that helps any."

"Do you want credit cards for this woman, too?"

"No. Just her past. And I need pictures for both people."

"That could be a long trek in a vast wilderness. Minus the manna, dig?"

"Why else would I come to you?"

"Hmm. If your Watkins woman had been charged with a crime last Wednesday, instead of being a victim, I could snatch her identity any number of places in the ether. But as it is, we might be looking for information that nobody has transmitted yet. Or stuff that requires us to have a name in order to start the search. Wonderfully vicious circle is it not? I might have to break into somebody's computer without them knowing it."

"Are we talking second-story work here?"

"No, Pilgrim. Physically and metaphysically, I always have both feet on the great bosom of Mother Earth."

"Sounds unstable, but it's totally your choice. I was offering to help out."

"Help out by coming up with a lot of what is rendered unto Caesar. Do we have a budget here, or can we get as enlightened as the universe will allow?"

"I need this one bad, Prophet. Enlightenment costs what it costs."

"Then the way shall be made clear. Can you shake off your tail?"

"If I have enough time, yes."

"Do it, and come and see me late tomorrow. Does your new phone have a number?"

"It does. But I called it a throwaway, yes? And that's what's about to happen."

"Then make sure it is truly put asunder. Don't give it to anybody else. It has my number in its memory now."

"I wouldn't ever give a cell phone to somebody else. That's like deliberately passing on a terrible disease."

"I don't reject that statement, Pilgrim. But it can be a hard road, getting rid of the electronic shackle. You sometimes pay a high price for your principles, I think."

"That's what Agnes says."

"Is Agnes a prophetess?"

"No, she's a secretary."

"Then she stumbles onto great truth with no grasp of what it might portend. Have I told you about the formation of a noncorporeal gestalt personality in the electronic ether, through—"

"See you tomorrow, Proph."

I looked at the phone and considered that maybe I should hang on to it for one more day, to call the Proph back and let him know when I was on my way to his place. Then I headed back out on Pierce Butler Road, took the 328i up to about 45, and threw the phone out the window. I watched in my rearview mirror as it bounced off the icy pavement, first in one piece and then in many. I smiled. Sometimes it's the little pleasures that matter.

Chapter Twelve

Backing Up Without Mirrors

After disposing of the devil's instrument, I headed back to the office. With a day and a bit more to wait before the Prophet had anything for me and no idea where Wilkie had disappeared to, I had no excuse not to go back and pretend to do some work. Agnes, of course, is quite capable of running things all by herself. All she needs out of me is an occasional signature and sometimes a judgment call on who we will or won't bond. But it's important to let her see now and then that I don't dump everything on her while I spend endless time at Lefty's pool hall. Leadership by example, and all that. The example being showing up. After all, if she ever got mad and quit, I might actually have to work for a living.

I thought about that signature business a bit. Valento had somehow gotten a bond with my name on it, without my signing it. I really wanted to find out exactly what went on there, but I hadn't figured out how to check into it yet. The Prophet couldn't help me. Like dinosaur-slash-Luddite me, bonding is a very pre-computer thing. The physical piece of paper is absolutely everything, and there is no substitute for somebody physically delivering it. So who was the somebody? Chris Parker, Valento's real PD, might be able to find out, if he had any reason to want to. But I had the distinct impression he had done as much for me as he was going to. I put it all in a dim corner of my mind, to wait for an inspired strategy.

Back in the office, Agnes was doing a computer version of the daily sudoku puzzle and nibbling on a granola bar that she had undoubtedly been nursing for several hours. She blushed and apologized when she saw that I had seen what was on her screen. I thought that was charming. She feels guilty if she's not grinding out some kind of work every minute of the day. Or maybe she feels guilty that she's enjoying herself. Sometimes the Protestant Work Ethic is a bitch.

On the corner of her desk was a shiny black Dell laptop. If that didn't tell me Wilkie had been there, the nearly empty coffee pot and the fresh handprint, where he likes to lean on my dingy wall, would.

"Is that what I think it is, Aggie?"

"Mr. Wilkie said you would want it."

"And where is *Mister* Wilkie?"

"You just missed him, Herman." She stared squarely at her screen.

"That's not what I asked you, is it?"

"No, but it seems to be what I'm going to tell you." She continued to stare resolutely straight ahead. "I don't know where he is, and that's the truth. I think he might be off to see his new computer date, but I'm really not sure. I finally got hold of Anne Packard, by the way." She turned away from the screen and gave me her "I did good, didn't I?" face.

"Don't change the sub —really? What did she have to say?" There weren't a lot of things Agnes could tell me that would make me totally lose interest in prying the truth about Wilkie out of her, but that was one of them. Was the ocean of strangeness that had come between Anne and me about to part like the Red Sea? My mind said no way, but that's not what my heart was telling me.

"I told her you had some kind of hot tip that she was in danger."

"That's a pretty good short version. And?"

"She didn't believe me. Or you, I guess. She said that was

one of the lamest ploys she had ever heard of."

"Well, rats. I thought it was rather good, besides being mostly true. Maybe you should have told her I have a recurring brain concussion and I'm supposed to have somebody with me for the next few days."

"Ooh, I like that."

"That happens to be totally true."

"Really? I never know when to believe you, Herman. I don't think she does, either, but I wish the two of you would get back together, all the same. I'd have tried the concussion story, if I'd known it."

"What else did she say?" Agnes knew perfectly well what I was hoping to hear, but it wasn't to be.

"She said to tell you that the planes from here to New York don't take any longer than the ones from New York to here." She hunched up her shoulders and gave me a sad smile of mute apology. It wasn't her fault. And if there were no problem except distance, I'd be on one of those flights in a heartbeat. I sighed and went back to a topic I at least knew how to attack.

"So Wilkie didn't say I should meet him anywhere?"

"Afraid not."

"And he didn't say where he's been."

"Nope."

"Okay. I'll try something else, then." I put my coat back on and picked up the Dell, still with no AC adapter. "You don't know anything about this thing, okay? Never saw it."

"That's what Mr. Wilkie said, too." She nodded with her whole upper body.

"Well, then, it must be right." I pretended I was Sgt. Preston of the Yukon and went back out into the arctic deep freeze, to follow Detective Armstrong's illegal advice.

First, though, I bought an AC adapter for Valento's computer, took it to the coffee house that Wilkie had liked, with the free wi-fi, plugged it in and fired it up. Then I used my

magical new password to send the identical email to each of the women that Valento had been keeping a file on.

I know where you live. I know where you work and where you shop and what you drive. I am coming for you, and when I do, I will take you as easily as plucking a grape. And I will use you and abuse you and then kill you slowly and with great pain. Be ready.

It was especially important to include the death threat. That made the email a felony, and even if they didn't believe it, the police or feds couldn't ignore it. It also gave the cops a reason to arrest Valento, even if he hadn't technically jumped bail yet. I was proud of myself. The next part of my plan was going to be a little trickier, though.

I parked two blocks away from Valento's digs and around a corner. I skated the rest of the way on the black ice sidewalks. Valento wouldn't know what my car looked like, and in the unlikely event that he was home, I didn't want him to find out.

There were no cars in the tiny parking area behind the building except a dirty ten-year-old Honda with a lot of frost on the glass. It had been there last time Wilkie and I came to visit, too. The mailbox was stuffed again, and the space behind the little glass in the door was still totally dark. Had I taken the time to re-lock the deadbolt the last time I was there? Somebody had. I got out my picks and went to work. Like any mechanical job, picking a specific lock is easier the second time. Once or twice more, and I'd be faster than somebody with a key.

I wasn't quite sure if the apartment looked or felt the same as the last time I was there or not. The stale beer and stale pizza smells seemed stronger than before, and there might have been even more trash. I touched my Beretta once to make sure I knew where it was and decided I would tarry there not one second longer than I had to. The built-in bed was still pulled out. I wiped down the Dell inside and out with some toilet

tissue, threw it back on the bed, and pushed the whole works into the wall. I noted with some satisfaction that there was no old AC adapter lying around. Bite your tongue, Wilkie.

Back at street level, I used the picks again to lock the door, and I was turning toward the mailbox when somebody came around the corner. She had her head down and was concentrating on navigating the ice, so I didn't think she saw me fooling with the lock. Even so, I'd need a cover story of some kind.

"Oh." She looked up and slid to a halt, eyes wide, mouth open in surprise. The proprietor of the antique shop around the corner. Had to be. It wasn't just that she didn't have a coat on, she just *looked* like antiques. I don't mean that she was all that old. She was probably pushing fifty and was doing a nice job of holding onto the good side of it. In fact, she was pretty and not at all frumpy. But she looked like a standard of beauty from a different age, as if she had stepped out of a fifties movie. Deborah Kerr, maybe, or Inger Stevens. Eve Arden, come to think of it. She had what used to be called strawberry blond hair that was mostly pulled up and back, except for a couple of dangling spit curls that framed her heart-shaped face. I thought of an old fantasy book by James Thurber in which one of the characters was frequently referred to as having an indescribable hat. She had indescribable hair, though it definitely looked professionally done.

And she had a small key tightly clasped between thumb and forefinger. The mailbox key.

"I, um, was just about to collect Mr. Valento's mail."

Her voice didn't actually shake, but it was damn nervous. My instinct was to calm her down by telling her, "Funny thing; so was I." But that wouldn't get me a whole lot of easy information, would it?

"Mr. Valento is gone, is he?" I said. "Where?"

"Oh, he doesn't tell me. I just, um…collect, um…the mail. Is all."

I didn't know what she was really up to, but it was obvious

that I had caught her red-handed at it. And it shook her up so much, she didn't even care who I was or what I thought I was doing there, only what I thought of her.

"Well then, by all means, collect it." I stepped back from the mailbox and put on my most official-looking stone face. "I came here to serve some papers on Mr. Valento. Do you have any idea where I might find him?"

"No. I'm sorry." She opened the box, dumped its contents into a paper shopping bag, and shut it again. Then she tried without success to pull her cardigan tight over her rather amply filled-out blouse. "Listen, it's freezing out here. Could we finish this discussion inside the store? I have to get back there anyway, to meet a driver from UPS."

"Sure." I made an "after you" gesture, and she turned and skidded away from me, leaving me to admire the way her hips worked the contours of a close-fitting pair of black pants. We turned the corner like a couple of clumsy dogs on wet linoleum, made it to the storefront door, and went in. She slammed the door behind us. A sign in the window said she was open for business, but there was nobody in the place but us.

Near the door were three big cardboard cartons with a lot of shipping tape and some complicated labels on them. "E-bay," she said, pointing at the boxes, "is the savior of small retail businesses everywhere." What she really wanted me to pick up on was the fact that there was actually somebody else on his way there, so she wasn't going to be alone in the shop for long.

Going inside was not so much like walking into another age as into dozens of them, all jumbled together. A Sargasso Sea of pop history. There was so much—well, *old stuff*—hanging from the walls and ceiling that it was impossible to determine the shape of the main room. Wood and iron tools whose function I couldn't imagine, enameled tin toys, clocks, lamps, bottles, faded prints and photos, wooden boxes with logos of long dead companies on them, dolls, model ships, and on and on. I gave up trying to even broadly classify it, much less take it all

in. But despite the visual chaos, it had a nice, cozy feel, as if each piece had been given a loving touch before it was finally assigned to its dusty space in the graveyard of lost memories.

"You must be Auntie Kew," I said.

She chuckled. "That's just a made up name. I'm Naomi, and I'm not anybody's aunt." She extended her hand and I took it. "Naomi Ford."

"Herman Jackson." I must have been more impressed by her than I realized. I actually gave her my right name. "But this is your place, yes? Your business?"

"My business and my building. I don't think—"

Her attention was suddenly directed to the far side of the sales area, where a big, scruffy-looking cat emerged from a jumble of weathered peach crates and wooden riding toys. Mostly white, it had a dark gray saddle that extended down over its shoulders and up over its jowls and eyes, forming a goofy-looking raccoon mask that didn't quite meet over its nose. It also had one half of a little Charlie Chaplin moustache and a huge plume of a tail that it held straight up, like a Samurai battle standard. It trotted across the room as if it had seen a beckoning tuna can and proceeded to tangle itself up in my legs. I reached down and gave it a rub behind one ear, and it looked up adoringly and gave me a loud purr.

"I don't believe that," she said. "Usually when there's a stranger in the shop, he hides in the darkest corner he can find."

"Maybe I'm not a stranger. Maybe we're old buds in one of his other eight lives."

"He seems to think so, anyway. Would you like a cup of tea, Mr. Jackson?"

"That's really nice of you. I would hate a cup of tea. But anything remotely resembling coffee would be wonderful."

"I've got some of that, I think, that 'remotely resembling' kind. Be back in a jiff." She disappeared into a back room and the cat followed her. I took off my coat and looked around. In

one corner, to the extent that the room had any corners, was a round oak table with carved lion's paws on its feet and three totally unmatched chairs around it. I draped my coat on one of the chairs and waited. I noticed that Naomi's own mail was laid out neatly on the burled maple top of an ornate buffet, but she had taken the contents of Valento's mailbox into the back room with her. Suddenly the reason for that dawned on me.

It took her considerably more than a jiff, but she did come back, carrying an enameled metal tray with two steaming cups and a plate of cookies on it. If she had been hoping I would get discouraged and leave while she was gone, she was out of luck. But she looked cheerful enough. She had worked on her hair a bit and changed her simple pearl studs for some dangly old-looking earrings. They also had pearls, but in tarnished silver settings. Maybe they were her equivalent of an employee ID badge.

"I took the liberty of throwing my coat over that chair."

"Good for you. Why don't you take the liberty of sitting in the one next to it? Do you take anything in your coffee?"

"Antique teaspoons and calloused thumbs. Beyond that, I'm a purist."

"That's good, because that's about all I have, minus the calluses. Do you really want a spoon?" She placed a cup in front of me and sat down across the table. The cups were blunt, roundy-cornered things in slightly muddied primary colors, with ridged saucers that matched.

"No, I was just being a smartass. It was nice of you not to point that out."

She didn't quite give me an approving look, but her eyes had a nice shine to them. She laid out some paper napkins.

"Nice cups." I lied.

"That's Fiestaware. They started making it in 1936, and kept on for about half a century after that. It's probably the most collected kind of dinnerware there is. Personally, I always thought it was rather ugly, but a lot of people really like it."

"My mother had a bunch of that stuff. Even as a little kid, I thought it was hideous."

She laughed, an easy, flowing ripple. "Well, isn't that just splendid?"

"Is it? What is?"

"We've only met, and already we're being brutally honest with each other."

"I guess that's a good beginning, at that. Was there a check?"

"Excuse me?" The smile vanished, replaced by the look of being caught with her hand in the cookie jar.

"Valento's mail. Did it have a paycheck in it?"

"Look, I don't know who you think I am, but—"

"I think you're his landlady, and he owes you money. Relax, okay? And I'm fine with you taking his mail, because if there is a paycheck, then it might tell me where he works. And I would very much like to visit him at work."

"You're not going to…?"

"No, I'm not going to. Take it easy."

"You don't really have any papers for him, do you?"

"More like a pair of handcuffs."

"Oh, dear. Then you're a policeman?"

"Bail bondsman. For you, not nearly so threatening. For him, maybe worse." I gave her one of my cards and what I hoped was a reassuring smile.

"I knew there was something wrong about that man. I *knew* it. He frightens me, Mr. Jackson."

"Then you have better instincts than a lot of women. I would dearly love to put him where he can't frighten you. Do you have any idea at all where he might be?"

"I really don't." She got a distant and rather sad look and took a sip of tea.

"How about where he works?"

"He's some kind of mechanic, but I don't know where. I see him with grease on his hands sometimes, and he gets it on the doorknob, too. Not much to go on, is it?"

"Not much, no. Oh, well. It seems we may as well just have a warm cup of whatever and a nice chat." What the hell was I playing at? Did I seriously think she knew more than she was telling me and would cough it up later if I drank some of her bad coffee? I don't know, but at that moment, I definitely wanted to stay there a while. Her little shop offered a certain serenity that I hadn't realized I needed until then.

"I would like that, Mr. Jackson. Yes, I definitely would."

"Herman. It's not a great name, but it's what I have. Tell me, if I had agreed to have tea instead of coffee, would you have read the leaves for me?"

"How could you possibly know that?" Her jaw dropped about halfway to her chest and stayed there.

"You remind me of somebody I once met who did that, I guess."

"Amazing. I can only do it for some people, and only sometimes. I never know when it's going to work. But yes, it has to be from tea leaves or dregs. I can't do a thing with a dirty coffee cup. Do you want to change your mind and have some tea?"

"I'll pass, but thanks anyway. I may not want to know my future just now. Before I forget it, by the way, I need to make a phone call, okay?"

"Of course." She looked like I had just asked her a trick question. "Why do you need my permission?"

"Because I don't have a phone."

"Oh." She laughed. "That's so rare these days."

"It's part of my religion."

"Over there." She pointed. I stared for a while at a wall covered with framed sepia-tone portraits, and eventually I spotted a wall phone in their midst.

"Oh, there. Not a cordless?" I got up and headed that way.

"What can I say? This is an antique shop."

"Naomi, you are my kind of people."

She went into the back room while I fished a card out of my pocket and punched in the number on it.

Chapter Thirteen

Time in a Dusty Drawer

I decided I would use the voice of a cheap mobster from the east coast that I had once bonded. The desk sergeant picked up on the first ring, and I asked him to transfer me to Detective Armstrong. He demanded to know who I was first, and I told him they call me No-Name Jack and that Armstrong would know me.

"Armstrong here. This better be good."

"It should oughta be, I got it myself."

"That's the worst accent I've ever heard."

"No, it ain't. It's plenty good enough so's you can say you didn't recognize the voice."

"We'll say so for now, anyway. What's the story?"

"The story, pal, is I'm in this bar over in Midway night before last? And I hear this guy, goes by the name of Ray Valentine or Vendetta or Valento or some such shit, tell some buddy a' his about wasting a broad down in Lowertown. Says he's got pictures of it on his computer—snuff pictures, he says— and would this guy like to go have a look-see."

"That's it?"

"Ain't that enough?" *Jesus, Armstrong, what do you need, a map?*

"Where's the computer?"

"In this guy's digs."

"And where are they?"

"What, you don't got a phone book?"

"Maybe it's enough, at that. I'll try it out. You know I have to ask. How can I get ahold of you again?"

"You kidding? You never hoid of a confidential source?"

"Not quite like this one."

"You musta never was in Jersey. See you, pal."

I was feeling rather pleased with myself after that, and when I rejoined Ms. Ford at the table, I helped myself to a cookie. It was a Girl Scout cookie, I think, the kind with the peanut butter filling, and it soaked up the bad coffee very nicely. As I was taking the first bite, the cat reappeared from the back room and jumped up on my lap.

"Stewball! You behave yourself." She started to get up. "I'm really sorry about him, Herman, sometimes he—"

"He's okay." I put down the cookie and gave the cat a little scratch behind both ears. It responded by butting its head against the bottom of my chin and giving me a ragged purr.

"You're sure?"

"Sure." The cat flopped against my chest. It must have weighed about twenty pounds. I rubbed him on the shoulder and chin, and the purr went to full outboard-motor roar. "We're great friends now. How did he get a name like Stewball?"

"He picked it. He was a tiny kitten when I got him. A stray, a true orphan of the storm. He followed me home from somewhere by the corner grocery on a day about like this, and I let him in and gave him some milk. He threw it up and collapsed. I mean, he was really sick. Or starving, maybe. And my car wasn't running, which is what it does best, so I couldn't take him to a vet. So I tried a remedy I had heard about. To get a little nourishment into him without making him sick again, I rubbed a little dab of butter on his nose. He licked it off, of course, and then he went to sleep. I did that a lot of times. And I wrapped him up in a fuzzy towel and sang to him."

"I thought cats didn't like music."

"Nobody told him. Anyway, I had to do *something*. I couldn't bear it if he had died and I hadn't done anything at all."

"So you sang to him and yourself."

"I guess that's what I did, yes. And his favorite song was 'Stewball.' You know, the folk song about the racehorse?"

"How did you know?"

"It made him purr."

"And he got well."

"And he got well." Her face lit up at the memory. "And then he got big and fat and sassy. Now he prowls around the shop catching things I don't want to know about and breaking merchandise, but I never scold him."

"It's nice to have a love."

"It is nice. And you know what else? If he had died back when I first took him in, it would still have been nice. You take love where and when you can get it, and you don't worry that it might not be forever." Her eyes were glistening now, and her mouth was slightly open in an expression that I couldn't read. What I did read, though, was that she was not the sort of person that would ever be involved with the scumbag upstairs.

"Naomi, would you go out to dinner with me tonight?"

"Absolutely."

⁂

Somehow the afternoon slipped away, as smooth and unnoticed as a master pickpocket. Stewball got tired of me when he saw that I didn't have a big enough lap for him to sleep on without dangling off in places. He went back to his secret corners, and I followed Naomi around the shop while she told me stories about her customers.

"Is it very, very old, your stock?"

"Mostly, no. Shops that sell really ancient stuff are very upscale. They sell things that were originally rich people's fancies—fine jewelry, serious art, stolen artifacts, and pretentious status items. That's not the sort of market we have around here. This is the scrapyard of popular culture, and the oldest

junk is bought by the oldest people. Nobody buys anything that was made before they were born, except an occasional interior decorator. Nobody is looking for any history except their own. They are looking for their own childhoods, because there's something back there that they lost. Let me show you something."

She went over to a heavy wooden cabinet with tiers of wide but shallow drawers, the sort of thing that architects and artists use to file their drawings. She opened one and pulled out a sheet of glossy, heavy paper that was printed with richly colored airplane pieces, slightly perforated, made to be punched out.

"During World War II, the hobby companies couldn't get balsa wood or rubber, so a minor industry grew up, making model kits out of printed paper. Airplanes, ships, tanks, whatever. Also farm buildings and forts. Some of them were really very well engineered, and beautifully printed."

"You see references to the wartime rubber shortage in old movies, sometimes. But I never thought about the balsa wood before."

"To a serious student of the printer's art or to a history museum, this is a pretty interesting piece, and it's in very nice shape. Not really what you would call valuable, though. But to somebody who was a young boy during the war, this is totally intoxicating magic. Pure gold. It transports him back to a world he had all but forgotten, and he would give almost anything to own it. The problem, of course—"

"Is that there aren't many people left who were little kids in World War II."

"Give that man a cookie. That's the problem, exactly. And it keeps moving forward, of course. There used to be an organization over in Minneapolis that called itself the Seventy-Five-Fifteen Club. They were regular customers of mine for military memorabilia for a while. Guess where the name came from?"

"The size of their club howitzer?"

"French boxcars. They were all ex-cavalry men, from the First World War. And a standard French railroad boxcar would carry exactly seventy-five troops or fifteen horses, but not both. I never saw their clubhouse, but it had a lot of my merchandise in it."

"And now it's gone."

"As gone as the five-cent cigar and the real malted milk. There is no point in me carrying World War I mementos any more, at all. Civil War, even less so. A couple years ago, I read somewhere that the World War II vets were dying off at some preposterous rate like a hundred a day. So pretty soon my olive drab Lucky Strike packs and original Rosie the Riveter posters are going to be drags on the market, too."

"So what do you stock, then?"

"Whatever I want to. Sometimes I think of myself as being a sort of a capricious historian. I save the artifacts of the people who are otherwise forgotten. So it won't be as if they had never been, you know?"

"Can you make any money that way?"

"Making money isn't everything, Herman."

"You're a very smart woman."

"I don't worry about being smart. I settle for having passion."

"It becomes you."

I told Naomi I needed to change clothes and would be back in an hour or so. Outside, the sun was already gone. During its brief visit, it had been brilliant, but it hadn't melted one cube's worth of ice off the streets. I drove, or slid, back to Trish Hanover's building, half out of control most of the time. I parked in front, illegally, and went straight to the ground floor restaurant.

I picked that restaurant because it seemed as if I should be keeping an eye on Trish's condo, if only on the chance that she might come back and explain things. But if I was honest with myself, I didn't expect it and maybe didn't want it, either.

What I wanted was an evening with Naomi.

The place had not opened for the evening, and judging by his expression of unvarnished malice, the maitre d' must have recognized me.

"We're not open." He probably thought the lack of a "sir" should tell me everything I needed to know.

"That's okay. I don't need a table until seven."

"Quite impossible." He made no attempt to hide the open appointment book with lots of white spaces in it. I had no doubt that seven o'clock on any other day was going to be impossible, too.

"My lady really likes this building, and she's dying to see what kind of restaurant is in it." I laid a crisp fifty-dollar bill on top of the book, with no finesse whatsoever. I kept a couple of fingers on it.

"Perhaps I have something, at that. Seven, you say?"

"Seven." I turned the bill loose. "And it would be nice to have a table where we could look up into the big atrium. I want her to see the fancy elevator."

"Not a problem, sir. Name?" Just like that, all the way back to "sir." And they say money won't make your sins go away.

I checked in briefly with Agnes, who was still playing deaf and dumb about Wilkie, then went to my townhouse, where I changed into black slacks, a dark blue shirt with black pinstripes, and my charcoal-gray sportcoat, the one with the soft fabric and the sharp lines.

I headed back to Auntie Kew's feeling like a dumb kid on a first date. Naomi saw me skidding up to the door through the storefront window, which had a "Closed" sign in it. She opened the door for me before I got to it.

She had changed her earrings yet again and had put on an elegant gold watch and a dark red dress in a leaf print pattern. It had a ruffled hem just above the knee, a closely fitted waist, and a scooped neckline that was downright daring. She filled it out perfectly.

"You look absolutely stunning." I meant it.

"So do you, Herman. I've been saving this dress for tonight, by the way."

"You lie."

"Yes I do. But I do it with style, don't you think?"

"I do. Let's go show the world, then."

She wrapped herself cleverly in some kind of camel-colored soft thing that could have been a cape, a shawl, or a huge scarf, or all three. Maybe it was indescribable. Whatever it was, it went well with her light tan shoes, which, considering the ice outside, looked a little risky.

"I'm parked a couple of blocks from here. Are you sure you're okay with those shoes?"

"These are absolutely the only shoes for this dress," she said, glancing down. "Kitten-heel, peep-toe slingbacks. Fun to wear and fun to say." She looped her arm in mine, and we went off into the night. Suddenly it didn't seem so icy.

Chapter Fourteen

Night Out

The restaurant actually turned out to be worth the extra fifty bucks. I had the rack of lamb, with a dark red wine sauce so savory, the little roasted potatoes died, just to jump into it. Naomi had a lobster salad, with greens that looked like they were from another planet. She seemed to like it. We had a table where I could see the wrought iron rail in front of Trish's apartment, but not the door itself. I hoped I wasn't too obtrusive about looking up that way.

"So, Naomi Ford, is there anything significant about your surname?"

"No such luck. The only thing I have in common with the Ford Motor Company is that neither one of us got a government bailout."

"That's good. I never was comfortable around billionaires."

"Well, then, you won't be disappointed."

"So instead of cars, you became an independent purveyor of used dreams. How did that happen, exactly?" I poured us more wine, while she contemplated the dessert menu.

"There aren't a lot of things you can do with a degree in American studies, are there? A purveyor of used dreams? I rather like that. The shop was my father's, originally. For him, it was a hobby business. He called it his escape pod."

"What was he escaping from?"

"His job, his marriage, his life. I think it changed over time. He was a stockbroker at his day job. He made a ton of money whether his customers did or not. And it got him a bleeding

ulcer, dangerously high blood pressure, and enough self-hatred and guilt to sink a battleship."

"So he needed a place to hide away."

"Wanted it, anyway. He bought the shop, and he remodeled the back so he could sleep there sometimes, which got to be most times. He made the shop quite nice, actually. He specialized in 1920s and 30s wooden and cast iron toys and opened by appointment only. Mostly, he worked on his bottle collection, and they weren't the antique kind. When I got older, I also realized he brought his floozies there."

"Floozies? That's a word I haven't heard in a while."

"Antique English."

"Does that go with the territory?"

"I'm an antique person. I can talk in antique English. It's not that I categorically disapprove of women with a free attitude toward sex. I approve of it, in fact. It's the lack of self-respect that I couldn't abide."

"His or theirs?"

"Both. My father would spout the classic soap-opera defense to my mother, the old, 'They never meant anything to me!' line. As far as I was concerned, that was the whole problem. They never meant anything to him or to themselves either. That's a misuse of a wonderful gift, Herman, a bad misuse."

"Did it lead to divorce?"

"They were hard core Catholics." She shook her head as if she still couldn't believe it. "It was fine to make a mockery of marriage, even to trash it, but unthinkable to give it up. So stupid. The Pope has a lot to answer for, you know?"

"A lot of Popes do. Tell me about your mother."

"My mother." She gave a sigh that came from some pit of sorrow about a mile deep. Then she took a long drink of wine. "My mother was a very beautiful woman."

"That would be logical, yes."

"Very cute, the way you snuck that in. Thank you. But I hope I'm not like her. She was so beautiful, she didn't need to

have any character. I resisted seeing that for a long time, but I finally had to admit she was authentically shallow. She wanted my father's money and status, and she wanted to go places where she could show them off. Beyond that, she didn't care about anything or anybody. She thought the antique store was a disgrace. She wouldn't go in it."

"And the women?"

"She knew about all of them. Sometimes I think that was the whole point of my father's affairs and one-nighters, letting her find out about them."

"So you grew up determined not to be like those women and not like your parents, either."

"You're a quick study, Herman."

"So I'm told."

"Does that go with being a bail bondsman?"

"Well, it goes with something I've been, anyway." Like a bookie in Detroit. But no matter how charming I found her, that was a place we absolutely couldn't go. And I also couldn't tell her that my own childhood toys were not paper airplane kits, but a baseball bat with nails poking out of it and a four-inch switchblade.

I debated telling her about my ambiguous brain damage. I finally decided it would probably sound like the worst pick-up line ever mouthed. *You're so lovely, my dear. Stay with me tonight in case I have another concussion.* Not good.

Then something up on the fifth floor caught my eye. A figure emerged at the balcony rail in front of Trish's condo. A man, for sure, but impossible to recognize from where I sat. He didn't run, but he moved quickly. He disappeared into the stairwell, emerged a couple minutes later in the elevator lobby. So my instinct had paid off, whether I wanted it to or not. The man left by the side door, the one the maitre d' had wanted me to use, so long ago.

"Oh shit, oh shit, oh shit." I stood up and reached for my wallet, then realized I couldn't possibly settle up the tab in

time. So I threw what I hoped was enough money on the table.

"Herman, what on earth—"

"Here's a bunch of money, just in case," I said. "But I'll be back. I absolutely promise I'll be back. Please, please wait for me." And I ran out. I hated doing it worse than death, but I had to know who that figure was.

Damned instincts.

Outside, my shadow man had already vanished. Having nothing else to go on, I headed south, toward the area where I had lost him the last time. That was assuming it was indeed the same guy. Come to think of it, I was only assuming that either one of them was the guy I really wanted. Armstrong, wouldn't be impressed by that.

Earlier that evening, back at my townhouse, I had debated whether or not to take a gun with me on my date. I decided it ruined the line of my sport coat, and I left it. Wilkie would find that hysterical. Ray Valento probably would, too. At the moment, I wasn't finding it even slightly amusing. I picked up my pace and tried to stay in mostly lighted areas, peering into dark ones. But sooner or later I would have to go into some of them or else give up the chase. I turned a corner and let the shadows claim me, pausing a moment to let my eyes adjust. They mostly didn't, and I plunged blindly on.

Under the old pedestrian bridge that sprung from the back of Union Depot, I glimpsed somebody two blocks ahead, moving east, toward a former cardboard box factory that had been made into artists' lofts. He either heard me or had excellent fugitive instincts, because he stopped to look back over his shoulder, then broke and ran south. The parking garage underneath the concrete deck that once held up roaring, steam-powered trains was now heavily under construction and renovation. The forest of concrete pillars that made a maze out of the original space was now thickened and made even more labyrinthine by countless shoring posts and small scaffolding. It was a good place to hide. That was where he

went. Pursuing him with neither light nor weaponry would be exactly like running in a pitch-dark room with an unpinned hand grenade.

I looked for something I could use for a weapon and found nothing. Should I have a closer look anyway? *That worked out so well for you last time, Herman. I'm sure you want to do it again.* Actually, I did want to. If I waited for a favorable time to chase the guy, it was probably never going to happen.

A gust of solid cold poked its fingers inside my coat and I slipped sideways on the ice. A bad night to be out. *That should be telling me something. This guy is not out for a stroll. Before he ducked into the scaffold area, he was headed somewhere warm and safe. His bolt hole, his sanctuary.* I tried to picture what lay to the east. The artists' lofts, but that didn't feel like his kind of place. In any case, I could easily check it out in the daylight. What else? The Lafayette Bridge, soaring over the whole area like the deck of an oversized aircraft carrier. And under it, a hodgepodge of old industrial buildings, mostly abandoned, all obscure and unfrequented.

I moved ahead and to the left, turning away from the river, staying in shadow, putting the street lamp between me and my quarry, so I wouldn't be backlit, past the former box factory. I surveyed the landscape of broken industry. Some single-story strip buildings had once been railroad freight transfer warehouses, with the floors built at a slope so it would be easier to wheel heavy loads from the freight cars down to the waiting wagons. Some had been converted to small offices or light manufacturing shops. Most were boarded up and abandoned, waiting for the wrecking ball. Beyond them stretched a real hobo heaven of scruffy brush and small trees. Finally I spotted a big cone-shaped structure that Public Works had once used to store salt and sand for the streets. It was made out of rusted steel sheets, with external ribs and no windows. But here and there, through a loose joint in the steel, I could see light bleeding out. I went closer, up to a six-foot high chain link fence

that surrounded the property. The fence had a big gate in front, chained and padlocked, and a lot of NO TRESSPASSING signs. I didn't try to climb over it.

The slits of light in the building were not large, but they were unmistakable. No way a mere storage shed should be lit up like that on the inside, in the dead of the night. As I got closer, I heard noises as well, a faint clanking of metal and an occasional hissing sound. A chop shop, maybe. Valento's job, where he got his hands greasy, and the same place he went to ground, a murderer taking refuge in a den of pirates.

As I stood watching, a steel overhead door rolled partway up and two men took positions in the opening, backlit by the fluorescents inside. They looked pretty nondescript, except that they both carried submachine guns.

"There!" One of them pointed straight at me. So the pirates had an alarm system, and I had definitely tripped it.

I thought suddenly of the photo reconnaissance fliers in World War II, who had the motto *Unarmed and unafraid.* Needless to say, they had a very short life expectancy. I decided not to emulate them. This night's mission was over.

I took off running, not stopping to see if they were following. When I rounded the corner by the carton factory, bullets slammed into the brickwork. Their guns were equipped with very good suppressors. Powder and shards of broken brick hit the back of my head, but there was no roar of muzzle blasts. I kept going.

Three blocks later, I ducked into an arched brick entryway and risked a look back. Nothing. My gunmen had decided not to go this far into civilization. I went an extra two blocks north, then turned around and headed back to the restaurant.

Naomi was gone.

Chapter Fifteen

Things That Go Bump

The pile of money was still on the table, but Naomi was nowhere to be seen. The waiter had left the check on top of the money.

I sank down at our table and drank the last of our wine. Then I counted the pile of cash and looked at the check. There hadn't been enough money after all. I put away the cash, took out a credit card, and signaled for the waiter.

"Sir?"

"Bring me a double Scotch, a revised tab, and a cyanide pill." I gave him the card.

"Yes sir." He seemed totally unfazed. Maybe he would do it, at that.

Two sips into the scotch, I heard the voice I had given up on.

"Herman, you're not driving me home if you get drunk."

The Scotch totally lost its flavor. "I don't want to, now. I thought you had gone, ditched me."

"Me? You were the one who left. I only went to the ladies' room. By any chance, are you going to tell me what's going on?"

"Yes. That, and a lot more, Naomi. Sit down. Let's order some dessert; this could take a while."

It was late when we finally got back to the antique shop. Naomi was less than thrilled by the news that she was living

downstairs from a homicidal maniac. But she seemed to take some comfort from the idea that he was probably busy jumping bail at the moment, and also had one set of cops who wanted to arrest him and another set who wanted to kill him outright. Still, all things considered, we stopped by my townhouse on the way back, and I picked up my nine millimeter and a spare magazine. I also took the .380 and put it in the glove compartment.

"You might as well park in the alley behind the shop," she said. "The lock on my back door has been all jammed up for ages, but at least it gets your car off the street."

I turned into the alley and put the headlights on high beam when I saw something near the building.

"You didn't leave anything open when we left, did you?"

"Of course not. Why would I?"

"I don't know, but isn't that Stewball by the back door?"

"Oh my God, yes it is."

The back door was partly open. The door was in a shadow cast by the fire escape, so we hadn't seen that right away. Naomi started to get out of the car, but I grabbed her arm and pulled her back.

"Get the cat in the car, if you can, and lock the doors. That's this little switch, here." I made sure she saw where I was pointing.

"All right. What are you going to do, Herman?"

"Go greet our guest. If I don't come back out in three minutes flat, you and Stewball get out of here, fast." I left the motor running, chambered a round in the 9 mm., and eased out on the rough ice.

I found a switch by the back door and turned it on. It lit up a corridor that led straight ahead to the shop, with doors to other rooms on both sides. I cocked my right elbow up, so I could hold the gun close to my face, and put my left arm straight out ahead of me. If somebody inside had a club, they might break a wrist or an elbow, but they wouldn't knock my

weapon away. Of course, if they simply shot me, that would be another matter.

I swept each room in turn, as fast as I dared, turning on lights when I could find them. Finally, I moved into the clutter of the antique showroom, which was even more cluttered now. Somebody had emptied drawers onto the floor and tipped furniture over. Not a really thorough trash job, though. Whoever did it had been in a hurry, or had been interrupted.

I wondered if Armstrong had gotten a warrant and visited the upstairs apartment already. I hoped so. I also wondered how good an idea it would be to ask him. Probably not very.

I finally made it all the way to the front door and found it ajar. Whoever had been there, I had just missed him. Again. Besides evil, this Valento character was damned annoying.

I hurried back out the alley door to tell Naomi not to take off with my BMW, thank you very much.

"You're not going to like what you find, but at least you won't be in any danger. There's nobody here but us."

She got out of the car. Clutching Stewball to her chest, she went inside, leaving me to shut off the engine and lock up. From the shop, I could hear a single, angry cry that could have been a shout or a sob or both. I went in after her, shut both doors to keep the cat inside, and took her in my arms.

"In a little while," I said, "you're probably going to tremble or maybe cry or both. If you do, that's okay."

"What about you, Herman. Don't you feel even a little shook up?" The tremble was creeping into her voice already.

"I've been dealing with bad people for a long time now. That doesn't make me happy about getting attacked, but it makes me a lot harder to scare. And make no mistake about it, that's what this is all about."

"Somebody wants to scare me?"

"Not somebody, our boy from upstairs."

"But why?"

"He knows he's being chased now. That makes him feel

vulnerable. He hates that, so he does what he has always done about it. He makes somebody else feel vulnerable. He knows you live here alone. If he had found you here—" Suddenly I realized I was saying far too much. The sobs found her then, and she buried her face in my chest. I held her tight and let her get it all out of her system.

After what seemed like forever, she backed away from me and wiped her eyes on her indescribable shawl.

"I want to ask you something, Herman, and I don't want you to take it the wrong way."

"Fire away."

"Stay with me tonight?"

"There's a wrong way to take that?"

She managed a laugh through the last of the tears. "I don't want you to think that I only asked you because now I need a bodyguard."

"Okay, I won't think that. But I also won't leave you unprotected until I nail this bastard."

"I was hoping you'd say something like that. What do we do about the doors? The jambs are all smashed at the lock bolts."

"Only the back one is smashed. The front one, he unlocked from inside. Do you have a hammer and some nails?"

"Antique, you might know."

"Well, it's probably an antique door, anyway. That ought to be just the ticket."

"Don't be bad-mouthing my building, Herman. It's old and so am I and I can't do anything about either one."

"Nor do you need to."

She disappeared in a side room, and I looked over the back door more carefully. A couple of well-placed nails would work a whole lot better than the original lock, but I didn't feel obliged to tell her that. When she came back, she not only had a claw hammer and a paper sack of square nails, she also had a bottle of champagne.

"I don't remember what I've been saving this for anymore,

and it's not chilled, but would you like a drink? The wine from dinner seems to have worn off, all of a sudden."

"That would be great."

I worked on the door and heard a loud popping of a cork behind me. When I finished, she handed me an ornate etched flute with silver on the rim. It was more than half full of foam.

"Happy days," she said.

"Happier than this one, anyway." We drank the warm foam.

"No, Herman, the proper response is, 'And long nights.'"

"I've heard that, yes. But I thought this one might be getting too long for you already."

"Well, it's definitely not what I had hoped for when it started." She ran an index finger around the silver rim on her glass, and for a moment I thought she was going to cry again. Then she stuck out her jaw and stiffened her posture and flashed me a defiant stare.

"I could leave, if you're feeling safe now and you want to be alone," I said.

"Like hell you could. You may have lots more practice dealing with bad people than I do, Herman, but I know one thing. If you let somebody rob you of your joy once, then it never ends. That's not going to happen."

"Well, I already said you're a smart lady."

"Yes, you did. Now, then. When you were checking the place out, did you see the bedroom?"

"Not very well. That's one where I didn't find the light switch."

"That would figure. I did tell you that my father had the place decorated originally, as a place to bring his floozies."

"I picked up on that, yes."

She giggled and took me by the hand. "Let me show you something."

We went to the hallway outside the bedroom door. She told me to stay there and to close my eyes. Several minutes later she said "Ta-daa! Okay, open them."

The room behind her was lit by a wall sconce over the head of the huge bed with silk and satin pillows. The lights in the room were all red. The walls were covered with richly brocaded fabrics and the ceiling was covered with mirrors in ornate gilded frames. I laughed out loud.

"You know, I've never seen this sort of thing in real life before."

"What sort of thing?"

"High class cat house décor."

"Good thing you said 'high class.' Do you know Gilbert and Sullivan's work, Herman?"

"Some of it."

"There's a line in one of the songs from *Trial By Jury*, 'She may very well pass for forty-three/ In the dusk with the light behind her.' What do you think?"

She faced away from the red light, reached behind her back to undo her zipper, and let her dress drop to the floor, covering her kitten-heel, peep-whatever shoes. She had obviously used the time when I had my eyes shut to get rid of her bra.

"Well?"

"Lady, if that's what forty-three looks like, then it must be the finest and sexiest possible age for a woman."

"Oh, I do so like a man who knows his lines. How fast can you get out of that outfit of yours?"

"Time me."

Chapter Sixteen

Wolves and Sheep

Stewball woke us the next morning, stomping heavily on my chest, chewing on my ear, and giving me his industrial-strength purr.

"Is he allowed on the bed?" I spoke to the lump of covers I assumed to be Naomi.

"Mmmph?"

"Stewball. Is it okay if he's up here?"

"I'd like to see you try to stop him."

"He's eating my ear."

"He wants you to get out of bed and feed him. He knows I won't do it for another hour."

"What does he eat?"

"Ears." She snuggled deeper in the covers and put a pillow over her head. I told Stewball I'd see what I could do.

I found my clothes in a heap on the floor, pulled on my pants and padded out toward the kitchen, the cold wood floor making me wish I had slippers. I couldn't find Stewball's dish or any cat food, so I opened a can of beef stew from the pantry and put half of it in a saucer.

"Here, cat." I put the dish on the floor. "Go nuts." From the way he tucked into it, I think he thought he had died and gone to cat heaven. I found an enameled metal teakettle, put fresh water in it and set it on the stove to heat. Then I went back to get more clothes, especially socks.

As I passed by the entry to the shop, I glimpsed a figure

peering in through the store window. I immediately forgot all about the socks. I grabbed my jacket out of the bedroom, threw it on, and pulled the 9 mm out of the inner pocket. Then I approached the front door in what I hoped was a stealthy manner, though I didn't really have a lot of cover. By then, whoever was out there was jiggling the doorknob. With the gun at high port, I tripped the deadbolt with my left hand and pulled the door quickly open.

"Jackson! What the hell are you doing here?"

"Armstrong. You forgot how to knock?"

"You meet more interesting people by entering unannounced. And I got a warrant that says I can. It covers the whole building, not just the upstairs apartment."

"How nice for you. Get your ass in here, will you? You're letting in half a cubic mile of arctic air."

He took his sweet time moving into the shop, and he left the door open. I put the gun in my pocket and slammed the door behind him.

"Is that the new chic, bare chest and great big gun?" he said. "It doesn't make you look a bit like Steven Seagal, you know."

"That's only because I don't have a pony tail."

"Are you going to offer me a chair and some coffee, Jackson?"

"No."

"Be that way, then. What the hell are you doing here, anyway?"

"None of your damn business."

"Please tell me you're not tampering with evidence again."

Naomi appeared in the back doorway, in a revealing dressing gown and some fuzzy slippers. "Who are you talking to, Herm—Oh!" She vanished back into the bedroom and shut the door.

"Holy shit, Jackson, is this for real? Is somebody who looks like that actually—"

"What I told you before."

"What was that?"

"Go fuck yourself, Armstrong."

"Oh, that. Well, I have to search this place, anyway."

"No you don't. There's nothing for you down here. And upstairs, you're probably too late. Our boy was back here last night. He partly trashed this place and then split in a hurry. He could still be upstairs, but I'm thinking he's most likely gone, and the item you want with him."

"Did you see him?"

"No."

"Then how do you know he's the one who trashed this place?"

"Oh, please, Armstrong. Are all cops this stupid?"

"What we are is insistent about usable evidence. You got any?"

"Somebody told me I should put it back, remember? But take your forensics people upstairs anyway. You might find evidence of a crime."

"That's not what the warrant says I can look for."

"Then *notice* it while you're looking for something else, okay? Jesus, do you want me to tell you how to tie your shoes, too?"

"If you told me how, it wouldn't work right."

"Well, some people are more trainable than others. Our boy Valento has a rap sheet longer than a loan shark's memory, by the way. His prints are in the system. Have you checked for them at Trish's place? Get a match there, and you can get a warrant that says whatever you want it to."

"Go tell my captain that you are replacing him as my boss, will you? I expect he'll be amused and delighted to hear it. But first, have you got a key to the upstairs pad?"

"I'll get one from the lady of the house."

Naomi dug a key out of a cluttered desk drawer in the shop office area, and I gave it to the cop. He headed back out the door. Over his shoulder he said, "Tell the lady bye for me, will you?" He held the door open way longer than necessary

and then was gone.

"Who was that?" Naomi was now wrapped in a much frumpier and more opaque robe.

"Cop. Looking for Valento, but he doesn't want to admit that yet."

"Nice guy."

"We must be talking about two different people. Want to go get some breakfast?"

"Let's wait until Mr. Charm leaves. I don't want to come back here and find that somebody new has trashed my place."

"I can buy that."

Armstrong was upstairs long enough for me to get fully dressed and have three cups of coffee and four cookies. By then, Naomi had also gotten dressed, again in smooth black pants, this time with a silky white blouse. She flipped the sign in her shop window around to read OPEN and unlocked the door.

"Do you think you want to do that just yet?"

"I sort of said it last night. If you let the bad guys make you hide in a hole somewhere, they've already won."

"Well put." I didn't ask her about what you do when hiding is your only realistic option.

Armstrong returned and put the apartment key into Naomi's hand. He held the contact for longer than he needed to, and I could see she was uncomfortable with it.

"Well?" I said.

"Well, what?"

"What did you find?"

"You know, you're lucky I can't arrest you for wasting my time, Jackson. There's not a damn thing up there. Quit poking your nose into police business."

"What makes you think I am?"

"Apart from the nonexistent laptop? Somebody has been messing with my computer at work." So the Prophet had done his work already. Good for him.

"Messing? How could you tell?"

"Some things are changed a little. Some things nobody but me would notice. That wouldn't be your work, too, would it?"

"How could that be? I'm the lowest-tech guy you'll ever meet. I don't even have a motor on my toothbrush."

"Consider yourself warned. You're not a cop and you had better get that through your head before you land in a shitload of trouble."

"I'll take it under advisement." Sure I would. Sometimes it takes me a disappointingly long time to figure things out. But when it comes to sizing up people, I've always found that my instincts are dead-on right, besides being instant. My instinct at that moment was that there was something very wrong about this cop. And I absolutely knew it would be a big mistake to tell him about the chop shop under the Lafayette Bridge, though I wasn't sure why. "Have a nice day, Armstrong. Can you find your car all by yourself?"

"Go to hell." And with nothing more clever to say than that, he left to climb into a fat blob of a brown Buick that was parked at the curb and drive off. I tried to see the plate number, but in the cold air, his exhaust hid it in a cloud of swirling white.

"What's his problem?" said Naomi.

"I don't know, but I promise you I'm going to find out. Now what about that breakfast?"

We were leaving the shop when a terribly withered and bent little white-haired lady came in the front door.

"Good morning, Mrs. Ellis. What can I do for you today?"

"I have something," said a tiny, quavering voice that seemed detached from the frail body. The woman opened her worn wool coat and produced a cut glass candy dish from some inner pocket. She held it out to Naomi like a gift of appeasement.

"You want to sell it?"

The wrinkled head bobbed in silent agreement.

"Well, let me see." Naomi held the dish up and turned it around a bit. "It's really a lovely piece, isn't it? I'm sure you'll be very sorry to part with it. I can give you ten dollars. How would that be?"

The head nodded again. Naomi disappeared in the back for a moment and returned with a crisp ten-dollar bill, which Mrs. Ellis quickly tucked away in a pocket. Then she shuffled out without another word. I held the door for her.

"You be careful on that ice, now," said Naomi

I shut the door again. "Is that thing she brought you really worth ten dollars?"

"Certainly not. It was junk when it was brand new, and it's twice as junk now. At best, it might bring a quarter at a flea market."

"Then why—"

"Because ten dollars is what she needs to buy her weekly half-pint of gin. She brings me something every week, and it's all junk."

"You think it's wise to encourage her?"

"I don't judge her. It's what she needs, and she has nobody else to turn to."

"You are some kind of fine person."

"Thank you. I do what I can."

"Are you still hungry?"

"Not really."

"Lets go back to bed."

"I thought you'd never ask."

Much later, we did go out for breakfast. Then I took her back to the store and told her I was going to go have a better look at the box factory and the possible chop shop, and it probably wasn't a good idea for her to come along. I walked her into her shop, checked it for interlopers, and then gave her the .380 Beretta.

"Wear something with a pocket and put this in it."

"I don't know anything about guns."

"I'll show you."

I gave her a quick course in the fundamentals of semiautomatic pistols and took her through a few dry firings. "The first time in your life you hold a loaded gun," I said, "your hand will shake. It's true for everybody, and nothing to worry about. Something about the awesome realization of having a thing of deadly power in your grip. It won't happen until you know it's loaded and has a round in the chamber. To compensate for it, you should always use a two-handed grip. Hold your arms well out in front of your body, and your feet spread wide, with one slightly ahead of the other, like a boxer's stance. And always, always peer down the sights. Like this, see?" I showed her, and then she tried it. "That from-the-hip nonsense is strictly for cowboy movies. Expect it to kick enough to knock your arms back a little and screw up your aim. Don't worry about that, either. Just bring it back down to where you can sight it and fire again."

"Again?"

"Damn right. If your life is in danger, you shoot to kill. And that means more than once."

"And how do I decide if my life is really in danger?"

"Don't decide, react. If you feel you're in danger, you are. If somebody gets inside your comfort zone, take him out. If you aren't prepared to shoot, the wolves will know it, every time. You have to be prepared."

"But you are coming back, yes?"

"Count on it."

"I think maybe I'll just lock up the shop."

"Okay. But carry the gun, too."

"I don't like it much, but I will."

On a whim, I decided to look at the upstairs apartment, both to see what if anything Armstrong had taken and to make sure the place was still empty. By now, the locks were old friends, and I was inside in, for me, record time. The place was

still empty, and if Armstrong had taken anything, I couldn't tell. Then I looked at the hide-a-bed and did a double take. There, bigger than sin, was the Dell laptop.

Chapter Seventeen

Things That Go Pop

Just to say I had, I stopped at my office and asked Agnes if she had seen or heard from Wilkie.

"You missed him again, Herman."

"Cute. Why do I think that when I find out what you two are up to, I'm not going to like it?"

"I can't imagine what you're talking about."

"If you see him, imagine something else. Tell him I think I've found out where our wayward boy is hiding."

Her eyebrows leapt to attention, and she started scribbling on a note pad.

"It's an old Public Works salt shed under the Lafayette Bridge, on this side of the river. I think it's being used as a chop shop, and you probably can't get in without an assault team. I'm going over there now to see what I can see, but I won't try to go inside until he's with me. He shouldn't try it on his own, either."

The pen continued to move for another half minute or so, and then she read her notes back to me.

"That'll work, Aggie." And maybe it would. Whatever Wilkie was doing, I was sure he wanted Valento. But for some reason, he didn't want me knowing how he was going about getting him. I could think of ways that might be perfectly all right, though not a lot of them.

"Do you still have your, um, *ailment*, Herman? Your head thing?"

"I guess. I don't think there's a way to tell when it's gone."

"Then take my cell phone with you. Please."

"So I can call for help after I pass out? All that will accomplish is losing your phone."

"No, what it will accomplish is making me less of a nervous wreck, worrying about you."

I thought about it for a minute. "You know, that I can maybe accept, Ag. I'll take it, but I won't turn it on. I don't want it going off if I find myself sneaking up on some bad actors with big guns."

"Thank you, Herman."

"Don't rub it in, okay?"

I left the BMW three blocks from the salt shed and scouted as inconspicuous a path there as I could. As far as the old box factory, it worked pretty well. I went inside and checked the building directory. No Valento or any name that I associated with him. I paced around the lobby and studied the security of the place. They had double locks on the inner and outer doors, with a lobby intercom for guests to press. The intercom had a camera above it, but it was the only one in the place, and it wouldn't be hard to block temporarily. Every lock was something I knew how to open, so if there was an unoccupied unit anywhere on the east end of the building, I could use it to stake out the chop shop. I returned to the building directory, and sure enough, both the third and the sixth floors had units with no names listed for them. I wrote down the numbers.

Back outside, beyond the abandoned freight houses, there was no more cover. I could only brazen it out, hoping I looked like a utility inspector or some such fool thing. I would know what kind when I heard it come out of my mouth. But there wasn't too much risk of that. Illegal businesses, including a "midnight auto parts" operation, tend to be nocturnal. If anybody was there during the day, he was most likely asleep or

stoned. But I had my radar on and my hand on my trusty nine, all the same.

There were no cameras around the building that I could see, but a couple of the fence poles and one of those gas pipe doohickeys with all the valves on it held what could definitely be the motion detectors I had probably tripped the night before. I went over to the one on the gas piping, took a wet rag out of a plastic bag, and put it over the gadget. I had brought several more rags, but I could only reach a couple of the other ones. It was also possible that part of the shed could be seen from at least one of the traffic cameras on the highway bridge above me. Anybody can monitor those things online, I'm told, if you know where to look.

The fence outlined a space that was more or less rectangular, while the building was round, so the distance from fence to wall was not constant. I went straight up to the part of the fence that was closest and climbed it, as if I were a carjacker breaking into an impound lot. Just like I used to do when I was a teenager, actually. There was no way to hide, so I didn't try. No barbed wire on the top of the fence. Somebody told me it's illegal these days, except for prisons. You're no longer allowed to give people minor cuts and lacerations just because they are breaking into your property to rob you blind.

As I had expected, the place stayed quiet. Close to the building, I saw small areas where the ice on the ground looked as if it had holes chipped in it that were later filled in with snow or slush. When I looked closer at one, I could see a round object about the size of a quarter just below the surface.

"Why, you vicious little bastards, you," I said to the objects. Toe-poppers is what they are called, crude little land mines made out of twelve-gauge shotgun shells. They wouldn't kill you, usually, but they would most certainly blow your foot off, and make a hell of a lot of noise, to boot. I was surprised to see them. People who have meth labs use them a lot. Of course, people who have meth labs are at least half crazy,

too. I usually expect auto thieves to have more couth. Maybe something more than illegal auto mechanics went on in the strange cone-shaped tin hut. Chop shoppers don't shoot at people indiscriminately, either.

The main door had a lock I could pick, but I didn't try it. Anybody who put crippling booby traps out in public, where anybody could trip them, was liable to rely on something even worse inside, where the consequences would not be so easily seen. Like a tiger trap or a deadfall. Something that would mess up more than just your foot.

I put a device the size of a large cell phone up against a curved wall and listened. It's a sort of electronic stethoscope that Wilkie and I use when we're about to break into somebody's bolthole. No more clanking noises, but I could still hear an occasional hiss. When I had first heard it, I took it to be from an acetylene cutting torch. Now that I had it slightly amplified, I no longer knew what to make of it. I walked around the perimeter, being careful of the little land mines, looking for one of the chinks in the wall I had seen light coming from, the night before. The one I found wasn't very big, but it let me get a small peek. Mostly, the interior was pitch black. But I could definitely make out the dim shape of a Shelby Mustang and the glimmer of its gold racing stripes. Armstrong wouldn't be impressed, but I was. I got the hell out of there. I had seen enough.

Back at my office, the wayward Mr. Wide Track had magically reappeared. I half believed he had migrated to an exotic retreat you don't bother to come back from. It didn't seem to occur to him that he owed me an explanation of where he had been, which told me there would be no point in asking, either. When and if he was ready, he would tell me.

"Agnes told me about the big tin shed. How sure are we that the guy we want is there?"

"I'm personally medium to high sure that he at least goes

there sometimes. I think that's where he was headed both the times I lost him. But as to whether he's there right this moment or any other exact time, we don't have a clue."

"Sounds like we need to do a stakeout, Herman."

"Unless you have some other line on the guy, that's exactly what we need to do."

"I don't have. I thought I did, but it didn't pan out."

"Some day when you're feeling generous, tell me about it, will you?"

"Why?"

"Never mind. I just thought friends did that sort of thing, you know?"

"Oh."

I waited for him to say more, but he was all done gushing for the day.

"There are a couple of empty condos over in the old box factory that could be used to watch the place. We could break in fairly easily, or we could get hold of the realtor who's trying to sell them, pretend we're cops, and let him know we're doing a stakeout. Which do you like?"

"Well, you know me, Herman. I'm a belt and suspenders man. I say we break in but have phony badges ready in case we get caught."

"Mr. Wilkie is thorough," said Agnes. If it had been my idea, she would pretend to be scandalized.

"You'll need a few more bodies."

"What do you mean, *I'll* need them?"

"I can't be there right away. I'm going to go see your least favorite person, the Prophet. And depending on what he has for me, I might have to go someplace else after that."

"Okay, I can get some extra breathers. Somebody with firepower, you think?"

"If we end up pretending the shed is Iwo Jima and we're the Marines, we could probably use it. Nobody who's trigger-happy, though. Our story is that we're bounty hunters and

we're after one guy only. We have no even slightly legal reason to shoot anybody else."

"We'll have badges. We could pretend we're busting the whole outfit."

"They might believe that, but the real cops won't. And sooner or later a bust, even a phony one, is going to run into them. Stick to what's easiest to sell. And make sure our people know the place we're looking at is booby trapped and wired for sound."

"Oh, yeah? What have they got in there, anyway?"

"I started out thinking it was a chop shop, but now I'm not so sure. For all we know, it could be a meth lab and a terrorist bomb factory, all in one. Just assume it's deadly."

"You're the boss."

"Hold that thought. You want a secret knock, for when I join you at the spy hole?"

"Sure. What do you like?"

"SOS. Three short intervals, three long, three more short."

"What does SOS have to do with anything?"

"Not a damn thing, but it's easy to remember."

"Fair enough. What happened to the laptop, by the way? Agnes said you picked it up."

"Yes I did. And after that, things got complicated." I told him about the whole business with Armstrong and the semi-ambulatory computer. "I don't know what's up with that guy, but I'm thinking we stay clear of him until we can find out."

"Sounds like a plan." There was a small gust of wind as he turned and headed for the door. He went off to recruit the Mean Street Irregulars and I went off to check on Naomi and keep my appointment with the Proph.

Chapter Eighteen

Enlightenment Found

"Can you close the shop for a while, Naomi? I'm going to go see a goofy character who sometimes sells me information, and I'd rather have you along than worry about you being alone here."

"I'd rather that, too. Let me put out some extra food for Stewball and lock up."

Five minutes later we were on our way. The Prophet's place is over on the far East Side, but because I didn't know yet if Armstrong had a tail on me, I went there via the West Side, which is really south. It's called the West Side, I'm told, because it's on the west bank of the Mississippi River. Rivers only have two banks, east and west, no matter how many different directions they actually run. So the West Side is actually south of the river and south of Downtown, and St. Paulites like that a lot, since it confuses the hell out of people from Minneapolis, who tend to look down their noses at our fine city.

Because the area grew up along a curving riverfront, that also means it has a lot of twisting and reversing and dead end streets where it's easy to spot a tail. There was a Taurus behind me for a while that could have been an unmarked prowler, but I lost him in the industrial flats around the Downtown airport. Satisfied that I was clean, I recrossed the river via the Robert Street Bridge, zigzagged through Dayton's Bluff for a bit, and finally headed for the East Side in earnest.

"You really know how to show a girl a good time, Herman."

"Did you like that? Remind me to give you my walking tour of Cathedral Hill sometime."

"Not in the winter."

"What kind of shoes are you wearing this time, by the way?"

"Low-heeled suede over-the-calf boots."

"That's good. We have a few boonies to go through."

"I'm ready."

Soon we were approaching a small two-story windowless brick building next to some railroad tracks. It had probably started its life as a switch house, and once it had windows all around the second floor perimeter. But those had been blocked in ages ago, and the ground level sprouted numerous crude additions in shapes that were not so easy to describe, built for purposes that were unfathomable. They were covered with an irregular array of slogans, painted in a variety of lettering styles. They changed from time to time, with newer ones simply going over the top of the ones that had faded. On the side of the building that I with my insider knowledge knew contained an entrance, I read, "THE LORD'S CROSS MIGHT REDEEM YOU, BUT YOUR OWN JUST WASTES YOUR TIME." On another wall, we had, "They shall beat their swords into plowshares/ And the plowshares into Common Shares/ And they shall STUDY POOR NO MORE/ But they have already lost the PEACE.

I went up to a sheet of plywood that said, "WELCOME TO THE HADES. IT'S NO PLACE FOR LADIES."

"What kind of person is this, again, Herman?"

"Harmless, is the thing to remember. Don't eat or drink anything here, though. You'll get hallucinations."

I moved the plywood sheet to one side, and we walked into an unlit vestibule lined with mirrors.

"This is a bad joss reflector, believe it or not," I said.

"Well of course. I could see that right away. What's joss?"

"It's a little like energy and luck all rolled together, I think. And it comes in good and bad. Here it maybe also comes in

vanilla and chocolate. Mirrors repel some varieties of it."

"Praise Yah!" said a voice from the black overhead.

"Yeah?" It was my standard answer. I was the only person who could get away with it. To Naomi, I said, "Say, 'Praise Yah!'"

"Are you serious?"

"He won't let us in, otherwise."

"Um, praise Yah," she said. "I guess."

"Welcome, Pilgrim," said the ceiling again. "Who's your fellow traveler?"

"Her name's Naomi. She's good people."

"Then welcome, Pilgrim and Good People. Enter."

We went around several sharp corners and switchbacks and eventually came to the Prophet's inner sanctum, which got a little weirder every time I saw it. The walls were now covered with something that could have been sound-deadening material or sheets of molded foam from a factory that makes padded bras or both. The ceiling had a huge part of it cut out, with a mechanical orrery hanging where it used to be. Planets and moons were kept in their proper relative positions by a complicated set of gears and levers, and in the center of it all, a black sun alternately flashed the time and temperature and a Coca Cola logo. Below that, the Proph's work station rose above the floor like part of the bridge of the Starship Enterprise, only with a lot of messy, tangled wires and strings of tiny lights. The Prophet presided over it all from a rattan cobra chair, which was mounted on rollers. He used the rollers a lot. He looked like Yapphet Koto, only with a Hassidic beard and long dreads. He ignored me, looked down at Naomi, and flashed her a grin that had about a dozen too-many teeth.

"Who is she that looketh forth as the morning," he said, "fair as the moon, clear as the sun, and terrible as an army with banners?"

"Um, hello. Herman says you're—"

"I am a brother to dragons and a companion to owls, eyes to the blind and feet to the lame. But always and constantly, I am a holy man and a bringer of truth. Will you have some?"

"Some truth?" she said.

"That, or some tea."

"No," I said.

"Let her speak for herself, Pilgrim."

"No, thank you," said Naomi. "I went to an alternate universe a couple of days ago."

"Ah, the Pilgrim has poisoned your mind, I think."

"I did, yes," I said. "It was the least I could do."

"Her loss. She has a good aura. Can you see it, Pilgrim?"

"I've told you before, I can't see auras."

"How little you grasp, sometimes. You see them and you read them. You just don't call them that."

"Have it your own way. Have you got something for me?"

"Always in a hurry. That way will not get you to enlightenment, Pilgrim."

"Well, I had enlightenment earlier this week. It hit me so hard, I woke up in the hospital."

"Clearly, it has been a profound week. I barely noticed it, myself. But yes, I have something for you."

He got up from his chair and handed me two paper files.

"The file on your Valento person is not very fat, I'm afraid. I need more time with him. He is very good at the art of vanishing. This is a man who walks on sandy beaches and leaves no footprint. Only three kinds of people can do that: the very innocent, the very holy, and the very evil."

"We can put this guy solidly into the evil category, without fear of contradiction."

"I gleaned as much from my studies. I found his criminal record, but I didn't print it because you said you already have it."

"I spoke without thinking, Proph. I have his Minneapolis rap sheet, but not St. Paul."

"Then you have all there is, except for some juvenile offenses that are sealed to all mere mortals."

"*What?*"

"He has not run afoul of Caesar's minions in the Saintly City."

"That doesn't seem possible."

"Unlike you, Pilgrim, I never trouble myself with what is or is not possible. I learn more that way."

"Maybe so. What else have you got?"

"This man does not deal with any of Caesar's agents at all. He has not filed an income tax return or paid his Social Security tax in this century. He has never registered for the draft. He has one credit card, a Visa, that he has used recently at a few East Side bars—the addresses and dates are in your file—and at Joe's Sporting Goods. Many several hundred dollars at Joe's."

"So he's armed now, if he wasn't before."

"I think you are wise to assume he was not buying a canoe paddle in the dark night of winter, yes. He has a checking account at U S Bank, but it is much neglected. He only runs about a thousand dollars a month through it. He pays his utilities and his Visa account by check, but not much else. He gets cash from ATMs all over the metro area, seldom the same machine twice in a row. He has no phone listed to himself, and if he does Facebook or any other social network, it is under some alias that I haven't found yet."

"Observe the lilies of the field," I said. "They do not Twitter, neither do they text."

"That's very good, Pilgrim. I will rob that from you shamelessly."

"Be my guest. What else?"

"He owns a classic muscle car and a prosaic hog motorcycle, license numbers in the file. He frequents biker bars, strip clubs, and sometimes native casinos. He has no known next of kin, including any mom. The Beatles would love him; he's a real nowhere man."

"Somehow I'm not surprised."

"Then I will be surprised for both of us. Unlike mighty Casey, I am not accustomed to striking out. I won't charge you for this one until I find something better. Are you planning on bringing some bad joss to this person, by chance?"

"Some very bad joss, yes."

"In that case, I may not charge you, period. A man like this puts the universe out of order. Something very serious needs to be done about him."

"What about our Jane Doe murder victim?

"A fatter file, if no easier trail. Your dead person is named Pamela Watkins. Hers is a tale of great promise, followed by one of great woe."

"Well, at the end, anyway."

"And well before then, also. She is a small town girl, an only child, born in 1979. Hiked the Gunflint Trail, sang in her church choir, worked on the yearbook, graduated high school with high honors. The all-American girl, the hope of the fair state, the observed of all observers. Came to the Twin Cities in 1997, to go to the Minneapolis College of Art and Design on a full-tuition scholarship. Disappeared in November of 2000, her senior year."

"Disappeared? You mean dropped out?"

"No, Pilgrim. To drop out, you talk to your student advisor, give notice, file papers, cancel the newspaper, put out the cat. You keep your universe in order and your options open. I mean she disappeared."

Naomi took the file from me and flipped to a page with photos. "She's pretty, but not stunning," she said. "She looks like a nice person."

"Don't look at the later photos, Naomi."

"The next time we see her," said the Proph, "is on a police blotter. Several of them, in fact. Solicitation, drunk and disorderly, shoplifting, grand theft auto, all several times, and finally aggravated assault, in 2008."

"That last one's big-league stuff," I said. "What was that all about?"

"Not to put too fine a distinction on it, Pilgrim, some guy patted her on the ass in a bar in Minneapolis, and she pulled out a hatpin and stabbed him in the gut, several times."

"Women still have hatpins?"

"Not usually. She may have thought it was less likely to get her charged with concealing a deadly weapon than a knife or an ice pick. The universe did not move that way, though. Her attorney managed to get the charge reduced from attempted murder, but even so, she went off to the house of sorrows for five to nine years. She did the five and got out on parole six months ago."

"Who was the guy she stabbed?"

"The trial record does not say."

"That's improper as hell. Who was the defense attorney?"

"A public defender. Her parents paid for her bail in all her sad ordeals, but it would seem they couldn't afford a really good shyster for a trial."

"So who was the court-appointed one?"

"Her name is Patricia Hanover."

Trish. "Jesus Christ."

"No, Patricia Hanover. But that's just as well, I think. Christ did not do so well pleading his own case, as I recall."

"You said the Watkins girl's parents always bailed her out. Are they still alive?"

"Their address is in the back of the file, Pilgrim. They still live in her home town."

"Which is?"

"A place called Bayfield, in the state of Wisconsin."

Chapter Nineteen

The Shore of Gitche Gumee

"The next day was Sunday, so Naomi had no issues with closing up the shop and coming with me. I still had no idea why Bayfield would be on a Map Quest on Valento's computer, but that was beside the point now. I wanted to find out what went wrong with Pam Watkins' world in 1996, and I figured the ones who could tell me were her parents.

As we were about to leave, I checked the upstairs apartment one last time, for both people and computer. I decided I'd been picking locks out in public about long enough, and I asked Naomi for her key. She dug into the same drawer as before and produced it, then paused as she was about to hand it to me.

"That's odd," she said.

"Is something wrong?"

"Not really. But there should be one more ring here."

"Ring? What kind of ring?"

"I didn't have a fob of any kind on this key, but you know those little spring-loaded shiny rings that you use to connect to a fob if you do have one? I had two of them on this key, for no special reason. Now there's only one. Now why on earth would that Armstrong person have taken one off? It's a lot of work, opening those things."

"Maybe he gave you the wrong key."

"It looks right. I just don't see—"

"Lets go try it."

The key worked like a charm. I did a quick tour of the

apartment, gun out. Maybe it was my imagination, but it seemed as if the Dell laptop was in a slightly different position than before. So I plucked a couple of hairs out of the top of my head and put one under each of two diagonally opposite corners of the computer. Somebody moving the thing would be unlikely to notice them and even more unlikely to take the care to put them back where they were. I went out in the hall and locked up.

"How does Stewball like riding in a car?" I said.

"He's one of the few cats I've ever seen who does like it. He sits on the dash or the rear window shelf and gets big eyes. It's like he has a need for speed."

"Let's take him with us. Then if we get delayed for some reason, you won't have to worry about him."

"Fine. We'll have to take a litter box of some kind, you know. He's not like a dog. He won't go off in the park and do his thing while you pretend not to watch."

"A box is okay. Trust me, my car will survive it. In fact, it's not even the most disgusting thing it's ever carried."

"Oh, really?"

"Don't ask." And even if it weren't true, I would have taken the cat along. I didn't think for a minute that we would get delayed in northern Wisconsin. But I did think it likely that Armstrong really had given Naomi the wrong key—his own. And if he had a key to one unit, he could have a key to the shop, too. Furthermore, if he did, he might loan it to somebody else. He was working way too hard at not being interested in Valento. That could merely mean that he was sloppy and lazy, but I didn't think so. It was almost as if he was protecting him. That might not be enough to imply an alliance, but then again, it might. I didn't want to come back and find Stewball missing or murdered. I was glad that idea hadn't occurred to Naomi. Maybe she would think of it later, maybe not. The cat rode with us, all the same.

⁂

We took the interstate as far north as Forest Lake, then turned east and crossed over the St. Croix River into Wisconsin. The river valley is beautiful, even in the winter. Farther east, there are no more rock cliffs or white water, but the landscape is still rolling and pleasant. Anywhere above latitude forty-four was glacier country about a billion years ago, and the land still shows it. Even the farm fields are not flat, and they are ringed with every imaginable kind of northern tree. In the summer, it's a heartbreakingly green country. It's an area you could fall in love with, as long as you never had any need to make a living, visit a museum, go to a play, vote for moderate political candidates, or eat at a gourmet restaurant. Or shoot serious pool. Come to think about it, maybe it's not so great, at that.

We stopped for brunch in the town of Spooner, at a place whose décor and menu are what I call "farm-wife chic." That's different from a greasy spoon. A farm-wife place is all about comfort food. They start every day by making about fifty gallons of gravy, and they will even ladle it on the French fries, but only if you ask for it. The mashed potatoes have real lumps in them, the pot roast falls apart when you stab it with your blunt-tined fork, and all entrées weigh at least three pounds. The waitress apologized that it being winter, they had no fresh fruit for their famous pies.

"Come back in August and try the blueberry," she said. "You'll dream about it the rest of your life."

"Beats the dreams I usually have."

She laughed.

"So what do you have instead?" I said.

"Stuff that doesn't have to be fresh. Coconut cream, chocolate, pecan, and lemon."

"Is it any good?" said Naomi.

"The pecan's okay. At least you can put a scoop of ice cream on that."

Naomi ordered the pecan, minus the ice cream, and I did, too. I made a mental note to give the waitress an extra nice tip

for her honesty, though it turned out the pie was very good, fresh ingredients or not. Maybe the blueberry really was worth a trip back in the summer.

"These people we're going to see," said Naomi over her first bite. "Do they already know their daughter is dead?"

"We don't know, so we have to proceed carefully."

"Oh, God, I hope we don't have to be the ones to break it to them."

"Amen to that. But if they don't know it yet, then it's high time somebody did."

After she finished her pie, Naomi reached across the table and took my now empty coffee cup. She swirled the last few drops around a bit, then put the cup down in front of her and peered intently into it.

"Madame Zenomi will now read the deepest secrets of your soul."

"You said you couldn't do it with coffee dregs."

"For you, Madame makes a special deal. I see here a tale of wandering and struggle, of lost love, of tragedy and sorrow."

"Do I pick one, or do I get all of those?"

"They are all one. But I see happier days over the horizon."

"Well, about time."

"I see a woman."

"You don't see any such thing."

"Her name is Anne."

My stomach suddenly lurched like a small ship being hit by a large torpedo.

"Where did you get that name?"

"Is in the bottom of the cup."

"I don't believe you."

"Oh, all right, then, you talk in your sleep."

"Oh, shit. Really? What can I say? I didn't ever mean to—"

"It's okay, Herman. It's not as if you called *me* Anne. Tell me who she is or was."

I took in a deep breath and let it out slowly. "She was my

girlfriend, before she moved away. She's a newspaper reporter, a damn good one. She got a job offer to write for the *New York Times*, and she took it. I thought our affair would survive the distance, but it hasn't."

She was quiet for a moment. Then she cocked her head to one side and said, "That's not so bad."

"It's not?"

"No. In fact, of all the reasons you can have for losing a lover, that's about the most no-fault one that I can think of. And carrying a torch is an honorable activity, as long as you don't get burned by it. It doesn't diminish me or you, and it doesn't detract from us."

"How do I not get burned by it?"

"Stick with me, kiddo, and maybe you'll find out."

"What else do you see?"

"I see a fear that I can't put a name to. Something that makes you constantly on your guard. Something you may or may not decide to tell me about someday."

"Unlikely."

"You didn't say, 'untrue.'"

"No, I didn't. What else?"

"I see that we have a long way to drive yet today, Mr. Secret Agent."

"We do, indeed. Let's get to it."

I paid the tab at an old-fashioned mechanical cash register on a front counter, while Naomi went to a C-store next door and bought a foil pouch of tuna for our passenger.

Crossing the parking lot I noticed a blob of a brown Buick back in a remote corner, with the motor running but nobody apparently in it. I reminded myself that GM made about a million of that particular model, so it might not mean a thing. After we were a block away from the café, it pulled out behind us. It stayed with us, one to two blocks back. Finally, well out of town, after we had taken the Highway 63 turnoff toward Hayward, it pulled into a gas station lot,

turned around, and went back the way it had come. I didn't mention it to Naomi.

I did mention my concussion, playing it as low-key as I could.

"My God, Herman, are you telling me you might black out at the wheel?"

"Not exactly."

"How can you not exactly pass out?"

"Well, I usually get a bit of a warning."

"*Usually*?"

"Yeah. I get enough time to pull over and stop, I think."

"*You think*?"

"Well, it's not like I've done it all that many times. And it's really not all that likely to happen again. I just thought if it did, you ought to know I didn't die, or whatever."

"*Or whatever*? It's a good thing I like you, Herman, because you are hauling some monumental luggage."

"Oh, good."

"*Good*?"

"Very good."

"What is?"

"You said you like me."

She gave me an exasperated sigh and crossed her arms over her chest. I smiled. I thought that had all gone rather well.

⌘

Nobody will ever tell you they happened to go through Bayfield on their way to somewhere else. It's out on a peninsula, and once you get there, there are only two places you can go: back the way you came or out onto Lake Superior. There's a highway that continues east from there, along the lakeshore and into the woods, but it really just takes you in a huge loop, back to where you started. I decided not to go out on the lake, though there was a plowed flat strip across the lake ice that I

assumed was used as a road out to Madeline Island, which was a dark hump on an otherwise white horizon.

The town was very old but well kept up, as if all the citizens helped with primping for the summer tourists. The result was either picturesque or cute, depending on how you feel about Victorian dollhouse post cards. The Watkins house was small, though it was a stone's throw from several huge Victorian mansions that were immaculately restored. A two-story box with a four-gable roof, it had never been fancy, even when it was new, which was probably at least a hundred years ago. But in the time since then, it looked as if it had never wanted for a fresh coat of paint or a neatly shingled roof. A Subaru Forrester sat in a small garage in the back. The door looked narrow enough that if you weren't careful, you could probably hit both sides of the opening at once.

I assumed Mrs. Watkins must have been watching us approach, since she answered the door almost immediately.

"Can I help you?"

"Hello, Mrs. Watkins. We need to talk to you about your daughter." I kept my voice as neutral as I could.

"Oh! Oh, my. Have they found the people who killed her?"

"I'm afraid not." *So they already know. Thank God for small miracles.*

"We're working on that," said Naomi. "Could we come in, please?"

"Yes, of course." She stepped away from the door to make room for us. Over her shoulder, she called, "Harold! Get your shoes on, we have company."

She showed us into a living room that might have been furnished from Naomi's shop, though it was neat as a pin and freshly cleaned. She sat us down on a frilly-looking sofa and brought us coffee and her husband, Harold. Her name was Lillian, and the two of them looked like every retired blue-collar couple I have ever seen. Not the "greatest generation," which Naomi says is dying off at a hundred a day, but a generation

or two later. Korean War or Vietnam. More likely the former, since there were some framed military medals on the wall. Simple but likeable people, now with a crushing burden of personal tragedy to carry for the rest of their days.

"So you two are police officers?" said Lillian.

"Not exactly," I said.

"We work with victims' advocacy groups," said Naomi. "Sometimes the police get a little overwhelmed, if you know what I mean, and—"

"Sometimes they don't give a damn, is what you mean," said Harold.

"Yes, well, whatever the reason, sometimes we help out with the investigation."

I couldn't believe it. Naomi was a better liar than I was.

"That detective," said Lillian, "the one who phoned us, um…"

"Armstrong?" I said.

"Yes, that's the one. He said in a case like this, where it's just a random murder out on the street, they really don't have much hope of solving it."

I exchanged a glance with Naomi, not sure what to make of that.

"It might not have been quite that simple, Mrs. Watkins," I said. "I was hoping you could tell us something about your daughter's past."

"She was going to be a great artist," said Harold. "Until that goddamned, um…" He bit his lip and forced back a tear.

"Until 2000?"

He squinched his eyes shut and nodded.

"Can either of you tell me what happened?"

"She was home from college, on Thanksgiving break, and she got attacked," said Lillian.

"Attacked, hell," said Harold, "she got kidnapped."

"Are you going to tell this, Harold, or are you going to let me?"

"You do it. You don't get as worked up."

"Well, she was home for Thanksgiving, like I said. It was her senior year, and we were so proud of her. She'd already been in lots of exhibits, and her instructors all said wonderful things about her. It made it all worthwhile. Harold's a plumber—"

"A *union* plumber," said Harold.

"Harold's a union fanatic, and he's always made good money. But when Pammy went off to school, even though she had a scholarship for tuition, she needed living money and money for art supplies. I didn't want her to work when she should be concentrating on her studies, so I took a job at the Suds Emporium, helping people weigh and sort clothes, and another one, part time, at the nursing home. It was hard at first, but I was glad to be able to help her.

"So anyway, she was home for Big Turkey Day. We gave her a new wool coat that she'd been wanting, even though it wasn't Christmas yet. She was wearing it downtown one night, walking to a tavern to meet some of her old high school friends. She never got there. Somebody came up behind her and knocked her legs out from under her and hit her on the head. Then he stuffed something in her mouth and handcuffed her and dragged her into a car. He drove out in the country somewhere and, um, well, had his way, I guess you'd say. Several times." She bit her lip, and we looked at the floor and waited. "And then he dumped her. Didn't even leave her nice new coat." She stopped to weep quietly for a while, and we let her. My instinct was to offer to come back some other time, but what time could possibly be any good for recalling an atrocity? Finally, she pulled herself back together, blew her nose in a tissue, and went on.

"That was the first time," she said.

"Excuse me?"

"She didn't recognize the bum, and the sheriff said just the kind of car wasn't enough to go on, so there was no arrest," said Harold.

"What kind of car was it?"

"One of those fancy sporty kinds, with stripes on it," Lillian continued. "I don't remember now."

"This is one of our suspects in her murder," I said, taking out a photo of Valento from the Prophet's file. "Do you recognize him?"

"No," said Harold, "and he better hope I never do. I'll take my old thirty-ought-six out of the closet and put some serious vent holes in the bastard."

"Calm down, dear." She pulled her reading glasses up from the chain she wore around her neck and peered at the picture. "I think that's somebody who went to school here, isn't it? I think he was a couple years behind Pammy. Maybe we should tell somebody."

"Like that worthless sheriff? He didn't do anything before, what's he going to do now?"

"You should let us handle it for now," I said.

"Yes, well anyway, the law didn't do a thing," said Lillian. "Three nights later, she was walking near the edge of downtown again. One of her friends was with her, going to buy her a drink and try to cheer her up. This time there were two men. They grabbed both the girls and threw them in a trunk."

"Same car?"

"No, a different one. A big car of some kind. They drove for quite a while, she said. She had a pair of jeans on, and she had a Swiss Army knife in the pocket. She managed to get the two of them loose, inside the trunk there, and she jimmied open the latch. She said they should wait until another car was behind them and then jump out. She saw some light in the lid crack after a while, and she opened the lid all the way. The car they were in sped up. There was a semi truck a quarter of a mile behind them, and she jumped out. She broke several bones hitting the pavement and scraped her face up real bad, but she got away. The semi driver stopped and helped her and called the highway patrol on his CB radio."

"What about her friend?"

"She was afraid to jump from a moving car. Pammy never saw her again. Nobody did."

"And nobody did anything about that, either?" said Naomi.

"Not the sheriff, anyway. We talked to the FBI, down in the Twin Cities, and they at least sent a man to talk to Pammy."

"Not the Wisconsin office of the FBI?"

"The sheriff said we should deal with that one, I'm not sure why. He came back a couple of times, but the second time, she had gone back to the Twin Cities, and we didn't have an address for her. Seemed like after that, we never knew where to find her except when she was in trouble."

"That's when Pam's life started to unravel?" I said.

"It surely did. She went back to the Cities, but she never went back to school. She had no heart for it anymore. She worked a lot of odd jobs, including some illegal ones. Got into the booze something terrible, sometimes drugs too. She thought we didn't know, but you could see it on her. Mostly she kept to herself, but when she did hang around people, they were the worst kind. Seems as though for a few years, Harold and I were driving down there every other month to bail her out of jail for something or other. It was a horrifying thing to see. Her classmates at the art school had graduated a long time ago, and I was still working my day jobs, so I could pay for her bail. Do you know how much that stuff costs?"

"Um, no idea." *It's not as if we're allowed to give discounts.* "So then, finally, she came unglued in a Minneapolis bar and—"

"Came unglued? Well, I guess you'd come unglued, too. She recognized the man."

"The one she stabbed?"

"You bet, that one. He was one of the two who had abducted her, the one with the big car. She was absolutely sure. And he talked like he was proud of it. So attempted murder was really the right charge, you see. She definitely wanted to kill that man."

"Did she tell the police that?"

"She tried to, but they wouldn't listen. Her lawyer told her not to even try for that as a defense. Said they'd get laughed out of court, maybe even get the judge mad at them for wasting his time."

"But that doesn't make any sense," said Naomi.

"Sure it does," said Harold. "Those assholes all stick together."

"Which assholes?" I said. But I was starting to think I already knew.

"Cops," said Harold. "The guy who abducted her, the guy she stabbed, the guy who God let live for no good reason I can see? He was a damned cop."

"What was his name?"

"They wouldn't tell her, said if she knew his name, she might try to ruin his *fine* reputation."

Suddenly a lot of things were starting to make sense.

Chapter Twenty

Speed and Ice

After we left the Watkins, we went to see the local sheriff, whose name, just like Gary Cooper in High Noon, was Will Kane. If he was proud of that fact, he did a good job of hiding it, along with everything else. He was considerably less than forthcoming. He said he didn't remember the incident in 1996.

I wasn't having it.

"You have so many abducted girls around here that they all blur together, or is old-timer's disease sneaking up on you?"

"Watch your mouth, mister big-city hotshot. We have one now and then. So does everybody else. What's that to you? You some kind of reporter? You researching a book?"

"FBI," I said.

"Bullshit."

But he paused a tiny moment and looked me over before he said it.

"Actually, I'm a bail bondsman chasing a skip. You seen anybody around here with a Shelby Mustang?"

"Never seen one in my whole life. This is a quiet place. Kids don't have expensive sporty cars and nothing much happens."

"Except for the occasional disappearing girl, whom you don't happen to remember."

"You know, Jackson, if I was to work at it, I could find a reason to arrest you."

"Well, it would be good if you worked at *something*. I didn't say the guy with the Mustang was a kid, by the way."

"Sure, you did."

"Nope. But go ahead and remember it that way, if you want to. That seems to be what you do best." I could see we were getting nowhere with the conversation, and I headed toward the door.

"You're a goddamn smartass and a troublemaker, you know that, Jackson?"

"I certainly hope so. See you around, sheriff."

Some people just aren't worth talking to.

I would have gone to the local high school next, and asked to see some old class photos, but it was Sunday. So we drove around and looked for a place to stay for the night.

We decided not to mention Stewball to the clerk at the motel we checked into. He was a well-behaved cat, after all. He wouldn't rat us out by shredding the curtains. And I would leave a nice tip for the maid, to suck her into the conspiracy. Interestingly, Stewball was also so accustomed to being an indoor cat that he didn't want to go outside at all. When Naomi opened the car door, he wouldn't leave it until she carried him. Not the worst instinct he could have.

I called my office and checked in with Agnes, giving her the phone number of our room. She said Wilkie was settled in at the surveillance site with a few helpers, including a guy named Lonesome George Lybrand. I knew him. He was an old bond customer, mostly arrested for second-story jobs or for holding the bag for heavier hitters. He really should have followed the example of people like Harold Watkins and become a plumber, because he was a lousy crook. But he wasn't crazy or stupid, he kept faith with his own people, and he knew how to handle a weapon. I decided he was okay for a limited engagement.

I told Agnes to call if anything developed. Less than five minutes later the phone rang. I picked it up and said, "Already?"

"The man you're looking for is holed up in a cabin on Madeline Island," said the receiver. The voice was not the sheriff or

anybody else I recognized.

"Who is this?"

"He's there now. Make a hard right at the ferry dock, and it's the second cabin on the left."

"Listen, if you—" The line went dead. I thought of the brown car that had followed us out of Spooner. I thought of a lot of things.

"Who was that, Herman?"

"Somebody who says Valento is out on the island across the bay."

"Do you believe it?"

"Well, I believe somebody is out there, anyway. I think they're waiting for me, and they want me in a remote spot."

"You mean it's a setup."

"Guaranteed."

"So what are you going to do?"

"I'm going to go see them, of course."

"*Herman!* Alone?"

"Wilkie couldn't get here for at least six hours. By then, it will all have fallen apart."

"That might not be the worst thing that could happen, you know." She scowled, then sighed, then said, "I'm going with you."

"You still have the .380?"

"Yes."

"Then I won't try to stop you. How about some dinner first?"

"What happened to needing to get there before it all falls apart?"

"This is different. This is a tactical delay. An hour or so is just enough time to let whoever it is get both careless and nervous."

"If you say so."

"I do. There's one other little thing I'm going to do first, though."

I dialed the Watkins' number, and Harold answered.

"Mr. Watkins? I was thinking about what you said about

your deer rifle, and I thought you might like to know where I'm going tonight and who I might run into."

I had no idea if he knew how to handle himself in a tight situation or not. But he was ex-military, so there was hope. And a .3006 is a lot of firepower. It was like grandma's chicken soup: it couldn't hurt. At this point, I needed any ally I could get. I gave Harold the particulars and left him to decide on his own plan of action, if any.

"You know," he said, "you two are the first people we've talked to who act like you actually care what happened to our Pam."

"And?"

"I've got your back."

⌘

An hour later, Naomi and I sat in the BMW at the top of the mainland ferry ramp and looked out across the ice. Black sky, white lake, with a broad, dark track where somebody had plowed a makeshift roadway. Farther up the coast, we could dimly make out huge blocks of pack ice jammed up on the shoreline, pushed by the great tracts of freezing lake. Their faceted sides gleamed in the cold blue light of a gibbous moon. But at the edge of the town, they had either been cleared away or weren't so bad to begin with. The edge of the ice was flat enough and solid enough to drive over. There were no other vehicles anywhere in sight and no place to go but out. I put the powerful headlights on high beam, threw the transmission into first, and departed the shore.

The surface was surprisingly rough, not at all like the slick skating rink I had expected. My tires made a funny noise on it, a cross between a rumble and a howl. I took us up to fifty in third gear and gave the wheel a little jerk, then a larger one, just to test the surface. We didn't spin out, but we did a little bit of a fishtail, despite all of BMW's fine suspension

engineering. I decided we could maybe track smoothly up to about 85. Above that, we would be on the edge of totally out of control. Off the roadway, the snow was drifted anywhere from a few inches deep to several feet. Here and there, a track from some snowmobile emphasized the hills and valleys of the drifts. If we got out there, we would be in a lot of trouble. I put the transmission in fourth, where I didn't quite have enough torque to break the rear end away, and we cruised along the rumble-strip.

Stewball had his hind feet on the console, front paws on the dash, and ears up at full alert. When the wind blew a wisp of powdery snow into my headlight beams, he jerked his head to follow it.

"He likes this," I said.

"He always did have more enthusiasm than sense."

"Maybe that's why we get along so well."

"I certainly hope not." She petted the cat, which he completely ignored. He had more exciting things on his mind.

After a while, the island ahead began to take on definition and detail, while the mainland receding in my mirrors became darker and more blurred. The square black shape behind us came up so fast, I almost didn't see it before it hit the rear bumper.

It was some kind of monster SUV, maybe a gen-one Humvee, heavy and high. If its lights had been on, they would have been shining right in my rearview mirror. But it was running blacked out, and damn fast. The first impact knocked us straight ahead, kicking us up to about sixty. It also gave us a little breather. But the driver quickly closed the gap and rammed us again.

If he was trying to get me to spin out into the snowdrifts, he didn't know what he was doing. You bump any car on only one corner of the rear bumper at highway speed, and even on dry pavement, you set up a harmonic oscillation that will end in a total loss of control. Hitting somebody straight on and

centered isn't good for anything but intimidation. Maybe that was all he wanted. Or maybe he wanted to run me up onto the island, going too fast to do anything but drive straight into some tree. I didn't care for that idea.

"Are you buckled in?" I said.

"Yes. Are we about to go airborne?"

"Not quite. Hang on to Stewball, and keep your gun handy. I'm going to try something."

I would worry about the legal consequences later. Right now, I was determined I would not become one more victim for Sheriff Kane to conveniently forget. I intended to take out the SUV.

I dropped the gearbox back down into third, feathered the gas pedal a bit to keep from spinning too badly, and pulled away from the black monster behind us. He would catch up sooner or later, of course, but I didn't need the extra distance for very long.

Then I felt it, the phantom ice pick at the base of my skull. It brought tears to my eyes. *Jesus Christ, not now. Let me avoid getting killed this other way first. Then I'll go quietly.* I gripped the wheel tighter. We were less than a mile from the island now.

When I had a lead of a quarter mile or so, I put in the clutch, jammed the wheel to the left, and put on the emergency brake. We skidded around in a full, high-speed spinout. I dropped the transmission all the way down into first, took off the brake, and hit the gas. The car snapped around in a full one-eighty, and I powered it into another forty-five or so before it lurched to a stop. I threw open the door and leaped out, leaning down against the front fender, with the engine block solidly between me and the oncoming vehicle.

My legs were getting weak, and I slumped down behind the fender and clenched my teeth, trying to hold off the pain behind my eyes. The SUV kept coming straight at us, speeding up. When it got within a hundred yards or so, I emptied the

clip, filling the windshield with lead.

It kept coming.

I fumbled in my pocket for a fresh magazine. Suddenly I lost my peripheral vision. Color perception went next, and as I jammed the new magazine into the grip, I began to feel very cold. The blackness was about to claim me again when I saw the windshield of the SUV explode outward. The vehicle swerved violently, hung on an ice ridge for an endless second, and rolled over. And kept rolling.

"What the hell…?" I didn't finish the thought before the universe went dark.

Chapter Twenty-One

The Adjustment Bureau

I couldn't help but be impressed with the truly rich variety of ceilings in the world. This one was plaster, with a bit of a swirl pattern troweled into it. It may have been white once. I decided I would call my memoirs *Ceilings I have Known*. Mom is probably still alive somewhere, so it might sell one volume.

This time, the doctor's name was Frost, and he was a poor substitute for Dr. Yang. But then, I was a long way from home, wasn't I?

"And how are we feeling?"

I grimaced. "You had to say 'we,' didn't you?"

"Answer the question, please." Like Dr. Yang, he pretended to have something very important to look at on a clipboard.

"I should warn you doc, I know this game already. I've played it before. I feel all right, and no, I have no idea where I am. But then, I didn't come here on my own, did I?"

"You're at Saint Mary's Hospital. Do you know where that is?"

"No."

"Do you know who you are?"

"I'm a famous ice road trucker. My friends call me Herman the Hammer." I looked past his over-serious face and saw Naomi, on the verge of laughing or crying or both. As soon as our eyes met, she came over and gave me a soft kiss on the cheek

"Welcome back, stranger." To the doctor, she said, "He's all

right, Doctor. Believe it or not, that's the way he talks all the time."

"I'll check back," said the man in white, and he let himself out.

"Good to see you again," I said. "Where on earth is Saint Mary's?"

"The City of Superior. Just across the bay from Duluth."

"That's a long way from Madeline Island. I assume we didn't walk?"

"You came here in the back of Mr. Watkins' Subaru. I followed in your BMW. I didn't care much for going that fast on the slippery roads, but I figured if he could do it, so could I. And I knew if I lost him, I'd probably never find this place on my own."

"How long have I been out?"

"Not so long. It's still Sunday night. Dawn is several hours away. I probably owe you a bit of an apology."

"Not for anything I can see."

"Maybe not. But I have to admit, when you told me about your brain injury, I wasn't sure whether to believe it or not. Maybe I wanted to think you had the world's most original pickup line instead, just for me."

"I like to think that for you, I'd have created something better. But anyway, now you know."

"Now I know." She gave me another kiss, this one quite long.

"So why aren't we both dead?" *Or in jail?* flashed into my mind. But I thought I knew the answer to that part, anyway.

"There were two men in the big SUV. You shot one of them in the shoulder. You might have hit the other one, too. We couldn't tell for sure. I was getting out of the car with my gun after you went down. I thought you must have been shot, and I was going to defend you. But Mr. Watkins was behind the other vehicle, in his Subaru. He stopped and shot through the back window and then shot out a back tire, and the monster

machine skidded out and rolled over. He says he only meant to shoot the tire. We couldn't tell if either man was dead. I said we needed to get you to a hospital, and we left."

"But you got a good look at the two guys in the Humvee? Was it Armstrong and Valento?"

"Yes, we got a look, and no, it wasn't. Not either one of them."

"Oh shit."

"Oh shit?"

"Definitely oh shit. What did the sheriff have to say?"

"We never saw him. By the time we were off the lake and headed out of town, he still hadn't shown up."

"The man who makes a career of seeing no evil continues to do so. Now *that* is interesting. Where's Watkins now?"

"He went back to Bayfield. He thought somebody ought to be there to tell our side of the story."

"He certainly didn't balk from playing his part in it, did he?'

"He did not."

"We should go thank him for that. Right now, in fact."

"It's still the middle of the night, Herman. And the doctor thought you should stay here a while."

"Doctors are so predictable."

"And?"

"I'm not."

"No, I can definitely see that, all right."

"And I'm too keyed up to sleep."

"Well, how many positions does that fancy bed have?"

I looked at the control box next to me. "Quite a few, I guess."

"Let's try vee-shaped first."

"You're not so predictable, either, are you?"

She chuckled.

Vee-shape turned out to be not workable at all, but arched turned out to be real killer bee. And then I really did sleep.

⌘

By the time we got back to Bayfield, the sun was up, if totally without any warmth, and the coffee shops were open. We put Stewball in the motel room and hung a "Do Not Disturb" sign on the door. Then we met the Watkins couple at one of the cafés and compared notes over steaming coffee and monster pancakes smothered in raspberries.

"I owe you a debt I can probably never repay," I said. "You saved my life twice in one night."

"That sounds like a bigger deal than it was," said Harold Watkins. "The first time was almost like a chance at getting my youth back. I didn't much like being in Korea, but I sure wouldn't mind being twenty-two again, you know? And the second business? Well, if I hadn't got you to a hospital in time, I was pretty sure your sweetie pie there would have blown me clean away. She sure acted like it, anyway."

Naomi blushed and looked at her plate.

"Looks to me like you two are a little more than *co-advocates*, if that's the word."

"It does look that way, doesn't it?"

"Well?"

"Very well, indeed." I decided a non-answer and a change of subject would be a really good idea just then. "What did our hard-working sheriff have to say about last night's doings?"

"Turns out, nothing happened," said Harold.

"Excuse me?" I said.

"Yeah. Ain't that a hoot? I gun somebody down, really blow the hell out of them, for the first time since that bitch of a winter at the Chosin Reservoir, and our fat, stupid sheriff says it's all in my head, never happened."

"And out on the ice?"

"All gone. The vehicle, the shell casings, even most of the skid marks. And that big Humvee ain't in any of the garages in town here, either."

"My, my, my," I said.

"Do you think this has anything to do with our Pammy,

Mr. Jackson?" said Lillian.

"Oh, you can count on that, Mrs. Watkins. Maybe her and a lot of other things."

"What are you saying, Herman?" said Naomi.

"That I have been much too modest in my thinking. Somebody went to a lot of trouble to take us out of the game here. And when that didn't work, they went to even more trouble to make it look like nothing ever happened. For a while I thought this was all about a chop shop operation. Or maybe it was also about one sick killer who uses a chop shop to hide in. But that's not big enough. It's time to talk conspiracy theory, people."

"Will Kane ain't smart enough for a conspiracy," said Harold.

"Not to run one, maybe, but he could still be part of it. Somebody followed us partway up here yesterday. When it was obvious where we were going, they turned around. I figure they called ahead, to set up a reception. That implies an organization with some size to it."

"All because of our Pam?" said Lillian.

"I don't think so. Make no mistake about it, Mrs. Watkins, we are looking for your daughter's killer. But there's something else going on here. Whoever was following us wouldn't have known *why* we were going to Bayfield, only that we were. And if all people wanted to do was keep us from finding Valento, it would have been a lot easier simply to tell him to go someplace else for a while. They wanted to protect something other than either a chop shop or a murder suspect. And they made the Humvee go away because either it or the people in it could be linked to that something."

"What?" said Harold.

"I don't know yet. Something we might find even if we weren't looking for it. Something we could find because we were looking for Valento. And it will be a thing with a lot of money attached to it. You don't try to kill somebody, make

your own people disappear, and buy a local sheriff and maybe a St. Paul cop, too, all over a bunch of car parts."

"What St. Paul cop?" said Harold.

"The one you talked to on the phone, Armstrong. We think he's dirty, but we're not sure just how."

"Like I told you, the bastards all stick together," said Harold. "Thank God you're not one of them. But you're not merely a victims' advocate, either, are you?"

"It's complicated," said Naomi. "You see, we—" I held up a hand to stop her.

"No, we're not." I looked Harold straight in the eyes. "I'm a bail bondsman. Valento has somehow obtained a phony bond with my name on it, and he's guaranteed to jump bail. In a way, he already has."

"So that's it? You're only here to protect your money?"

"No. It started out that way, but then it got personal."

"But our Pam isn't personal for you," said Lillian.

"Yes, she is. I think she died because she was involved with a friend of mine. And I think to some extent, it's my fault." I paused to let that sink in.

"You have to understand, bonding is a funny business, in a lot of ways. I'm part of the criminal justice system, but I'm really not, because I'm neutral. Or I'm supposed to be, anyway. It's a little like being at a prize fight where lethal weapons are allowed. I'm not really involved in the contest, but I rent out neutral corners to the people who are. Sometimes I rent them to people who are meaner than a junkyard dog and sometimes I rent them to folks who wouldn't kill a fly if you held it down for them. And when they're done using the neutral space, they go off to trial. They get convicted or acquitted, and either way, it's none of my business. Absolutely none.

"But sometimes you can't let it go at that. Sometimes the system isn't capable of anything remotely resembling justice, and the temptation to play God gets to be overwhelming. And suddenly you quit being just a bondsman."

"And become what?"

"The Adjustment Bureau."

There was a long silence after that. Finally, Harold cleared his throat and said, "So, what has the big, big conspiracy money attached to it? Drugs?"

"It does, but I'm not seeing any other hints of that. It's something else, I think."

We were all silent for a while.

"Sheriff Kane didn't like it when you said you were an FBI agent," said Naomi.

"No, he did not. He was shook up by it at first, before he looked me over and decided I must be faking it."

"So what does the FBI get involved with?"

"Bank robbery," I said. "Kidnapping. Any crime involving interstate commerce. Catching spies, but only if they don't go overseas. Blatantly assassinating people like John Dillinger and Clyde Barrow. I think they're all gone now."

"What about human trafficking?" said Naomi. "Do they get involved with that?"

The Watkins traded a look.

"They're supposed to, anyway. It's a form of kidnapping. What are you thinking?"

"The sheriff said they get a missing girl case now and then."

"Yes he did, didn't he? Now wouldn't it be interesting to find out what 'now and then' really means?"

"Are we going to call the real FBI and get them involved, then?" said Naomi.

"We need a lot more information before we can call in the feds and expect them to take us seriously," I said.

"Can we help?" said Lillian.

"Sure," I said. "You can go over to your local newspaper and check their back issues for disappearing girls over the last few years. Go back as far as you can stand to."

"I don't know if I can run one of those micro-fish things," said Harold.

"Somebody there will help you, you can bet on it. People like to show off what they know, especially if it's something hardly anybody ever asks about."

"I guess maybe they do, at that. What are you going to do?"

"Lillian said she thought Valento's photo looked like one of Pam's old classmates. We're going to see what we can find out at the high school. Let's make this place our fallback meeting spot. Don't go back to your house until we're all together again. Not before we know what we're up against. If you see my car out in front of this place, come in and compare notes. If not, check at the school. Or call us on Naomi's cell phone."

"And visa-versa. If we're not here, we'll probably be over at the *Daily Press*, in Ashland."

"Sounds good. And Harold, do you have a short gun, something besides the deer rifle? Something you can conceal in your clothes?"

"Sure. I've got an Army Colt Model 1911 yet. I snuck it out with—"

"You don't have to tell him that, Harold. I'm sure Mr. Jackson has a fine imagination. And Mr. Jackson, thank you *so much.*"

"For what? I haven't accomplished a thing yet."

"For getting us involved. After all that time of feeling helpless and forsaken, we finally get to do *something* to help Pammy. It feels good." Harold nodded silently.

"Just don't forget the artillery, okay? We don't know who all is a target now."

Chapter Twenty-Two

Jack the Ripper's School Days

Bayfield High School was easy enough to find. A prim, two story building of dark brick, white mortar, and solid proportions, it was built into the side of a hill, so the entrance had a walkout-basement effect. It looked too big for the size of the town. It must have pulled kids in from a broader area, but still, it showed that the locals weren't afraid to invest in education. I rather liked that.

A cheery, white-haired receptionist named Cheryl, who looked considerably older than the building, fixed us up with an empty library table and school yearbooks from 1984 to 2000. I went from late to early and Naomi tried from 1984 forward. By the time we met, at about 1992, we still hadn't found anything useful.

"I'm afraid I'm not very good at looking at young people's pictures and imagining what they'll look like as adults," she said.

"I have the same problem," I said. "I keep hoping we're going to find a picture of Valento as a senior, so it's not quite such a big stretch of the imagination. But whatever class he was in, he should be in the roster in the back of the book, and I'm not finding that, either,"

We found lots of pictures of Pam Watkins, in this or that club or activity, radiating youthful energy and good will. But as for her sinister possible classmate, we were staring into a total void. After a couple of fruitless hours, Cheryl, the receptionist,

came and offered to get us some coffee or tea from a vending machine. We said that sounded wonderful.

"Are you having any luck?" She returned with steaming white paper cups in quilted brown heat-absorbing sleeves.

"Absolutely none," I said. We hadn't told her who we were looking for or why, and she hadn't asked. Now I took out my photo of the adult Valento and showed it to her. "This is who we're after, several years older."

She gave it a long look. "You're police, aren't you?" she said.

"Something like that," said Naomi.

"Why do you say that?" I said.

"I think I remember this boy. Seems to me he was always in trouble with the police."

"That would fit, yes," I said. "His name is Valento."

"No, I don't think so. It starts with a vee, all right, but that's not quite right." I traded glances with Naomi. No wonder we had totally struck out.

"And you won't get anywhere looking at senior pictures," she said, " because if I'm thinking of the right person, he never made it that far. His teachers were more eager than he was for his sixteenth birthday, so they could kick him out for good. But something else happened, I think. I can't quite..." She took the 1997 volume and started leafing quickly through it.

It took her a while, but finally she pointed triumphantly at a photo in the sophomore class of 1994. "That's him, I think. I thought it was a little more recently than this, but my memory does that to me sometimes. I'm pretty sure that's him."

I looked and gradually agreed. There was a lot of baby fat on those young cheeks, and no lines on the forehead at all, but the glinting, predator's eyes were unmistakable, as was the permanent cynical sneer.

"Walesa was his name," said Cheryl. "Roy Walesa. It sounded like a vee name, you see, but it wasn't, it was one of those Eastern European W's. In a place like this, where the majority of our student names are Ojibwa or Lakota, you remember

that sound. That of course, and the fact that he was always in trouble. I said that before, I guess."

"What kind of trouble?"

"Just about any kind a boy that age can get into. Fighting with the boys, grabbing the girls, stealing cars, bringing liquor to school functions, vandalism, torturing animals. I couldn't begin to count how many times the police came to take him out of class."

"You said his teachers were dying to expel him. Did they?"

"No. There was some other trouble that beat them to it. He only had one parent, as I recall, but I don't remember if it was a single mom or single dad. Whichever one it was, he or she died in a house fire."

"A fire that was set by the kid?"

"I can't honestly say I know that. I don't think anybody does, but a lot of people thought so. It was the sort of thing he would do, anyway. Anyway, we never saw him at school after that. There was a rumor that he had gone to live with his older brother."

"What was his name?"

"The brother?" She shook her head. "I didn't know that. Whatever it was, I don't think he ever went to our school. He had some kind of repair garage, as I recall, out in the sticks someplace. But the boy could just as well have gone to some foster home in another town, too. We wouldn't know unless somebody asked to have his school records transferred. I don't think anybody did. That's all I know, I'm afraid."

"That's a lot," I said.

"Thank you so much," said Naomi.

"You didn't say why you're looking for this person."

"No," I said. "We did not."

"Well, whatever it is, be careful. Even when he was a kid, you could tell he was evil. Dangerous and vicious. Just no sense of right or wrong whatsoever."

"Sounds like you know him, all right. Thanks again."

⌘

After we left the school, I cruised past the raspberry restaurant. There was no Subaru parked nearby, so I went on. I went past the Watkins' house, saw no new vehicles or lights, and kept going.

"What now?" said Naomi.

"Public library. See if we can find a 1994 phone book. Maybe the older brother with the garage had an ad in the Yellow Pages."

"You know where the library is?"

I nodded. "There were fliers in the school lobby."

"And if we find an ad for a garage that might be the one, then what do we have?"

"Maybe something, maybe nothing. If he went there once when he was in trouble, he might do it again."

"If it's still there."

"Yes. If. Let me tell you how I think the early story lays out. Our boy with his original Polish name is a real candidate for the young Antichrist, as nasty as they come. He gets busted for a lot of stuff that there's no record of now, because he was a juvie. Finally, he caps his young career by torching his own house and killing his only parent. He's not *quite* old enough to drop out of school, and the authorities really don't know what to do with the little bastard. And then somebody comes up with a special plan."

"What kind of somebody?"

"Maybe the brother, maybe our deaf-and-dumb sheriff, maybe a player we haven't seen yet. Somebody who looks at the kid and sees raw talent that can be molded in useful ways. But first—"

"First they have to get him out of the system."

"That's right. And they have to make him dependant on *them*. So they find him a place to lay low, a place that's legitimate on the face of it, but only if his new handlers make it

so. And they let him accumulate a big debt, get a lot of future promises out of him. They begin to groom him."

"What about the brother?"

"He might not even be a real person, but if he is, it would make things simpler. A maverick one-stall grease monkey who needs money and connections, maybe? Easy to recruit, easy to keep in line. And every scam that uses wheels needs a mechanic."

"That looks like the library," she said, pointing.

We pulled up in front of a small but tall building, made mostly out of some kind of pink stone, as was a grand front stairs that looked as big as the building it lead to. Four big columns held up a cornice and gable with an inscription that proudly proclaimed the place to be a Carnegie Library. It looked a hundred years old and it looked brand new. It had a nice collection of books and regional pamphlets, but unfortunately, no old phone directories. The librarian couldn't remember anything useful, either. We went back to the bar/grill/coffee shop where we had started the day. This time, the Subaru was parked at the curb, and we joined the Watkinses for coffee and burgers.

⁂

"This part of the state has one or two girls disappear a year," said Lillian Watkins. "Once in a while, three, but not usually. If you add in the Duluth and Superior area, the number goes to six to eight. That's been true since 1985. Before then, there wasn't one a year."

"And guess what happened in 1984?" Said Harold.

"Will Kane got elected sheriff for the first time," said Naomi.

"Bingo," said Harold.

Damn, I like a smart woman.

We filled the Watkins in on the results of our own probing, including my speculation about the school days of Valento, a.k.a. Walesa.

"So what do we do now?" said Harold.

"Well for right now," I said, "I should go back to St. Paul. I've got a partner doing a stakeout there, and he really doesn't know what he's up against. You two should find a place to lay low for a while. Get out of town if you can. This thing could get a lot uglier before it gets nice."

"I've seen ugly before," said Harold. "It doesn't scare me. After you lose your only child, nothing can scare you anymore."

"No, I guess it couldn't. Just be careful, okay?"

"Okay. I got an old Army buddy, has a cabin on the lakeshore, west of here. Maybe I'll go borrow it for a while. Maybe the missus and I will go do a little snowmobiling."

"Make sure your machine has rearview mirrors, will you?"

"That, I will. And along the way, I'll keep a sharp lookout for a Humvee with a shattered windshield."

"Well, if you find it, get hold of me before you do anything."

"Fair enough. How do I do that?"

"Um—"

"I have a cell phone," said Naomi. She wrote her number on a card and gave it to Lillian.

"Speaking of phones," I said, "do you still have a name and number for that FBI agent who talked to you back in 2000?"

"I thought you might ask," said Lillian. She pulled a card out of her purse and gave it to me.

We couldn't think of anything else to say, so we stood up and exchanged handshakes and then hugs. It felt as if we were going to war together.

We went back to the motel to collect our luggage and our cat. Stewball was happy to see us but was busy kicking at something on his ruff that he didn't like. He was wearing a collar. He had never had a collar before.

I unbuckled it and took it off, and I saw that it had a round metal medallion attached to it, the kind people put their pet's name and their own phone number on. Instead of that, this

one simply said, "GET OUT WHILE YOU CAN!"

Naomi was looking over my shoulder as I read the tag.

"I'd say it's a little late for that," she said. "Wouldn't you?"

Chapter Twenty-Three

Home Fires

The trip back south was uneventful. It was late on a Monday afternoon by then, and if there was such a thing as an open country rush hour, I wasn't seeing it. The rear bumper on my BMW was mashed up and ugly, but I still had all my taillights and plates, so I wasn't worried about attracting the interest of any highway patrols. Any time I had a stretch of straight road more than a mile long, I let the car go as fast as it could and still track straight, and the miles melted away. Stewball loved it. This time, we were not followed. Naomi put her seat back, pulled her coat over her face, and let the machine noises lull her to sleep. I figured she was entitled. By the time we were again passing through Spooner, she and Stewball were both solidly out of it. I stopped at a superstore gas station and got out as quietly as I could. I filled the tank and bought myself some cheapuccino and factory-made chocolate cupcakes. That's a combination I have found to be not quite as potent as adrenalin, but not far behind it. And no matter what kind of jerkwater place you buy it at, it's always the same. I also got fresh doughnuts, a cup of hot water and some green tea bags, a warm fish sandwich, and a pint of milk, for when the rest of my troops woke up. I drove on.

It was well after dark when we crossed the St. Croix, but the western sky had lost all its stars, as they disappeared in the general orangish glow over the metro area. It looked as if the city had been firebombed while we were gone, and the embers

were still burning. I thought of the pictures I've seen of London during the blitz. I looked over at Naomi and saw that she was awake now, and looking at the same thing.

"We're under siege, aren't we, Herman?"

"Yes, we are. That message on Stewball's collar was pure bullshit. The bad guys would like to have us on the run, but no matter what we do, they are going to come after us. And the worst part is that we don't really know who or what we're up against."

"So what do we do?"

I gave her another look, trying to see if she needed a sugar-coated answer. I decided she didn't.

"I honestly don't know yet. If all we had to worry about was Valento, we could leave him to the Minneapolis cops, but that's only if we knew where he is, which we don't. With Armstrong, we can't rely on any cops, Minneapolis or St. Paul, and we don't know where he is, either. And we probably also have a bunch of other players that we don't know, period. It's like the quest for the Holy Grail. Nobody's ever seen the thing, but we all think we'll know it when we see it. And then we'll know what to do."

"What if there are more bad guys in this play than heroes?"

"There almost certainly will be. That's why we had better be smarter, and get that way really soon, because this is a war. And if we rely on somebody else to fight it for us, we're going to lose"

"That's an honest answer, anyway."

"At this point, that's as good as it gets."

She threw off her coat, stretched, and sniffed. Soon she was gobbling doughnuts shamelessly, and appreciating the tea. Stewball was down in the foot well, curled up in a tight ball. He opened one eye for a moment and then went back to sleep. I guessed he didn't care if his fish sandwich got cold.

"Where are we going first, Herman?"

"Wilkie's stakeout."

"Is he somebody you trust?"

"Completely."

"Then I do, too."

⌘

We pulled into the parking lot for the Lowertown loft condos, and to my surprise, Wilkie came out of the building to meet us.

"Everything okay?" I said.

"Everything's quiet, anyway. I brought you a key."

"A key? How did we come to have one of them?" I took the shiny brass item from him and put it in my pocket.

"Miss Agnes thought we ought to go legit. She talked the condo owner into renting it to her for two months, said she needed a place to work on a movie."

"He probably thinks it's a porn flick."

"Are you kidding? Who could talk to her and suspect her of anything sleazy?"

"You've got a point. This is Naomi, by the way."

"Is she, um…"

"Yes. She's very um."

"Then I'm pleased to meet you, ma'am." Sometimes he amazes me by managing to talk just like the square world.

"Nice to meet you, too, Mr. Wilkie."

"I hope you weren't driving Herman's precious Beemer when the ass end got dipped into that barrel of ugly. It looks like shit."

Then again, sometimes he doesn't.

"No, he did that all by himself."

"Lucky for you. Who's the rug?"

"The rug's name is Stewball," she said. "He sleeps in six languages and purrs in four."

"Bring him in. We probably have some slope-head chicken he would like."

"Now, there's an image," I said.

Up in the sixth floor condo, there were more guys hanging around than at an open poker game. Most of them looked lost, but a few were gathered around a display of video monitors on an inside wall. Four screens showed the salt shed from different angles and three more showed parking areas and grounds around it.

"You've been busy, Wide."

"Damn right."

"Do I want to know what we're spending here?"

"Actually, you do. You remember Jeff, at the electronics department at Best Buy? He set up all this stuff. I told him it was for a sting operation that's so super-secret, we couldn't even use the equipment from our own agency."

"Which is?"

"I told him FBI."

"Oh good. If you're going to impersonate a law enforcement officer, you might as well go high class."

"That's what I thought, too. Anyway, Jeff ate it up. He actually loaned us most of this stuff. It belongs to customers who think it's being repaired right now."

"What about all the warm bodies?"

"You have a lot of fans, Herman, my man. These are all people you helped at some time or other. We don't have to pay them unless they shoot somebody."

"*What?* Who did you put a bounty on?"

"It's not like that. I told them we would repay them for the bullets, is all. Also, I buy them pizza and Chinese. There's lots of leftovers, if you're interested."

"Any beer?"

"Of course."

"Jesus, what an operation."

"Thank you. I worked hard, setting it up."

"And what have you found?"

"Tell you what I haven't found, Herm. I haven't found a string of hot cars going in and truckloads of auto parts going out."

"No, I was wrong about that. What about Valento? His real name is Walesa, by the way."

"If he's in there, he hasn't budged since we started watching."

"How about a fat brown four-door Buick?"

"It's hard to tell colors with those funny sodium yard lights, but it could have come and gone a few times. We have video recordings we can check. There have also been a couple of nine-passenger vans in and out. Nobody in them but the drivers, bringing some boxes."

"Groceries?"

"Could be. If so, it's for a fairly big number of people."

"Shit."

"Double shit. You know what's funny? All of the vehicles going in had one of those stupid diamond-shaped yellow tags people used to have years ago, that says 'Baby On Board.'"

"Maybe that's a sort of gate pass."

"That's what I think, too. A password."

"Maybe we should get one." I looked at Naomi.

"They were big in the sixties and again in the eighties," she said. "I'm sure I have at least one around."

"One of the vans also has FBI painted on the side," said Wilkie. "That's mainly why I decided to tell our buddy Jeff that's who we were."

"Oh shit, again," I said.

"Try some kung pao beef. You'll feel better."

"I doubt it."

"I take it you ran into some kind of bad shit up north?"

"You have no idea," said Naomi.

"Give me one," said Wilkie.

We sat down at a folding card table littered with half-empty white cardboard cartons and boxes of cold pizza, and I gave Wilkie a quick recap of what we had found in Bayfield, including our adventures on the ice road and the disappearing Humvee. "Somebody has a lot to protect," I said, "and they're not done doing it yet."

"That could fit a lot of things, Herm. You think the salt shed could be a transfer point for abducted girls?"

"Well, we're right across the river from an airport that mainly handles private traffic. It would be handy, for sure. You snatch girls from the northern boonies, collect them here, maybe get them trained, then fly them out to wherever."

"What do you mean, 'get them trained?'"

"You know what I mean. And it's just as ugly as you think it is."

Wilkie suddenly went a little pale, which surprised me.

"Where does Valento fit in all this?" said Naomi. "Bad as it is, a human traffic operation isn't murder."

"No," I said, "but it can lead to it, easily enough. People with no respect for human dignity don't have much for human life, either. And this looks like a big enough operation to have a few loose cannons. I'm thinking Valento is just another one of the troops, probably a snatcher. But now and then he runs off the rails and takes a victim for himself."

"Or his keepers give him one," said Wilkie. "Throw your mad dog some red meat now and then, just to keep him loyal."

"Could be. It could also be that he's become a liability to them, though. If they hadn't gotten him the phony bond, I'd say they might even throw *him* to us."

"Don't hold your breath," said Wilkie. "We need to raid that place, Herman, the sooner the better."

"I agree. But first we need to find out if we can trust the feebs. If the real FBI is bent too, then we are well and truly fucked."

"So how do we find that out?"

"I'm thinking about it."

"Maybe we walk into their offices and ask them," said Naomi.

"Gee, Herman, I don't know why I never think of these plans," said Wilkie.

"You're probably too devious."

"I think I like that just fine."

"And I like the idea," I said. "I think we need some hardware that's a little more sophisticated than what our boy Jeff can get us, though. You suppose the Prophet is open this hour of the day?"

"Who knows when sleeping time is on his planet?"

"We're about to find out."

"So, when do we raid the shed?"

"Soon."

"How soon?"

"Very soon." *What the hell is his problem, anyway?* "Meanwhile, though, if one of those vans leaves the shed with some women on board, stop it, absolutely. Any way you can, legal or illegal."

"I can definitely handle that part, Herm."

Chapter Twenty-Four

Tickling the Dragon's Tail

If the Prophet was annoyed at being visited in the middle of the night, he gave no sign of it. He praised Yah!, welcomed us in his usual enthusiastic manner, and, of course, offered us some of his highly suspicious tea.

"Your travels must have been rewarding, children," he said. "Naomi's aura has waxed even brighter than before."

I still didn't see her aura, but she gave him a shy smile that was utterly charming.

"I need some high-tech hardware, Prophet."

"Lo, the anointed priest of all Luddites wants to tech up and get down. Truly, the axis of the universe has shifted, and events of great pith and moment are about to occur."

"I certainly hope so. I need a bug that can be planted quickly and easily in a very secure building."

"Just a plain vanilla bug, audio only?"

"Yes."

"What kind of range does it have to have?"

"Half a mile would be nice, but I could live with a lot less for the sake of keeping the size down."

"For a given size battery, you can have range or durability. Does it have to last a long time?"

"A day is probably plenty."

"Then I'll give you the range. And the device has to go through a security check to get in the building?"

"Yes."

"You want a phone clone. It looks like a regular cell phone, which it also is, but when nobody is watching, you pull a panel off it and stick it to wherever you can. And like a seed of chaos, your bug is planted."

"Stick it with what?"

"Chewing gum, double-face tape, a magnet, whatever you like."

"I like the tape."

"Then you shall have it. And I'll give you a classy plastic chassis, so if somebody is scanning you with a quantified metal detector in and out, they won't notice that you left something behind you."

"Sounds like just the ticket."

"When do you need this marvel of the brave new world?"

"Well, if I needed it tomorrow—"

"You'd ask me tomorrow. Of course. You know, sometimes I think you are one big karma debt, Pilgrim. You are sure you won't take some tea? This is going to take a little time."

An hour and a half later, we left with the goodies. I had pretended to sip some tea, but I drew the line at pretending to be in another universe.

The next morning, I parked at a meter a block away from the Federal Building downtown and fired up a device that fit nicely in my shirt pocket. It was a one-frequency radio combined with a signal-activated tape recorder. Naomi put the decoy phone in her purse and headed for the building. Inside, she went through two security checkpoints. At one of them, she had to show a guard that her phone was not the kind that can take pictures. She finally managed to get to an FBI office, where she asked for Agent James Douglas, which was the name we had gotten from Lillian Watkins. She was politely told that no such person was around, and could somebody else help her?

"No, I have to talk to that agent."

"Perhaps if you told me what this is all about?"

"I don't think so. If I can't talk to Agent Douglas, I'll just go back to northern Wisconsin."

"Is there a number we could call you at?"

"No. If you don't want to help me, I'm gone."

"But surely you can see—"

"Goodbye."

At that, she was asked to wait just a short while, and wonder of wonders, the elusive Agent Douglas was produced. I heard footsteps and doors and finally an interview.

She told the agent she was the older sister of a young woman who had vanished from the Bayfield area a month before.

"Why didn't you go to the Milwaukee FBI office, miss?"

"Well, I pestered our sheriff, Mr. Kane, about the case a lot, I'm afraid, but he said he had no information. Finally, he gave me your name. He said you were running a task force on abducted girls from the north country and might be able to help."

"He may have been too optimistic, miss. There is no task force and I have no such kind of case. But why don't you give me the pertinent information, and I'll look into it."

She gave him the info the Watkinses had pulled from the newspaper, plus a lot of completely phony stuff about who Naomi was and where she lived. She also gave him a bug. While she was ostensibly looking for a tissue in her purse, she peeled it off her cell phone and stuck it on the bottom of the agent's desktop. It was about the size of a business card, but an eighth of an inch thick or so, and it was voice-activated, so it gave off no signal when it was just sitting there. Then she gave him a phony hotel phone number and left. We figured no agent, straight or bent, would tell her anything useful until he had a chance to check her and her story out. What we wanted to know was what he would do before that.

She could hardly have been out of the building before he called Sheriff Will Kane.

"What the hell is wrong with you, Kane? How long you think this operation is going to hold together, you start giving my name out to people? Sending a relative of the goods *here*? Judas priest, man. Now we've got another one we have to get rid of."

The bug wasn't sensitive enough for me to hear the other side of the conversation, but what I got was enough.

"What the hell you mean, you didn't? She was just here. In *my* office. She knew my name, and she had—Huh? Huh? *Huh?* Not at all? Oh, shit!"

He hung up the phone loudly and shouted, "Secure the building! Stop that woman who was just in my office. Get her, *now*."

Naomi slipped into the BMW and we pulled quickly out into traffic.

"Well?" she said.

"You were fantastic."

"And?"

"We are well and truly fucked."

⁂

Back at the loft condo, Wilkie was not happy.

"We've got to go in there, Herman. If you won't come along, I'll go on my own."

"Wide, we don't have any idea how many people we're up against, we can't use the excuse that we're apprehending Valento because we haven't established that he's there, and we can't trust the cops or the feds. That all adds up to a really good way to walk into about a ten-year prison sentence *if things go well* and a death trap if they don't."

"You didn't used to be so chickenshit, Herman."

"You didn't used to be crazy."

"Herman, there's people in that shed."

"Well, yeah. I mean, we would hardly be having this

conversation if there weren't."

"No, I mean there's a certain person."

"Wide, what the hell are you talking about?"

"Trish."

"Excuse me?"

"I think they've got Trish Hanover."

"How on earth—?"

"She disappeared the night you were in the hospital, remember? And Valento's laptop told us she was setting a trap for him."

"Yeah, but—"

"I called her cell phone, Herm. Some asshole laughed and told me he had her. And I'm damn well going to get her back."

"Back?"

"Well, I mean—"

"Oh my God. I can't believe I didn't see it before. You two are an item, aren't you? She's the woman you met through the online matchmaking service."

"Yeah, so?"

"She's a nice person. I'm happy for you."

"And?"

We were interrupted by the radio in my pocket, and for the next two hours or so, we put off our own discussion and listened while Agent Douglas made quite a lot of phone calls. Apparently he had no worries about the security of his office phone at all. Big mistake. Better yet, as he was talking to somebody at the salt shed, he gave the guy the number of his personal cell phone. Why thank you, very much. And as he made his hurried plans, I began to see the pieces of one of my own. It was chancy as hell, but it was possible.

"What are you thinking, Herman?"

"Every wall has a crack in it *somewhere*."

"Yeah, and?"

I sighed and thought of a series of cartoons I saw when I was a kid. A couple of ragged, emaciated guys are in a dungeon

cell, with their arms and legs spread out and chained to the walls, so their feet don't even touch the floor. One of them looks at the other and says, "Now, here's my plan..."

I felt like that guy as I looked at Wilkie and said, "Let's go get your girl out of there."

Chapter Twenty-Five

Special Ops

I looked over my troops. Besides Lybrand, there was Joe Carmody, also know as Plug, Fingers Martin, Slip Mulligan, Kenny Fender, and October Jones. Not exactly a group you would pick to save the world. But they were what I had. All but Jones were ex-cons, some of them repeaters. Basically, the favor I had done for each of them was the same: I believed in them when nobody else did. Or at any rate, I wrote bonds for them when nobody else would. They didn't have enough property to sign over as security against a skip, but I sized each one of them up and decided he would show up for trial. I had bet on them, in a word, and apparently they remembered that. So I called them to attention and told them the bad news.

"What we're about to do could get us shot, locked up in a federal pen, or both, and there's not a damn penny to be made from it. If anybody wants out, say so now. I won't question your motives."

"I will," said Wilkie.

"Is this important to you, Herman?" I wasn't sure which one of them said it.

"Yes."

"Damned important," said Wilkie.

"Then we're in." They all nodded in agreement. A whole roomful of people with just as little sense as me. No wonder the bonding business is thriving. I sighed again and started giving out assignments.

"We need a van that looks like the one you've been watching go in and out of the shed, complete with the FBI marking on the side."

"That would be my bag," said Fender. "How quick do you need it?"

"No later than seven tonight, with a road test behind it, a full tank of gas, and the letters already on it and the paint dry."

"Piece of cake. You want some armor plating, too?"

"You can do that?"

"Not all over, but some."

"Great. Do it. Don't put on so much weight that you make it slow, though."

"I'll soup the engine a little while I'm at it, and beef up the suspension."

"You've got time for all that? How the hell did you get caught, anyway?"

"Bad partners."

"Pity. Okay, go for it. Wilkie, you go see your buddy Jeff again and get us some hands-free radios that we can use to stay in contact during the operation. Make sure they're on a frequency that is not popular with law-enforcement types. Two of the rest of you, come with me."

Lybrand and Carmody stepped up. I picked up Wilkie's cell phone and dialed a number from my dim past.

"Dave's Sewing Machine Repair," said the phone.

"Hey, Dave. Herman Jackson."

"Who?"

"I wrote a bond for your nephew once, back when he was a runner for—"

"Oh yeah, yeah. Been a while. I never really thanked you properly for that. How've you been?"

"Fair to mid, thanks." That was my way of telling him I was not calling on a secure line, if there was such a thing in the world anymore. If I had been, I'd have said, "I'm cool."

"Listen," I said, " I have a bit of business for you."

"What kind?"

"The kind you like."

"Big, fancy sewing machines?"

"Yeah, but portables, and automatics."

"Fix you right up. I'll be at the shop for another hour or so. How soon can you be here?"

"Fifteen minutes."

"I'll look for you."

I left Naomi at the condo, so she could legitimately say she had no knowledge of any illegal arms transactions.

Dave's "shop" was a three-stall garage tucked under a shabby 1920s bungalow in St. Paul's little Rust Belt, near the former Whirlpool washing machine factory and the former Hamm's Brewery. The garage was built into the face of a steep hill, and the house on top of it faced the other way, toward the street. Down at alley level, a crudely painted sign advertised walk-in small appliance repair. Both the sign and the business itself had been the subject of a long battle with the City's zoning administrators. For some reason, that particular piece of property wasn't supposed to have any businesses, though it was impossible to imagine that a home shop would ruin the neighborhood. The final compromise had been that the garage could stay in business if Dave built a small parking lot for his customers in the back yard, fronting the alley, which he did. It was all very hilarious, in a way, since good old Dave couldn't fix a sewing machine if his life depended on it.

We found Dave sitting behind a counter amid assorted small appliances and tools. After introductions and vouchers of reliability, he asked me what I needed.

"What does the FBI use for high-prejudice operations?"

"M-16s, mostly. Glocks for hand guns. Sometimes the more exotic stuff, but I don't have that."

"M-16s are good. Everybody recognizes them as US federal. I also want jackets and hats with FBI logos, Kevlar vests,

and a thousand rounds of ammunition, all in extra magazines."

"I can only give you about six hundred already in mags. What are you mobilizing for, if you don't mind my asking?"

"Entebbe, I think."

"Nice operation, as I recall. Very professional."

"Yeah. Maybe I should hire the Israeli Army to do this one for me."

"You want I should make some calls?"

"Nice thought, but I probably can't afford them. We'll go home grown, and if it comes off right, we won't fire a shot, and you can have all the stuff back again in a few days."

"Yeah, seems to me I've heard that one before. My policy is that I'll buy back whatever hasn't been compromised at half a buck on the dollar."

"Works for me." I loved that word, "compromised." What he was telling me was if we shoot anybody, we'd better be damn sure to pick up the spent shells, or else don't bother coming back to him.

He got up and locked the door we had come in through, as well as the three small overhead doors. Then he inserted a key into what looked like an ordinary electrical receptacle. There was a groan of machinery, and most of a side wall of the garage tipped up and inward, like an old-fashioned overhead door. Behind it was a sort of cave, carved into the limestone ledge rock under the front lawn of the house. Dave found a light switch near the opening, and the place lit up to show me rough walls arrayed with every type of gun I had ever seen or heard of.

"I'm a little overstocked on anti-tank weapons right now, Herman. I can make you a hell of a deal."

"Some other time, maybe. Not a lot of tanks in my neighborhood just now." I seriously wondered if he had another room with tanks and APCs, too.

We picked out half a ton of weapons and gear and let Dave close the cave wall. Then I drove the BMW into the garage,

and we loaded our small arsenal into the trunk. Now I had all the elements I needed except a formal rehearsal and a few crucial phone calls. One of them had to be fairly long, so I figured I should make it from someplace where I didn't care if the location was traced. I left my troops and their gear at the loft, took my fancy new tape recorder out to the main terminal at Lindbergh Field, and fired up a pay phone. All the people I needed were available. That was nice. I do so hate talking to machines.

⌘

Finally, I picked up Naomi and drove her back to her shop to look for the "Baby on Board" placard.

"It all looks different," she said.

"You mean somebody's been here again?"

"No, not that. Sometimes you go off and do some things, experience some powerful feelings, and the whole world changes. You come back and look at the things that used to be familiar and comforting, and you don't recognize them anymore."

"Trust me, things will be comforting again."

"I'm not positive I want them to be. You are quite an adventure, Herman."

"Thank you, I think."

"So what happens tonight?"

"Tonight, yes. Tonight we get to show off our knowledge of classical literature. We run a Trojan horse operation. We are welcomed through the gates, and then we throw open the doors of the van and leave our dopey hosts wondering what the hell hit them. Shock and Awe, the Army calls it. Leave them so stunned they don't know how to react."

"And if they aren't quite that stunned?"

"Then we blow enough of them away that the others get scared and quit."

"Blow them away? You mean kill them."

"I'd like to avoid that, since we don't really know who we're dealing with. But yes, there is that distinct possibility." I didn't turn away from her intense gaze.

"What if somebody in the shed is an undercover policeman or agent?"

"Then he'd better have enough sense not to shoot at us. Just like the rest."

"I think I like the first way better."

"Me too."

"Is there a part in all this for me?"

"Yes, and it's important," I said.

"I hope your friend Wilkie appreciates all this."

"It's not a question of appreciation. He would do it for me. If I were rescuing you, he would be right there, no questions asked."

"Then I will try very, very hard to do it right."

We had a long hug and then headed back to the staging area.

Chapter Twenty-Six

Shock and Awe

The van was a perfect match for the one on the video recordings, even down to the amount of dirt on it. We went to an empty corner of a parking ramp and practiced getting out of it and deploying in a hurry. There was no way to guess how long it would take people to recognize that they had been invaded. Our assumption would have to be that we would be spotted right away. If so, the van would be an immediate target, and I wanted us out of it as fast as possible.

"When I say go, I want everybody out and ten feet away from the van in every direction, in two seconds flat. That's whether the vehicle has stopped moving or not. You take an area that fans out from whichever door you went out of, and within that, you take out anybody you see. Subdue them if you can, but be ready to shoot them if you can't. Make all the noise you want, including shooting at the roof. We want intimidation, and we want it fast. Listen to your radios. Wilkie will leave the van before the rest of us, and he will be able to read the situation and tell you if you need to go someplace different than you are. Questions?"

There were no questions, but there were a lot of bewildered looks. I'd have liked questions better.

The first run-through was terrible. Instead of leaping out of the van, people stepped out. Some of them actually paused to close the doors behind them. Wilkie and I shared a pained look, and I seriously wondered if we would have to abandon

the operation, after all.

"Listen, idiot children," said Wilkie, "the van is full of nitroglycerine and you are all on fire, okay? You don't want to step out, you want to *fly* out. And if you can't manage that, I'll damn well *throw* you out later, when we're at highway speed. Everybody got it?"

I drove into another part of the ramp, came to a screeching stop, and we tried it again. Lybrand had an old leg injury, and he simply couldn't move very fast, so we decided he wouldn't go on the mission. Kenny Fender, who had gotten the van for us, piled out of his door in a summersault, sprang to his feet screaming like a banshee on meth, and waved his gun around in every direction. At first I thought about telling him he couldn't go, if he couldn't control himself any more professionally than that. But then I thought having a scary crazy person here and there might not be such a bad idea, at that. I let him be.

We tried some more, and they got better. On a scale of one to ten, with ten being a Navy SEAL team and one being Laurel and Hardy, my squad was maybe a four point five. They had to be reminded to turn on their radios and take their weapons off safety, but they moved pretty well. As we practiced, they got up to about a six, and I decided it would have to do. We checked out of the ramp, picked up the rest of our gear, and drove to the salt shed.

Wilkie was at the wheel. I was next to him, with Naomi next to me. Everybody else was in back, and a block away from the shed, everybody but Wilkie hunched down out of sight. Wilkie stopped at the gate, got out and cut the padlock with an iron jaws, and then drove up to the big corrugated door and blew his horn.

I cringed. The horn was the one thing we hadn't tested, and it didn't sound the same as the one on the other van. Would anybody notice or care?

I held my breath.

We waited long enough for me to start sinking into total despair. Then the big door rolled slowly open, screeching and rumbling.

"Radios on now, people," I said.

When the opening was high enough, Wilkie hit the gas and drove smoothly inside. Near the left-hand side of the door, a pot-bellied guy with a lumberjack shirt and about two years worth of hair and beard held a control box that dangled from an overhead cord. He gestured to Wilkie to stop behind a white line that was painted on the dirt floor. Wilkie drove a full van-length beyond it. The guy punched the "close" button on his controller and came stomping angrily up to the driver's door of the van.

"Goddamn it, I told you to stop back there. Same as all the other—"

Wilkie reached through the window and punched the man in the nose, hard. The guy gave out some kind of "aaagh" sound but didn't go down, so Wilkie opened the door into him. As he was getting out, he said to me, "Take it, man!"

I quickly slid over behind the wheel and floored the gas pedal. Behind me, I could hear Mr. Potbelly becoming even sorrier that he had bitched at Wilkie, but I didn't look back. I had a complicated interior to read in a very short time, and I gave it my full attention. The inside of the shed was poorly lit, and the view was obscured even more by jets of steam that came gushing out of the big dirt floor at irregular intervals. That explained the hissing I had heard, some kind of strange system for heating road sand, maybe, now just used for general heating. In our own headlight beams, I could see some structures against the far wall that could only be called cages.

As we got closer, I saw the landscape of a nightmare. Inside the cages, lit by a few industrial floodlights, were some shapeless, huddled figures on bare mattresses. One young woman was up, wandering around as if she was in a trance, naked except for a dirty bathrobe that hung open at the front. Another

clung to the bars at the front of the cage, and as we approached, her mouth opened and tears began to stream down her face. One might think that their treatment had just been careless and makeshift, but I didn't buy it. I believed they were meant to be intimidated by every aspect of their new life, including their Spartan housing, ragged clothes, and drugs that were total downers. Hell, they were meant to be outright terrorized, and they obviously were. I found it hard to take my eyes away from the captive women long enough to size up the rest of the setup in the shed. I headed for the back wall, pedal to the floor. Over my shoulder, I said, "Get hot, people! Target coming up." I heard rounds being chambered.

To the left of the cages were some crude plywood enclosures with doors but no windows, probably field offices or a bunkhouse for the more privileged staff. On the other side of the big shed, some vehicles were lined up facing the center of the building, including a van, a brown Buick, and Valento's Shelby Mustang. I skidded around into a right-hand turn and a stop, broadside to the cages, blocking the other vehicles, and yelled, "Go!" All the doors of the van flew open, and my crew of phony feds piled out. Two men went out the back, the others out the side doors. We could hear Wilkie's voice in our ear buds, saying, "Nobody on the main perimeter, guys. Head for the plywood sheds." They did. I went to the cages, with Naomi behind me.

There were six women of varying ages in the cages, including Trish Hanover. Compared to the last time I saw her, she looked like hell, to say the least. Dark makeup streaked down from her eyes like prison tattoos, and she looked spaced out and lifeless, like the rest. But she didn't seem injured. There was a lot of noise in the echoing metal building by then, but when Trish saw my face, I could see her mouth my name. Her lower lip trembled.

My people deployed even better than I had hoped. As men began to pour out of the plywood bunkhouse, Kenny Fender

ran straight at them, just as he had in practice, screaming and spraying bullets at the ceiling. The bad guys didn't know what the hell to make of him. Most of them dropped their weapons and held their hands up in placating gestures. My other guys quickly flanked Kenny and knocked the wind out of anybody who hadn't already dropped his weapon. Then they knocked their feet out from under them with M-16 butts or booted kicks and took away their Uzis and Tech-tens.

"You ain't supposed to be here for another half hour," said one who hadn't been hit yet. "We ain't ready yet."

"You're ready," said Carmody. He jabbed the man in the solar plexus with his rifle muzzle and took his pistol away as he started to go down.

"What the hell is going on, man?" said another, looking at the FBI jackets. "You guys are supposed to be on our side."

"In another life, tool," said October Jones. "We're not on your side, and we're not afraid to kill you here and now, either. Assume the position."

Fender screamed again and sprayed bullets at a corner where three men were trying to get out of sight. One went down with blood gushing from a leg wound. The other two dropped their weapons without being told.

One man managed to get past our guys and ran toward the cages, waving an Uzi. "It's a bust!" he screamed. "Kill the bitches." As he fumbled with a padlock, I ran up behind him and stuck the muzzle of my rifle behind his ear.

"Drop your gun now and open the rest of those locks, sleazeball, before I take away your ability to do either one."

He dropped his gun but made a big show of fumbling with a ring of keys. I hit him on his left forearm with my rifle butt, hard. "That would mean '*now*,' asshole." It had the desired effect.

Taking her cue from the open doors, Naomi was right behind me, guiding the women to the van and helping them in, giving them blankets to wrap themselves in.

One of the people we had sapped a moment earlier got back up, picked up the Uzi that my key-man had dropped, and was holding it against Trish Hanover's head. He seemed to think that was a good idea for all of about ten seconds, until he looked up and saw Wilkie glaring at him over the barrel of an M-16.

"He won't talk," I said. "He'll just kill you. I would say you have less than two seconds to live."

The man dropped the Uzi and put his hands up. Wilkie, with his M-16 still trained on him, came over, kicked him in the crotch, and then in the stomach. Trish flew over to her rescuer, arms outstretched, but Naomi grabbed her and pulled her toward the van. "We have to get you out of here, now."

With all the women safely in the van, Naomi got behind the wheel and headed for the big door. I sprinted ahead of her and hit the "open" button on the controller. She didn't slow down as she went out, and she didn't stop afterwards. The plan was that no matter what happened in the shed, she and the abducted women were gone, clean. I watched her taillights speed off into the night. Then I heard gunfire behind me.

Leaving the big door open, I raced back inside. I didn't know who had opened fire first. One of the thugs, blood soaking one pants leg, was rolling around on the floor in agony. The others were stretching their arms up, making an exaggerated show of surrendering.

Somebody said, "You can't just shoot us. We got rights. You got to—"

"Oh, now you're going to tell us what we have to do?" said Wilkie. "You fucking idiot. You lost every damn right you ever had when you snatched those girls." He went back over to the man he had kicked earlier and jerked him upright by his shirt. "Where the hell is Valento?"

My crew was busy tying the rest of the gang to the cage bars, using the plastic one-use ties that are actually made for electrical work.

"Where?" said Wilkie again. He stuck his Glock in his belt and punched the man in the nose, probably breaking it. Then he wrapped a hand around one of the man's ears and started to squeeze.

"He's here someplace," said the man, spitting out blood between his words. "I don't know where, exactly, I swear."

"Throw a grenade in the shack!" I said. Not that we had any grenades, but it seemed like a good threat to make. Two more men came running out, hands in the air, but they weren't the two we wanted. Then we heard the engine. Something smooth, big, and well muffled. The Buick left its place at the wall and sped toward the big door, tires throwing gravel behind it.

At least three of us whirled around and sprayed the departing car with lead from our M-16s, but it kept going. Wilkie and I ran to the door and fired some more, but it was clearly too late. Our quarry was gone. On the ground just past the door, I could make out a fresh trail of some kind of liquid.

"We hit either the gas tank or the radiator," I said. "Maybe we can track him."

"Let's get our loose ends tied up here and give it a try."

"Sounds good. Time to leave, anyway."

Back inside, I asked where the official gangland phone was, and after a little more of Wilkie's persuasion, one of the goons produced a cell. I took it and dialed Agent Douglas on his personal cell phone.

"What the hell are you calling me now for?"

"For a slight change of plan."

"What? Who is this?"

"The voice of doom. And the new plan is that you are not going to move everything and everybody out at eight o'clock because everybody is already out."

"Look, whoever you are, you had—"

"Do you want to hear how to save your sorry ass, or do you want to threaten and bitch?"

"Um."

"Good. So the new plan is this: if you get down here in the next fifteen minutes, you can go back to pretending you are a real FBI agent, and you can take credit for a very impressive bust of a human traffic ring. Don't wait too long, though, because the camera crews from Channels Five, Four, and Eleven are already on their way. If you show up late, it might be a little hard for them to draw the right conclusion. And if you don't have a good story for them, I'll have to give them the recording of all your phone calls from this morning."

"You're bluffing. You don't have—"

"Are you in your office?"

"Yes."

"Look under your desktop, in the knee well."

"And then what?" After a brief pause, he added, "Oh shit."

"Give the man a cookie. He knows an 'oh shit' when he sees it. I'll be watching the news. Make it work the way I want, or you'll be making even bigger headlines." I hung up, wiped off the cell phone, and threw it in some dark corner. As long as it didn't have my prints on it, I didn't care if it got found or not. Then we went over to the remaining vehicles. All the keys were in them. I tossed my M-16 to Plug Carmody, and Wilkie did the same with his. We kept the Glocks. He and I took the Mustang. The rest of the crew took off in the van. As we headed out, we could see the TV camera trucks in the distance. We could hear sirens off somewhere, too. I supposed some neighbor had called 911, and the local cops didn't know they weren't invited to this party. That was fine.

I had figured we wouldn't have time to sort out the fired guns from the clean ones right away, so the plan was for my guys to dump all our phony FBI gear and weapons in the back room of my office, where Agnes was waiting for them. She would put everything in my office safe for now. If we hadn't found a spare vehicle at the shed, then the crew would have gone back to the condo on foot, as fast as they could. This was much

better. The safe was originally built for a railroad freight house. It wasn't big enough to hold a boxcar, but a mere ton of junk would disappear in it quite nicely.

Meanwhile, Wilkie and I followed the trail of leaking fluid. It was continuous enough that whatever the stuff was, we fully expected to come upon a stalled vehicle soon.

A quarter of a mile away from the shed, the trail went into a parking ramp. We took a ticket from the automated dispenser and cruised in, guns drawn. The damn pipes on the Mustang were so loud, there was no way we were going to sneak up on anybody, but at least we had our guard up. On the top floor, the trail ended.

"Whatever the leak was, they found a way to plug it," I said.

"Looks that way. Damn shame. I thought we had them."

"We will. But not today, Wide."

"Yeah. How are you liking these wheels, by the way?"

"The Mustang? Overrated. Stupid muscle cars are all alike. Nice drive train, but the ass end is just way too light for all that power. On slippery streets, it's as helpless as a pig on a hockey rink."

"Probably we shouldn't keep it, then."

"No, probably not. But we're damn sure not giving it back to Valento."

"Nah, he'd just use it to get in trouble."

We looked over the rail around the entire perimeter of the ramp, to be sure the streets below were deserted. Then Wilkie stood outside the car while I got in, put it in first gear, and peeled off. Twenty yards from the ramp edge, I threw the shifting lever into the neutral bridge and jumped out. The car crashed into the guardrail, smashed most of it, and nosed out over the street below. But it didn't fall.

As I was picking myself up, Wilkie came over and said, "Damn! They really made that rail strong."

"Afraid so."

"Hell, it's never like that in the movies."

"You suppose the movie makers would lie to us?"

He went over to the car and kicked the rear bumper in disgust. Then he kicked it again. On the third try, the car teetered, lurched a little, ground some concrete off the edge of the floor slab, and finally dropped six stories. The gas tank didn't explode on impact, but the chassis did crumple very nicely when it hit the frozen ground. We left quietly by the stairs at the other end of the ramp.

"It ain't like ripping that bastard's face off," said Wilkie, "but it felt good."

Chapter Twenty-Seven

Across the River and Into the Trees

We walked back to Lowertown, keeping to the shadows, and retrieved my BMW. Then we drove to United Hospital. On the back side of the building complex, at a loading dock, Naomi was standing in front of the duplicate-phony FBI van. To my surprise, Trish was with her. We stopped and got out. Wilkie ran over to Trish and wrapped her in a hug that should have broken about three vertebrae. Naomi was flushed with excitement, and she gave me a kiss.

"Everything go all right?" I said.

"Just the way you said it would. I told the admitting nurse at the Emergency Room that these were abducted girls who needed to be checked out and that I didn't have authority to sign them in, but the FBI would have somebody else there shortly. I gave them one of the cards that I got from Agent Douglas's office. Then I said I had to move the van out of the emergency driveway, and I pretty much left before anybody had time to argue with me. God, it was exciting!"

"How come Trish is with you? She's got to be just as beat up, demoralized, and pumped full of chemical downers as the others."

"I know. But once she knew I was going to meet you and Wilkie, she wouldn't stay."

"Maybe we should let them check her out at Region's Hospital."

"Why didn't we go there in the first place? It would have been closer."

"That was the whole idea. I didn't want you to go to the first place somebody else would look. I wanted to get a security net of nosy reporters in place before anybody bad finds the girls."

"At least one TV truck was pulling up as I left."

"Did they see you?"

"Maybe, but they didn't film me."

"Then we're gold. The calls I made from the airport paid off." I looked over at Trish and Wilkie, shamelessly embracing each other. Maybe Trish would be all right at that. In any case, I could see that Naomi was right; she wasn't going to leave Wilkie. "Let's get out of here before those two get arrested for indecent public behavior."

"What about the van?"

"We leave it. There's a jug of bleach in my trunk. We need to douse the driver's seat and the dash, but then we just abandon it, keys and all. If we're lucky, maybe somebody will steal it. Take the 'Baby On Board' sign, though."

"I already wiped the van down for fingerprints. Isn't that good enough?"

I shook my head. "If somebody wants to ID us bad enough, they'll check it for DNA, too. Bleach wipes out everything. But we don't care about the traces from the passenger seats. Everybody will know who the snatched girls are, anyway. Wilkie? Time to go, man."

"I haven't done the bleach thing yet," said Naomi.

"No, but I figure I'll need to tell him more than once."

That was putting it mildly.

⁂

There was a lot of background noise at Lefty's Bar and Pool Hall, much of it from my own people, but you could still make out the audio from the TV over the bar. The whole crew was there, except for Lybrand, whom we had left back at the condo to record the night's doings, though I really wasn't sure why.

And even though we had missed the two people we most wanted to apprehend, we allowed ourselves a modest celebration. It had, after all, been a hell of an operation. We got all the kidnapped women out and none of our people got arrested or shot or even injured. Maybe we weren't as good as the SEALS, but we didn't need to hire the Israeli Army, either.

On the nightly news, the site of our little commando raid was getting a lot of play. There were some real FBI vehicles there by then, plus about a dozen cop cars, and a bunch of greasy-looking thugs were being led away in cuffs. One agent in particular was getting the featured spot in front of the camera, talking to reporters.

"Is that our man Douglas?"

"That's him," said Naomi.

"He puts on a good act on short notice, I'll give him that. All that phony crap about how hard he worked on this bust actually sounds believable."

"You think he'll get off Scot free?"

"God, I hope not. It's a horse race, basically. We need to get the truth to every branch office that his stupid agency has, faster than he can get a bunch of misinformation put out."

"Can we do that?"

"I don't know. He knows we have recordings of his phone calls from today, so he'll already be working on inventing a new spin for them. We need something else."

"What if we can't get it?"

"We got Trish, didn't we?"

"You're right. We're dynamite."

"Naomi, we are positively thermonuclear."

The TV screen cut to the emergency entrance at United Hospital, and another FBI agent, looking considerably less sanguine than Douglas, talked to the camera. I scarcely dared to believe it. Things were working, at least for now.

But of course, it couldn't stop there. Sooner or later we had to catch up with Armstrong and Valento, and I had no idea

how we were going to do that. Could we put a tail on Douglas? Tracking an agent who was actually trained in tracking seemed like pushing our luck. So while the rest of my group tossed back boilermakers and sang Irish songs of drinking and blackguarding, my own euphoria began to bleed away rapidly. I stared morosely into a flat beer and thought black thoughts. Now and then, Naomi squeezed my arm.

Then she reached into her purse and pulled out her cell phone. She flipped it open and said, "Yes?" She listened for a while. "Yes, he is. Hold on."

She handed the phone to me. "It's Harold Watkins. He says he's found the garage in the woods."

Chapter Twenty-Eight

The Last Dogsled to Nome

I told Harold not to approach the garage until Wilkie and I got there, and he sounded a little miffed that I hadn't trusted him to already know that. The shot-up Humvee was outside the garage, he said, and though the place looked abandoned, there was smoke coming out of the flue stack.

"There could be some people headed that way, ahead of us," I said, "possibly in a shot-up Buick. Don't mess with them and don't let them see you."

"Okay. I've got a good sniper blind, about a hundred yards from the place. I'll lay low there and keep an eye on things." He gave me directions for finding his friend's cabin, and we agreed that I would call him from there as soon as we arrived. I had no idea what we would do when we got there, but we had completely run out of options in the Twin Cities. All the action was back up north. And if there was a God, the garage in the woods was where He told Valento and Armstrong to go to ground.

Before we headed there, we made one more stop at Naomi's place and checked the upstairs apartment again. It was still empty, but the Dell laptop had definitely been moved. I flipped it open and fired it up.

The email opened right up, which surprised me. Nobody had changed my password to anything else. But it didn't look as if it had received any new messages since I had last looked at it. It was all stuff I had seen before. The history file of Google also looked unchanged.

"He doesn't keep very much on the desktop," said Naomi. "Let's take a look at the hidden files."

"How do I do that?"

"Here, let me." She did some mysterious things with the keyboard and touchpad, and pretty soon we were looking at an old-fashioned, multi-tiered outline of file names. It looked like there were hundreds of the damn things, maybe thousands. Just on spec, we opened one labeled Black Book. It had nothing in it but a single document page with the line, "Thought you were smart, didn't you, asshole?"

"Decoy," I said.

She nodded. "And there could well be some others that are not only decoys, but things that also trigger hiding or erasing the files that we really want."

"Really? Our garden variety sleaze ball could do that?"

"Or find somebody to do it for him. That's what you would do."

"Rats. Yes, I would." I sighed and looked over the seemingly endless list of files. And suddenly my eye stopped, and I remembered what the young techie at Best Buy, Cherri, had said to me about hiding something in a boring-looking folder. For there, staring back at me, was something labeled "2008 Tax Returns." And the Prophet had told me that Valento had never filed a tax return in his life.

"Pay dirt," I said.

It wasn't a file, it was a folder, a branch point on the big outline. And inside it were bunches and bunches of simple documents, each a separate file, most of them quite short. In a phrase from a different world, the folder was a bulletin board, a letter drop where Valento, Armstrong, and sometimes even Douglas left messages for each other, though not with their own names. Instead of entrusting them to the chancy airways of email, they had just left them on the one machine, and they had each dropped by now and then to check the postings and leave some more. Nice, deeply incriminating stuff. Meetings,

operations, payments, sometimes even the names of women they had kidnapped. It went back years. There was a lot of stuff about Pam Watkins and how unfortunate it was that she could identify not one but two of them. Trish also appeared by name, in the newer stuff. The plan for her had been to sell her somewhere in Asia and then kill her soon after she got there.

"Can you move all this out to the computer desktop?"

"Of course, Herman. Do you want to give it a new name?"

"Call it Doomsday."

She did, and we closed all the files, shut the computer down, and took it. On our way back to the condo, I left it with Agnes, along with the recorder that had all the good, dirty phone traffic on it. I showed her what it contained and made her promise not to tell anybody else that she had it. She looked insulted. I also looked at the armory in my safe and picked out two M-16s that hadn't already been fired, two more Glocks, and some extra magazines. I didn't know if we were headed for Armageddon, but it wasn't impossible, either.

We rendezvoused with Wilkie at the condo, transferred to his Ford Explorer, and headed north. Stewball stayed with the remnants of our surveillance crew at the loft. He seemed to be a big fan of leftover Chinese. When we left, he had his head stuffed inside a white cardboard carton. Trish came with us. I worried about her. She should be ready for about two days of sleep and a month with a psychotherapist by now, but she was having none of it. She had her mouth set in an unvarying grimace, and her eyes were wild and luminous. Was she still running on adrenalin? When she finally crashed, it could be an ugly sight. And in the meantime, it could be dangerous.

As we merged onto I-35 northbound, I said, "This has to be the strangest double date I've ever been on."

"Cheer up, Herm," said Wilkie. "If everything works out right, we might get to shoot somebody."

"And to think I was afraid we might be headed for some trouble."

"Nah. Why would you think that?"

"My dour nature, I guess."

"Oh, that shit. You ought to get rid of that."

"It's sort of like your repressed anger Wide. Nobody's made me an offer for it."

As we settled into cruising speed, I leaned over and whispered in Naomi's ear, "How does Trish seem to you?"

"She scares me."

That made two of us.

An hour and a half later, we drove into a blizzard. At first it was just powdery, crystalline flakes, and the wipers could handle it fine on their lowest intermittent setting. Then it got thicker and turned into fat, heavy blobs that built up on the edges of the blades and the perimeter of the windshield. Wilkie put the wipers on full speed and fooled with the heater controls a bit to keep us from fogging up. Soon the road had a continuous sheet of white stuff streaming across it from left to right. No bare pavement was visible anymore at all, and steering was strictly by the shape of the shoulders. Now and then the Explorer would shudder when a stronger gust of side wind hit it. Sometimes we would hit a drift that had settled on the road, several inches deep. We slowed down to 50 and plodded on. I offered to relieve Wilkie at the wheel, but he was determined to tough it out. I couldn't help but wonder if he was trying to impress Trish, who snuggled up against his right side and squeezed his arm now and then.

"Here's to the man on the trail tonight," I said. "May his grub hold out, may his dogs keep their legs, may his matches never misfire."

"Robert Service?" said Naomi.

"Jack London."

"The man knew," said Wilkie.

I wondered if it was too late to stop somewhere and buy some industrial-strength parkas and mukluks. And waterproof matches.

⁂

It was past three a.m. when we got to the town of Bayfield. The streetlights made yellow cones of illumination in the snow-filled darkness. We were the only vehicle moving, anywhere. We went through the deserted downtown and then took Wisconsin Highway 13 east, into open country. A few miles later, at a place that a sign called Star Bay, we turned onto a secondary road that looked as if it had been plowed no more than two or three times the entire winter, none of them recently. You could tell where the roadway was, but only just. I said a nice little silent prayer of thanks for the fine engineers who had invented four-wheel drive. Soon the trail turned back east and the woods closed in around us. Off to the right, the night somehow got even blacker than it had been, and I assumed we were looking out across Lake Superior. At a tin mailbox that said Cramden, we turned again and headed toward the lake.

The cabin was a big A-frame, with one gable facing the lake. There was a light over the door, and when we got closer, a yard light flashed on, illuminating a Subaru Forester and two snowmobiles. We pulled in ahead of the Subaru, put every bit of outerwear we had back on, and stepped out into the blast of the storm. Two steps out of the vehicle, I had ice in my bone marrow. I wondered for a moment if our Kevlar vests were actually heat conductors, rather than insulators. Maybe I should have asked good old Dave for the Antarctic version.

Wilkie was ahead of me, and when he got within ten feet of the front door, it flew open to reveal Lillian Watkins with a double-barreled shotgun against her shoulder.

"Who the hell are you?" she said. Then she saw me and relaxed. We all hurried inside and slammed the door in the face of the howling white beast behind us.

"Thank God you're here," she said. "Harold isn't answering his cell phone anymore."

Chapter Twenty-Nine

Hunting Party

Lillian handed out heavy sweaters, stocking caps, fur-lined mittens and felt-lined boots to those of us who didn't really have warm enough clothes for the occasion. "We'll go the last quarter mile or so on foot, so the engine noise doesn't give us away," she said. "Do you like cross-country skis or snowshoes?"

"Which one is harder to fall down on?" I said. She rolled her eyes. From a big pile of gear by the door, she handed me a pair of snowshoes, the kind that look like they were made out of varnished wicker ware. She gave Wilkie a pair that were the same but bigger. Trish and Naomi picked out cross-country skis with over-the-boot bindings. We all found bungee cords to strap our new foot gear on our backs. I adjusted the strap on my M-16 so it could go over the whole works.

"I assume everybody knows how to run a snowmobile?" said Lillian.

Blank faces, all around. It was starting to look like a long night.

"I'll show you," she said, "and I'll drive one of them. I have to go anyway, since I'm the only one who knows where it is. One person should stay here, in case Harold calls."

"Not me," said Trish. She pulled the Glock out of her pocket and checked to see that it had a round in the chamber. Whether it was a wise thing to do or not, she had come for blood, and she was not going to leave the wet work to somebody else if she could help it.

"I'll stay," said Naomi.

"Stay protected and warm," I said. "Like, between two mattresses, with nothing but a Glock poking out. I'm coming back to check."

"I'll hold you to that." She wrapped her arms around the big pile of clothes that made me look like an oversized wool penguin and gave me a kiss on the cheek.

"Jesus, and you thought Trish and I were disgusting," said Wilkie. "That's so fearsomely sweetsy-cutesy, I could just puke."

"Better not, Wide. It's liable to freeze on you. Let's go see if we can finish what we started." We waddled to the door and plunged back out into the fury of the storm.

Lillian gave us a crash course in the workings of powered sleds. They turned out to be much simpler and easier to run than I would ever have imagined. No clutch, no gears to shift, nothing tricky of any kind. And the seats, she said, were heated. Wow. None of that, of course, would keep me from tipping the stupid thing over, but at least I could make it go.

I didn't get to find out, though. Wilkie wanted to try his hand at it, and I let him drive one machine, with Trish on the back. It was a Polaris that looked bigger than the other one, an Arctic Cat with a paint job that looked like it had been done by a California hot rod artist. I got on the zoot machine behind Lillian, our guide, and we were off.

Our headlights only let us see twenty feet or so, before they were swallowed up in swirling white incandescent fuzz. The whole world looked like a black and white *sumi* ink painting with electric highlighting. You could get disoriented in it very quickly. Now and then the dark shapes of trees would leap into our light beams and then quickly disappear on one side or the other. They looked like construction paper silhouettes, but most of them were big enough to do us serious damage if we hit one. Fortunately, Lillian had an old track to follow, though it was rapidly getting filled back in.

The seat really was heated, although it took a while for it to get started. It was surprising at first, like a long-suppressed memory of when you were a little kid and couldn't get your snow pants off fast enough to make it to the bathroom. I didn't like it much.

After ten or fifteen minutes, Lillian shut off her headlight and slowed down. Wilkie, about twenty yards behind us, did the same. We swung around into the middle of a little grove of pines and stopped.

"From here, we hike," said Lillian, killing her motor.

We sat sideways on the seat cushions of the snowmobiles and struggled with putting on the unfamiliar footgear. Lillian didn't wait for us. Her man was out of communication, and she was by God going to find out why. She was wearing new-style snowshoes, the kind that look like old electrical conduit and rubber inner tubes, and she was running. She still had the double-barreled shotgun. By the time Wilkie and I got our snowshoes on, she was already out of sight, but her tracks were easy enough to follow, even in the storm.

After what seemed like a long and exhausting trek, the tracks headed up a large hill to a ridge that had a lot of downed timber on top of it, all buried in fresh snow. Near the crest, the tracks disappeared into a black hole, like a wide, low cave. We followed them.

It wasn't really a cave, just a sheltered hole under a lot of big tree trunks. Harold Watkins was on the far side of it, using the timber for a sniper's bench. Lillian was beside him now, and she made a gesture to show us everything was all right.

"You're okay?" I said.

"Keep your voice down." He gestured in the direction that his rifle was pointed, and I looked through some gaps in the piled-up wood.

The landscape sloped gently down away from us, and a hundred yards below there was a big tin prefab pole barn with a faded sign over an overhead door that simply said "Auto

Repair." The shot-up Hummer was alongside the building. Heavy tire tracks went from it forward and back, around the building and out the driveway, making me think the vehicle had been towed there and left. Beyond the Hummer, in front of a big overhead door, was the familiar brown Buick, now also noticeably shot up. *Tallyho.*

"I turned off the ringer on the cell phone when the Buick showed up," he said. "Two guys got out, and I was afraid they might hear if I got a call. Turns out, you can't feel it vibrate, either, when it's in your parka pocket."

"Only two guys?"

"Yeah. I think they're alone in the building. Nobody came to the door to meet them. They had to unlock it themselves, and even though there was smoke coming out of the chimney, there were no lights on until they turned them on."

Lights still peeked into the darkness from small windows that were probably too high and dirty to look into.

"When did they get here?"

"Maybe an hour ago. One of them has a limp. Did you guys do that?"

"One can only hope."

"They fooled around with the Hummer for a while, started it up but didn't go anywhere. Now the snow's probably too deep for the Buick. I'd say they're trapped, except for the Hummer."

"Is that good?" said Wilkie.

"You ever hunt a trapped animal before?" said Harold.

"No."

"You don't want to, either."

"If the Hummer ran but they didn't go anywhere in it, they're either waiting for reinforcements or evac," I said.

"What kind of evac?" said Wilkie.

"I'd guess a chopper. That flat field behind the building looks big enough for a landing pad, and there's a shred of orange cloth flapping around that could be a windsock. There won't be anybody flying until the weather breaks, though. We

should deal with them before that happens." Everybody else in the group nodded.

"How do you want to play it?" said Wilkie.

"Well, we don't have a Trojan horse this time, do we?"

"We could smash the door open with the Hummer."

"And be sitting ducks inside it," I said. "Let's see if we can get them to come out. Go down there nice and quiet. Get ourselves flat against the wall on either side of the big door. Harold, once we get there, call Naomi back at the cabin and let her know we found our quarry. Don't even try to be quiet about it. Then take your rifle and shoot out the tires on the Hummer. After that, start putting some rounds through the walls of the shed. If they come out any way except with their hands up, we cut them down. No chit chat, no hesitation, no remorse."

"I like it," said Trish. She had a look on her face I had never seen before, couldn't have imagined on her. You wouldn't ever want to face a woman with a look like that and a gun in her hand.

"I like it, too," said Harold.

"Here we go, then."

We went back out of the sniper's hole the way we had come in, then took a long dogleg along the snowy ridge so we wouldn't leave any tracks pointing straight at Harold. I led the way, with Wilkie and Trish close behind. Lillian stayed with her husband. I was starting to like the snowshoes. Once you got used to walking flat-footed with your feet far apart, they worked well. Trish was faster on her skis. Now and then she got carried away and glided past me, then stopped and waited for me to catch up.

We went down to the driveway, a couple hundred yards away from the building, then turned and headed straight at it, walking in the tracks from the Buick. There were no windows on the front of the building, and we didn't try to hide, only to be silent. Ten yards in front of the big door, we split, with

me taking the right-hand side and Wilkie and Trish the left. I looked back at where Harold must be and nodded with my whole upper body.

I could hear Harold talking on his cell phone, despite the roar of the wind, and I thought I could hear voices inside the building, as well. Angry voices, arguing. Then the crack of the rifle split the night, and one corner of the Hummer dropped. Then another, and a third. Harold was a damn good shot. After the next two bullets slammed into the side of the building, there were muffled shouts from inside. I took off my heavy mittens, chambered a round in my M-16, and brought it to my shoulder.

The big overhead door rolled slowly upward, screeching on old, rusted bearings. First a strip and then an ever-growing rectangle of yellow light spilled out over the snowy driveway.

Nobody came out.

Chapter Thirty

Top of Nothing

Back in Detroit, the shiny chrome city of my youth, my Uncle Fred, the bookie, taught me every game known to mankind that you can play for money, including bridge. He didn't play Goren, exactly, he played Fred. And I always remember a strategy that he called the "top of nothing lead." That was when your hand was absolute crap, but you had the lead whether you wanted it or not. So you would lead the highest card in your longest suit and assume that everybody else's cards would lie in a way that would make that work, precisely because they *had* to, or you were doomed anyway. It was amazing how often it worked. Which was nice to remember, because Wilkie and I were about to play our own top-of-nothing.

I saw him unfastening his snowshoes, and I did the same with my own, then picked up the M-16 again. I put an extra magazine in my left hand and shouldered the weapon. Across the entry apron from me, Wilkie made a sweeping gesture with his left hand, telling me to lay down a spray of suppressing fire, so he could run inside. It was a dumb idea, but I didn't have a better one. And there was no way to argue with his gesture. He did a countdown with the fingers of his left hand—three, two, one, closed fist—and I swung out into the door opening and pulled the trigger.

The interior was like most small-time repair garages, which is to say it was an incomprehensible jumble of junk. Hard to

make sense of it in a quick glance, and even harder to pick out the figures of people hiding in it. I put my weapon on full automatic and laid down a spray of bullets from left to right, emptying the magazine. Then I yelled, "Go!" Wilkie charged into the opening with his own weapon blazing as I quickly dumped the empty magazine and put in the fresh one from my left hand.

Heavy automatic fire came back at us from the center of the room. Somebody, probably Valento, was hunched over a metal workbench. He had what looked like a Tech Ten in each hand and was firing wildly in every direction. A blast hit Wilkie squarely in the torso and sent him sprawling backwards across the concrete floor. Then I caught a round in the chest. My Kevlar vest stopped it, but the impact still knocked me backwards and took my breath away. My legs buckled like wet noodles. I dropped my M-16 as I was falling, and I couldn't move well enough to get the Glock out of my pocket. I was surprised at how calm I was, considering that I was about to die.

Sprawled on my back as I was, I had a view of the bench and Valento, who now seemed to be out of bullets. As I was struggling to get mobility back, a figure stepped out of the shadows behind him. Armstrong. He calmly lowered his service nine millimeter and shot Valento in the temple.

Valento's head dropped to the bench top, but he didn't fall over or back. I could dimly see that he had rope wound around his arms and wrists. He had been tied to the bench, just for us to shoot at and also to shoot at us.

"See how everything works out in the end, Jackson? Valento goes out with blazing guns, showing what a bad guy he was, and I have to shoot him in the line of duty. The world is saved from the infamous murderer-rapist and I'm a hero. Of course, it would have been okay if he had killed you as well, but I'll take what I can get."

"What you can get is dead, asshole. Like the dog you are." Trish had her Glock out in front in a classic two-handed grip,

and she was steadily advancing toward Armstrong, despite still having her skis on. "You killed Pam, not him, you son of a bitch. I was there, remember?"

"Look, we can—" But he didn't finish. When she was within about twenty feet of him, she opened fire. And whether because of that or because of the maniacal look on her face, he did not shoot at her. He turned and ran, straight through the little office in the back and out the door into the storm. Trish emptied her gun at his fleeing back, paused just long enough to put a fresh magazine in the Glock, and went after him.

Thirty seconds later, I heard a lot of gunfire outside.

I struggled to make my body move. As soon as I could work my legs again, I leaned forward and got to my knees, then to my feet. Every movement made my chest hurt like hell, but when it hit a certain nasty level, it didn't get any worse. It wasn't pleasant, but I could live with it. I stumbled past the very dead Valento to the back door, getting a little more sure of myself along the way.

Outside, the snow was deep. Really deep. I sank in up to my knees on the first step and knew that I would never catch anybody if I didn't get my snowshoes. Going back through the garage, I saw Wilkie beginning to shake himself into action.

"You going to be okay, Wide?"

"I think so. Don't wait to see, man. Go help Trish."

I snatched up my snowshoes and headed toward the rear. I could almost run by then, though I was still short of breath. At the door, I laid the snowshoes out in front of me, hunkered down on them, and fastened the bindings as fast as I could. I realized that I had left my M-16 by the big door, and I decided not to take the time to go back after it. I pulled a Glock out of my pocket and plunged forward.

The snow was finally letting up, and the visibility wasn't too bad. I could see the tracks of the man with no snowshoes and the woman on skis easily enough, and as more of my strength returned to me, I started running as well as I could with a set

of wicker bedsprings on my feet. I didn't get very far.

Just over the first large hill, Trish lay sprawled face down in the snow, her skis pointing in odd directions, her right arm still extended, with the Glock in it. I stuck my own gun back in my pocket, bent down, and rolled her over.

"Can you hear me, Trish?"

"I got him, Herman." Her voice was faint, and she obviously had trouble opening her eyes, but she was smiling. "I put at least one bullet in that bastard, maybe two. He's walking wounded now. You can catch him, easy."

"How many did he put in you, Trish?"

"Not too many."

"Please don't tell me you didn't wear your vest?"

"Okay, I won't tell you. Get out of here, will you? Get him, Herman. Please, please get him. No way he lives, after what he has done."

I shook my head. "No way you die, if I can help it."

"God damn it, Herman, go!" The extra effort made her cough, and when she did, she spat up blood.

I looked behind me and saw Wilkie, not moving terribly well but coming, all the same.

"She needs a medic, Wide. She's hit."

"I'll get her to one. You go do what we came here for, okay?"

"You're sure?"

"Never been surer of anything. Go, man."

As I was handing Trish over to Wilkie, she said, "I'm sorry, Herman."

"Don't be."

"No, I mean about your head."

"Huh?"

"Get out of here, man," said Wilkie.

I got.

Chapter Thirty-One

Reckoning

The storm had quit altogether by then, and the clouds actually let a bit of moonlight through, here and there. On the brilliant white landscape, it was enough. I followed the tracks easily, and now and then I saw dark stains on the snow that might have been blood. If so, then I should be catching Armstrong soon. He didn't have snowshoes or skis, and stomping through that kind of deep snow had to be totally exhausting even for somebody who was not wounded. I watched the perimeter of the trail with great attention, looking for places he might have dropped back to ambush me. As I approached a grove of small pines, I slowed down and led with my gun.

The grove looked strangely familiar, and suddenly I knew why. It was where we had left the two snowmobiles. Only now, there was one. I took off my snowshoes and climbed on the other one, the Arctic Cat, and desperately tried to remember everything Lillian had shown me.

Throttle on the right-hand handlebar grip, brake on the left. Key and ignition in the middle. I turned the key and the engine popped into life. I thought I would give the throttle a couple of twists and rev up the engine, the way bikers do before they peel off. Wrong move. At the first twist, the sled leaped out from under me and almost dumped me in its track. But when I let go of the throttle, it settled back to a motionless idle, and I climbed back to the front of the seat. I didn't know where the bungee cords for my snowshoes were anymore,

and I looked for a place to stow the clumsy items. Finding none, I settled for laying them across my lap. Then I shifted my weight forward and fed the machine some gas, this time concentrating on opening the throttle smoothly. I won't say I looked very skillful doing it, but I roared off and managed to stay on the seat.

Whipping around to follow Armstrong's track, I took my first turn too sharply and almost tipped over. After that, I assumed a crouched position with my butt in the air, like a professional jockey, and shifted my weight with every smallest maneuver. I didn't know if that was the correct way to ride or not, but it seemed to work. To hell with the heated seat. I found the headlight switch, turned it on, and swung into the fresh track from the Polaris.

I had no idea how far ahead of me Armstrong was or how fast he was going. With only one person to carry, my own machine was terrifyingly fast, and I felt confident about catching him. His track wasn't very straight. At one point, going around a small hill, he had obviously dumped the machine and had to pull it upright and start over. I couldn't feel smug about that, since I was running on the verge of out-of-control all the time. Any time I thought I wasn't, I gave it more gas. It wasn't quite as dangerous as the bullets from Armstrong's gun, but it felt close.

The track wandered through a lot of small groves, not in any consistent direction, and I dared to hope that Armstrong might be getting disoriented and close to passing out. Then a couple of small trees leaped into my headlight, too fast for me to react. I held on tight to the grips and mowed one of them down. It was a jolt, but I didn't crash or stall. My snowshoes fell off my lap and into the snow, and I didn't stop and go back for them. *Worry about your own stability, Jackson, not his.*

Then, on a broad, open hilltop, Armstrong's track made a sweeping left turn and joined two older tracks that were running close parallels. *Shit, shit, oh shit.* He was following

our earlier tracks. Back to the cabin. Back to Naomi. For the first time in my life, I desperately wished I had a cell phone. I swung into the new track and opened the throttle as far as it would go.

The same trees that had looked like black silhouettes on the way out now seemed bigger and more solid. I was glad that it had been Lillian, not me, who had broken the original trail. I kept the throttle open and flew over it. It felt much shorter this time, and soon I could see the big A-frame in the distance. The front door was open, and the light from inside illuminated a Polaris snowmobile with nobody on it. Armstrong was inside, with Naomi. *If that asshole hurts her, I'm going to shove my Glock up his ass and pull the trigger until it doesn't work anymore.*

No. Wrong thinking. Attack somebody in a rage, and you'll probably screw it up. And even if you don't, you'll mess up your head for the rest of your life. Isn't that what Wilkie had told me, back at Lefty's, so long ago? As I approached the yard in front of the cabin and let my speed bleed off, I made a concentrated effort to slow down my breathing and calm my mind. *Cold, Jackson. Get very, very cold. Cold and deliberate. Focused, but not hot. And get a script that you can follow whether you feel like it or not. Now.*

I shut off my machine, took the key, and headed toward the rectangle of light, watching the dark corners beside it for somebody who could be waiting to ambush me. But I didn't really expect Armstrong to be there. He would be inside, where he figured he had his biggest trump card. As I got closer, I took the key out of the Polaris, as well. The seat was sticky and shiny with what I assumed was blood.

On a sudden inspiration, I went over to Wilkie's Explorer. We had brought extra weapons along, and I opened the door as quietly as I could to take a Glock out of the glove compartment. I fed a round into its chamber, and dropped it into my right-hand coat pocket. Then I raised the Glock that I had been using and went in the cabin door.

In the big center room of the cabin, Armstrong made no effort to hide. He had Naomi in front of him, holding a fistful of her hair in his bloody left hand. With his right hand, he was pushing his gun up against her chin.

"I'm so sorry, Herman. I thought it was you at the door, and—"

"Can that, bitch," said Armstrong. "You know the score here, Jackson. I want your gun and I want the keys to that Explorer, or she dies. Gun now."

"Okay, detective." I held up my left hand with the palm toward him, fingers spread. "Don't hurt her."

"Gun, asshole."

"Sure. Whatever you say." I tossed my Glock at him, harder than I needed to. He had to move his leg a little to keep from getting hit with it. Not much of a diversion, but it was as much as I would get. And it was what I had planned. His eyes followed the gun, and as they did, I pulled the other Glock out of my pocket, raised it, and fired. To hell with the small talk.

I normally shoot my own gun at the target range at thirty feet. Armstrong and Naomi were more like half that distance from me, and the Glock had a higher muzzle velocity than my usual gun, so I needed to aim a little bit lower than I was used to.

My first shot went over his head and into some glass at the other end of the cabin. The second one caught him in his right shoulder. He didn't go down, but he jerked back and dropped his arm. Naomi was alert enough to lurch away from him, even though he was holding her hair. When she did, I put four rounds into his chest, and he went down in a heap. I walked over to him and stood on his right hand, which was still holding his gun.

"Wearing a vest, Armstrong? Too bad it's not bigger." I kept my foot on his gun hand and shot him in the face twice. He didn't twitch after the second shot.

Naomi was shook up but otherwise seemed okay. Even so,

I was glad that I did not have another attack of head pain, because if she were all by herself, she wouldn't know to send an ambulance to the garage. I found the cabin's phone and dialed 911, wondering where the call would go, up here in the boonies. Wherever it was, what a lot of fine things I would have to tell them.

Chapter Thirty-Two

Final Arguments

I told the 911 operator that nobody at the cabin needed any medical attention, but we needed an ambulance, hearse, or dump truck to take away a body.

"There's another site, though, an auto repair garage in the woods, where they need an ambulance ASAP," I said, "and I don't know how to tell you how to get there."

"Could somebody else have called from there, sir?"

"Somebody named Harold Watkins, maybe?"

"Yes, sir. Is that the place?"

"That's it."

"We tracked it on his cell phone. The ambulance may already be there."

"And to think I bad-mouthed those things."

"Ambulances? I don't understand, sir."

"Doesn't matter. Look, I'm hanging up now, so I can call Harold and find out how people are doing there, okay?"

"No sir, not okay. Stay on the line until the authorities arrive."

"I promise I won't leave this location."

"Sir, please—"

"I'll call you back." Nice lady, but I needed to talk to Watkins.

Harold didn't pick up right away. When he finally did, he said the ambulance had already arrived, along with about a dozen state highway patrolmen and sheriff's deputies. He had called as soon as he saw Wilkie and me go down. Fortunately,

both the cabin and the repair garage were in Douglas, not Bayfield County, so we were not dealing with people from Will Kane's office.

"Has anybody said anything about the M-16s and the empties from them?"

"What M-16s, Herman? What empties?"

"You're a good man, Harold. I always said so. How's Trish?"

"She's alive. They're putting new blood in her now, and taking her to the hospital you were at when your head blew a fuse. Your friend Wilkie went with them. That's about all I can tell you. How about the cop that Pam stabbed, Armstrong? Is he dead?"

"As the proverbial doornail."

"So now you've been to the Chosin Reservoir, too."

"I guess I have, at that."

"Trust me, you'll handle it fine. You're a good man, too, Herman."

"Thank you for that. I have to hang up now and call the nine-one-one lady back, before she has an anxiety attack and orders an air strike on me. The snowmobiles are both here at the cabin. How shall I go about getting you here?"

"We'll catch a ride with one of the troopers. I'll see you at the hospital, probably."

"I'll be there."

⁂

The Douglas County Sheriff was named Roger Stanton, and though he didn't have a name from a character in an old western movie, he looked like one. He was tall and angular, and the way his gun belt hung on him reminded me of a young Steve McQueen. He also had freckles, and one of those faces that would always look like it belonged on a dumb kid, no matter how old he got. That must have been a problem for him, and I hoped he didn't try to overcompensate for it.

He didn't much care for people coming all the way from the Cities to shoot somebody in his county in the middle of the night, but he couldn't quite come up with a legal reason for disliking me.

I kept my story simple and fairly close to the truth, if less than complete. Wilkie and I had come to the north woods chasing somebody who had skipped on a bond, and we were helped by the parents of one of the skippy's former victims. We didn't know that Armstrong was in cahoots with our quarry, and it was a big surprise when I had to shoot him to save Naomi. Sheriff Stanton would find out about the human traffic ring and the other crooked cops and feds soon enough, but I didn't feel like complicating things for him just then. And of course, I said absolutely nothing about the assault on the salt shed in St. Paul.

"And just exactly how did you know your bail jumper was headed here?" he said.

"Anonymous tip." I said it loud enough to be sure Naomi could hear it in the next room.

"I'm so sure. Aren't those handy, though? And you always take your girlfriend along when you go off to shoot somebody?"

"What can I say? She likes the action."

"Uh huh. Well, you better hope you're enough for her."

"I do hope that, yes."

He chased me around the what-are-you-hiding barn for another hour or so, then questioned Naomi separately. I thought the blood Armstrong had splattered on her gave her a nice credibility.

Finally Sheriff Stanton said, "Well, it would have been a lot cleaner if you had shot this guy when he was shooting at you, back at the garage. But even here, it was clearly self-defense. I don't see any basis for arresting anybody here. Looks to me like you and the lady have had enough grief for one night."

The paramedics took the body away, and the sheriff's people took a few more pictures and left. I got the spare set of keys Wilkie keeps in a magnetic box on the trailer hitch housing,

and Naomi and I drove the Explorer to Saint Mary's Hospital in Superior.

⌘

Trish had taken three bullets, one of which had stayed in her, but none of them had hit a bone or a vital organ. Her biggest problem was losing a small ocean of blood and going into shock. Her official prognosis was good. The doctors worked on her for a little over two hours. Afterwards, she was conscious, and they let Wilkie talk to her for a while, but not Naomi or me. I think he told them he was her common-law husband. And for all I knew, maybe he was.

Out in the OR waiting room, I asked Wilkie for a recap.

"She's going to make it, Herm. She has all the signs of being in two wars and a train wreck, but she's going to be okay."

"This is good. Did you tell her Armstrong is dead?"

"Yeah, I did. Perked her right up."

"I'm glad." I wondered, though, if she would ever get the innocent twinkle back in her eyes. Some lines can never be uncrossed.

"Listen, Wide, I have to make a lot of things happen back home in a short time."

"Yeah, I figured that. You want to borrow the Explorer? I'm going to stay with Trish."

"How about if you give us a ride to the bus depot in Duluth?"

"I guess I could leave her for that long. Sure."

⌘

When we got to downtown Duluth, the next bus for St. Paul wasn't leaving for over three hours, so Naomi and I strolled down the street and killed some time in the Lake Superior Railroad Museum attached to the old train depot. She took my picture looking out of the cab window of a big steam locomotive called a Mallet, that had about thirty drive wheels and

a boiler two blocks long. Then she joined me in the cab.

"What do you think it was like, actually being the one who ran a monster like this?" she said.

"I think I would have liked it. I mean, look at this wall of levers and valves and pipes and gauges and *stuff*. Not an electronic component or a computer anywhere."

"Sounds like your bag, all right. And all day you'd get to watch the world's biggest cast iron phallic symbol surging across the countryside ahead of you. I bet steam engineers were some of the horniest bastards around."

"You think you'd like to have been Casey Jones' girl?"

"I think maybe I am. It's nice."

"Hold that thought for about three hundred miles."

"It'll be hard."

"The way you talk, Naomi. I'm shocked."

"No, you're not."

As aphrodisiacs go, escapes from nearly certain death are even better than steam engines, though it was unlikely that she realized that.

"Tell me, Herman—"

"I'll haul no caboose but yours, my dear."

"No, tell me about the bond. What happens with that now?"

"Well, assuming Sheriff Stanton is nothing like his neighbor to the east, Valento's body should even now be in the Douglas County Morgue, and getting a copy of the death certificate from them should be no problem. Once I have that, getting the bond released is easy."

"And you'll never know who wrote it in the first place?"

"Oh, I think I know."

"Really? Tell me, because I certainly don't."

"Agnes, my secretary wrote it." She looked at me in astonishment. "She wrote it because Wilkie asked her to, and she likes him and wanted to help him with his normally terrible love life. And Trish, who may be the only love he has ever had, asked him to ask Agnes because she wanted to

help Pam Watkins. She had been Pam's public defender and hadn't been able to keep her from getting railroaded into the slammer, so she felt she owed her. And when Pam got out of prison hell-bent on revenge, she offered to help. They cooked up a scheme to get Valento out of jail and lure him to Trish's apartment."

"To kill him?"

"Absolutely."

"But Trish had no experience with anything of the sort. And Pam had only tried it once and had failed."

"Having no experience never stopped any killer in history. But in this case, it should have. They probably had the silly notion that if they merely pointed a gun at somebody, he would be afraid and would do what they said. They might not have been outgunned, but they were definitely overmatched and out-eviled."

"And to make matters worse, something went wrong and Wilkie wasn't there," she said.

"And Armstrong was. We'll probably never know the real chain of events, but I think I might have screwed things up when I chased Valento through Lowertown and Trish hit me on the head to get me to back off."

"You can't be serious. *Trish* hit you?"

"You bet. She apologized for it when she was bleeding all over the snow, but Wilkie changed the subject. She hit me on the head, and it's quite possible that Pam got murdered and Trish abducted when Wilkie was busy getting me to a hospital. That's all pure speculation, mind you, but it fits what I know."

"Oh dear, oh dear, Herman. So you really meant it when you told the Watkinses that Pam's death was personal for you."

"The Prophet would even call it a karma debt."

"Does Wilkie know you've figured all this out?"

"If he does, he's keeping quiet about it. Knowing him, he may keep quiet about it forever."

"Wow, Herman. Just wow."

"Wow is what it is, all right."

"I just have one other question."

"No, I haven't ever had sex in an abandoned train car in a museum."

"You really do know how to read people, don't you?"

⁂

Two days later, we were sitting on an ornate bench in the Como Conservatory, under the old center dome. Naomi had a sketchpad on her lap and was making a charcoal drawing of the monster palms and ferns that leaped away from us, right up to the bottom of the glass dome that looked like a transparent version of the nose of a zeppelin. Small birds flitted here and there, emphasizing the lofty space of the place, and mist drifted around the upper fronds.

"It's really nice," she said, "being surrounded by all this lush greenery in the depth of the winter."

"It's probably primal, even. Here comes somebody who doesn't think so, though."

The FBI agent's shoes clicked on the flagstone of the path through the jungle. He looked like someone who had just had his ice cream cone smashed by the town bully. He was carrying a metal briefcase. When he got close enough to recognize Naomi, his scowl deepened.

"Well, if it isn't Agent James Douglas, Junior G-man," I said. "How's your day going, Agent?"

"Eat shit and die. Who the hell are you, anyway?"

"Doom. I told you that already. John Q. Doom."

"I'll find out, you know. And when I do, being a smartass is just one of the things you're going to be sorry for."

"I'm sure. But meanwhile?"

"Meanwhile, there's ten grand in this case. What you asked for. Where's the damn laptop?"

I reached under the bench, produced a cloth book bag, and handed it to him. He pulled the Dell out and threw the bag on the floor. Then he opened the computer and turned it on. After punching a few keys and doing a few touchpad strokes, he grunted, shut it off, and slammed it shut.

"You want to count the money?" He held out the case to me.

"I trust you. Just put the case on the bench."

He hesitated for a moment, possibly trying to think of some really rude and insulting way of complying. Finally he dumped it on the end of the bench, spun on his heel, and strode away.

"And a nice day to you, too," I said to his retreating back. He flipped me the bird.

"You want to go now?" said Naomi.

"Finish your drawing. We have lots of time. Commune with the rain forest."

Half an hour later, she folded up the sketchbook and put it in the book bag, and we strolled through some more greenery.

"I assume you left the briefcase on purpose?" she said.

"You bet. There's no telling what Douglas put in it besides money. And I don't want my prints on the case, either."

"Then why did you have him bring it in the first place?"

"Otherwise, he would have known that all I wanted was for him to have the laptop, so he could be found with it. Now he thinks *he* wanted it, because he had to pay for it."

"And how do you know he will be found, with the laptop or any other way?"

"Yesterday I took the computer to The Prophet, along with the phone recordings we made on the day of the great salt shed raid. He put all the nice, damning stuff on YouTube, along with handy keys for identifying the speakers and writers. I don't know if it's viral yet, but a lot of people have seen it. He also sent a special copy to *The New York Times*."

She chuckled. "Won't they trace it to the Prophet's YouTube account?"

"He used the FBI's account."

"You've got to be kidding. The FBI has a YouTube account?"

"They do now."

This time she laughed out loud. "I wonder how many hits they've gotten."

Chapter Thirty-Three

The Defense Rests

The next morning, Stewball nibbled on my ear and purred, in what was rapidly becoming a routine. I got up and fed him, though to his chagrin, it was only dry cat food. Still, Purina said it was their best, and he only fussed a little before he settled into inhaling it.

The morning *Pioneer Press* had the entire front page taken up with a story about FBI and SPPD personnel caught in a sex-traffic ring. There was a photo of our man Douglas being led off in cuffs, while another agent carried the poisoned Dell laptop. Ah, the free press. Well, sometimes it is, anyway. Plant the right seeds, and they will blossom all over page after page. As I was pouring the first coffee of the day, Naomi joined me, wearing delightfully little. The early morning sun through a high shop window backlit her blond hair and reminded me of when I had first seen it and found it indescribable. I still did. She gave me a kiss and then went into the office corner of the shop and fired up her computer. Soon she was back with a couple of pieces of paper.

"I got you a present, Herman."

"And I appreciated it, too. But what are the pieces of paper?"

"Boarding passes."

"What are we boarding?"

"A big airplane. Have a look."

I looked, then did a double take, and finally looked back at her. She had that sly smile that became her so well.

"New York?" I said.

"New York, Herman. We are going to say goodbye to Anne Packard."

Not so long ago, that would not have seemed like a good thing to do at all. But now, it definitely did. In fact, it seemed like the only thing to do.

"What a fine idea," I said.

And I was reminded of a story my Uncle Fred used to tell. Like all his stories, it had a moral.

It seems a couple of bored croupiers are hanging around a dice table when a pretty blonde walks in the casino and puts down $20,000 on a single roll of the dice, betting that she will roll craps, which is a two, three, or twelve.

"I hope you don't mind," she says, "but I feel luckier when I'm naked." She promptly strips off everything but her earrings and shoes. Then she picks up the dice and shakes them in her fist, saying, "Come on, babies, mama needs a new dress."

She throws the dice and immediately claps her hands, jumps up and down, and squeals with delight. "I won, I won!" She hugs both the croupiers and kisses them on the cheek. She also scoops the dice back up and kisses them, too.

One croupier numbly counts out $140,000, the standard seven-to-one payoff for craps. The woman quickly gathers up her winnings and her clothes and hurries away.

"So, what did she throw?" says one croupier.

"How should I know?" says the other. "I thought *you* were watching."

And the moral? According to Uncle Fred, it is that not all blondes are dumb. And I do so agree. But I think it's also that if you have one who lets you see her naked, even in the dusk with the light behind her, don't waste your time looking at something else.

Acknowledgements

Many thanks to Katrina C. Randall of Liberty Bail Bonds, for her technical advice about the mechanics of bonding. Thanks also to my faithful critiquers, Rebecca Kanner and Sandy Stephanson, and, as usual, to my indispensable beta reader, Margaret Yang.

Author's Notes

All of the characters in this book are the products of my fevered imagination. Bayfield County and Douglas County are real places, of course, and presumably they have real sheriffs, though I have never met or even seen them. The sheriffs portrayed in this book are in no way meant to resemble them, nor to reflect on the integrity of their offices.

A story needs a lot of sites. Lefty's Pool Hall, Herman Jackson's office, The Prophet's strange digs, Dave's Sewing Machine Repair, and the repair garage in the Wisconsin woods are fictitious locations, though not, I trust, implausible ones. The storage shed for road salt, just east of Lowertown, has not existed for several decades and was never as big as described here. Something quite like Auntie Kew's Antiques exists in the Midway area, though not by that name. All other locations in the book are real, and are rendered as accurately as I could manage, though Lowertown itself is mostly as I remember it from the 80's and 90's, when I was the city building inspector there. Since then, large parts of it have been gentrified almost beyond recognition. I wanted the older, more sinister version. Like Herman, I don't always embrace progress.